MW01581083

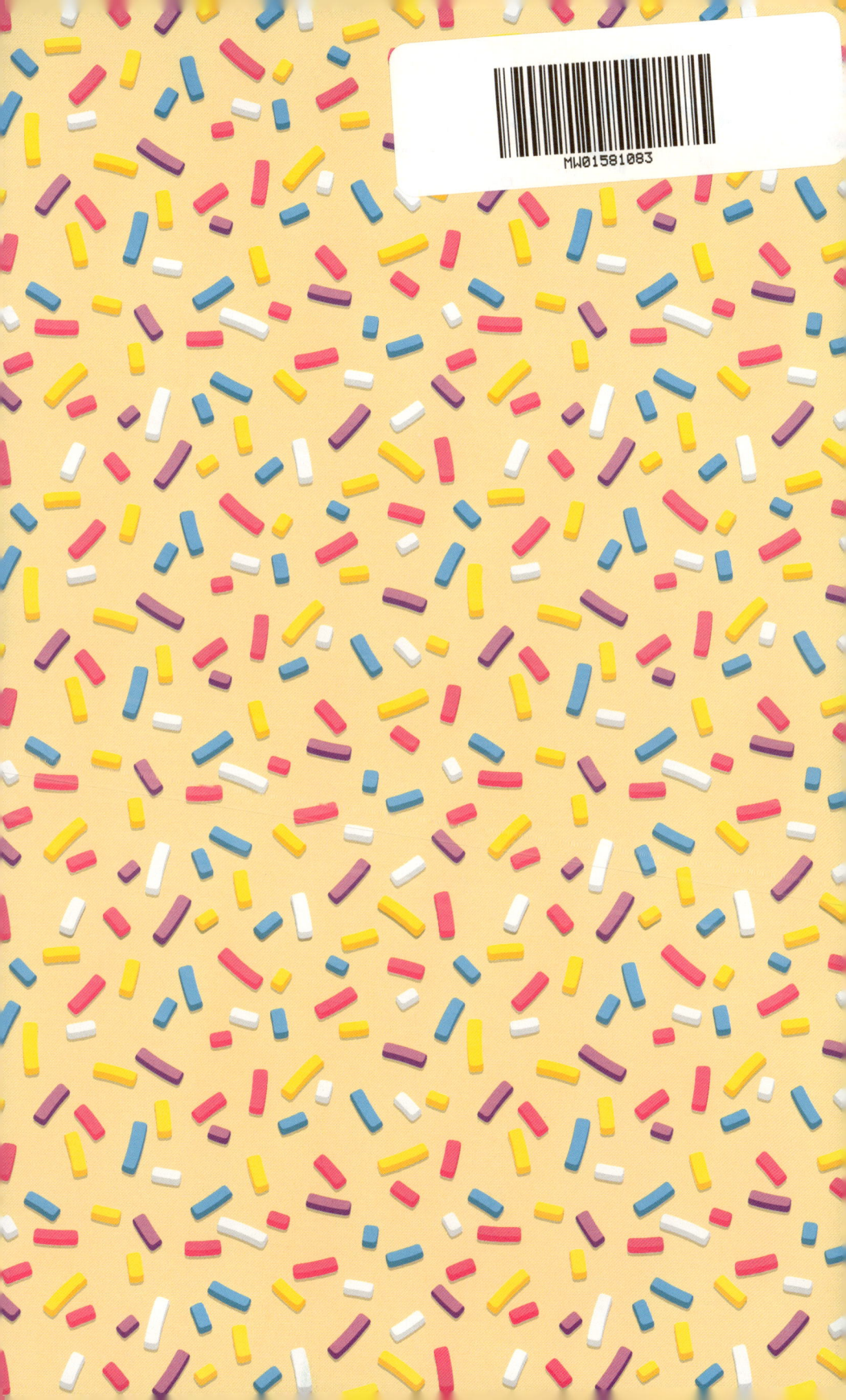

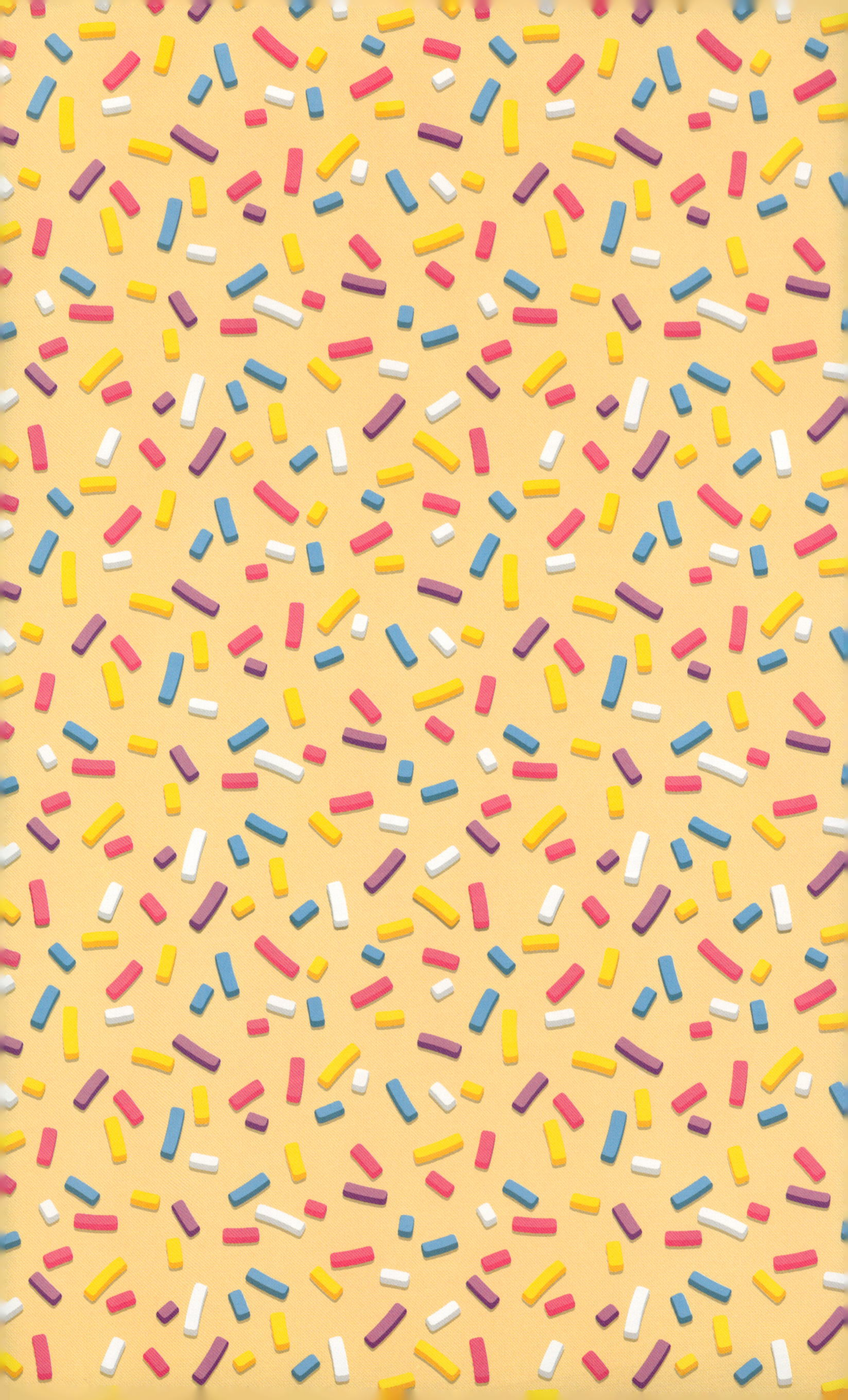

Alexis
Cool
as a
Cupcake

This book is a work of fiction. Any references to historical events, real people, or real places are used fictitiously. Other names, characters, places, and events are products of the author's imagination, and any resemblance to actual events or places or persons, living or dead, is entirely coincidental.

SIMON SPOTLIGHT
An imprint of Simon & Schuster Children's Publishing Division
1230 Avenue of the Americas, New York, New York 10020
For more than 100 years, Simon & Schuster has championed authors and the stories they create. By respecting the copyright of an author's intellectual property, you enable Simon & Schuster and the author to continue publishing exceptional books for years to come. We thank you for supporting the author's copyright by purchasing an authorized edition of this book.
No amount of this book may be reproduced or stored in any format, nor may it be uploaded to any website, database, language-learning model, or other repository, retrieval, or artificial intelligence system without express permission. All rights reserved. Inquiries may be directed to Simon & Schuster, 1230 Avenue of the Americas, New York, NY 10020 or permissions@simonandschuster.com.
This Simon Spotlight edition August 2025
© 2025 by Simon & Schuster, LLC
All rights reserved, including the right of reproduction in whole or in part in any form.
SIMON SPOTLIGHT and colophon are registered trademarks of Simon & Schuster, LLC.
For information about special discounts for bulk purchases, please contact Simon & Schuster Special Sales at 1-866-506-1949 or business@simonandschuster.com.
Simon & Schuster strongly believes in freedom of expression and stands against censorship in all its forms. For more information, visit BooksBelong.com.
The Simon & Schuster Speakers Bureau can bring authors to your live event. For more information or to book an event, contact the Simon & Schuster Speakers Bureau at 1-866-248-3049 or visit our website at www.simonspeakers.com.
Text by Tracey West
Cover and Character Design by Manuel Preitano
Art by Giulia Campobello at Glass House Graphics
Assistant on inks by Marzia Migliori
Colors by Francesca Ingrassia
Lettering by Giuseppe Naselli/Grafimated Cartoon
Supervision by Salvatore Di Marco/Grafimated Cartoon
Book design by Laura Roode
The text of this book was set in Comic Crazy.
Manufactured in China 0425 SCP
10 9 8 7 6 5 4 3 2 1
ISBN 9781665971492 (hc)
ISBN 9781665971485 (pbk)
ISBN 9781665971508 (ebook)
This book has been cataloged with the Library of Congress.

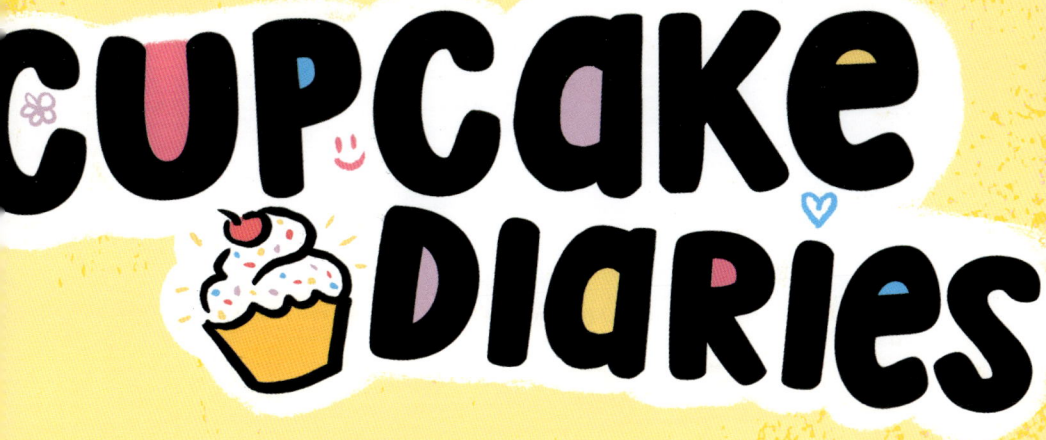

Alexis Cool as a Cupcake

By
Coco Simon

Illustrated by
Giulia Campobello
at Glass House Graphics

Simon Spotlight
New York   Amsterdam/Antwerp   London
Toronto   Sydney/Melbourne   New Delhi

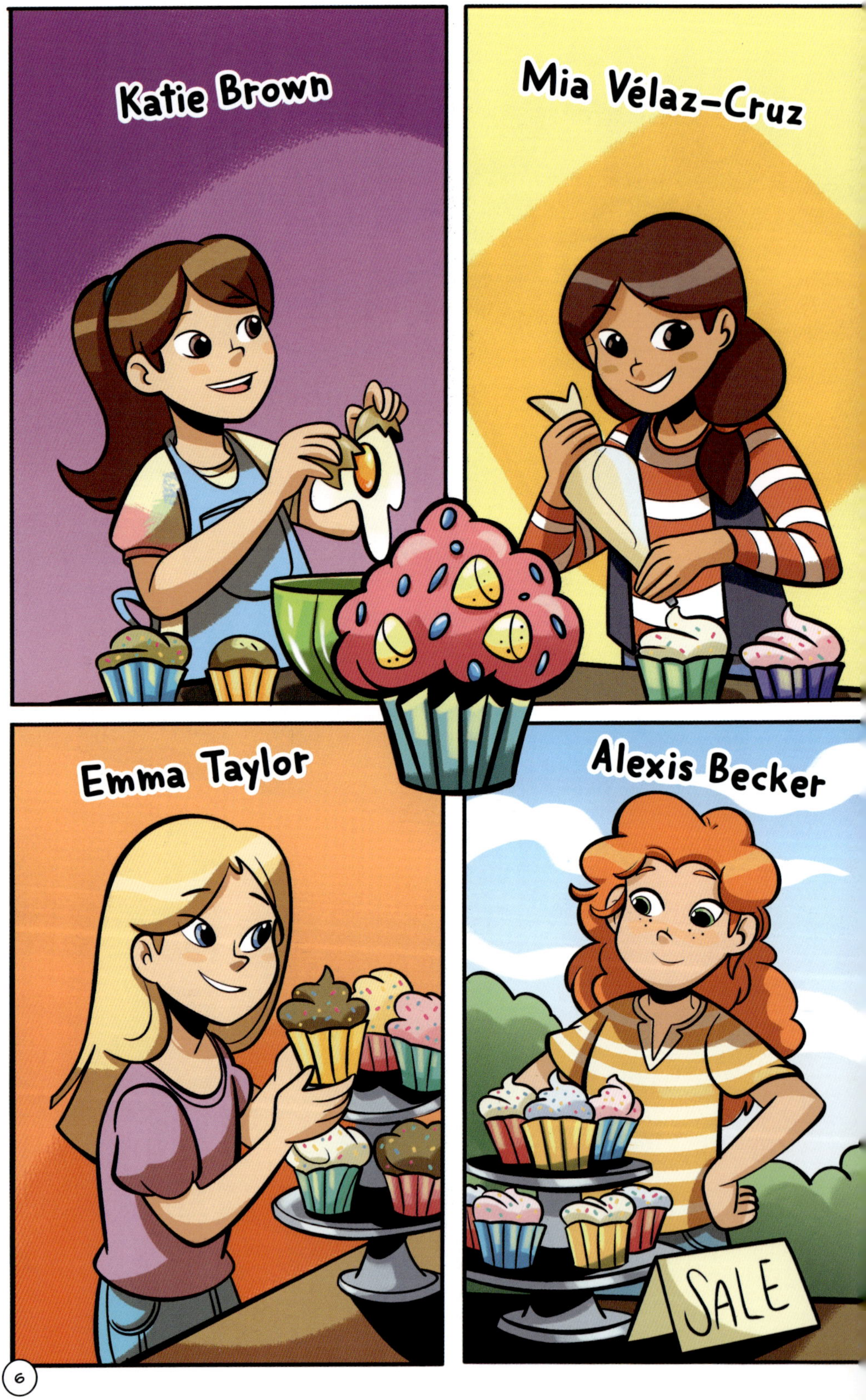
Katie Brown
Mia Vélaz-Cruz
Emma Taylor
Alexis Becker
SALE

Chapter 1

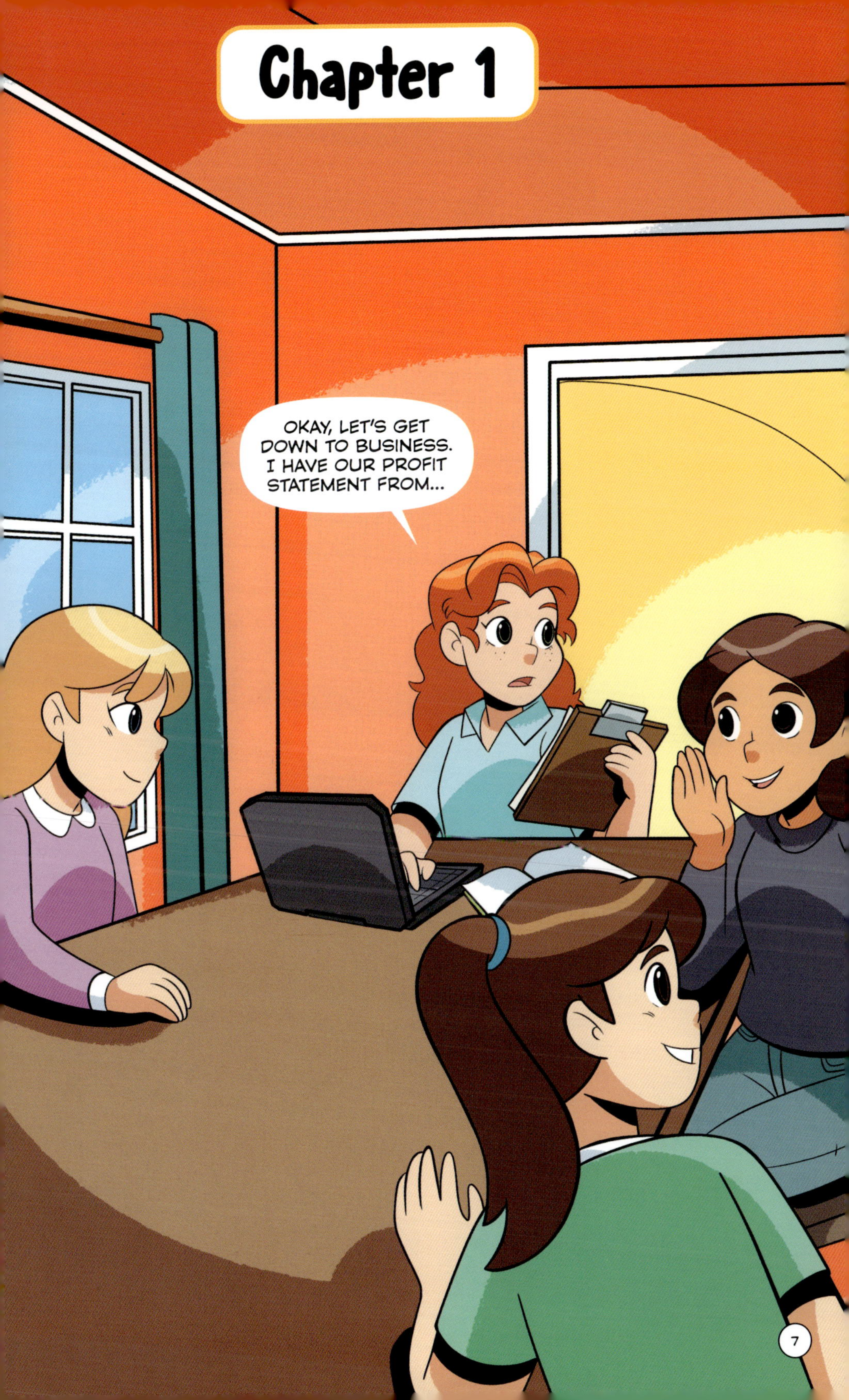
OKAY, LET'S GET DOWN TO BUSINESS. I HAVE OUR PROFIT STATEMENT FROM...

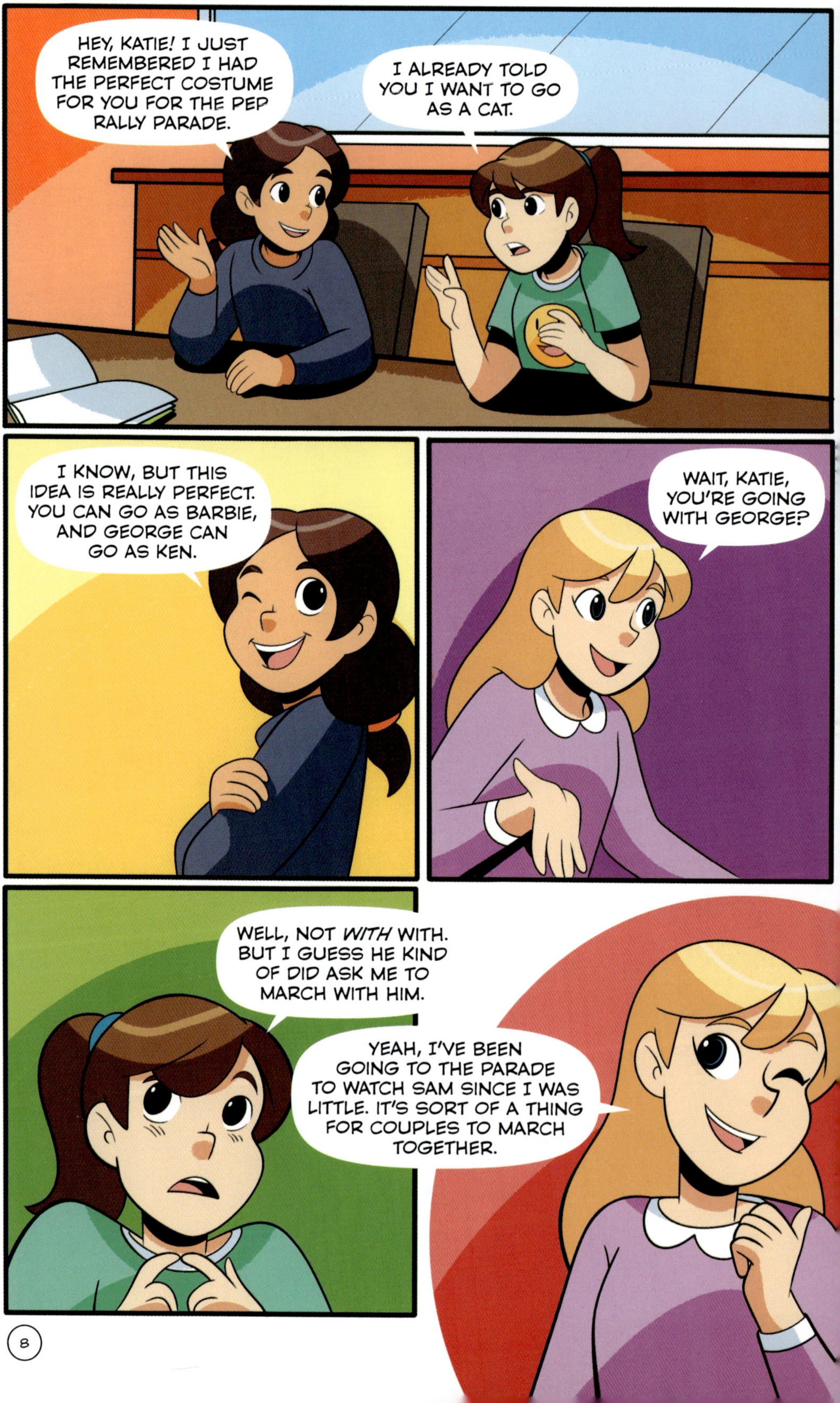
HEY, KATIE! I JUST REMEMBERED I HAD THE PERFECT COSTUME FOR YOU FOR THE PEP RALLY PARADE.
I ALREADY TOLD YOU I WANT TO GO AS A CAT.
I KNOW, BUT THIS IDEA IS REALLY PERFECT. YOU CAN GO AS BARBIE, AND GEORGE CAN GO AS KEN.
WAIT, KATIE, YOU'RE GOING WITH GEORGE?
WELL, NOT *WITH* WITH. BUT I GUESS HE KIND OF DID ASK ME TO MARCH WITH HIM.
YEAH, I'VE BEEN GOING TO THE PARADE TO WATCH SAM SINCE I WAS LITTLE. IT'S SORT OF A THING FOR COUPLES TO MARCH TOGETHER.

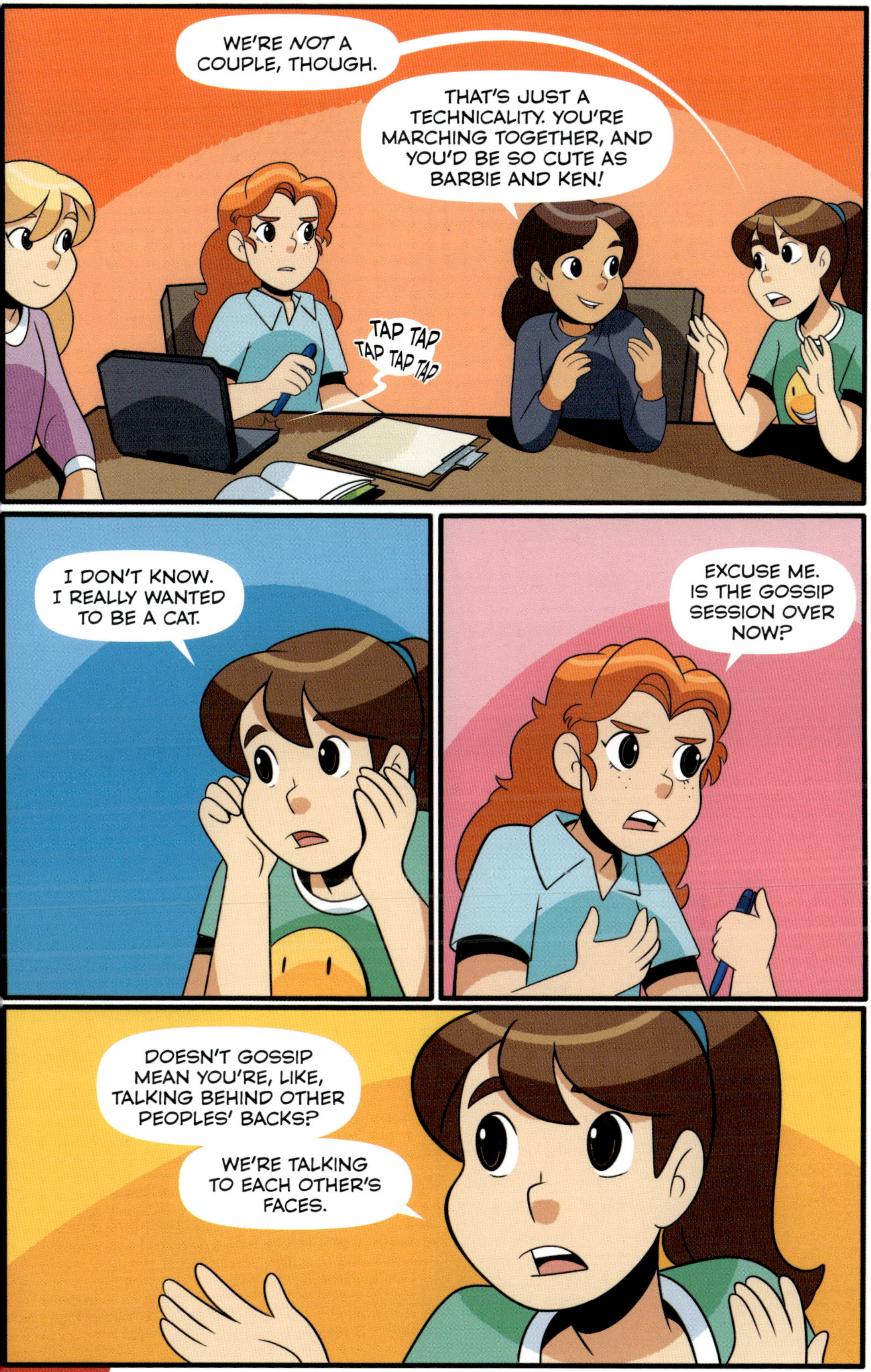
WE'RE *NOT* A COUPLE, THOUGH.
THAT'S JUST A TECHNICALITY. YOU'RE MARCHING TOGETHER, AND YOU'D BE SO CUTE AS BARBIE AND KEN!
TAP TAP TAP TAP TAP
I DON'T KNOW. I REALLY WANTED TO BE A CAT.
EXCUSE ME. IS THE GOSSIP SESSION OVER NOW?
DOESN'T GOSSIP MEAN YOU'RE, LIKE, TALKING BEHIND OTHER PEOPLES' BACKS?
WE'RE TALKING TO EACH OTHER'S FACES.

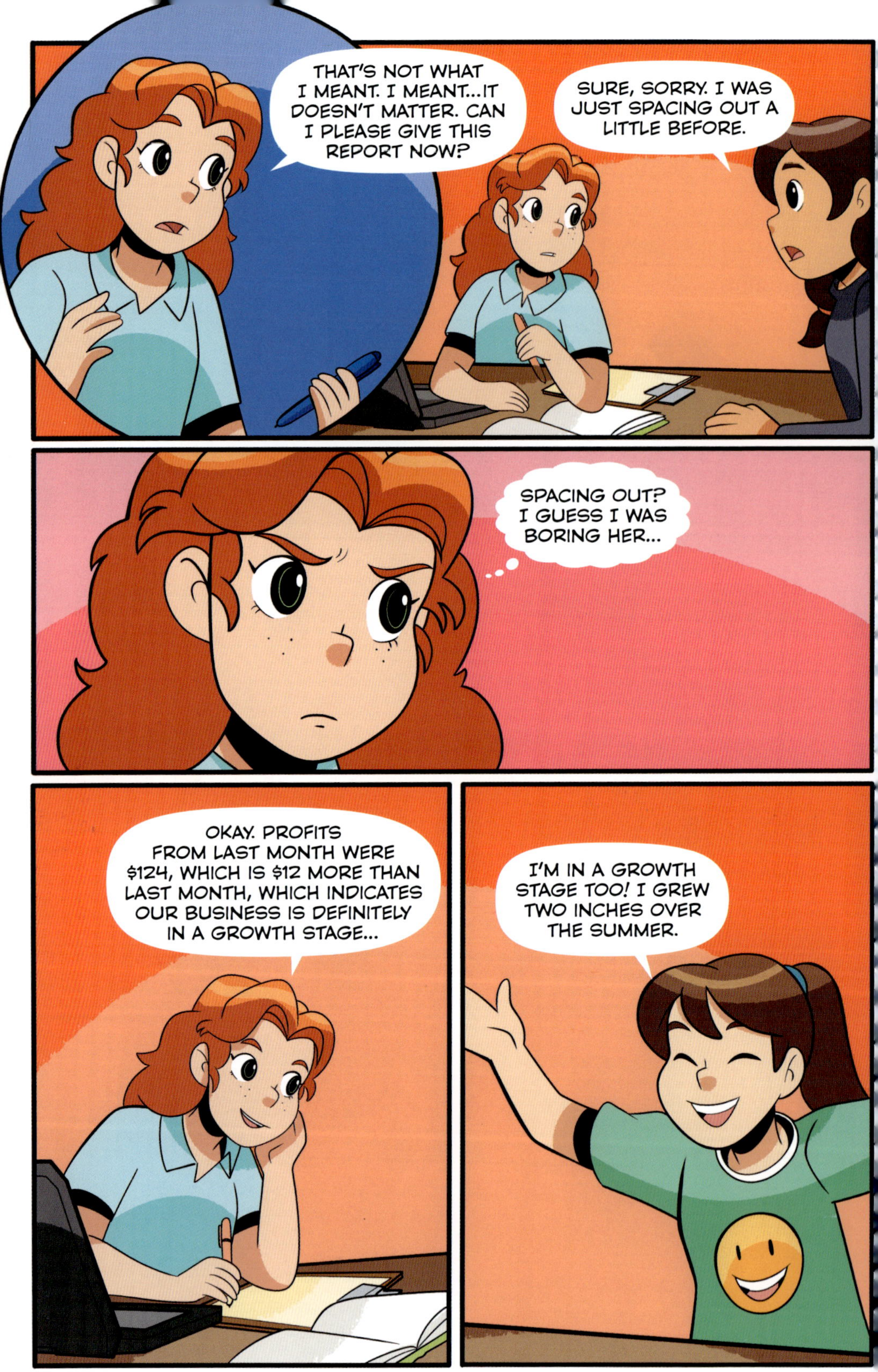
THAT'S NOT WHAT I MEANT. I MEANT...IT DOESN'T MATTER. CAN I PLEASE GIVE THIS REPORT NOW?
SURE, SORRY. I WAS JUST SPACING OUT A LITTLE BEFORE.
SPACING OUT? I GUESS I WAS BORING HER...
OKAY. PROFITS FROM LAST MONTH WERE $124, WHICH IS $12 MORE THAN LAST MONTH, WHICH INDICATES OUR BUSINESS IS DEFINITELY IN A GROWTH STAGE...
I'M IN A GROWTH STAGE TOO! I GREW TWO INCHES OVER THE SUMMER.

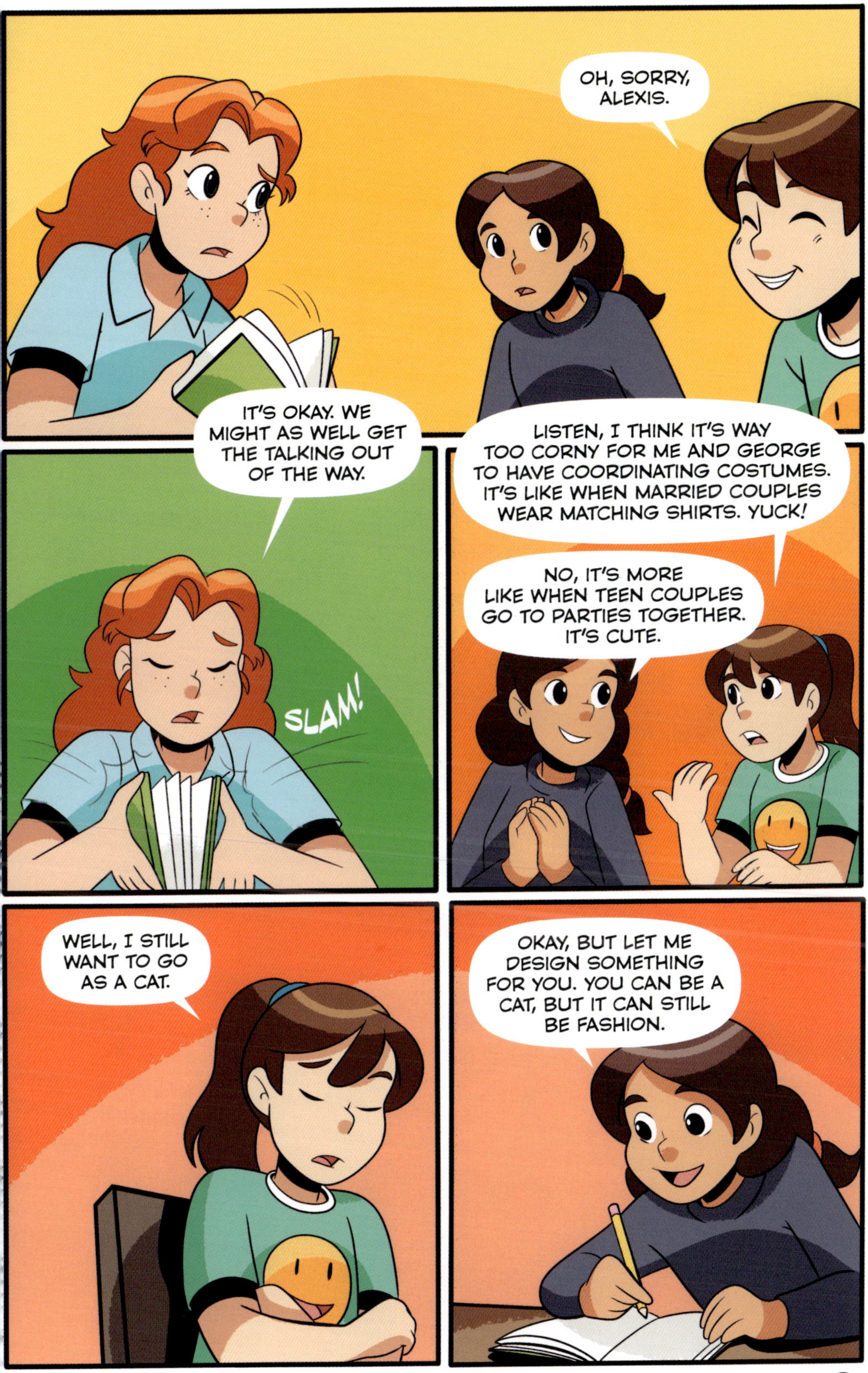
OH, SORRY, ALEXIS.
IT'S OKAY. WE MIGHT AS WELL GET THE TALKING OUT OF THE WAY.
SLAM!
LISTEN, I THINK IT'S WAY TOO CORNY FOR ME AND GEORGE TO HAVE COORDINATING COSTUMES. IT'S LIKE WHEN MARRIED COUPLES WEAR MATCHING SHIRTS. YUCK!
NO, IT'S MORE LIKE WHEN TEEN COUPLES GO TO PARTIES TOGETHER. IT'S CUTE.
WELL, I STILL WANT TO GO AS A CAT.
OKAY, BUT LET ME DESIGN SOMETHING FOR YOU. YOU CAN BE A CAT, BUT IT CAN STILL BE FASHION.

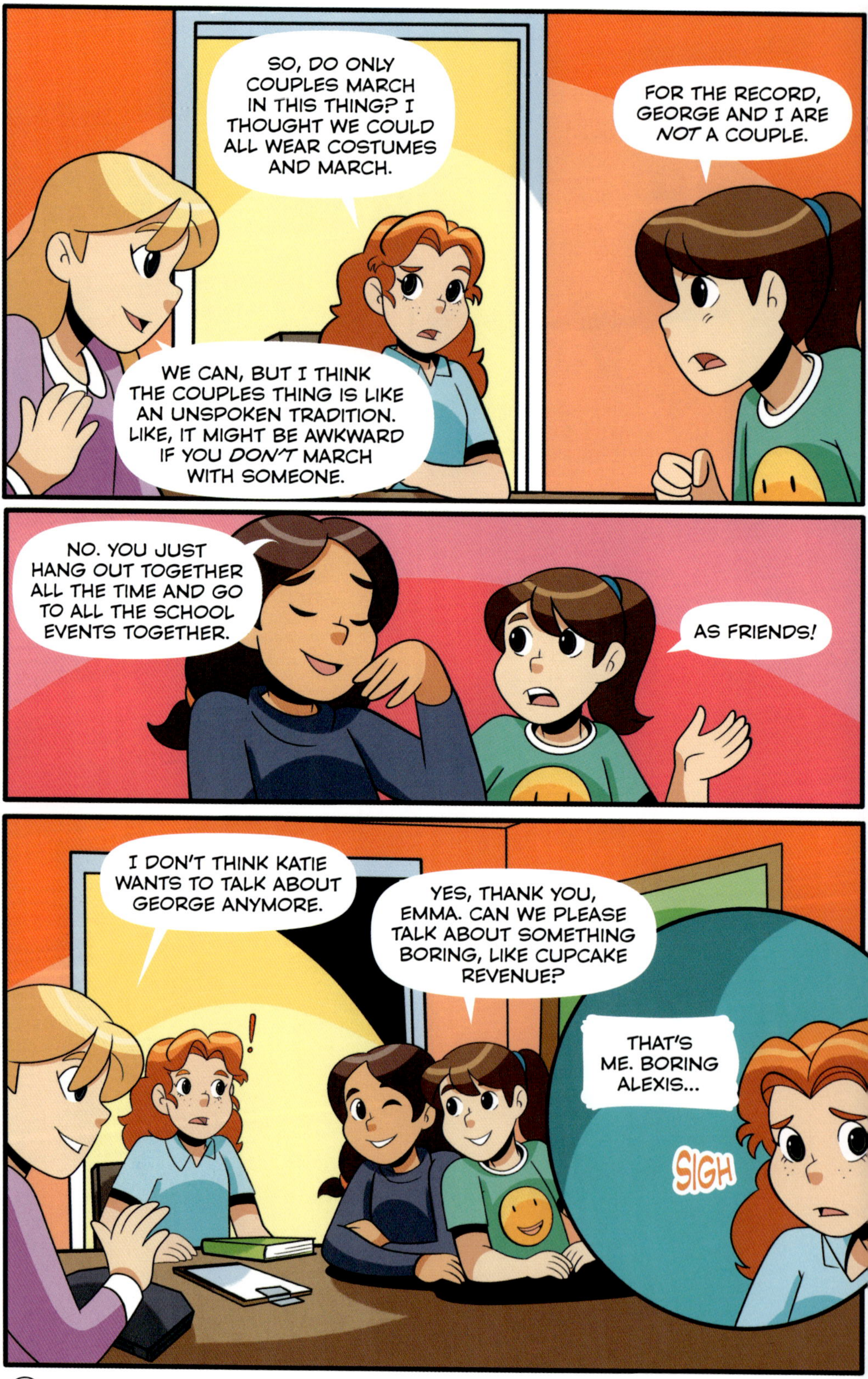

SO, DO ONLY COUPLES MARCH IN THIS THING? I THOUGHT WE COULD ALL WEAR COSTUMES AND MARCH.
WE CAN, BUT I THINK THE COUPLES THING IS LIKE AN UNSPOKEN TRADITION. LIKE, IT MIGHT BE AWKWARD IF YOU *DON'T* MARCH WITH SOMEONE.
FOR THE RECORD, GEORGE AND I ARE *NOT* A COUPLE.
NO. YOU JUST HANG OUT TOGETHER ALL THE TIME AND GO TO ALL THE SCHOOL EVENTS TOGETHER.
AS FRIENDS!
I DON'T THINK KATIE WANTS TO TALK ABOUT GEORGE ANYMORE.
!
YES, THANK YOU, EMMA. CAN WE PLEASE TALK ABOUT SOMETHING BORING, LIKE CUPCAKE REVENUE?
THAT'S ME. BORING ALEXIS...
SIGH

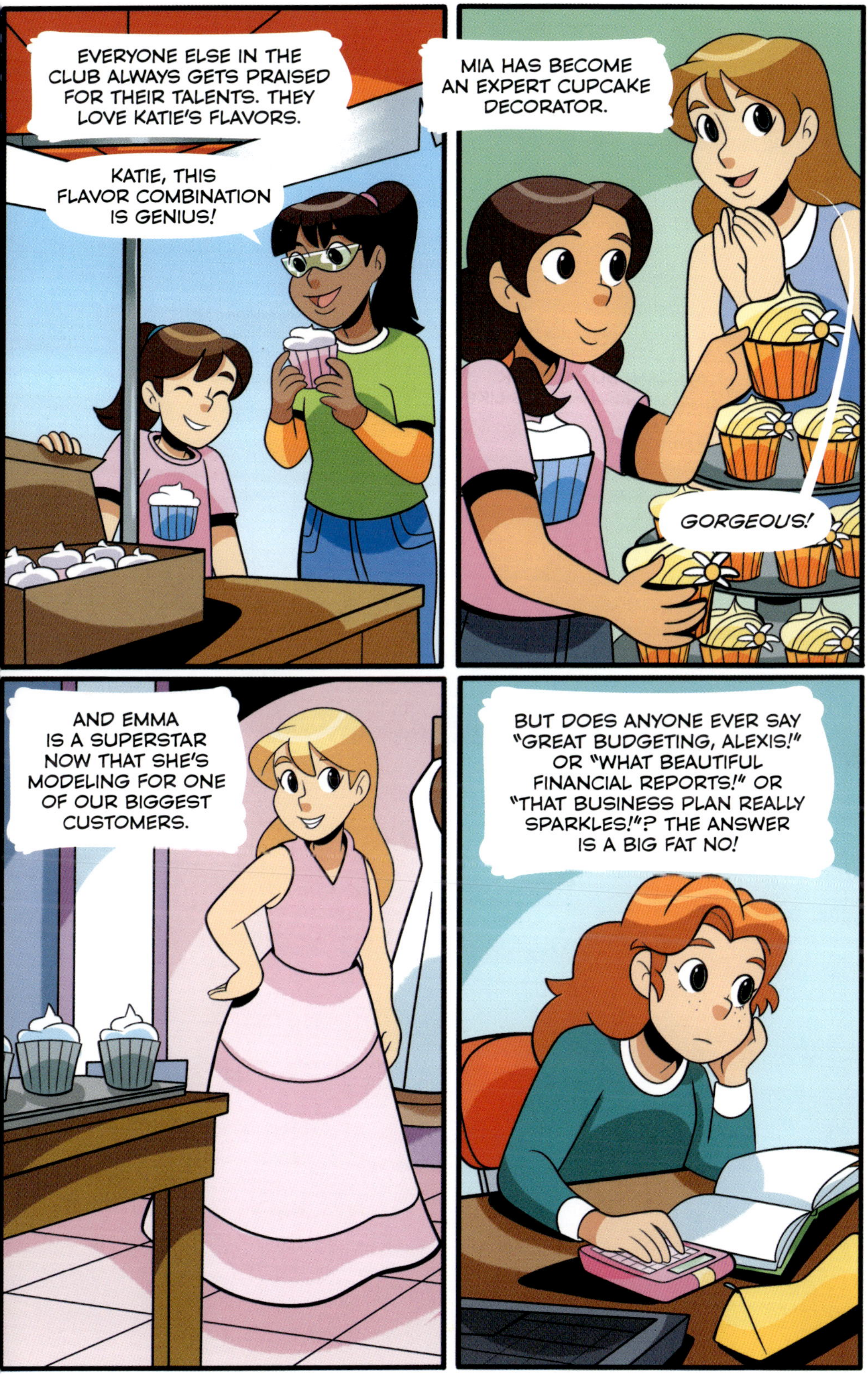
EVERYONE ELSE IN THE CLUB ALWAYS GETS PRAISED FOR THEIR TALENTS. THEY LOVE KATIE'S FLAVORS.
KATIE, THIS FLAVOR COMBINATION IS GENIUS!
MIA HAS BECOME AN EXPERT CUPCAKE DECORATOR.
GORGEOUS!
AND EMMA IS A SUPERSTAR NOW THAT SHE'S MODELING FOR ONE OF OUR BIGGEST CUSTOMERS.
BUT DOES ANYONE EVER SAY "GREAT BUDGETING, ALEXIS!" OR "WHAT BEAUTIFUL FINANCIAL REPORTS!" OR "THAT BUSINESS PLAN REALLY SPARKLES!"? THE ANSWER IS A BIG FAT NO!

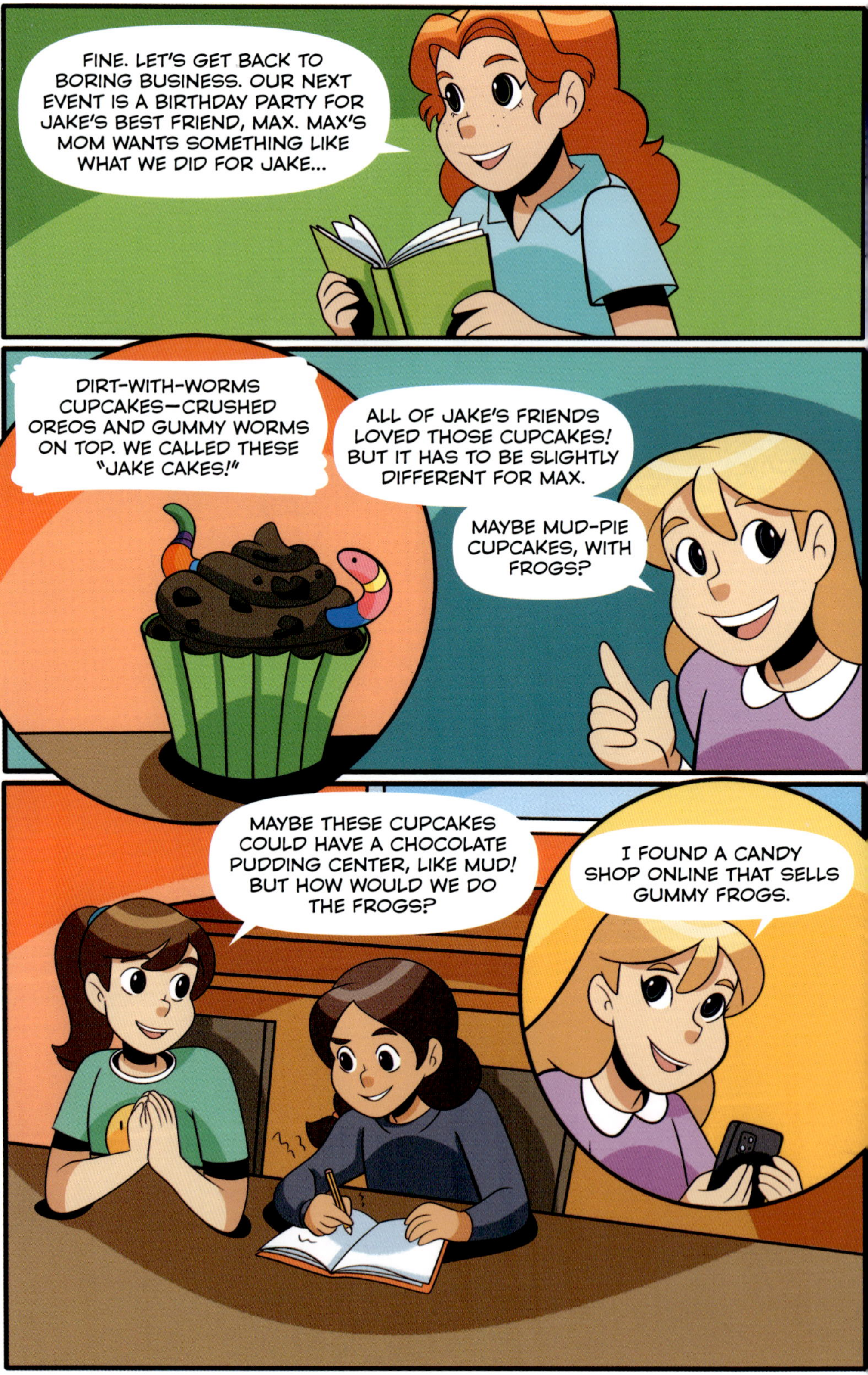
FINE. LET'S GET BACK TO BORING BUSINESS. OUR NEXT EVENT IS A BIRTHDAY PARTY FOR JAKE'S BEST FRIEND, MAX. MAX'S MOM WANTS SOMETHING LIKE WHAT WE DID FOR JAKE...
DIRT-WITH-WORMS CUPCAKES—CRUSHED OREOS AND GUMMY WORMS ON TOP. WE CALLED THESE "JAKE CAKES!"
ALL OF JAKE'S FRIENDS LOVED THOSE CUPCAKES! BUT IT HAS TO BE SLIGHTLY DIFFERENT FOR MAX.
MAYBE MUD-PIE CUPCAKES, WITH FROGS?
MAYBE THESE CUPCAKES COULD HAVE A CHOCOLATE PUDDING CENTER, LIKE MUD! BUT HOW WOULD WE DO THE FROGS?
I FOUND A CANDY SHOP ONLINE THAT SELLS GUMMY FROGS.

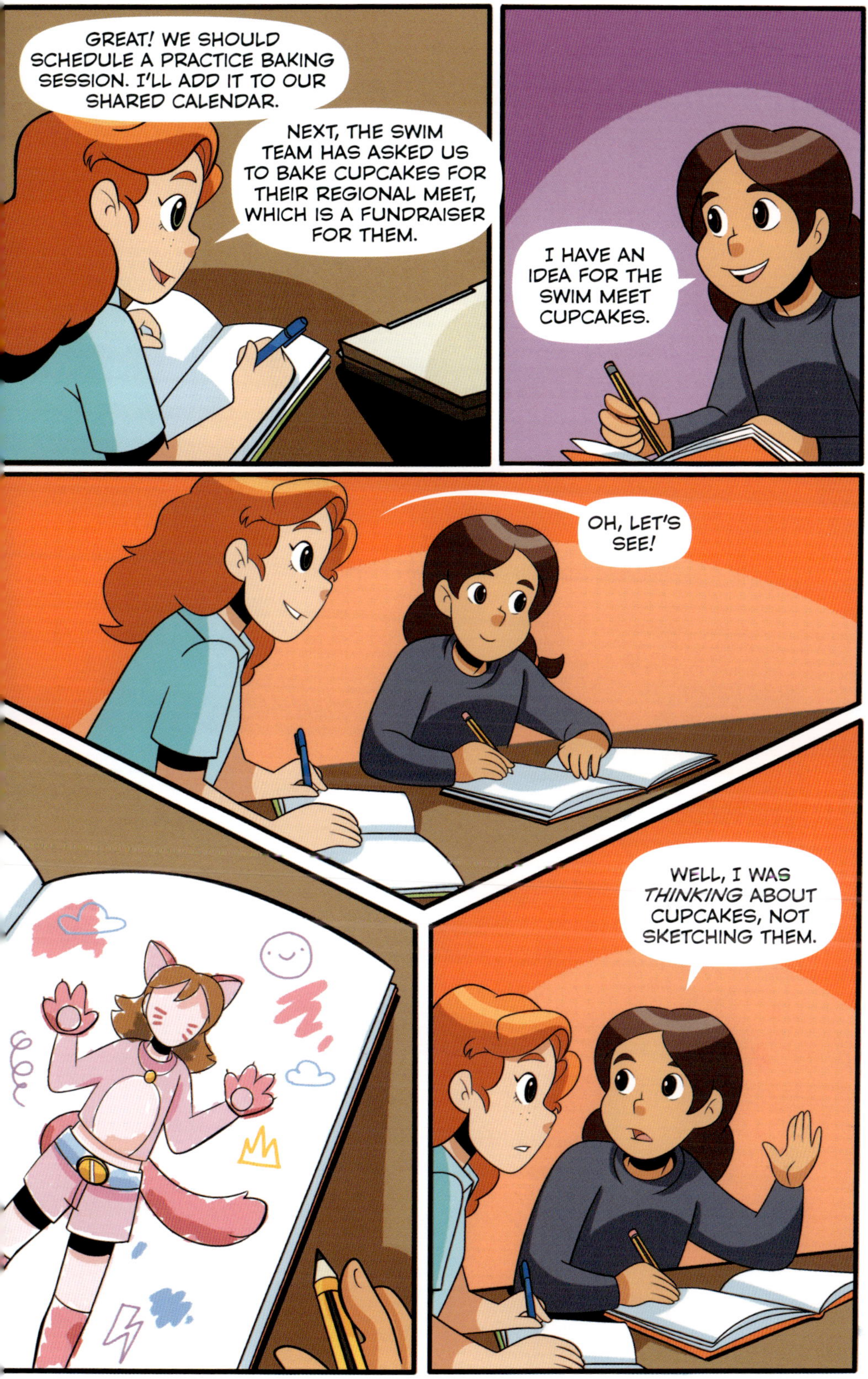
GREAT! WE SHOULD SCHEDULE A PRACTICE BAKING SESSION. I'LL ADD IT TO OUR SHARED CALENDAR.
NEXT, THE SWIM TEAM HAS ASKED US TO BAKE CUPCAKES FOR THEIR REGIONAL MEET, WHICH IS A FUNDRAISER FOR THEM.
I HAVE AN IDEA FOR THE SWIM MEET CUPCAKES.
OH, LET'S SEE!
WELL, I WAS *THINKING* ABOUT CUPCAKES, NOT SKETCHING THEM.

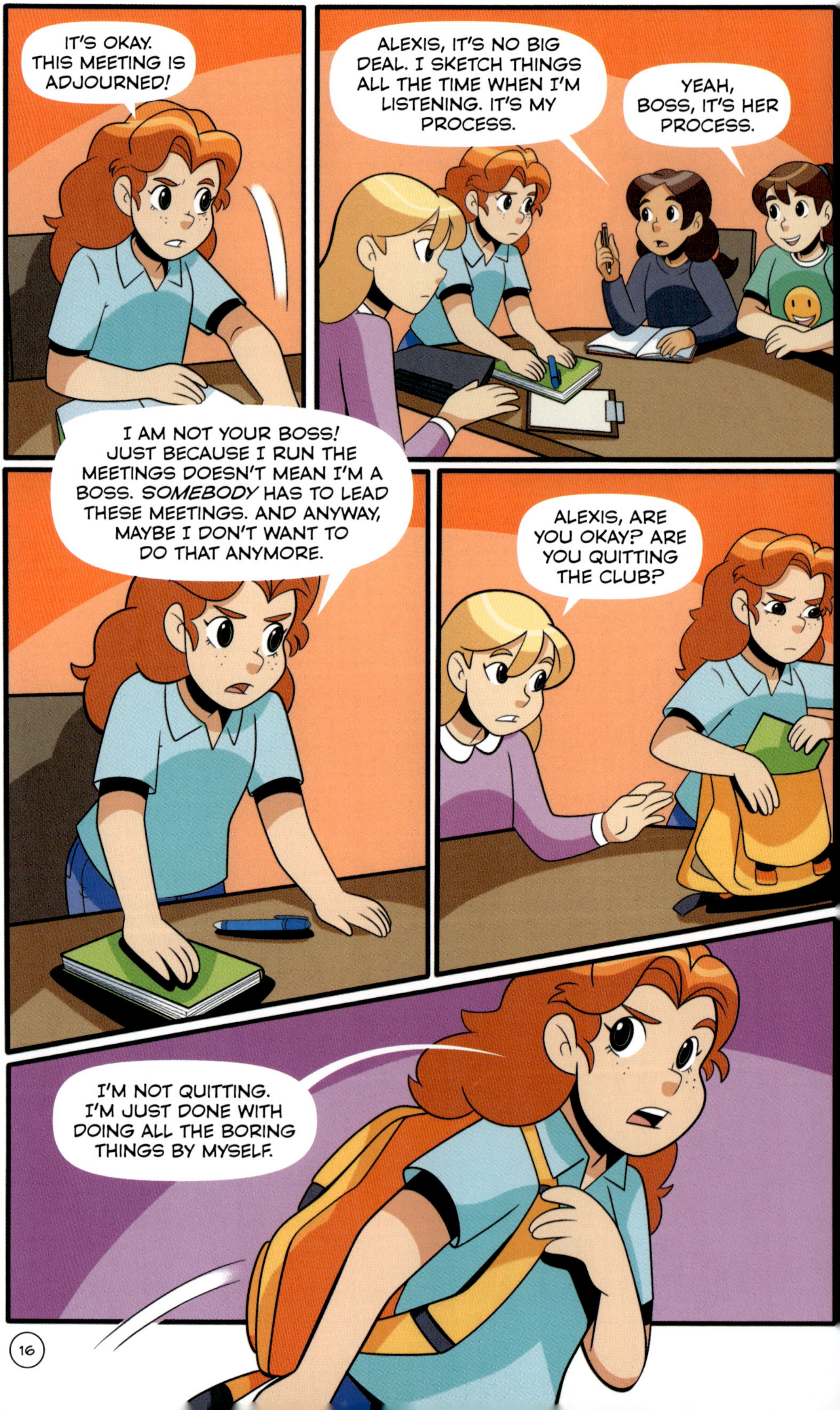
IT'S OKAY. THIS MEETING IS ADJOURNED!
ALEXIS, IT'S NO BIG DEAL. I SKETCH THINGS ALL THE TIME WHEN I'M LISTENING. IT'S MY PROCESS.
YEAH, BOSS, IT'S HER PROCESS.
I AM NOT YOUR BOSS! JUST BECAUSE I RUN THE MEETINGS DOESN'T MEAN I'M A BOSS. *SOMEBODY* HAS TO LEAD THESE MEETINGS. AND ANYWAY, MAYBE I DON'T WANT TO DO THAT ANYMORE.
ALEXIS, ARE YOU OKAY? ARE YOU QUITTING THE CLUB?
I'M NOT QUITTING. I'M JUST DONE WITH DOING ALL THE BORING THINGS BY MYSELF.

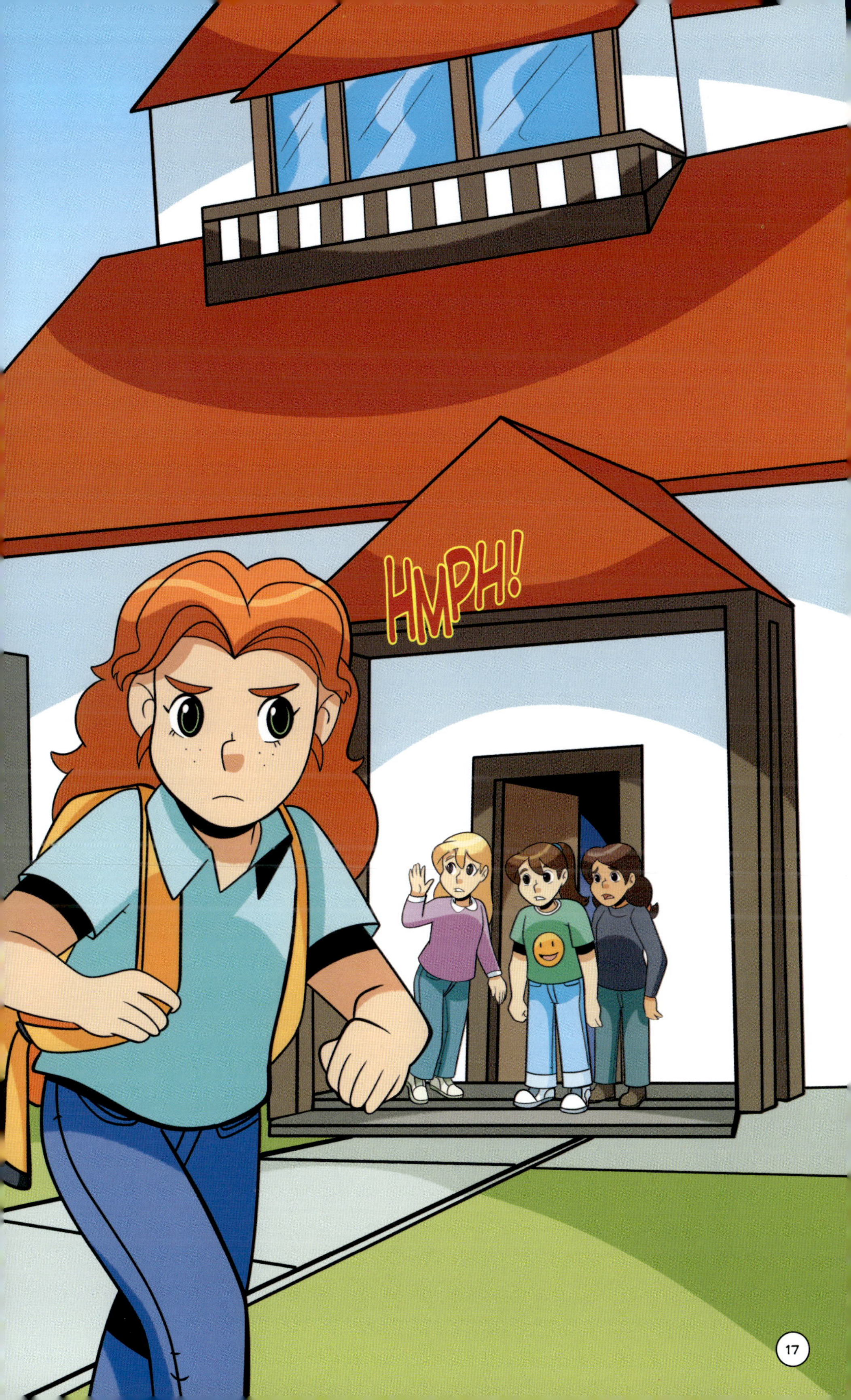
HMPH!

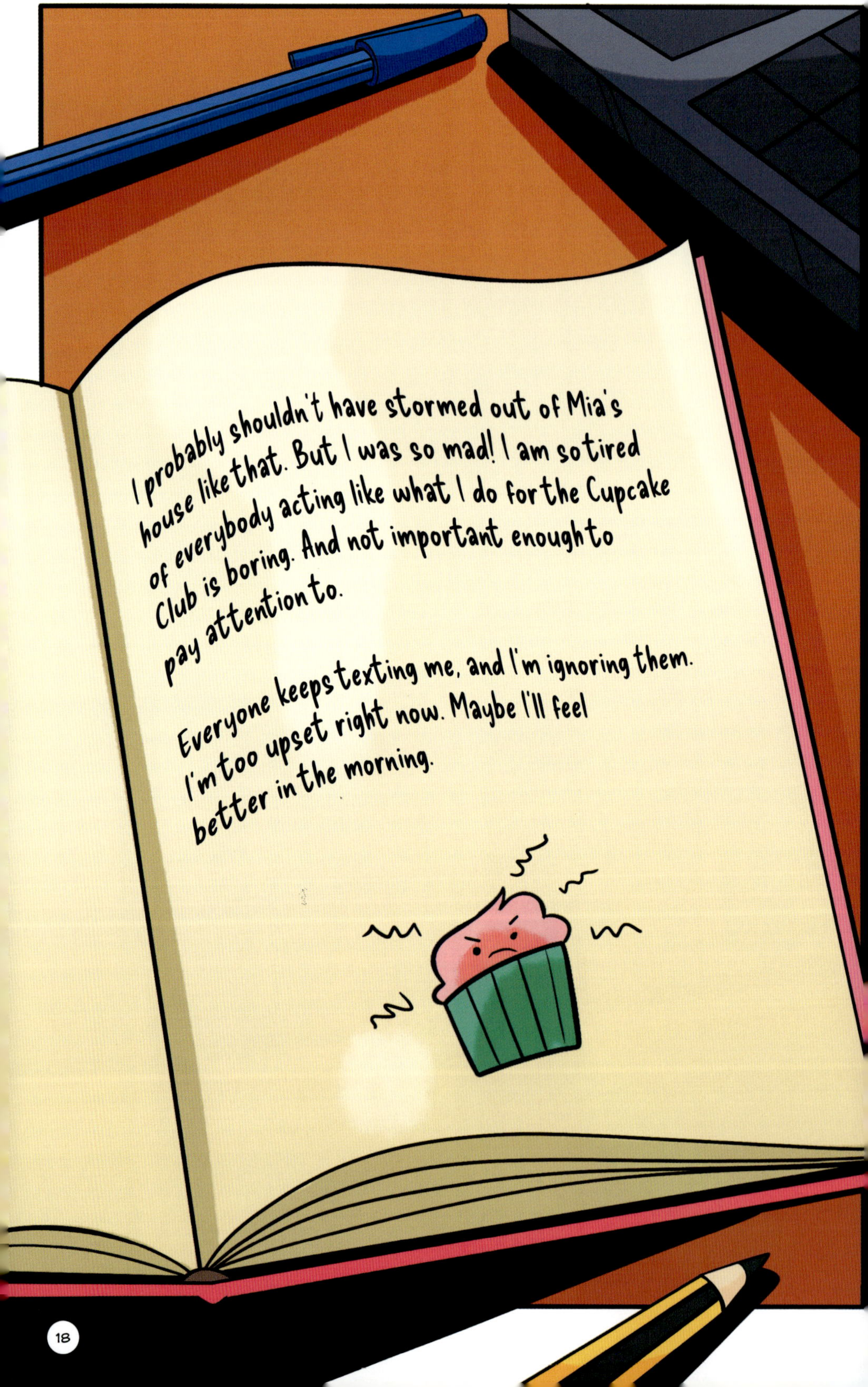
I probably shouldn't have stormed out of Mia's house like that. But I was so mad! I am so tired of everybody acting like what I do for the Cupcake Club is boring. And not important enough to pay attention to.
Everyone keeps texting me, and I'm ignoring them. I'm too upset right now. Maybe I'll feel better in the morning.

Chapter 2

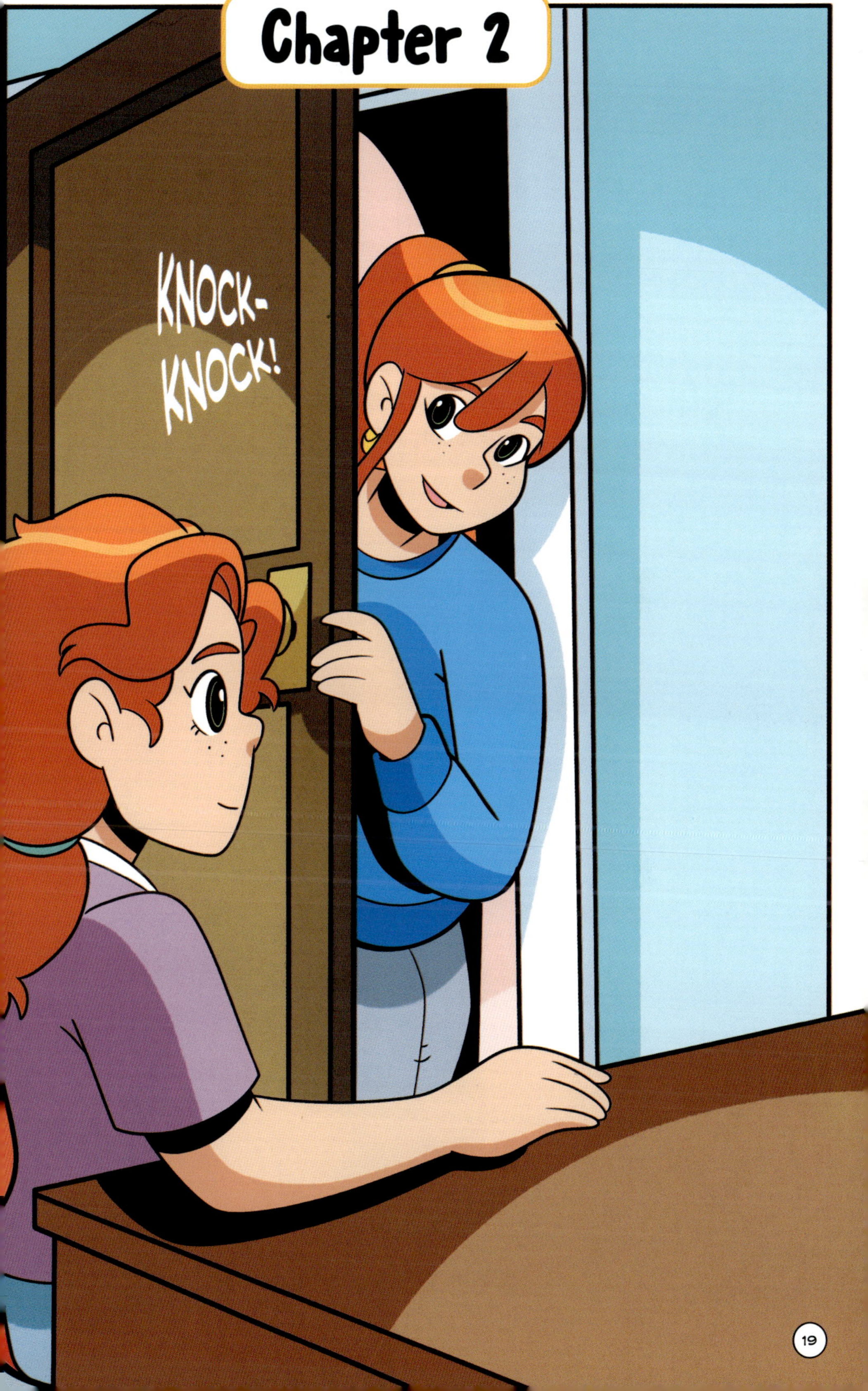
KNOCK-
KNOCK!

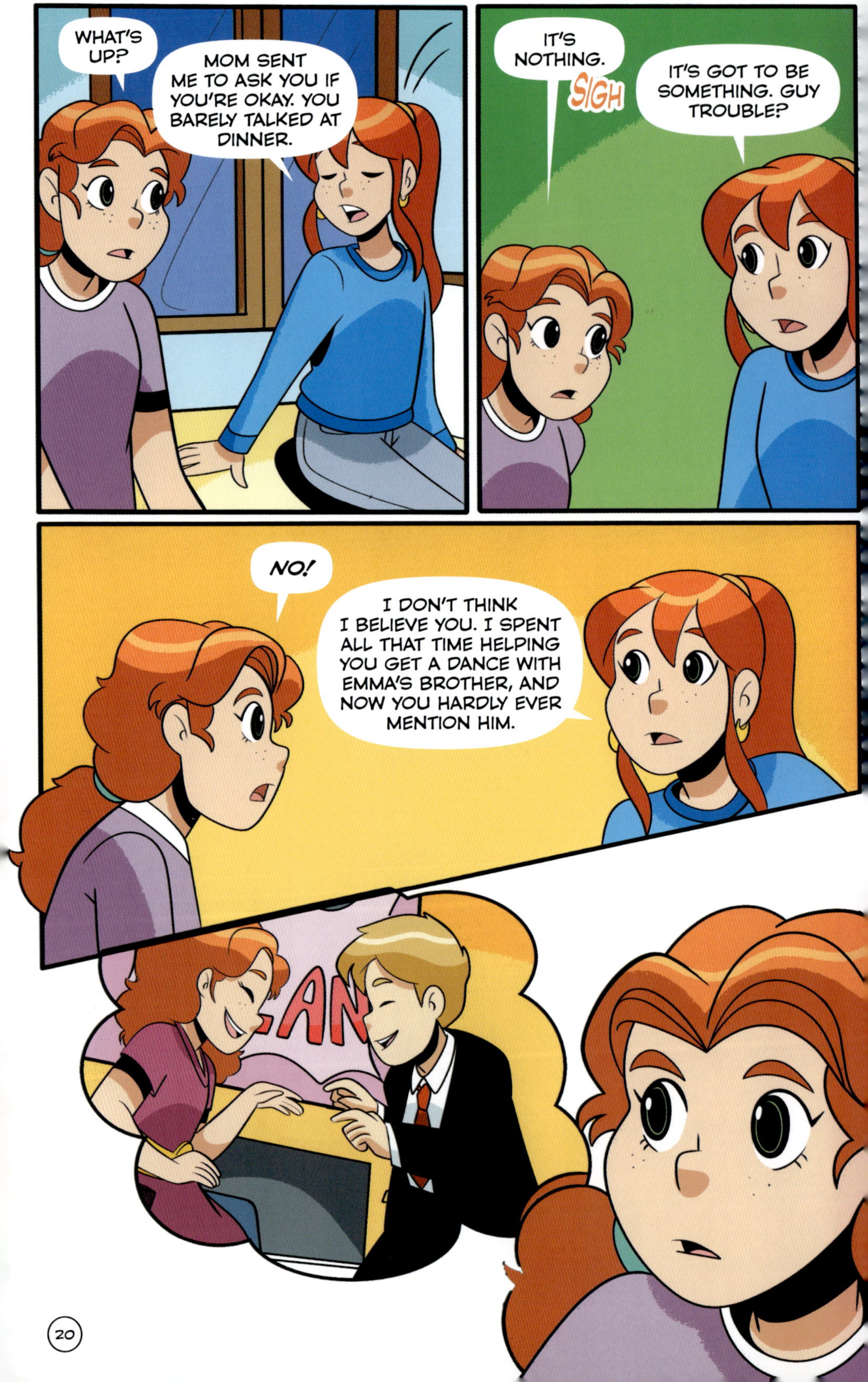

WHAT'S UP?
MOM SENT ME TO ASK YOU IF YOU'RE OKAY. YOU BARELY TALKED AT DINNER.
IT'S NOTHING.
SIGH
IT'S GOT TO BE SOMETHING. GUY TROUBLE?
NO!
I DON'T THINK I BELIEVE YOU. I SPENT ALL THAT TIME HELPING YOU GET A DANCE WITH EMMA'S BROTHER, AND NOW YOU HARDLY EVER MENTION HIM.

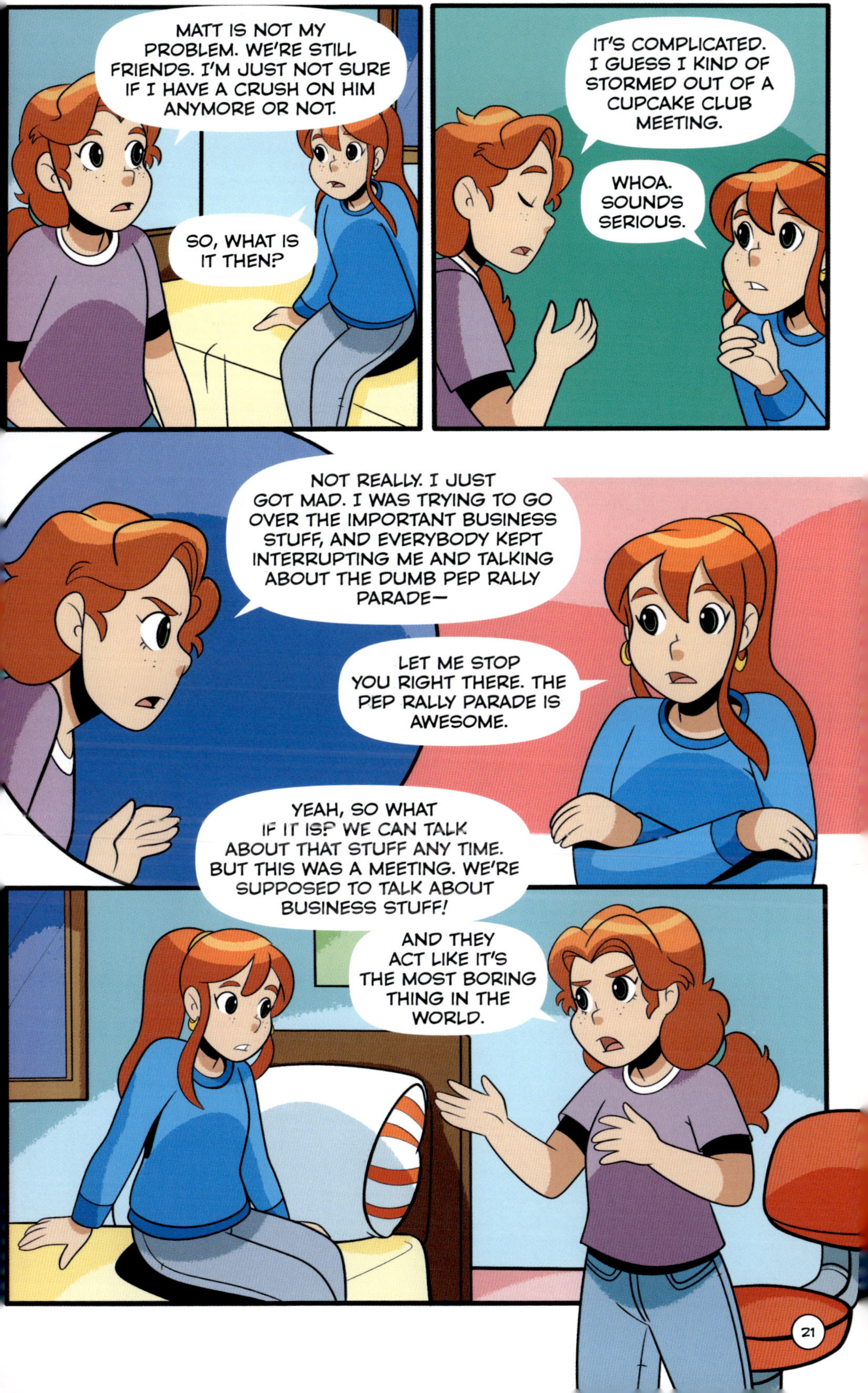
MATT IS NOT MY PROBLEM. WE'RE STILL FRIENDS. I'M JUST NOT SURE IF I HAVE A CRUSH ON HIM ANYMORE OR NOT.
SO, WHAT IS IT THEN?
IT'S COMPLICATED. I GUESS I KIND OF STORMED OUT OF A CUPCAKE CLUB MEETING.
WHOA. SOUNDS SERIOUS.
NOT REALLY. I JUST GOT MAD. I WAS TRYING TO GO OVER THE IMPORTANT BUSINESS STUFF, AND EVERYBODY KEPT INTERRUPTING ME AND TALKING ABOUT THE DUMB PEP RALLY PARADE—
LET ME STOP YOU RIGHT THERE. THE PEP RALLY PARADE IS AWESOME.
YEAH, SO WHAT IF IT IS? WE CAN TALK ABOUT THAT STUFF ANY TIME. BUT THIS WAS A MEETING. WE'RE SUPPOSED TO TALK ABOUT BUSINESS STUFF!
AND THEY ACT LIKE IT'S THE MOST BORING THING IN THE WORLD.

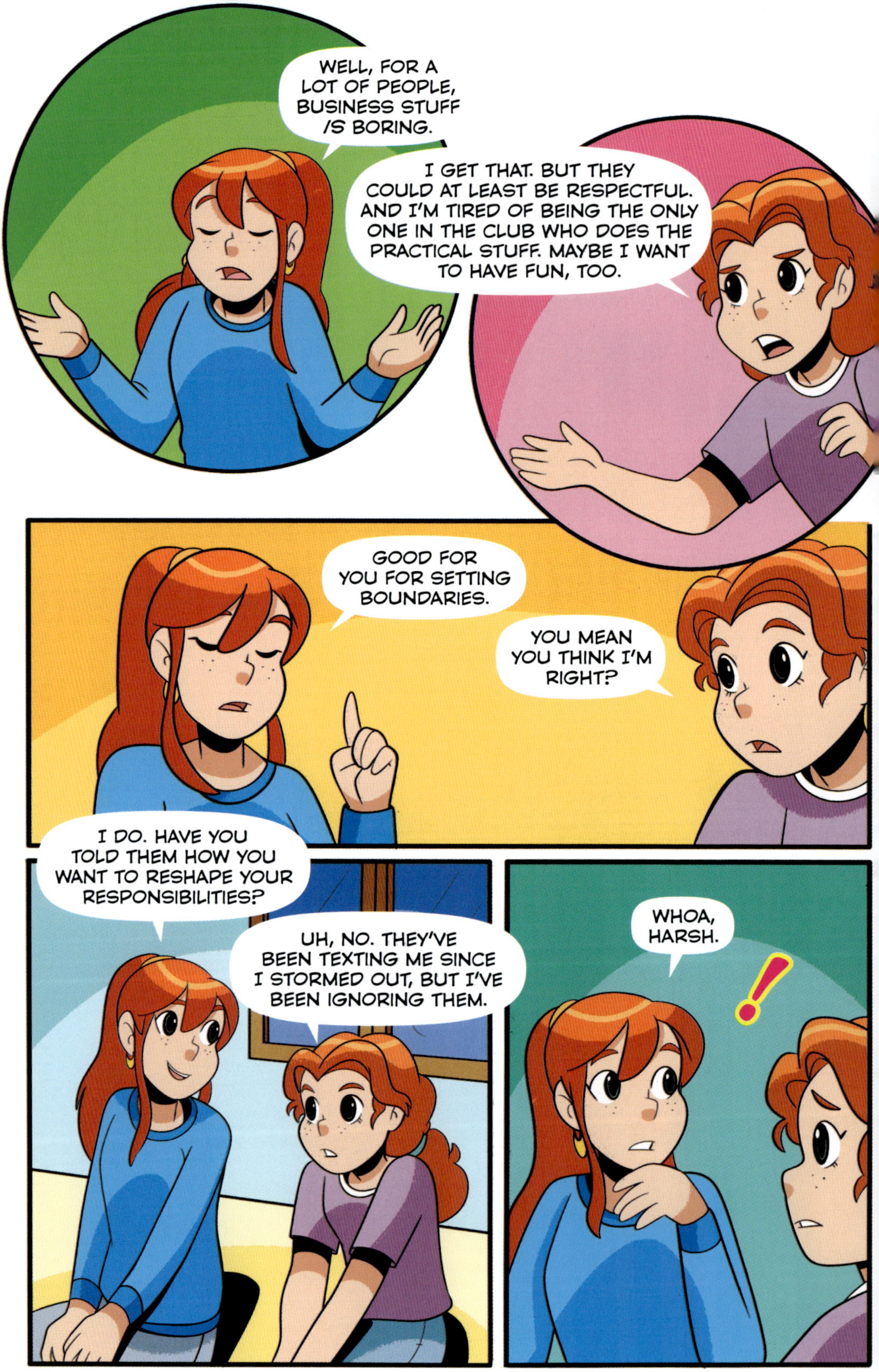
WELL, FOR A LOT OF PEOPLE, BUSINESS STUFF *IS* BORING.
I GET THAT. BUT THEY COULD AT LEAST BE RESPECTFUL. AND I'M TIRED OF BEING THE ONLY ONE IN THE CLUB WHO DOES THE PRACTICAL STUFF. MAYBE I WANT TO HAVE FUN, TOO.
GOOD FOR YOU FOR SETTING BOUNDARIES.
YOU MEAN YOU THINK I'M RIGHT?
I DO. HAVE YOU TOLD THEM HOW YOU WANT TO RESHAPE YOUR RESPONSIBILITIES?
UH, NO. THEY'VE BEEN TEXTING ME SINCE I STORMED OUT, BUT I'VE BEEN IGNORING THEM.
WHOA, HARSH.
!

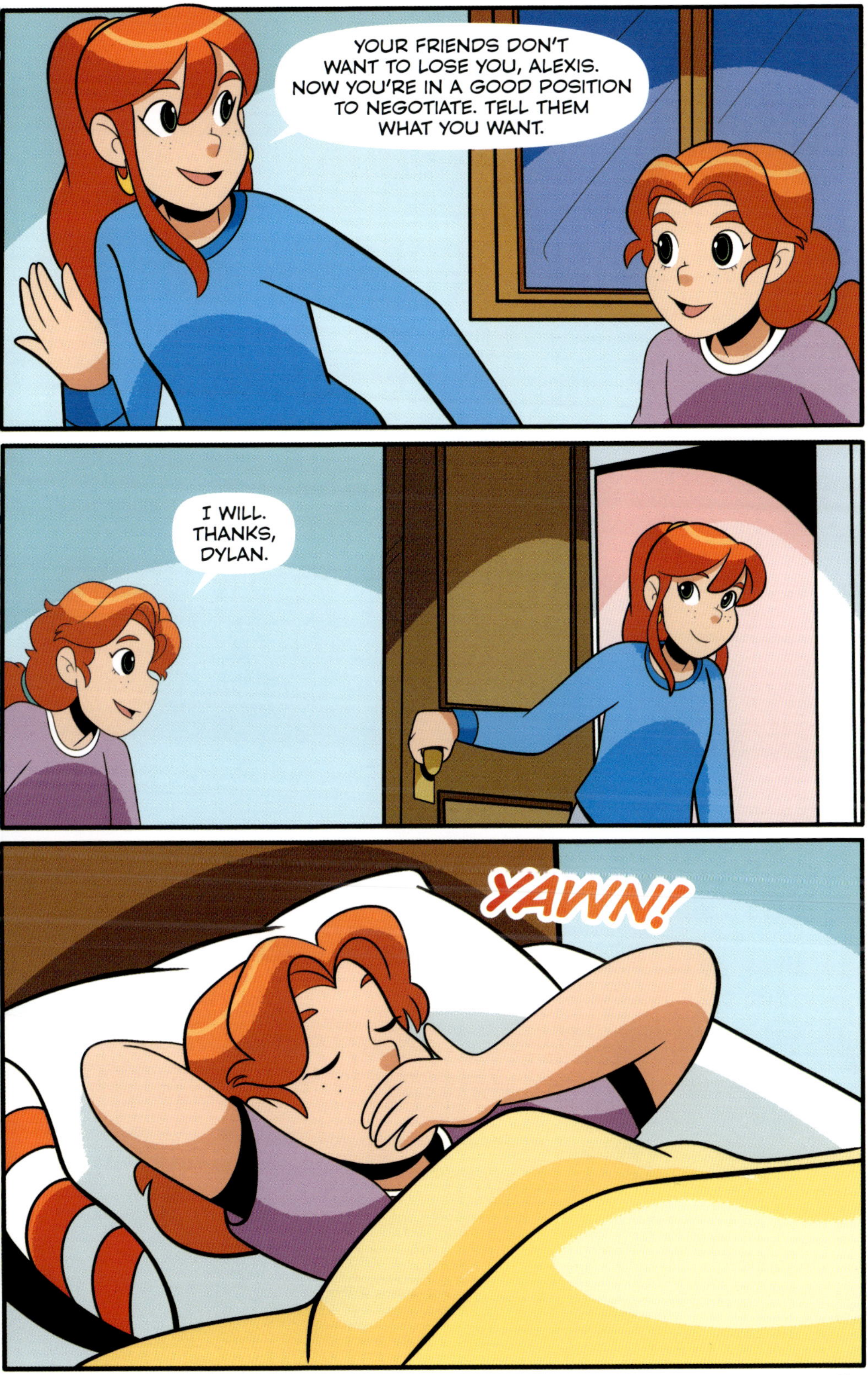
YOUR FRIENDS DON'T WANT TO LOSE YOU, ALEXIS. NOW YOU'RE IN A GOOD POSITION TO NEGOTIATE. TELL THEM WHAT YOU WANT.
I WILL. THANKS, DYLAN.
YAWN!

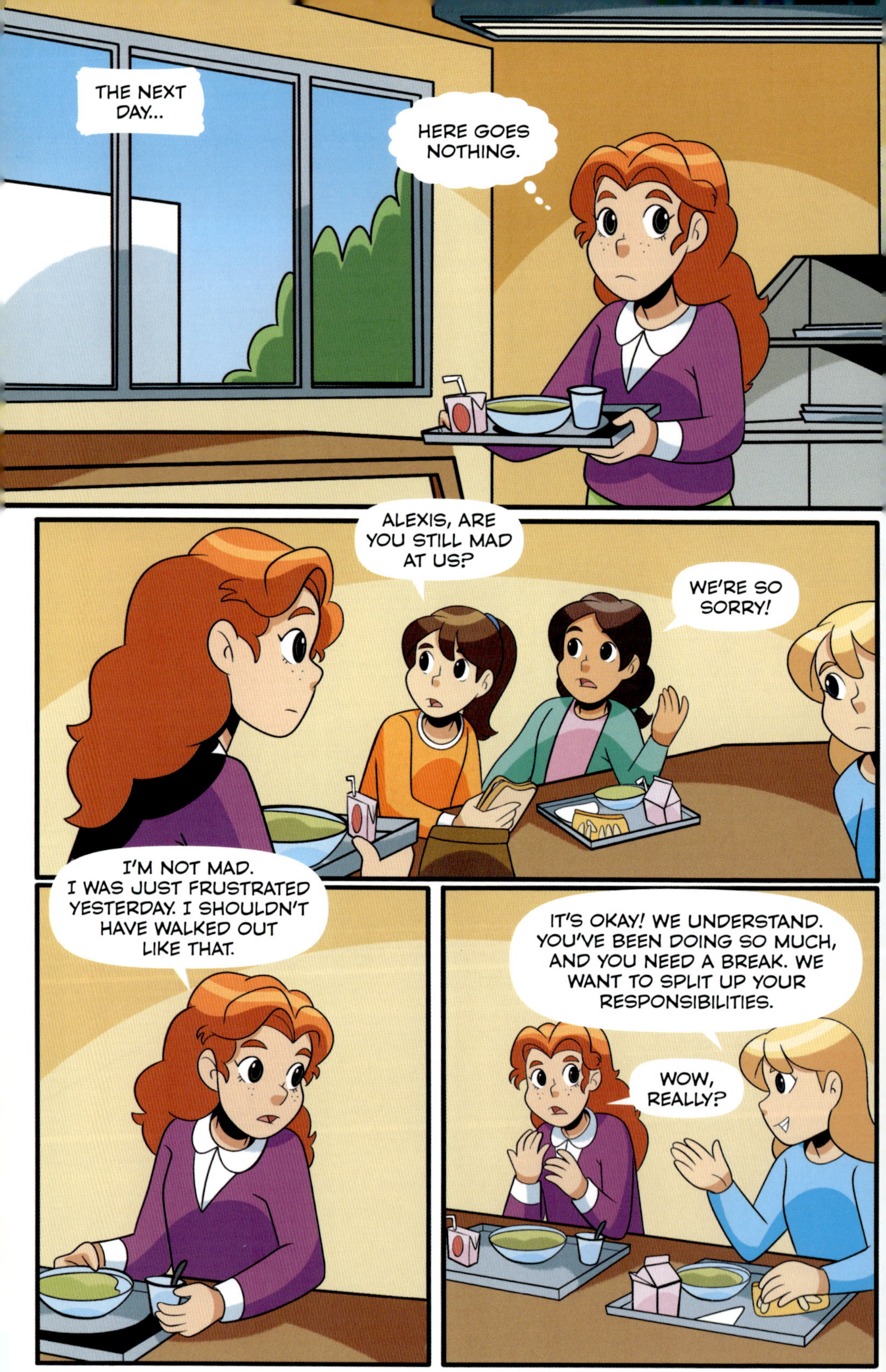
THE NEXT DAY...
HERE GOES NOTHING.
ALEXIS, ARE YOU STILL MAD AT US?
WE'RE SO SORRY!
I'M NOT MAD. I WAS JUST FRUSTRATED YESTERDAY. I SHOULDN'T HAVE WALKED OUT LIKE THAT.
IT'S OKAY! WE UNDERSTAND. YOU'VE BEEN DOING SO MUCH, AND YOU NEED A BREAK. WE WANT TO SPLIT UP YOUR RESPONSIBILITIES.
WOW, REALLY?

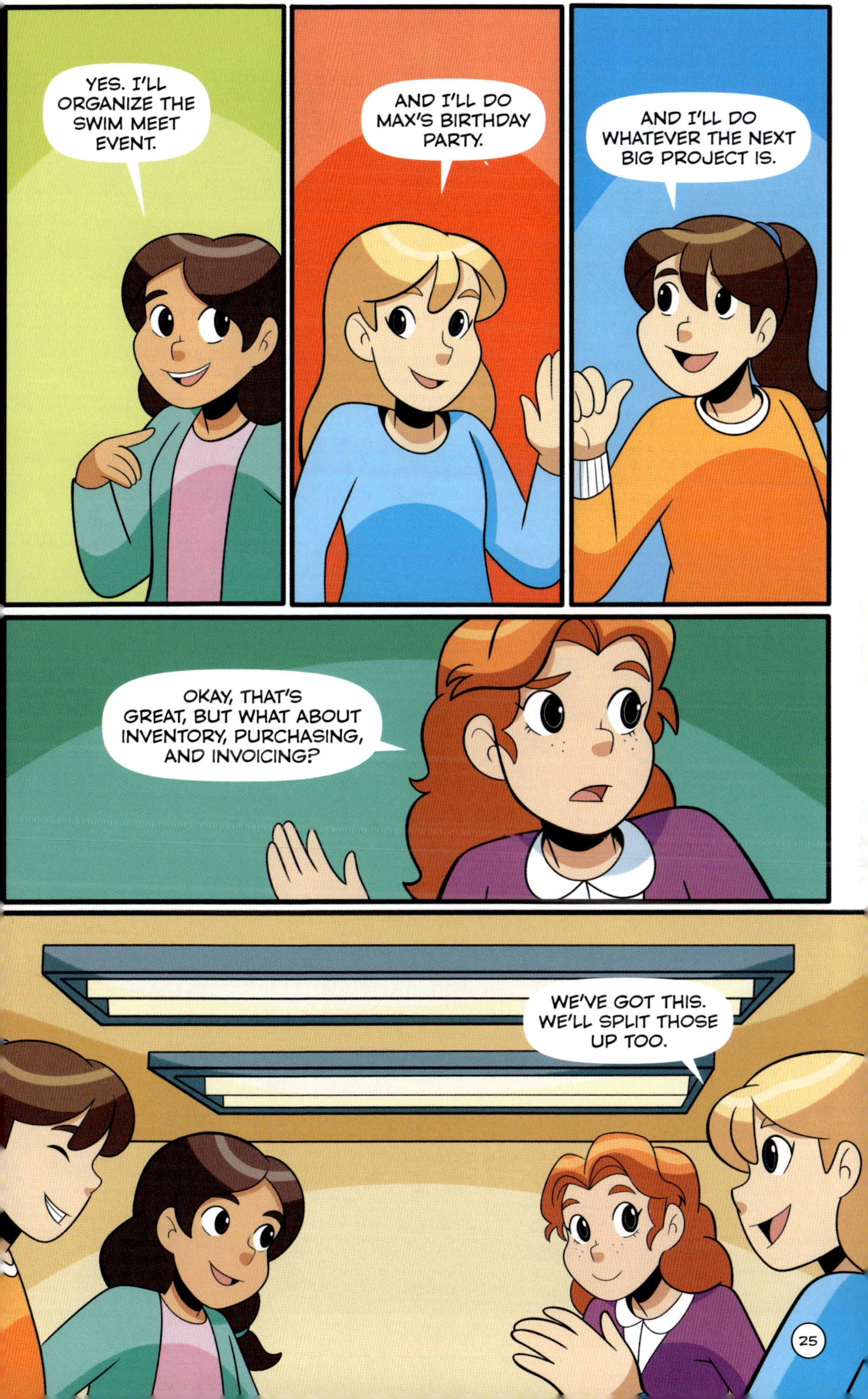
YES. I'LL ORGANIZE THE SWIM MEET EVENT.
AND I'LL DO MAX'S BIRTHDAY PARTY.
AND I'LL DO WHATEVER THE NEXT BIG PROJECT IS.
OKAY, THAT'S GREAT, BUT WHAT ABOUT INVENTORY, PURCHASING, AND INVOICING?
WE'VE GOT THIS. WE'LL SPLIT THOSE UP TOO.

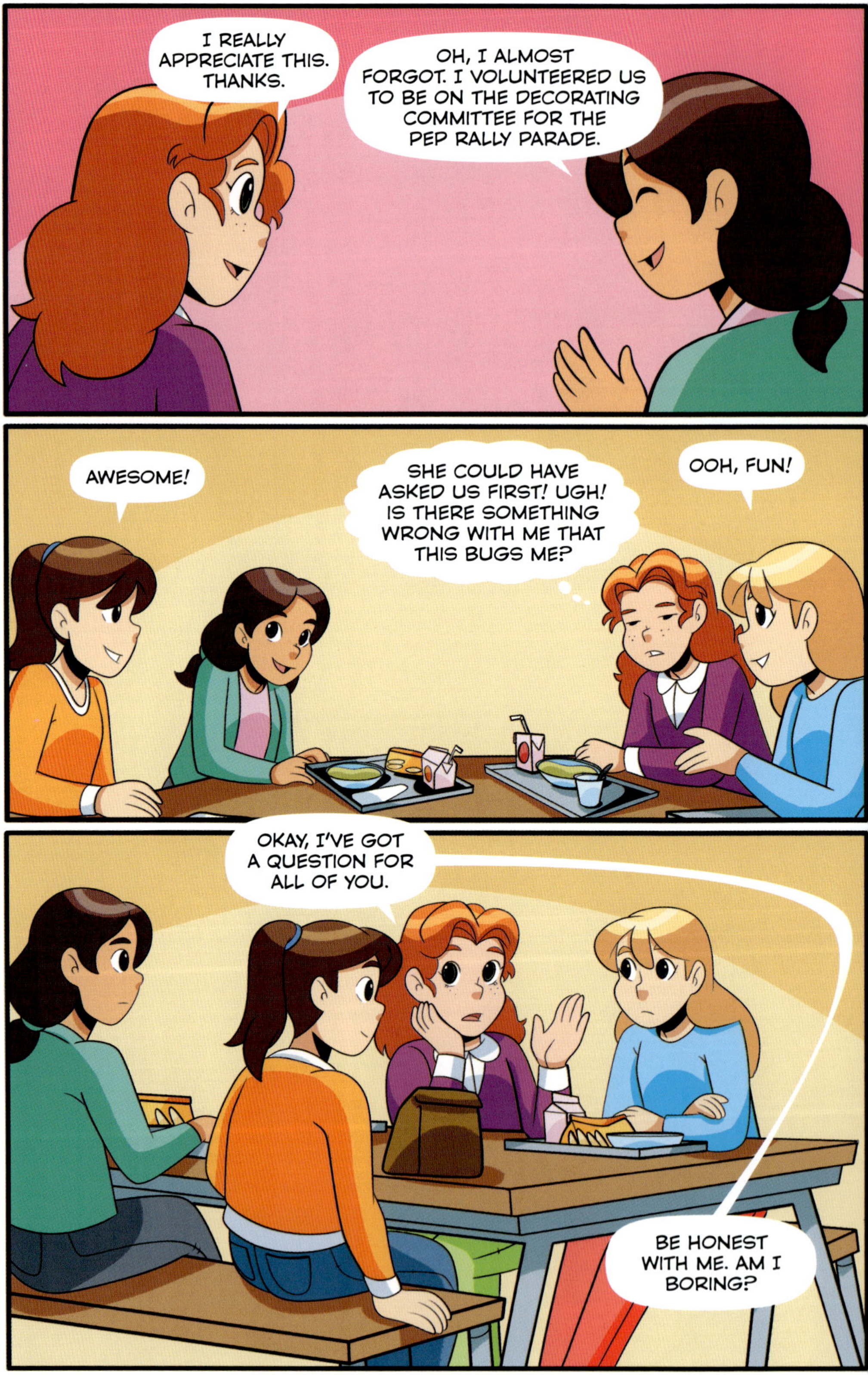
I REALLY APPRECIATE THIS. THANKS.
OH, I ALMOST FORGOT. I VOLUNTEERED US TO BE ON THE DECORATING COMMITTEE FOR THE PEP RALLY PARADE.
AWESOME!
SHE COULD HAVE ASKED US FIRST! UGH! IS THERE SOMETHING WRONG WITH ME THAT THIS BUGS ME?
OOH, FUN!
OKAY, I'VE GOT A QUESTION FOR ALL OF YOU.
BE HONEST WITH ME. AM I BORING?

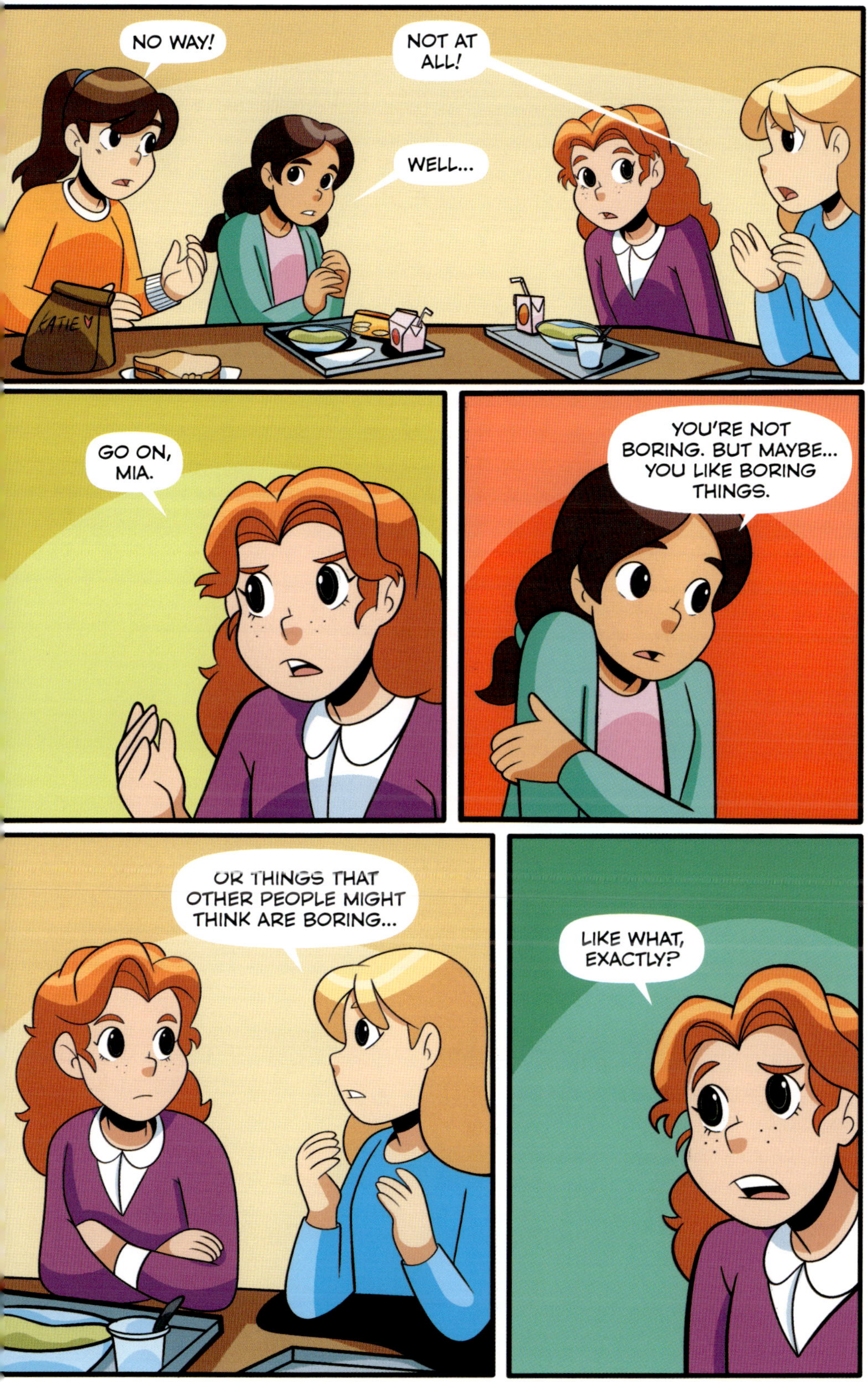
NO WAY!
NOT AT ALL!
WELL...
KATIE
GO ON, MIA.
YOU'RE NOT BORING. BUT MAYBE... YOU LIKE BORING THINGS.
OR THINGS THAT OTHER PEOPLE MIGHT THINK ARE BORING...
LIKE WHAT, EXACTLY?

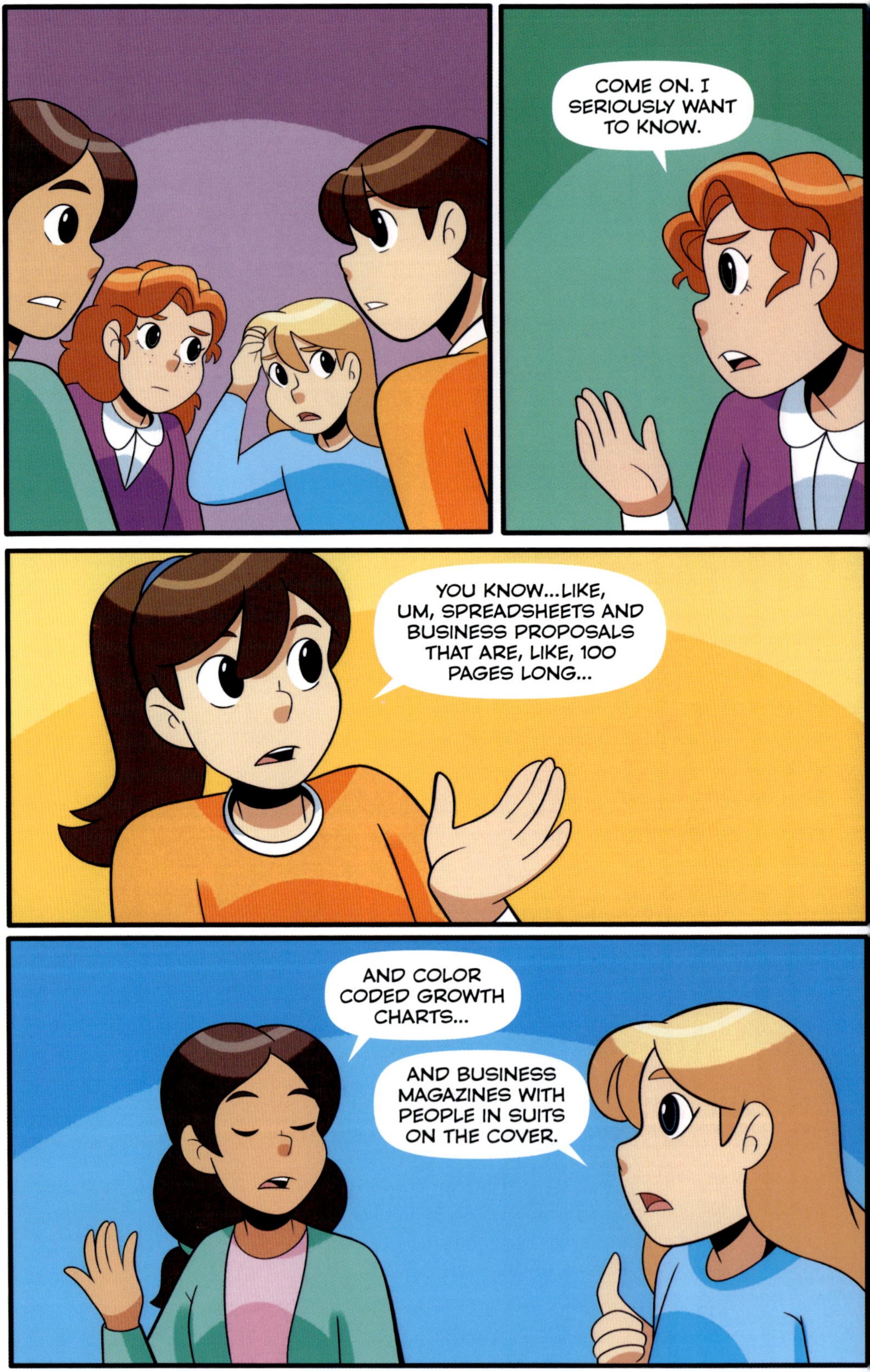
COME ON. I SERIOUSLY WANT TO KNOW.
YOU KNOW...LIKE, UM, SPREADSHEETS AND BUSINESS PROPOSALS THAT ARE, LIKE, 100 PAGES LONG...
AND COLOR CODED GROWTH CHARTS...
AND BUSINESS MAGAZINES WITH PEOPLE IN SUITS ON THE COVER.

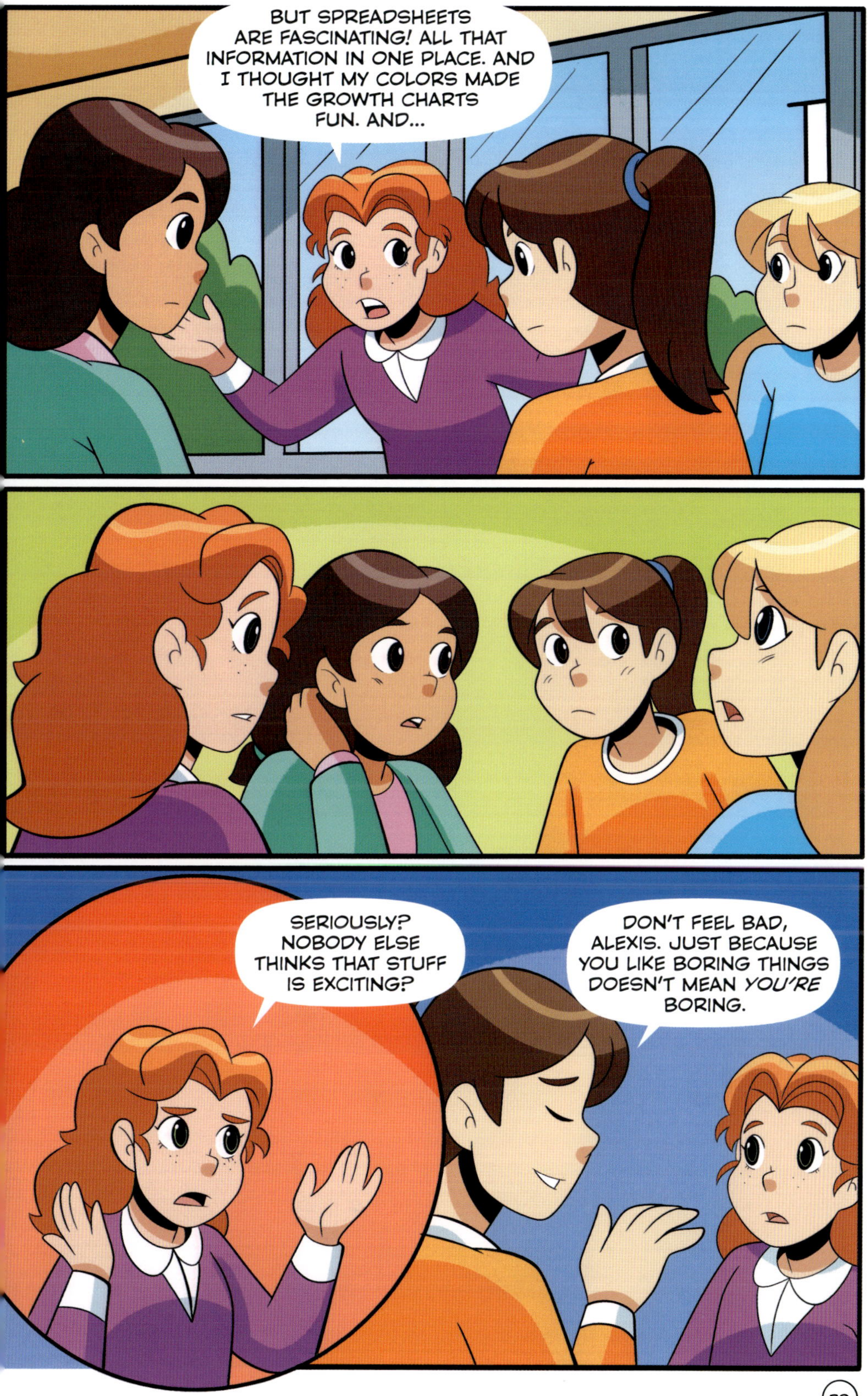
BUT SPREADSHEETS ARE FASCINATING! ALL THAT INFORMATION IN ONE PLACE. AND I THOUGHT MY COLORS MADE THE GROWTH CHARTS FUN. AND...
SERIOUSLY? NOBODY ELSE THINKS THAT STUFF IS EXCITING?
DON'T FEEL BAD, ALEXIS. JUST BECAUSE YOU LIKE BORING THINGS DOESN'T MEAN *YOU'RE* BORING.

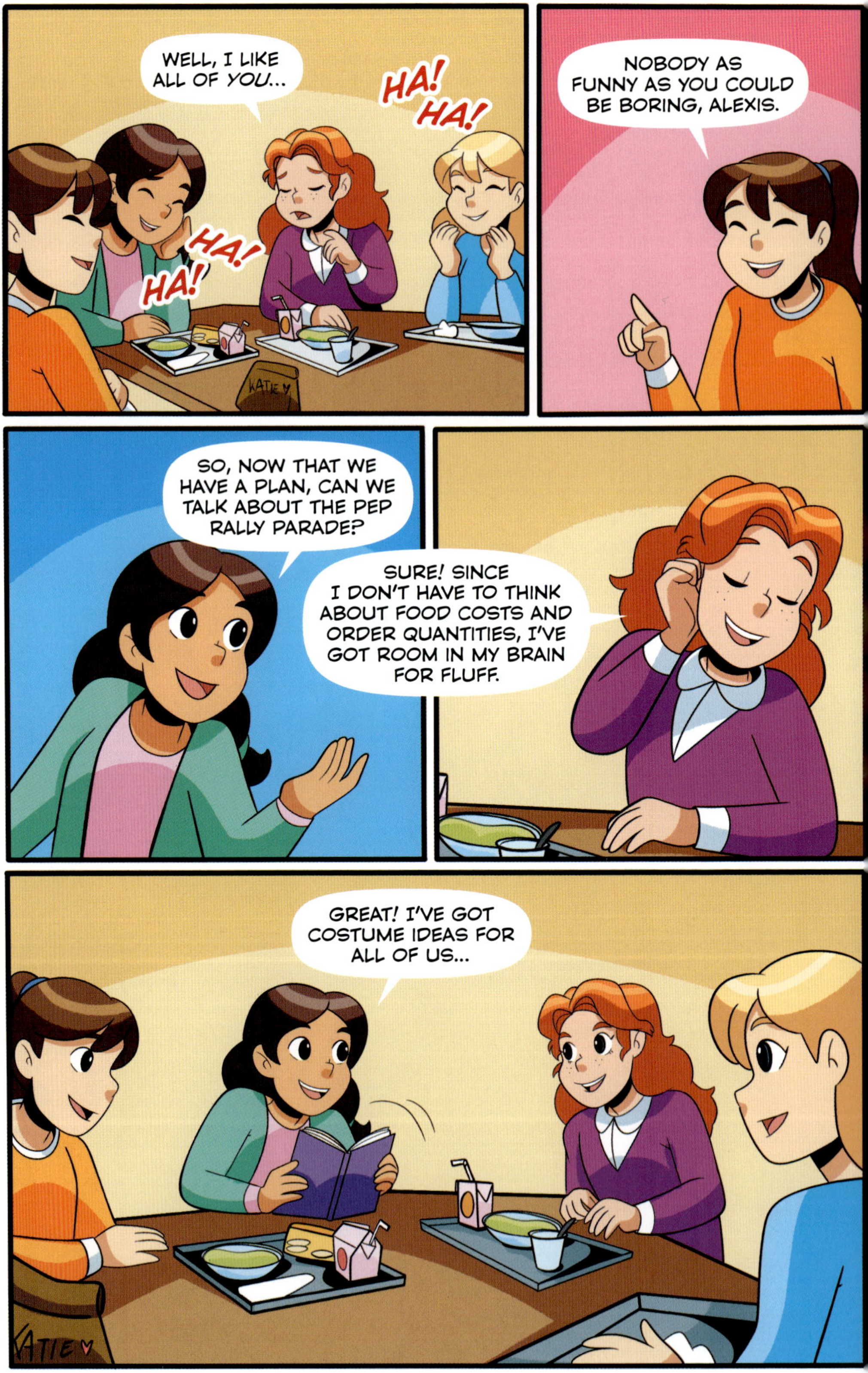
WELL, I LIKE ALL OF YOU...
HA! HA!
HA! HA!
KATIE
NOBODY AS FUNNY AS YOU COULD BE BORING, ALEXIS.
SO, NOW THAT WE HAVE A PLAN, CAN WE TALK ABOUT THE PEP RALLY PARADE?
SURE! SINCE I DON'T HAVE TO THINK ABOUT FOOD COSTS AND ORDER QUANTITIES, I'VE GOT ROOM IN MY BRAIN FOR FLUFF.
GREAT! I'VE GOT COSTUME IDEAS FOR ALL OF US...
KATIE

Chapter 3

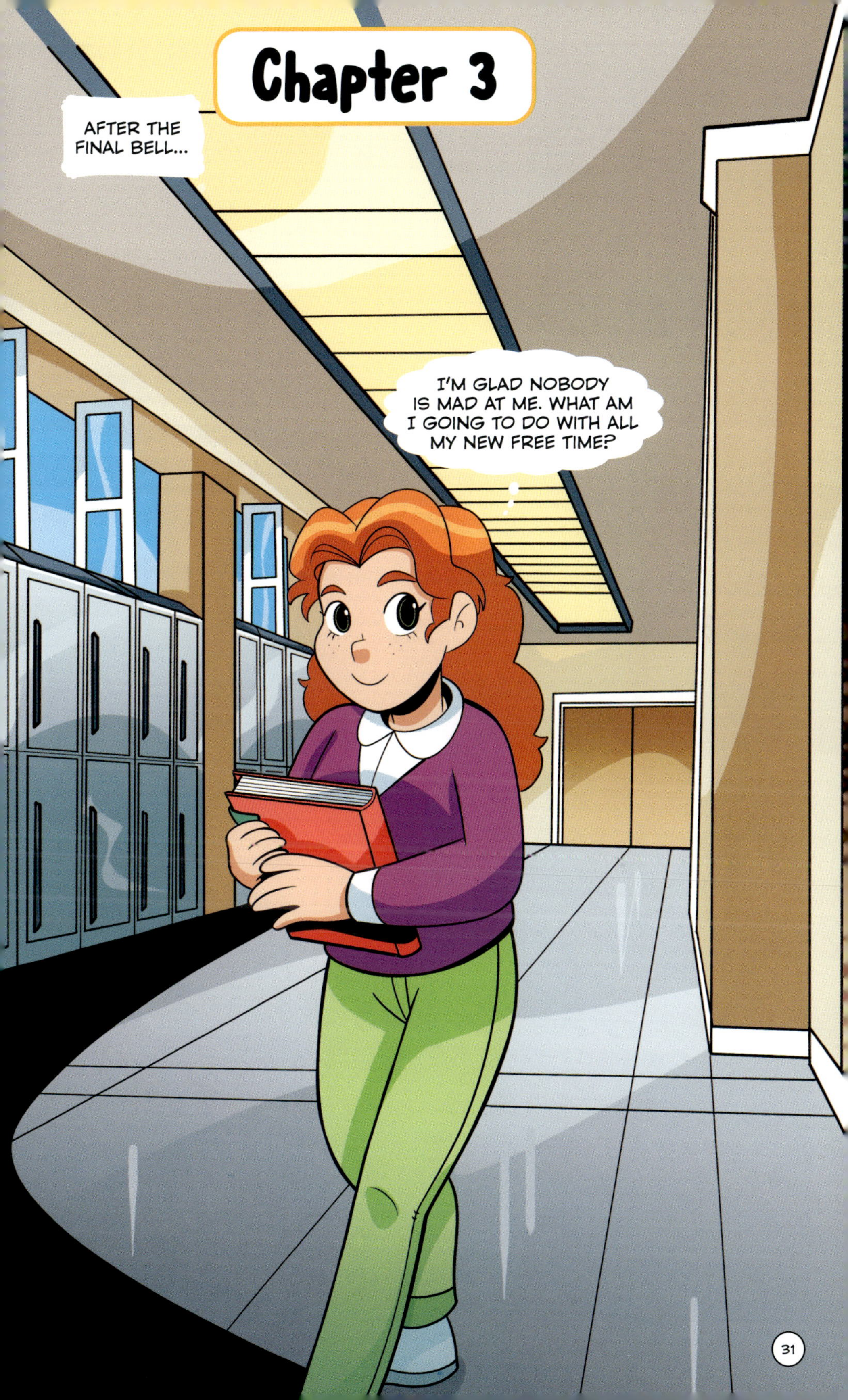

AFTER THE FINAL BELL...
I'M GLAD NOBODY IS MAD AT ME. WHAT AM I GOING TO DO WITH ALL MY NEW FREE TIME?

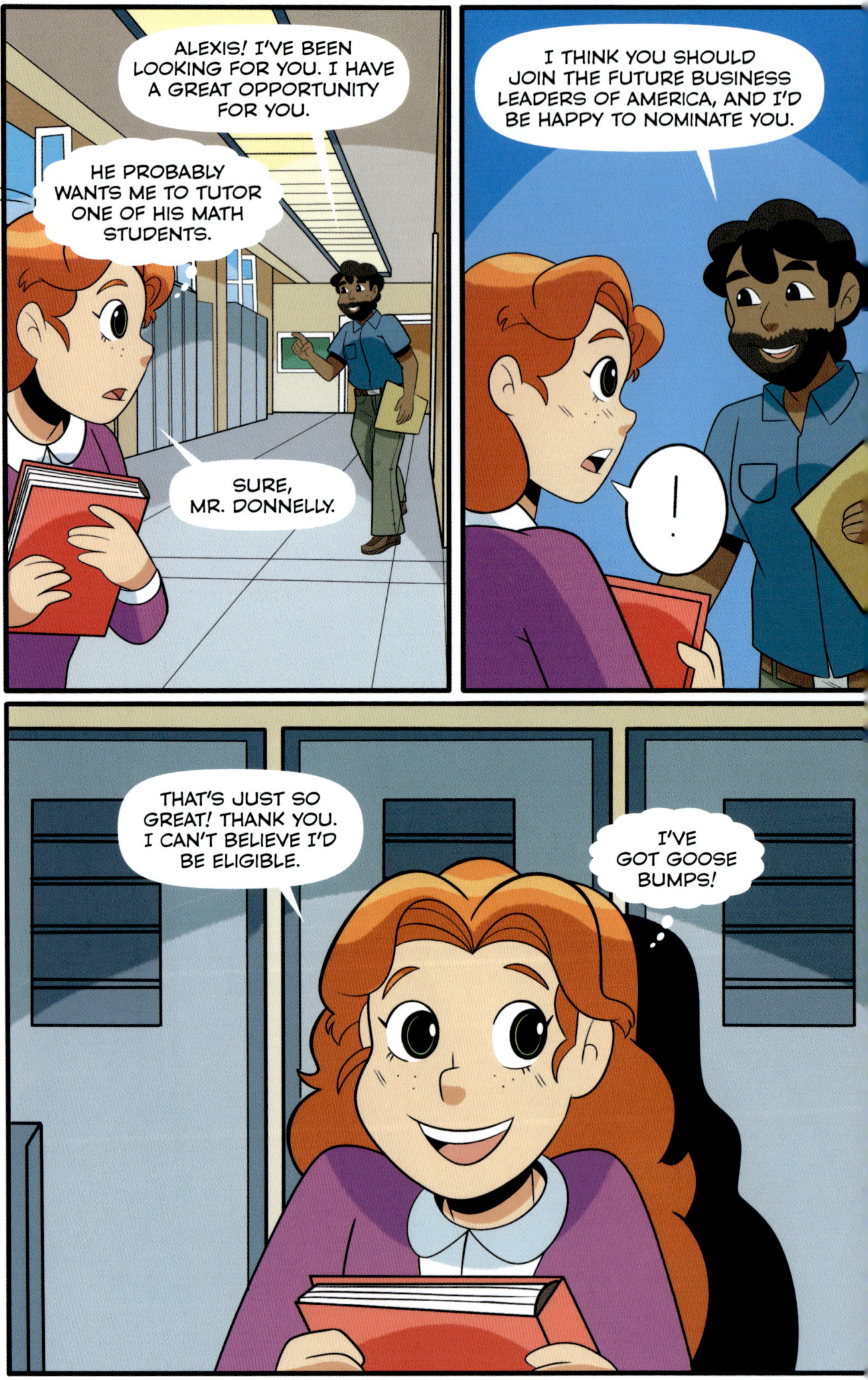
ALEXIS! I'VE BEEN LOOKING FOR YOU. I HAVE A GREAT OPPORTUNITY FOR YOU.
HE PROBABLY WANTS ME TO TUTOR ONE OF HIS MATH STUDENTS.
SURE, MR. DONNELLY.
I THINK YOU SHOULD JOIN THE FUTURE BUSINESS LEADERS OF AMERICA, AND I'D BE HAPPY TO NOMINATE YOU.
!
THAT'S JUST SO GREAT! THANK YOU. I CAN'T BELIEVE I'D BE ELIGIBLE.
I'VE GOT GOOSE BUMPS!

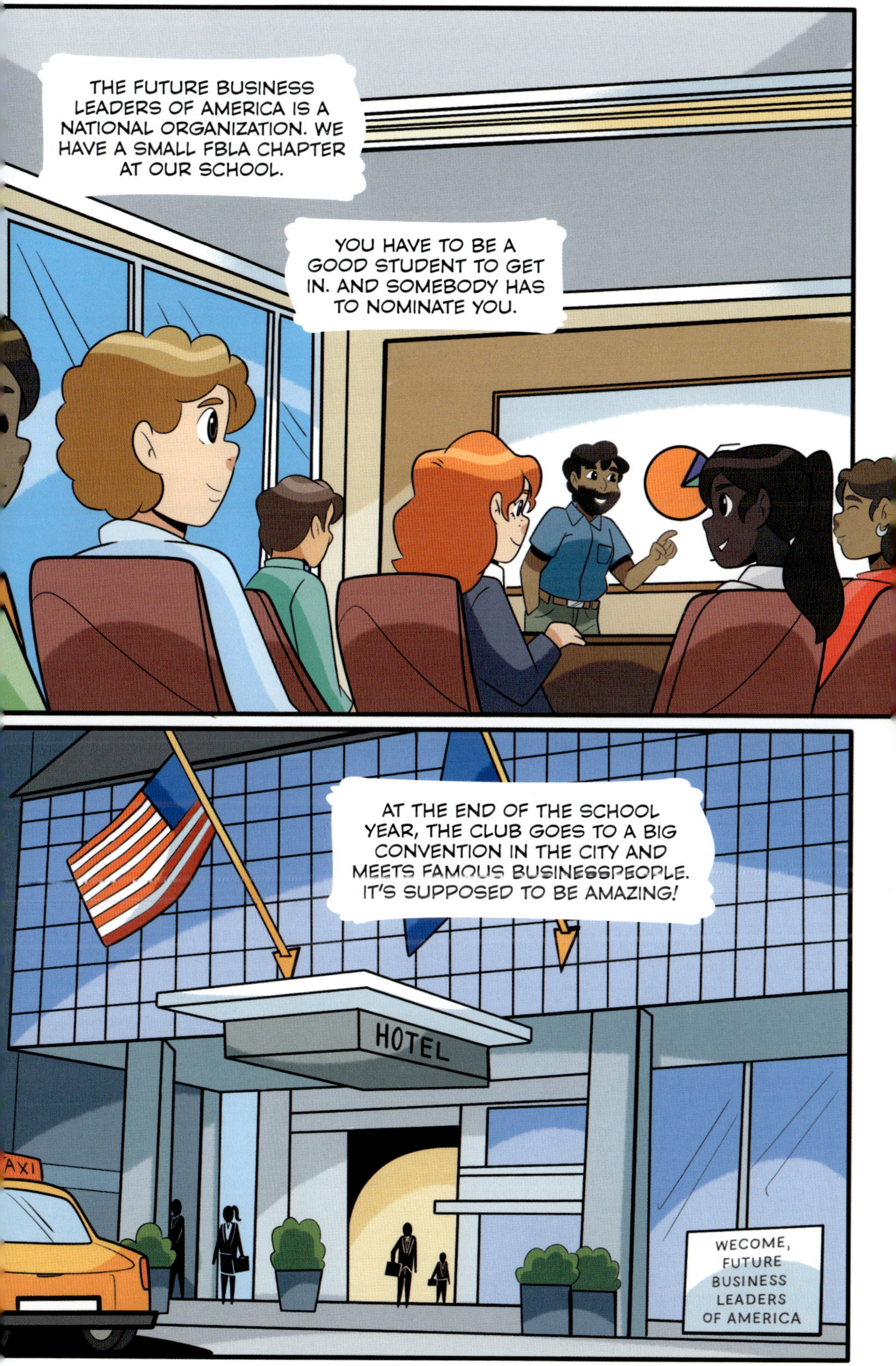
THE FUTURE BUSINESS LEADERS OF AMERICA IS A NATIONAL ORGANIZATION. WE HAVE A SMALL FBLA CHAPTER AT OUR SCHOOL.
YOU HAVE TO BE A GOOD STUDENT TO GET IN. AND SOMEBODY HAS TO NOMINATE YOU.
AT THE END OF THE SCHOOL YEAR, THE CLUB GOES TO A BIG CONVENTION IN THE CITY AND MEETS FAMOUS BUSINESSPEOPLE. IT'S SUPPOSED TO BE AMAZING!
HOTEL
AXI
WECOME, FUTURE BUSINESS LEADERS OF AMERICA

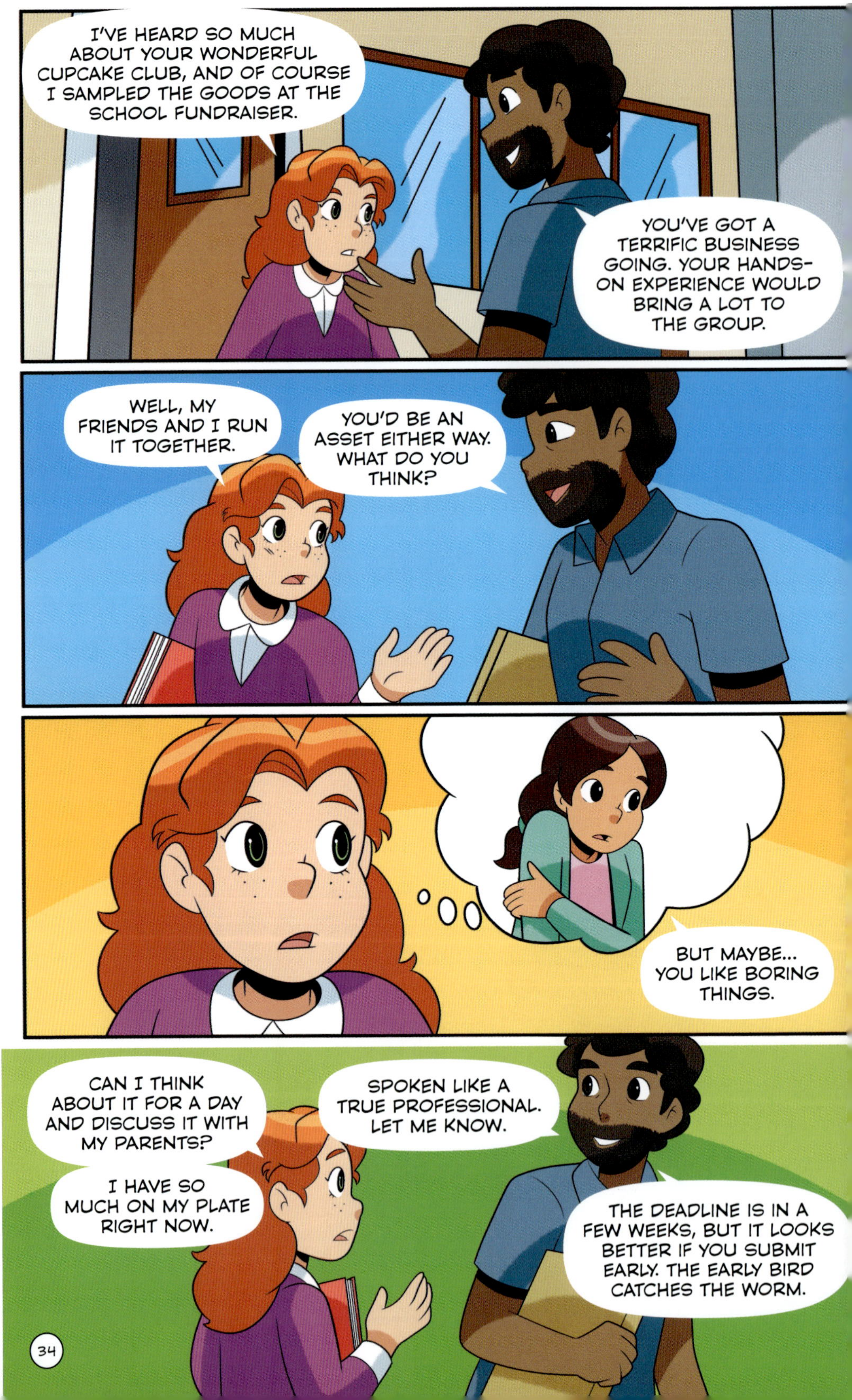
I'VE HEARD SO MUCH ABOUT YOUR WONDERFUL CUPCAKE CLUB, AND OF COURSE I SAMPLED THE GOODS AT THE SCHOOL FUNDRAISER.
YOU'VE GOT A TERRIFIC BUSINESS GOING. YOUR HANDS-ON EXPERIENCE WOULD BRING A LOT TO THE GROUP.
WELL, MY FRIENDS AND I RUN IT TOGETHER.
YOU'D BE AN ASSET EITHER WAY. WHAT DO YOU THINK?
BUT MAYBE... YOU LIKE BORING THINGS.
CAN I THINK ABOUT IT FOR A DAY AND DISCUSS IT WITH MY PARENTS?
I HAVE SO MUCH ON MY PLATE RIGHT NOW.
SPOKEN LIKE A TRUE PROFESSIONAL. LET ME KNOW.
THE DEADLINE IS IN A FEW WEEKS, BUT IT LOOKS BETTER IF YOU SUBMIT EARLY. THE EARLY BIRD CATCHES THE WORM.

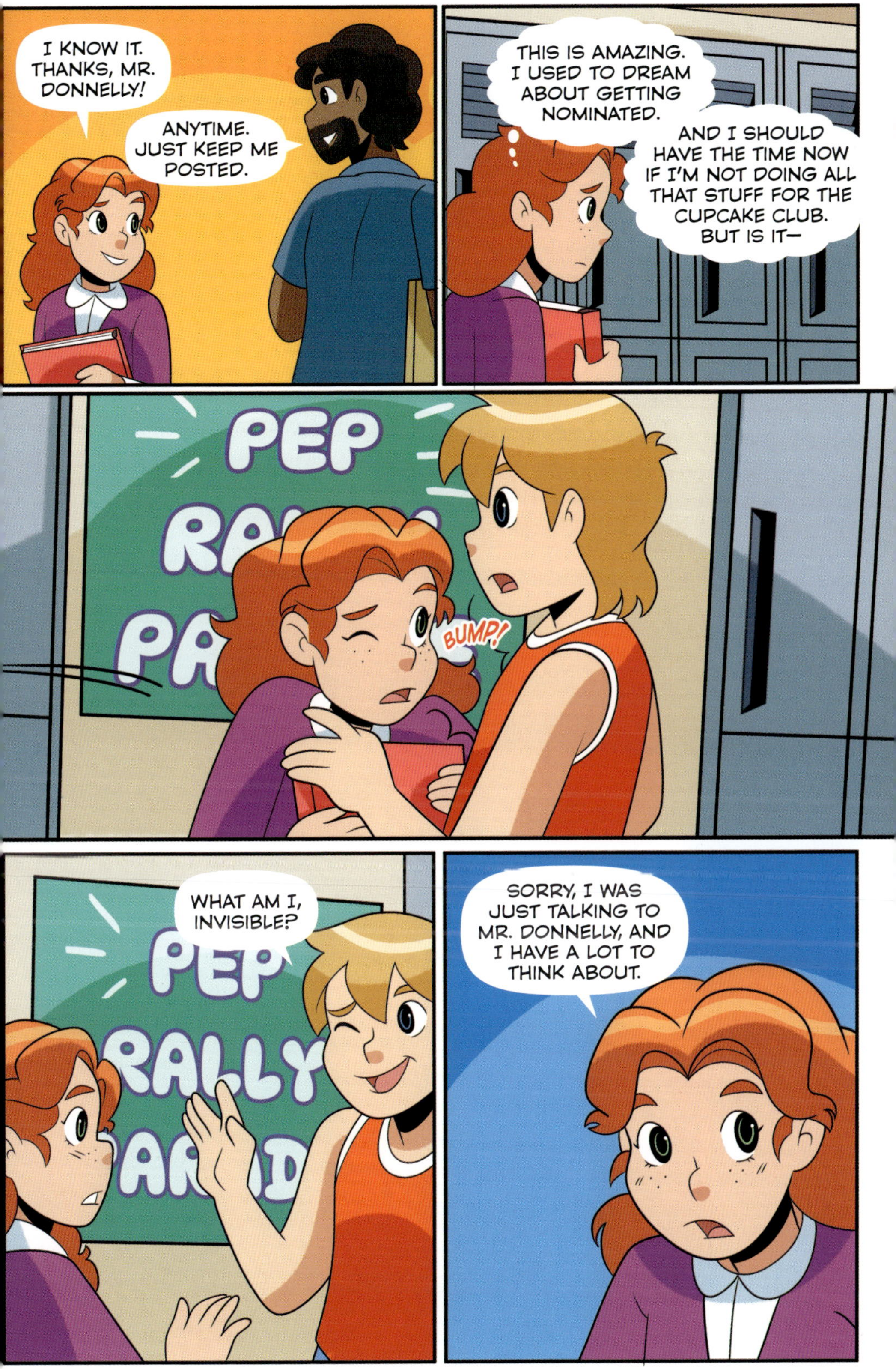
I KNOW IT. THANKS, MR. DONNELLY!
ANYTIME. JUST KEEP ME POSTED.
THIS IS AMAZING. I USED TO DREAM ABOUT GETTING NOMINATED.
AND I SHOULD HAVE THE TIME NOW IF I'M NOT DOING ALL THAT STUFF FOR THE CUPCAKE CLUB. BUT IS IT—
PEP
BUMP!
WHAT AM I, INVISIBLE?
PEP
RALLY
SORRY, I WAS JUST TALKING TO MR. DONNELLY, AND I HAVE A LOT TO THINK ABOUT.

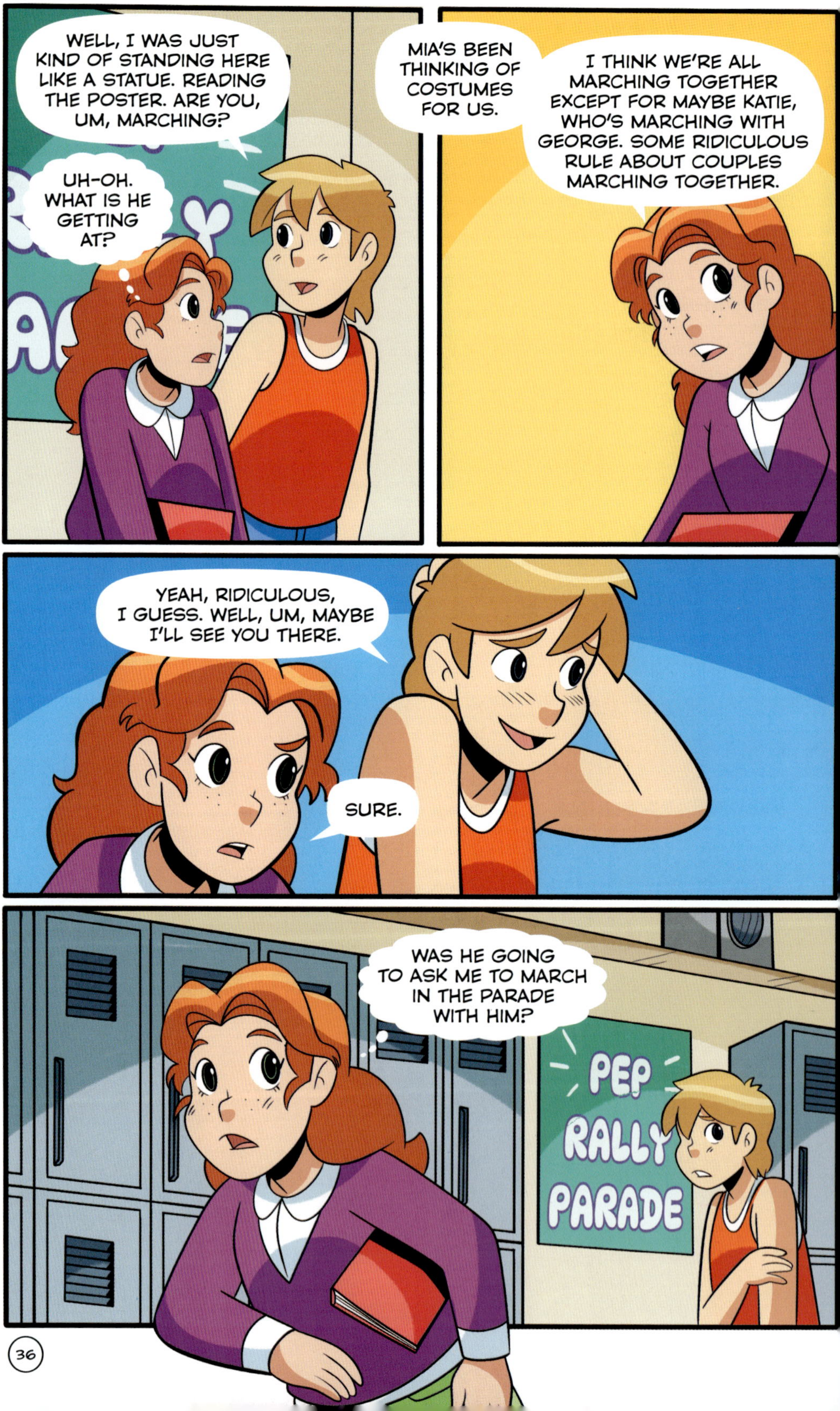
WELL, I WAS JUST KIND OF STANDING HERE LIKE A STATUE. READING THE POSTER. ARE YOU, UM, MARCHING?
UH-OH. WHAT IS HE GETTING AT?
MIA'S BEEN THINKING OF COSTUMES FOR US.
I THINK WE'RE ALL MARCHING TOGETHER EXCEPT FOR MAYBE KATIE, WHO'S MARCHING WITH GEORGE. SOME RIDICULOUS RULE ABOUT COUPLES MARCHING TOGETHER.
YEAH, RIDICULOUS, I GUESS. WELL, UM, MAYBE I'LL SEE YOU THERE.
SURE.
WAS HE GOING TO ASK ME TO MARCH IN THE PARADE WITH HIM?
PEP RALLY PARADE

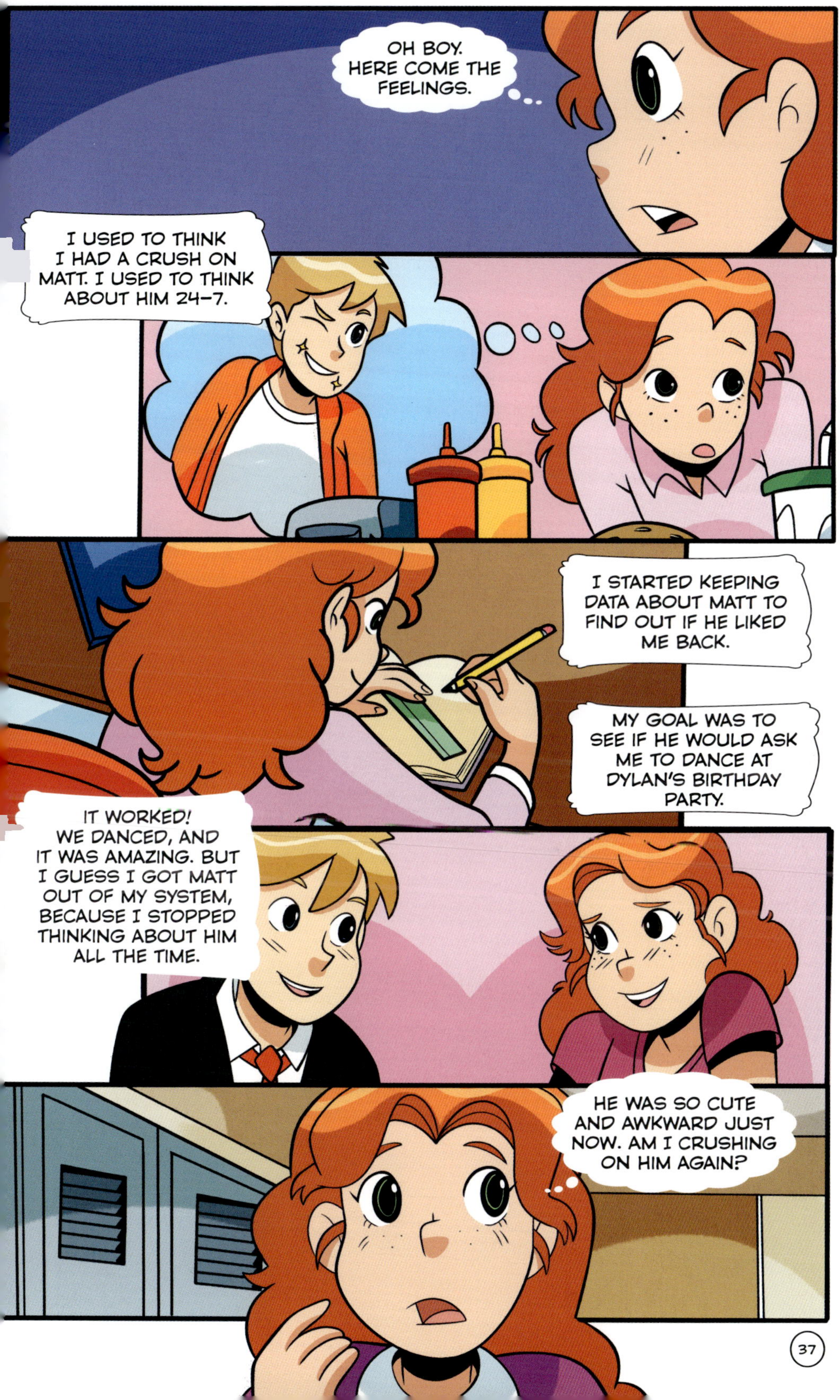
OH BOY. HERE COME THE FEELINGS.
I USED TO THINK I HAD A CRUSH ON MATT. I USED TO THINK ABOUT HIM 24-7.
I STARTED KEEPING DATA ABOUT MATT TO FIND OUT IF HE LIKED ME BACK.
MY GOAL WAS TO SEE IF HE WOULD ASK ME TO DANCE AT DYLAN'S BIRTHDAY PARTY.
IT WORKED! WE DANCED, AND IT WAS AMAZING. BUT I GUESS I GOT MATT OUT OF MY SYSTEM, BECAUSE I STOPPED THINKING ABOUT HIM ALL THE TIME.
HE WAS SO CUTE AND AWKWARD JUST NOW. AM I CRUSHING ON HIM AGAIN?

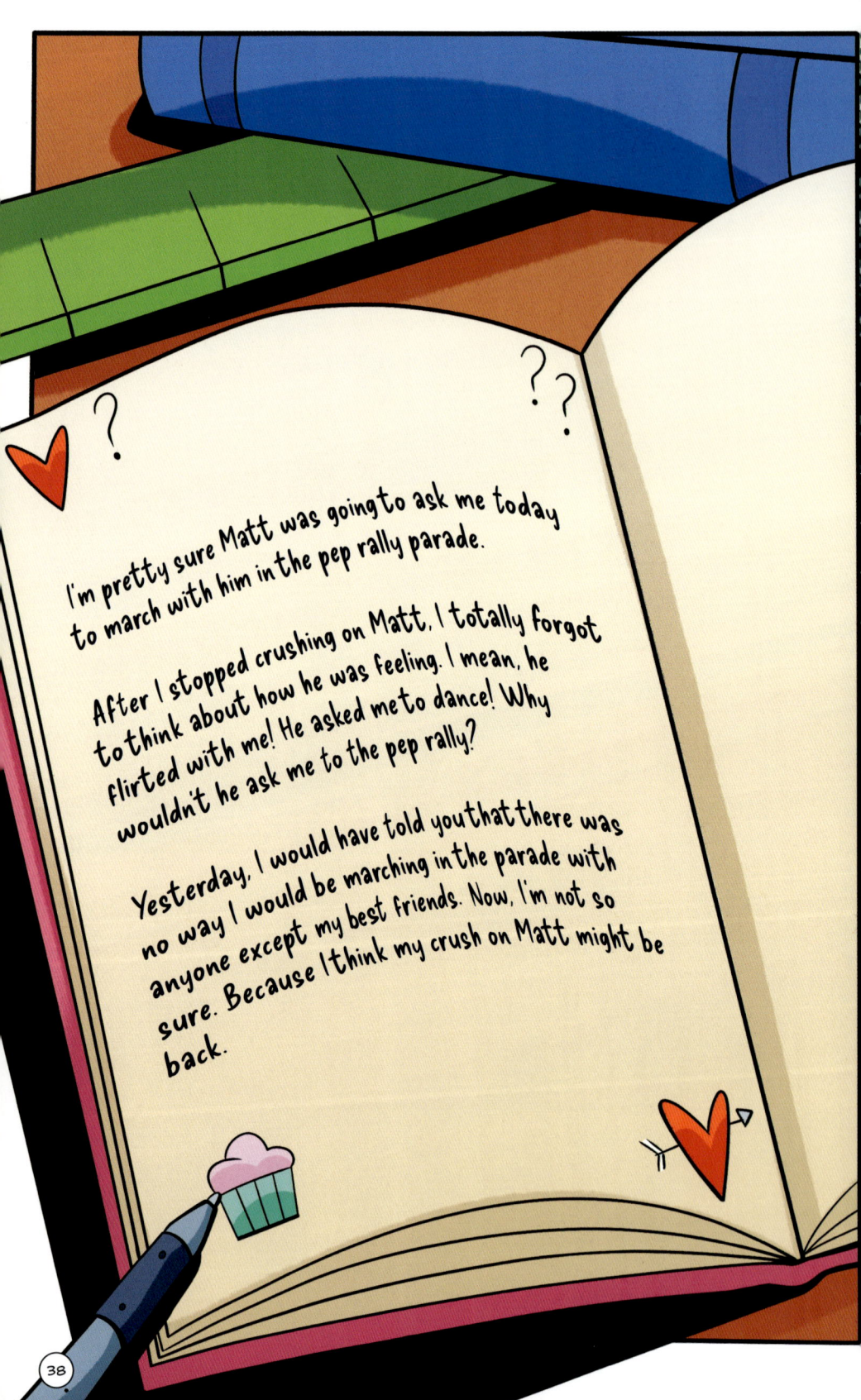

I'm pretty sure Matt was going to ask me today to march with him in the pep rally parade.

After I stopped crushing on Matt, I totally forgot to think about how he was feeling. I mean, he flirted with me! He asked me to dance! Why wouldn't he ask me to the pep rally?

Yesterday, I would have told you that there was no way I would be marching in the parade with anyone except my best friends. Now, I'm not so sure. Because I think my crush on Matt might be back.

Chapter 4

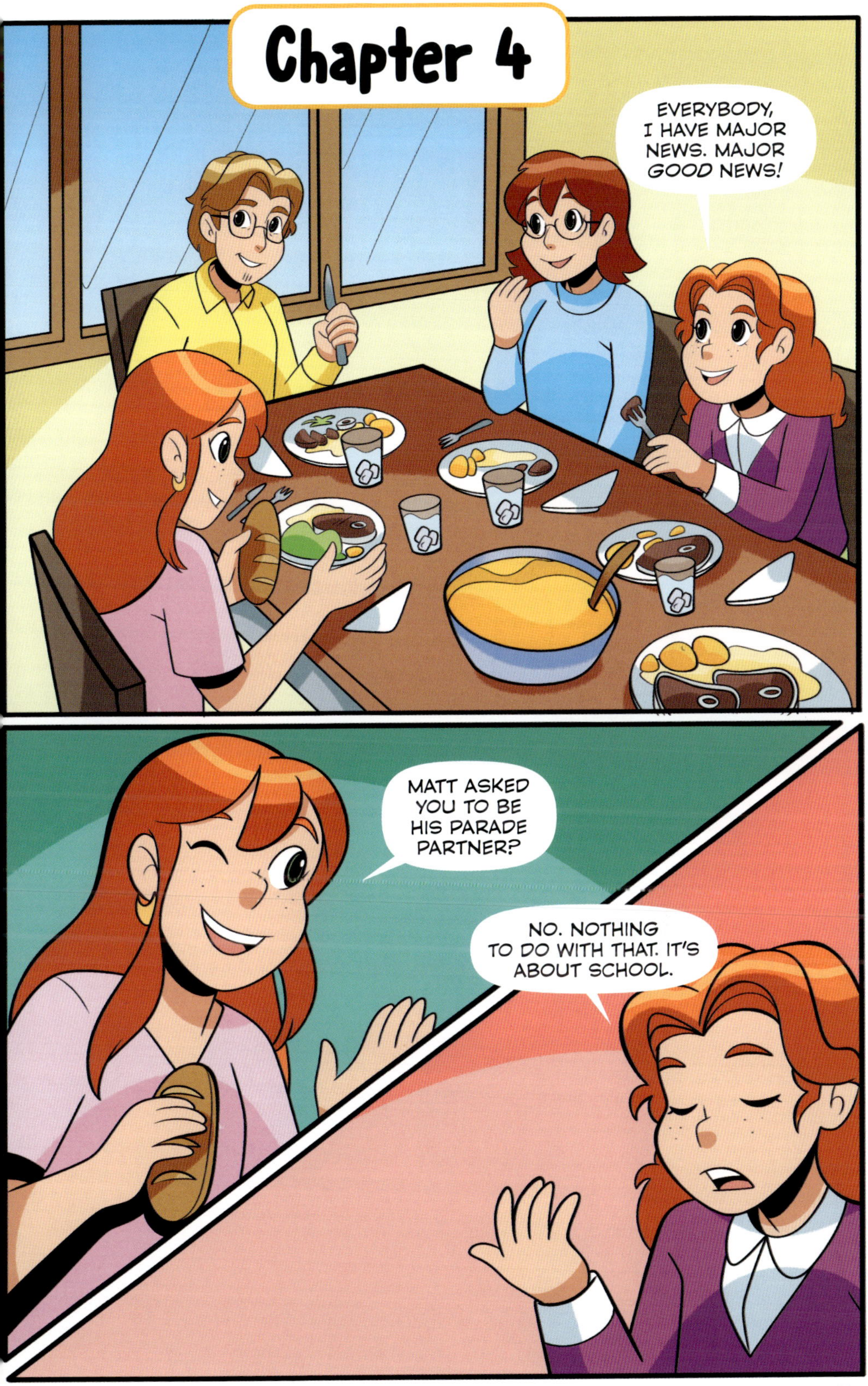
EVERYBODY, I HAVE MAJOR NEWS. MAJOR *GOOD* NEWS!
MATT ASKED YOU TO BE HIS PARADE PARTNER?
NO. NOTHING TO DO WITH THAT. IT'S ABOUT SCHOOL.

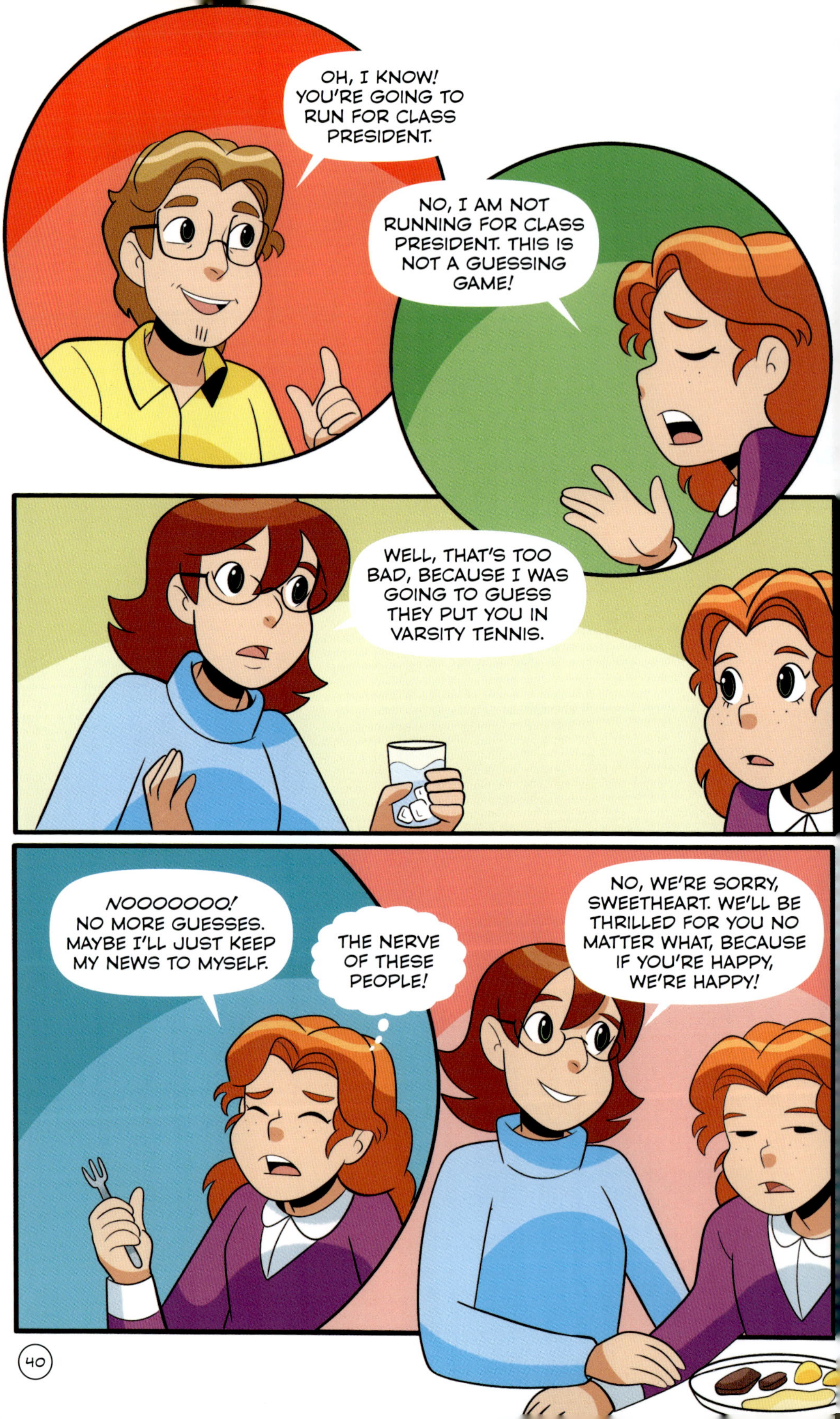
OH, I KNOW! YOU'RE GOING TO RUN FOR CLASS PRESIDENT.
NO, I AM NOT RUNNING FOR CLASS PRESIDENT. THIS IS NOT A GUESSING GAME!
WELL, THAT'S TOO BAD, BECAUSE I WAS GOING TO GUESS THEY PUT YOU IN VARSITY TENNIS.
NOOOOOOO! NO MORE GUESSES. MAYBE I'LL JUST KEEP MY NEWS TO MYSELF.
THE NERVE OF THESE PEOPLE!
NO, WE'RE SORRY, SWEETHEART. WE'LL BE THRILLED FOR YOU NO MATTER WHAT, BECAUSE IF YOU'RE HAPPY, WE'RE HAPPY!

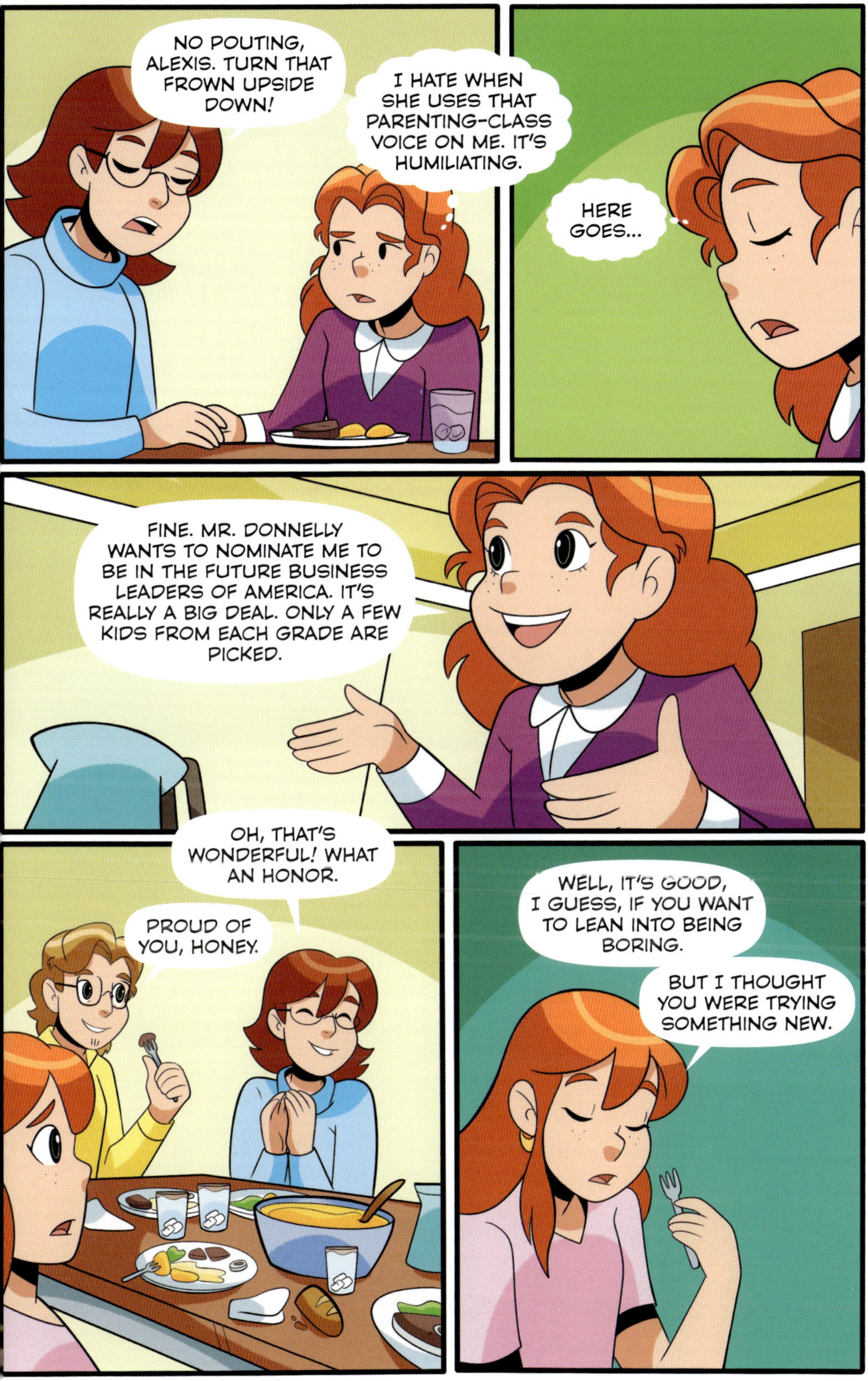
NO POUTING, ALEXIS. TURN THAT FROWN UPSIDE DOWN!
I HATE WHEN SHE USES THAT PARENTING-CLASS VOICE ON ME. IT'S HUMILIATING.
HERE GOES...
FINE. MR. DONNELLY WANTS TO NOMINATE ME TO BE IN THE FUTURE BUSINESS LEADERS OF AMERICA. IT'S REALLY A BIG DEAL. ONLY A FEW KIDS FROM EACH GRADE ARE PICKED.
OH, THAT'S WONDERFUL! WHAT AN HONOR.
PROUD OF YOU, HONEY.
WELL, IT'S GOOD, I GUESS, IF YOU WANT TO LEAN INTO BEING BORING.
BUT I THOUGHT YOU WERE TRYING SOMETHING NEW.

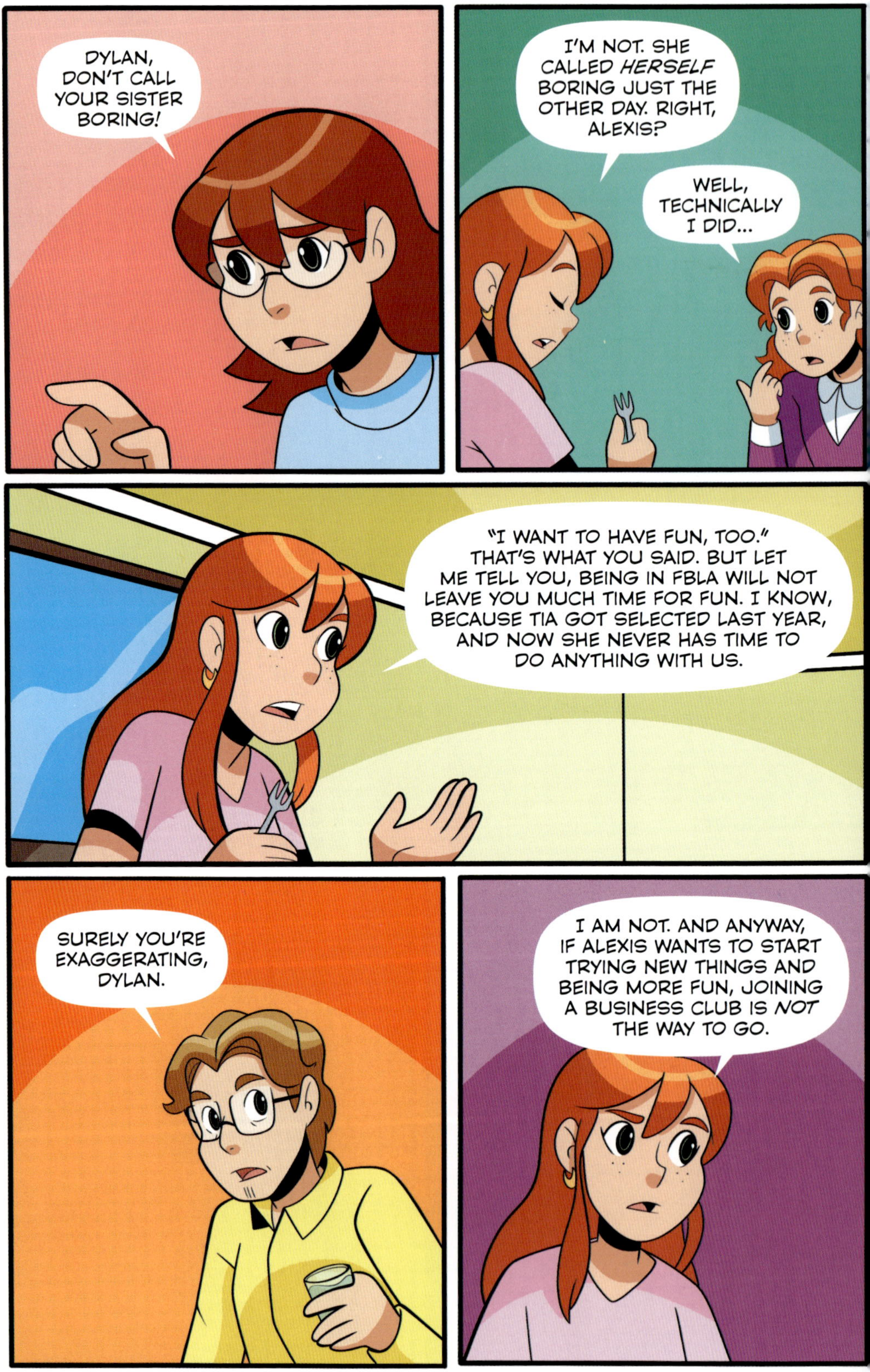
DYLAN, DON'T CALL YOUR SISTER BORING!
I'M NOT. SHE CALLED *HERSELF* BORING JUST THE OTHER DAY. RIGHT, ALEXIS?
WELL, TECHNICALLY I DID...
"I WANT TO HAVE FUN, TOO." THAT'S WHAT YOU SAID. BUT LET ME TELL YOU, BEING IN FBLA WILL NOT LEAVE YOU MUCH TIME FOR FUN. I KNOW, BECAUSE TIA GOT SELECTED LAST YEAR, AND NOW SHE NEVER HAS TIME TO DO ANYTHING WITH US.
SURELY YOU'RE EXAGGERATING, DYLAN.
I AM NOT. AND ANYWAY, IF ALEXIS WANTS TO START TRYING NEW THINGS AND BEING MORE FUN, JOINING A BUSINESS CLUB IS *NOT* THE WAY TO GO.

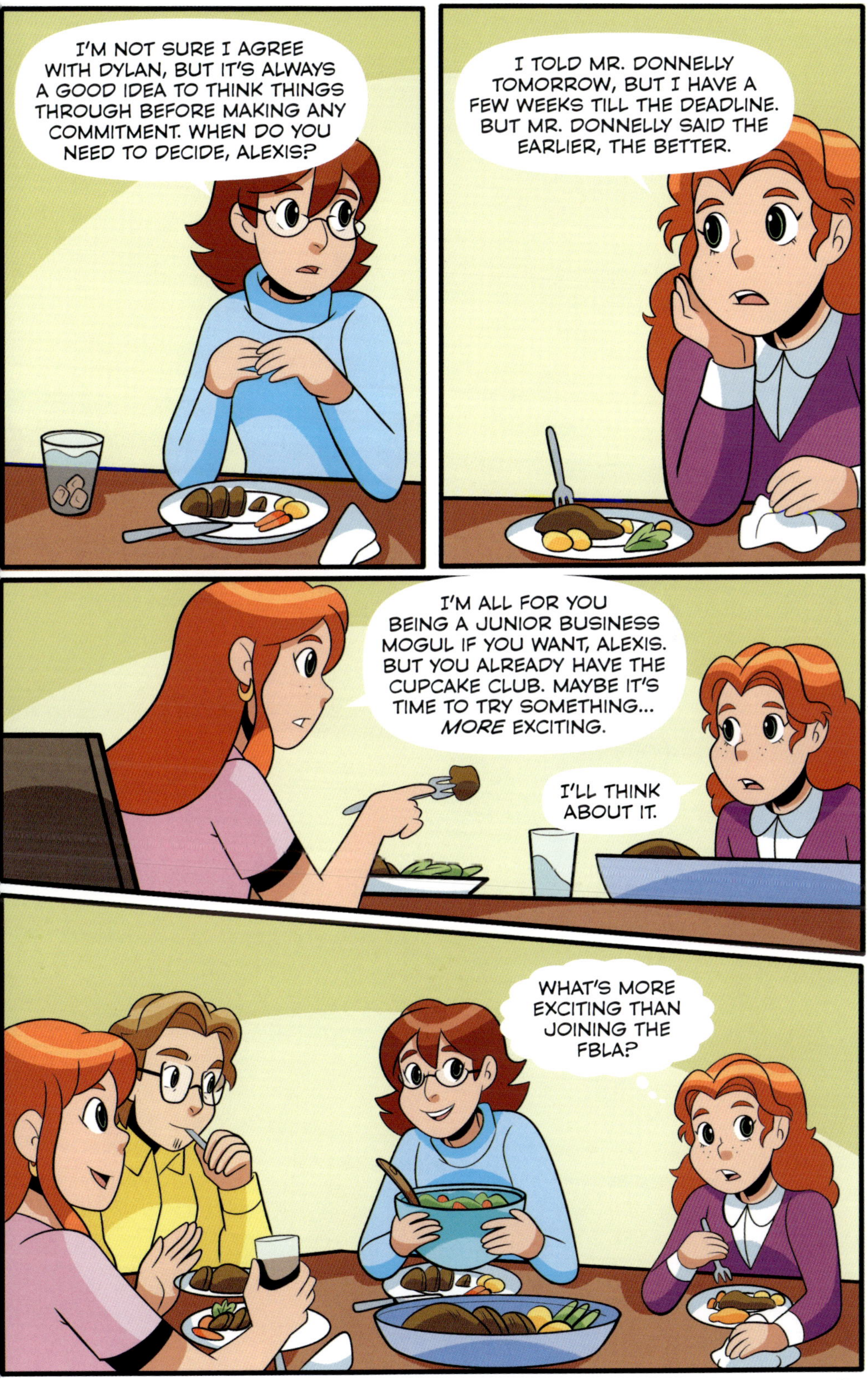
I'M NOT SURE I AGREE WITH DYLAN, BUT IT'S ALWAYS A GOOD IDEA TO THINK THINGS THROUGH BEFORE MAKING ANY COMMITMENT. WHEN DO YOU NEED TO DECIDE, ALEXIS?
I TOLD MR. DONNELLY TOMORROW, BUT I HAVE A FEW WEEKS TILL THE DEADLINE. BUT MR. DONNELLY SAID THE EARLIER, THE BETTER.
I'M ALL FOR YOU BEING A JUNIOR BUSINESS MOGUL IF YOU WANT, ALEXIS. BUT YOU ALREADY HAVE THE CUPCAKE CLUB. MAYBE IT'S TIME TO TRY SOMETHING... *MORE* EXCITING.
I'LL THINK ABOUT IT.
WHAT'S MORE EXCITING THAN JOINING THE FBLA?

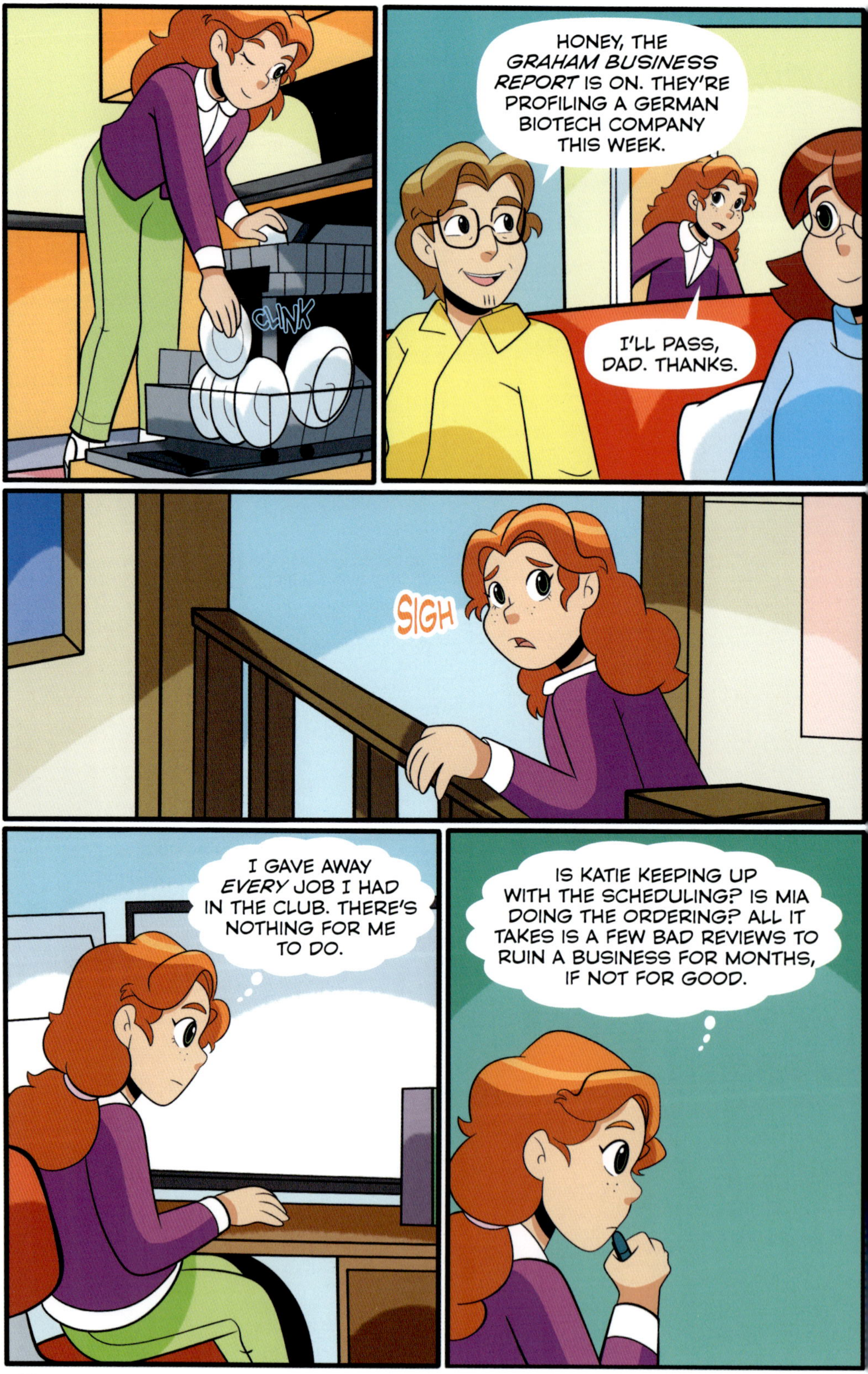
CLINK
HONEY, THE *GRAHAM BUSINESS REPORT* IS ON. THEY'RE PROFILING A GERMAN BIOTECH COMPANY THIS WEEK.
I'LL PASS, DAD. THANKS.
SIGH
I GAVE AWAY *EVERY* JOB I HAD IN THE CLUB. THERE'S NOTHING FOR ME TO DO.
IS KATIE KEEPING UP WITH THE SCHEDULING? IS MIA DOING THE ORDERING? ALL IT TAKES IS A FEW BAD REVIEWS TO RUIN A BUSINESS FOR MONTHS, IF NOT FOR GOOD.

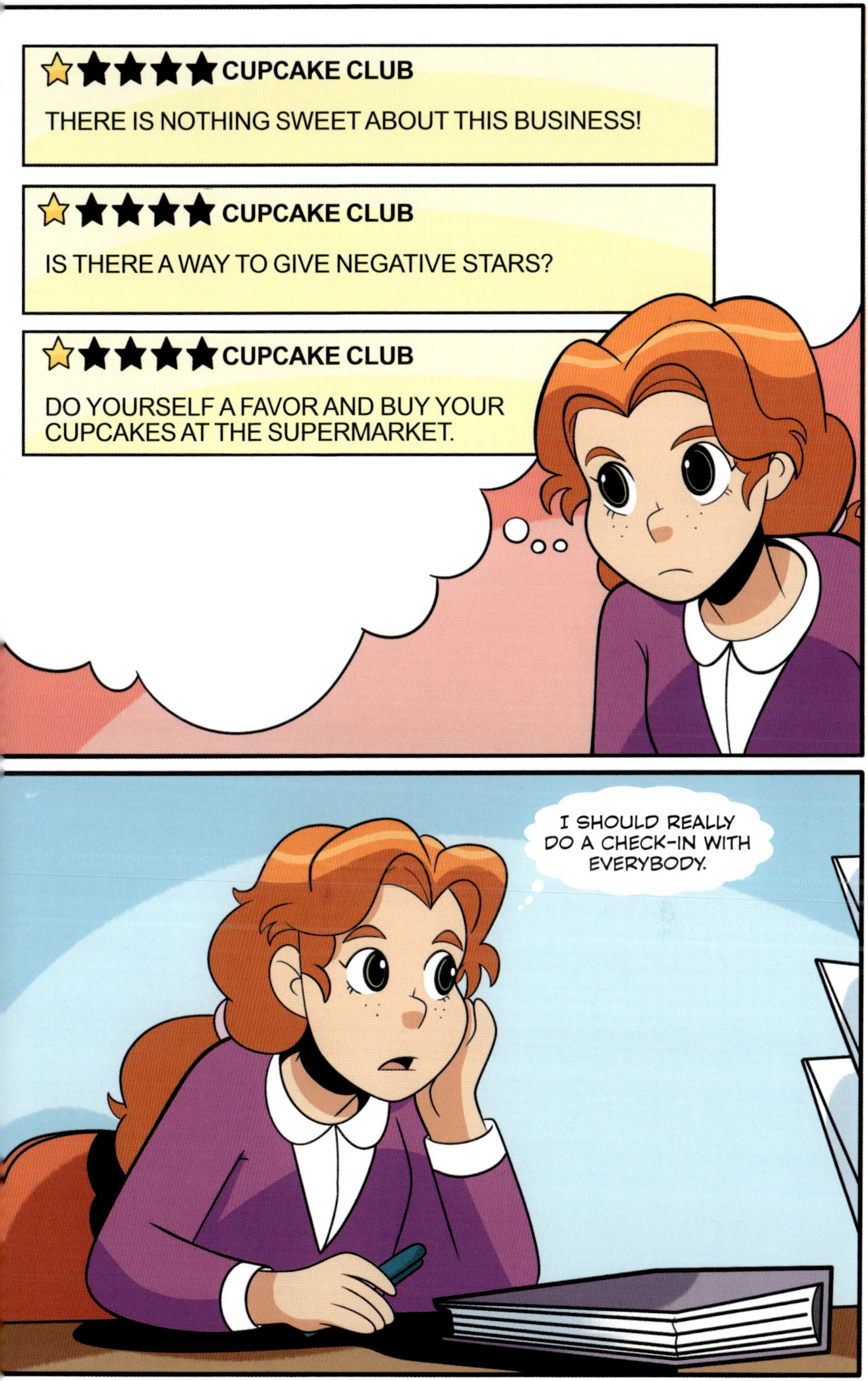
CUPCAKE CLUB
THERE IS NOTHING SWEET ABOUT THIS BUSINESS!
CUPCAKE CLUB
IS THERE A WAY TO GIVE NEGATIVE STARS?
CUPCAKE CLUB
DO YOURSELF A FAVOR AND BUY YOUR CUPCAKES AT THE SUPERMARKET.
I SHOULD REALLY DO A CHECK-IN WITH EVERYBODY.

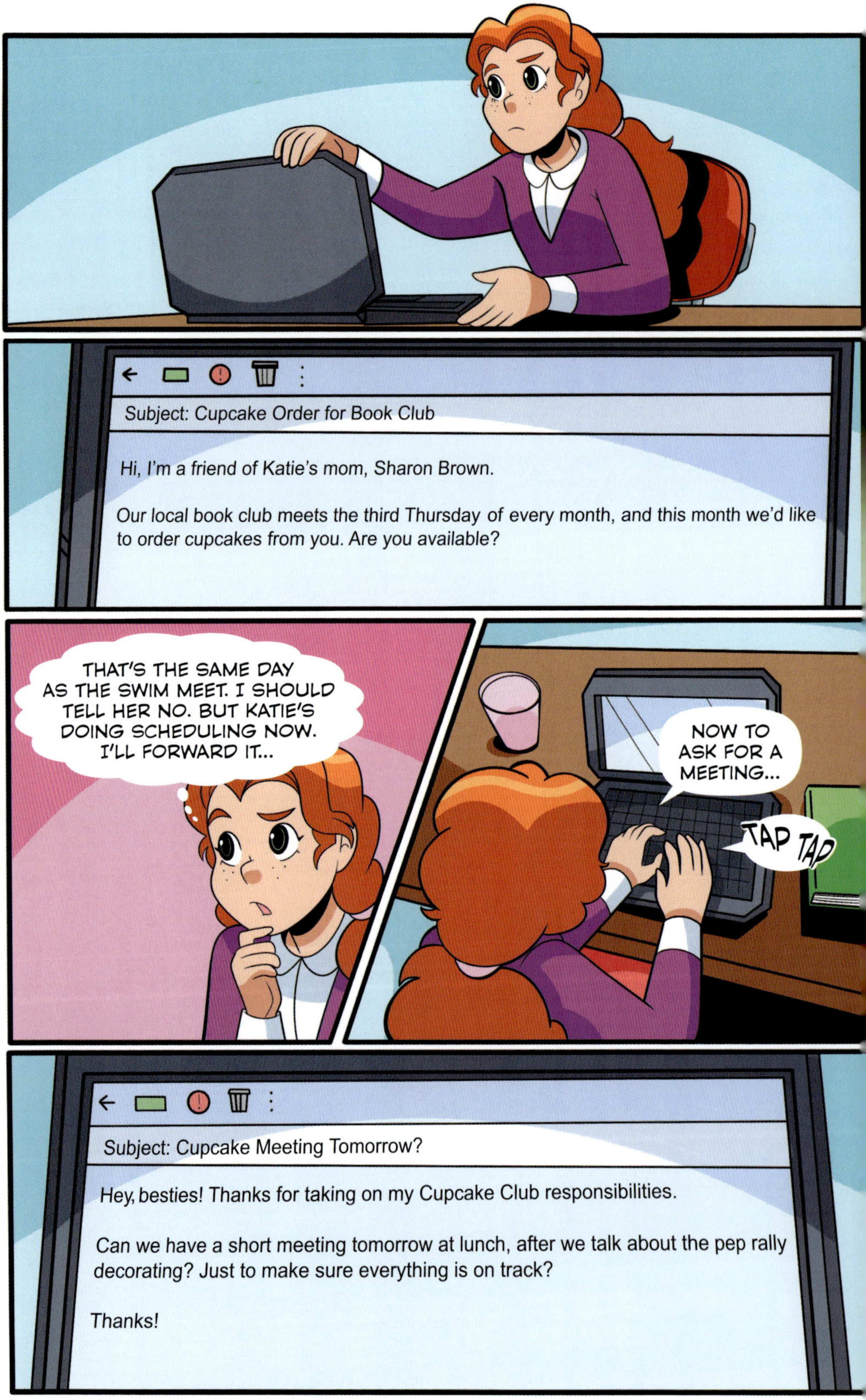
Subject: Cupcake Order for Book Club
Hi, I'm a friend of Katie's mom, Sharon Brown.
Our local book club meets the third Thursday of every month, and this month we'd like to order cupcakes from you. Are you available?
THAT'S THE SAME DAY AS THE SWIM MEET. I SHOULD TELL HER NO. BUT KATIE'S DOING SCHEDULING NOW. I'LL FORWARD IT...
NOW TO ASK FOR A MEETING...
TAP TAP
Subject: Cupcake Meeting Tomorrow?
Hey, besties! Thanks for taking on my Cupcake Club responsibilities.
Can we have a short meeting tomorrow at lunch, after we talk about the pep rally decorating? Just to make sure everything is on track?
Thanks!

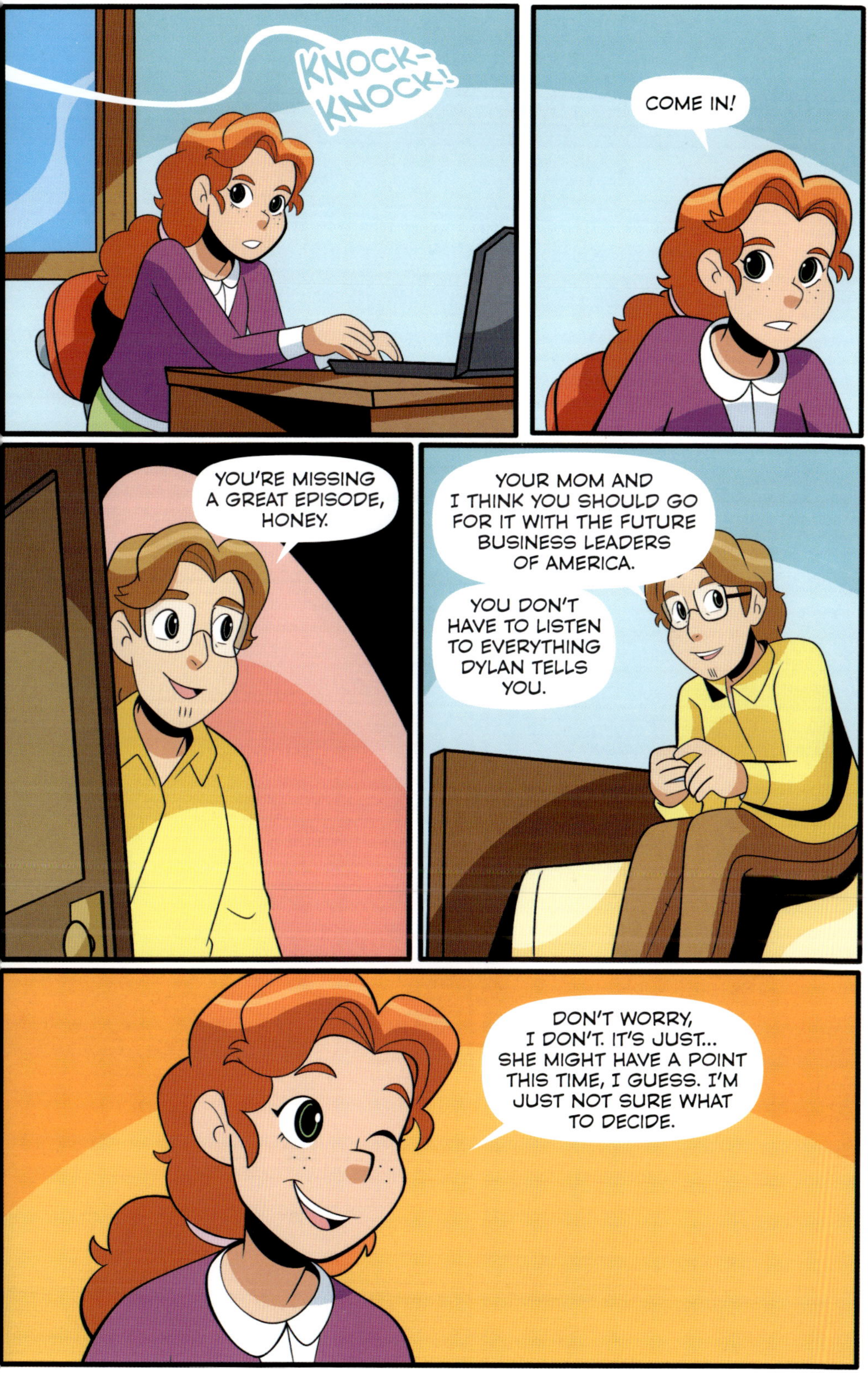
KNOCK-KNOCK!
COME IN!
YOU'RE MISSING A GREAT EPISODE, HONEY.
YOUR MOM AND I THINK YOU SHOULD GO FOR IT WITH THE FUTURE BUSINESS LEADERS OF AMERICA.
YOU DON'T HAVE TO LISTEN TO EVERYTHING DYLAN TELLS YOU.
DON'T WORRY, I DON'T. IT'S JUST... SHE MIGHT HAVE A POINT THIS TIME, I GUESS. I'M JUST NOT SURE WHAT TO DECIDE.

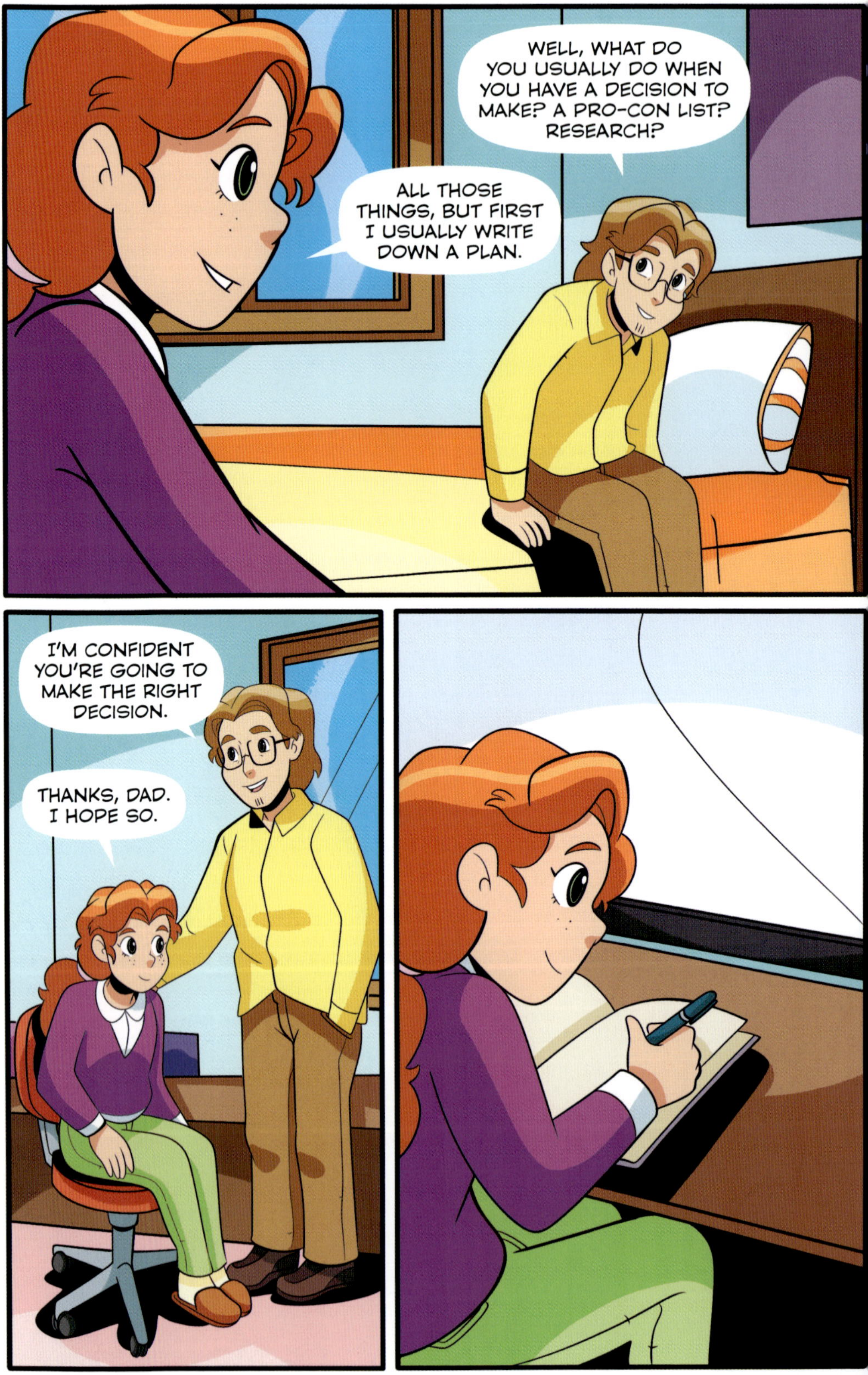
WELL, WHAT DO YOU USUALLY DO WHEN YOU HAVE A DECISION TO MAKE? A PRO-CON LIST? RESEARCH?
ALL THOSE THINGS, BUT FIRST I USUALLY WRITE DOWN A PLAN.
I'M CONFIDENT YOU'RE GOING TO MAKE THE RIGHT DECISION.
THANKS, DAD. I HOPE SO.

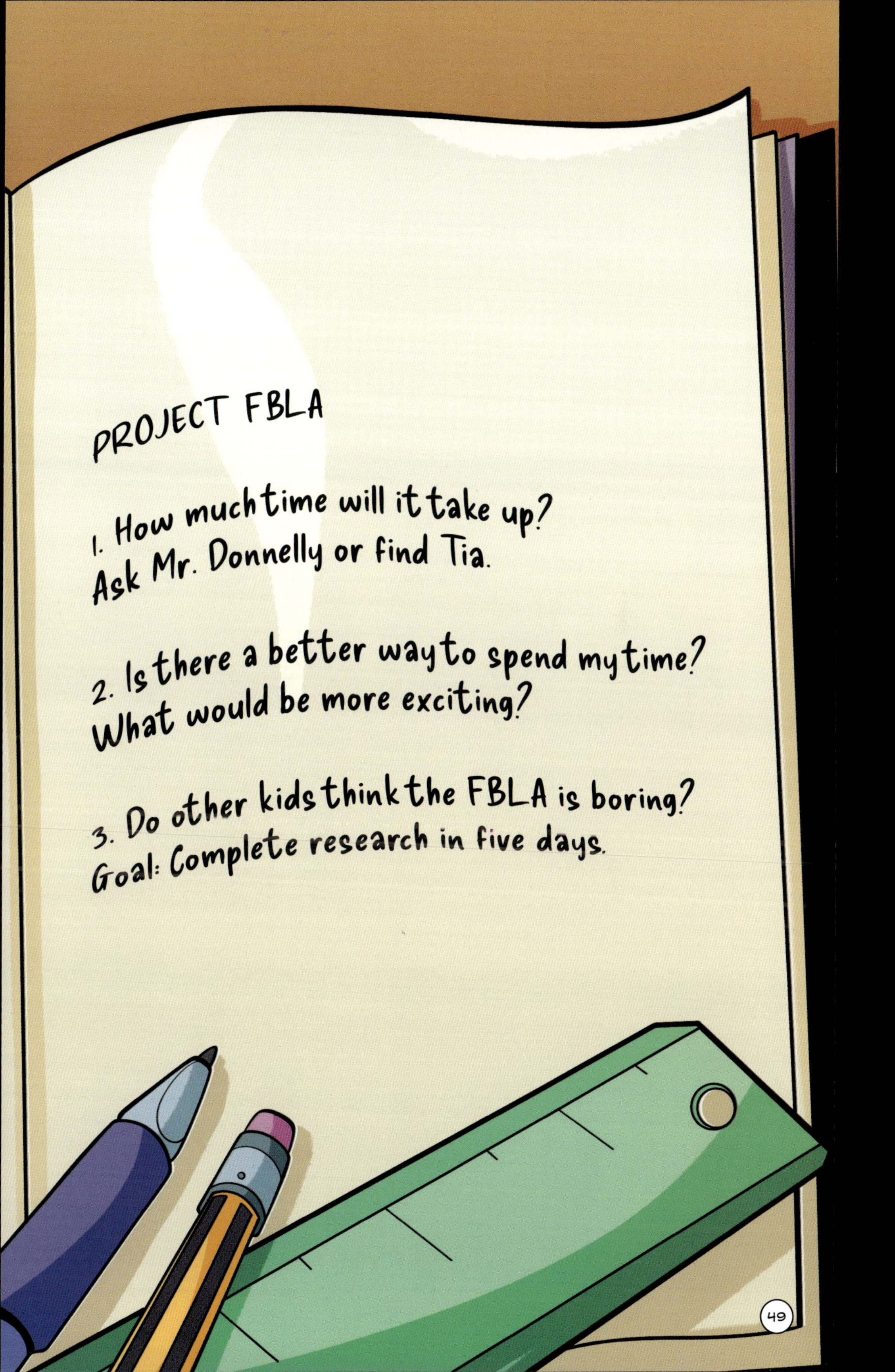
PROJECT FBLA
1. How much time will it take up?
Ask Mr. Donnelly or find Tia.
2. Is there a better way to spend my time?
What would be more exciting?
3. Do other kids think the FBLA is boring?
Goal: Complete research in five days.

Chapter 5

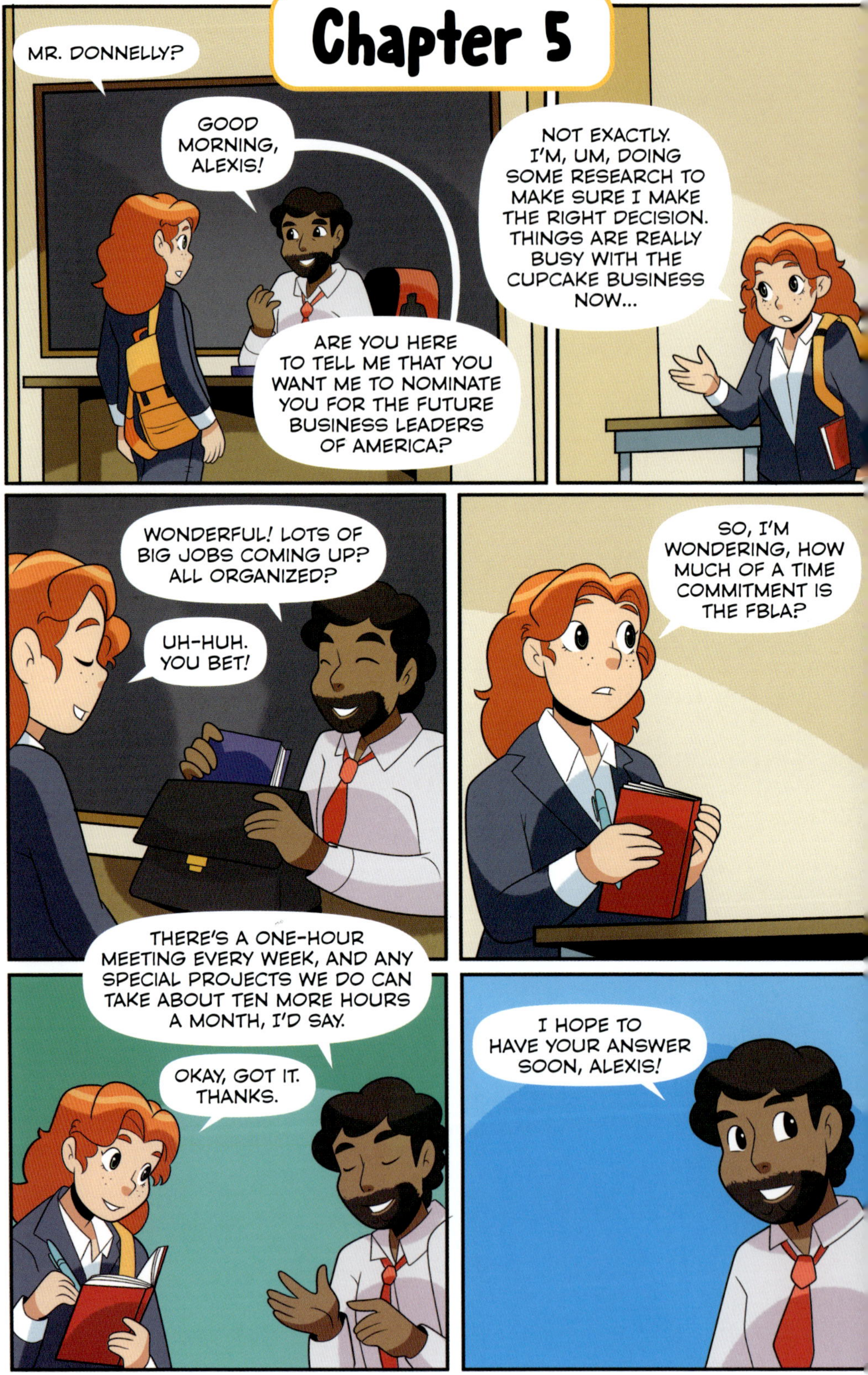
MR. DONNELLY?
GOOD MORNING, ALEXIS!
ARE YOU HERE TO TELL ME THAT YOU WANT ME TO NOMINATE YOU FOR THE FUTURE BUSINESS LEADERS OF AMERICA?
NOT EXACTLY. I'M, UM, DOING SOME RESEARCH TO MAKE SURE I MAKE THE RIGHT DECISION. THINGS ARE REALLY BUSY WITH THE CUPCAKE BUSINESS NOW...
WONDERFUL! LOTS OF BIG JOBS COMING UP? ALL ORGANIZED?
UH-HUH. YOU BET!
SO, I'M WONDERING, HOW MUCH OF A TIME COMMITMENT IS THE FBLA?
THERE'S A ONE-HOUR MEETING EVERY WEEK, AND ANY SPECIAL PROJECTS WE DO CAN TAKE ABOUT TEN MORE HOURS A MONTH, I'D SAY.
OKAY, GOT IT. THANKS.
I HOPE TO HAVE YOUR ANSWER SOON, ALEXIS!

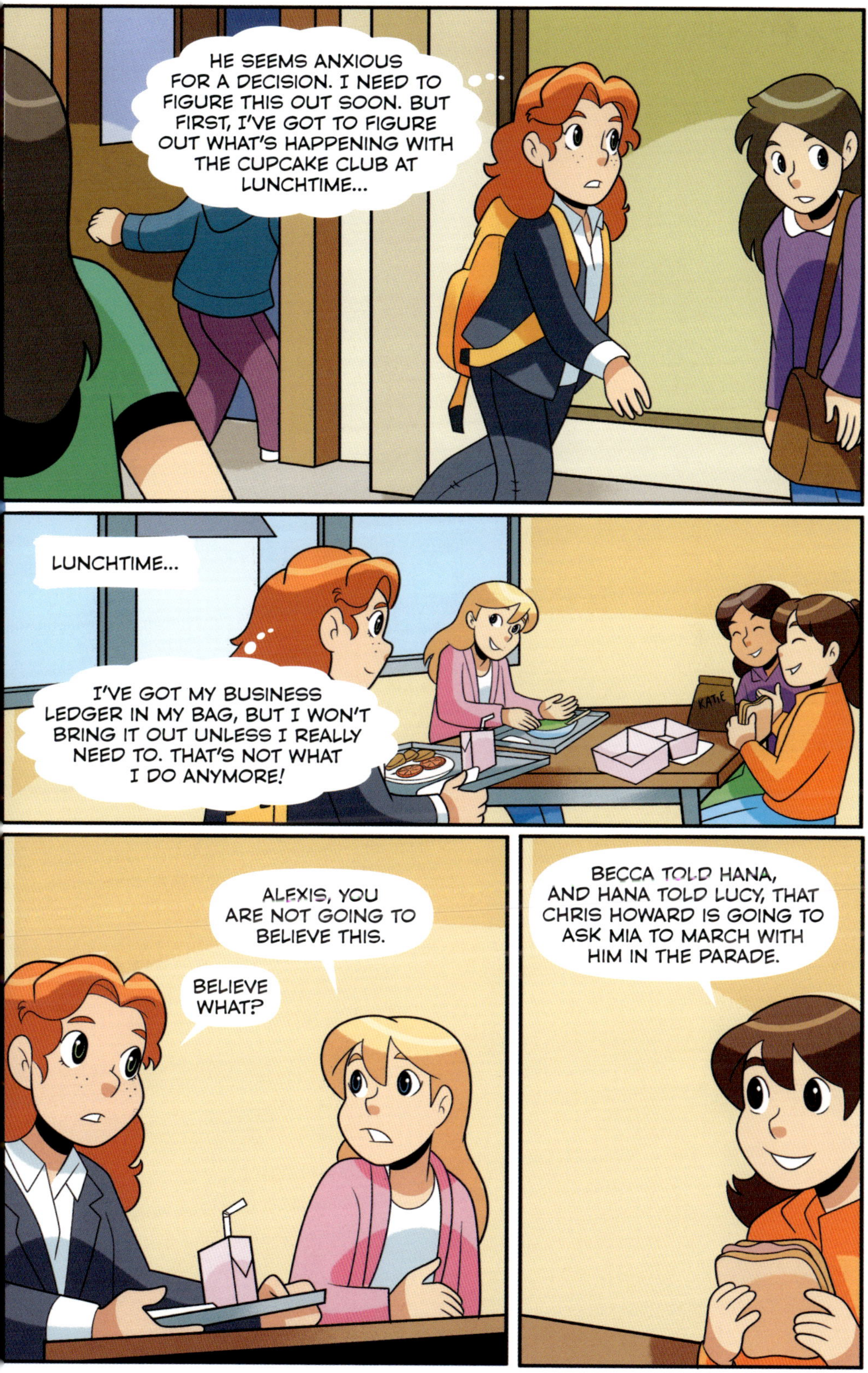
HE SEEMS ANXIOUS FOR A DECISION. I NEED TO FIGURE THIS OUT SOON. BUT FIRST, I'VE GOT TO FIGURE OUT WHAT'S HAPPENING WITH THE CUPCAKE CLUB AT LUNCHTIME...
LUNCHTIME...
I'VE GOT MY BUSINESS LEDGER IN MY BAG, BUT I WON'T BRING IT OUT UNLESS I REALLY NEED TO. THAT'S NOT WHAT I DO ANYMORE!
KATIE
ALEXIS, YOU ARE NOT GOING TO BELIEVE THIS.
BELIEVE WHAT?
BECCA TOLD HANA, AND HANA TOLD LUCY, THAT CHRIS HOWARD IS GOING TO ASK MIA TO MARCH WITH HIM IN THE PARADE.

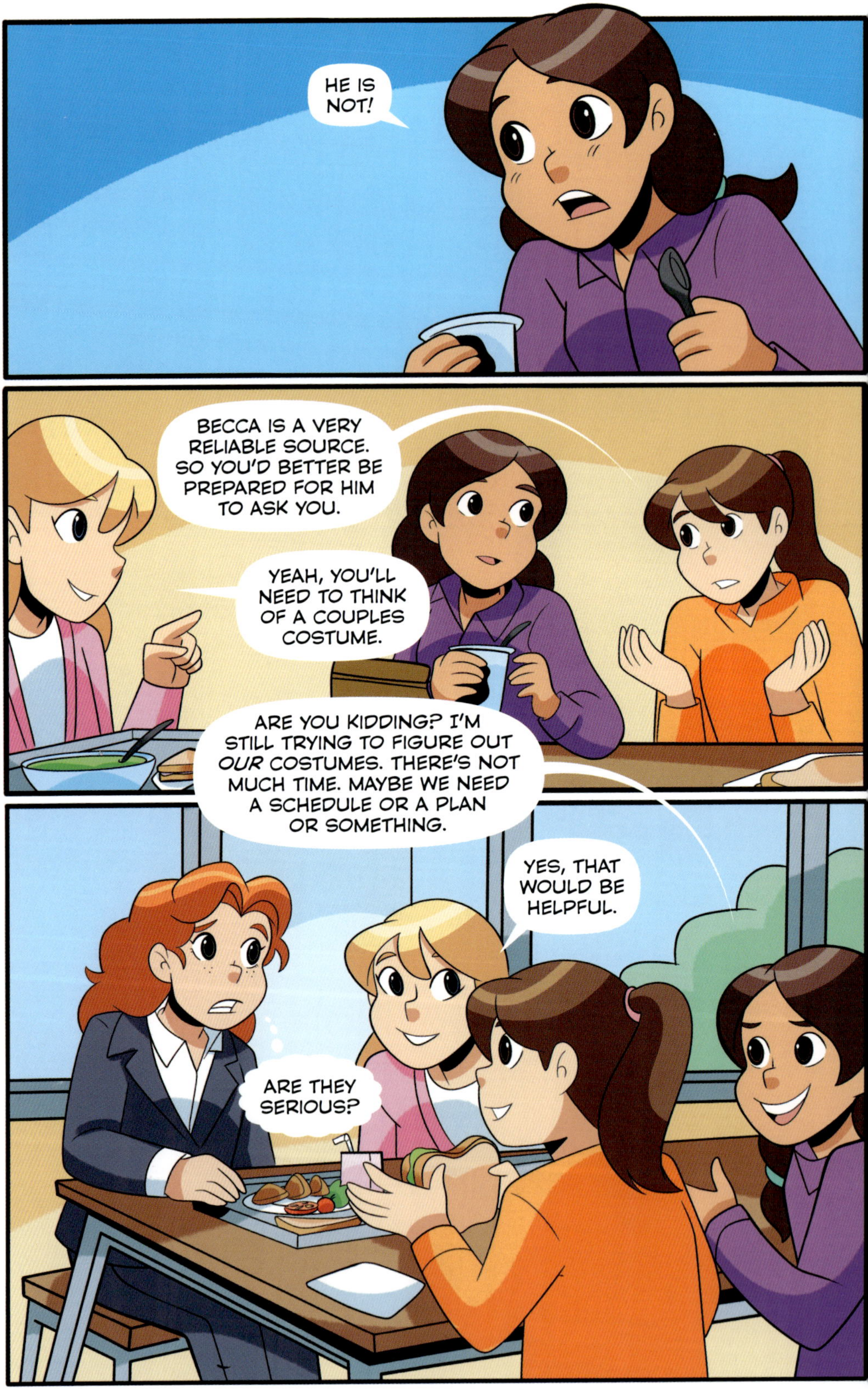
HE IS NOT!
BECCA IS A VERY RELIABLE SOURCE. SO YOU'D BETTER BE PREPARED FOR HIM TO ASK YOU.
YEAH, YOU'LL NEED TO THINK OF A COUPLES COSTUME.
ARE YOU KIDDING? I'M STILL TRYING TO FIGURE OUT *OUR* COSTUMES. THERE'S NOT MUCH TIME. MAYBE WE NEED A SCHEDULE OR A PLAN OR SOMETHING.
YES, THAT WOULD BE HELPFUL.
ARE THEY SERIOUS?

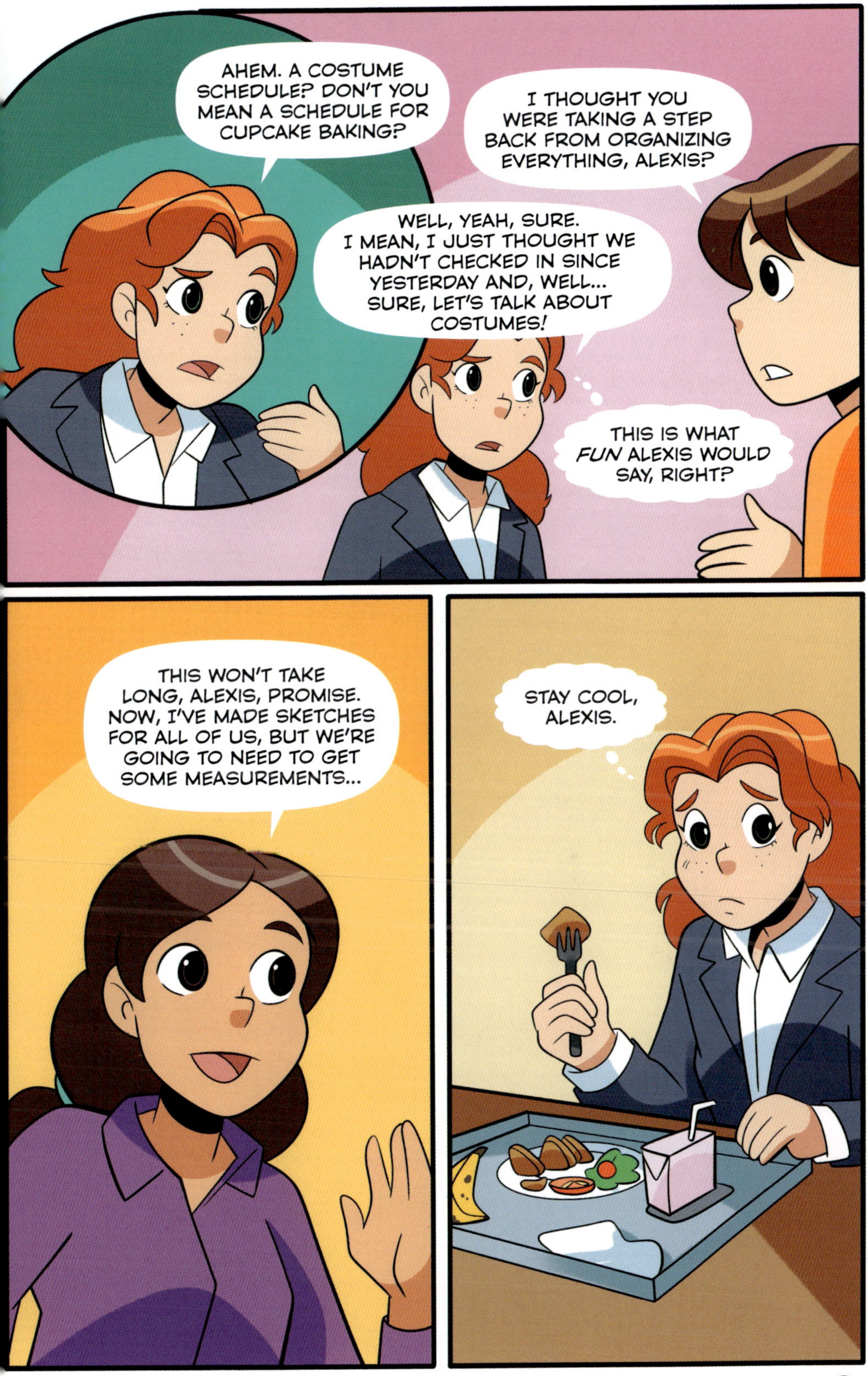
AHEM. A COSTUME SCHEDULE? DON'T YOU MEAN A SCHEDULE FOR CUPCAKE BAKING?
I THOUGHT YOU WERE TAKING A STEP BACK FROM ORGANIZING EVERYTHING, ALEXIS?
WELL, YEAH, SURE. I MEAN, I JUST THOUGHT WE HADN'T CHECKED IN SINCE YESTERDAY AND, WELL... SURE, LET'S TALK ABOUT COSTUMES!
THIS IS WHAT *FUN* ALEXIS WOULD SAY, RIGHT?
THIS WON'T TAKE LONG, ALEXIS, PROMISE. NOW, I'VE MADE SKETCHES FOR ALL OF US, BUT WE'RE GOING TO NEED TO GET SOME MEASUREMENTS...
STAY COOL, ALEXIS.

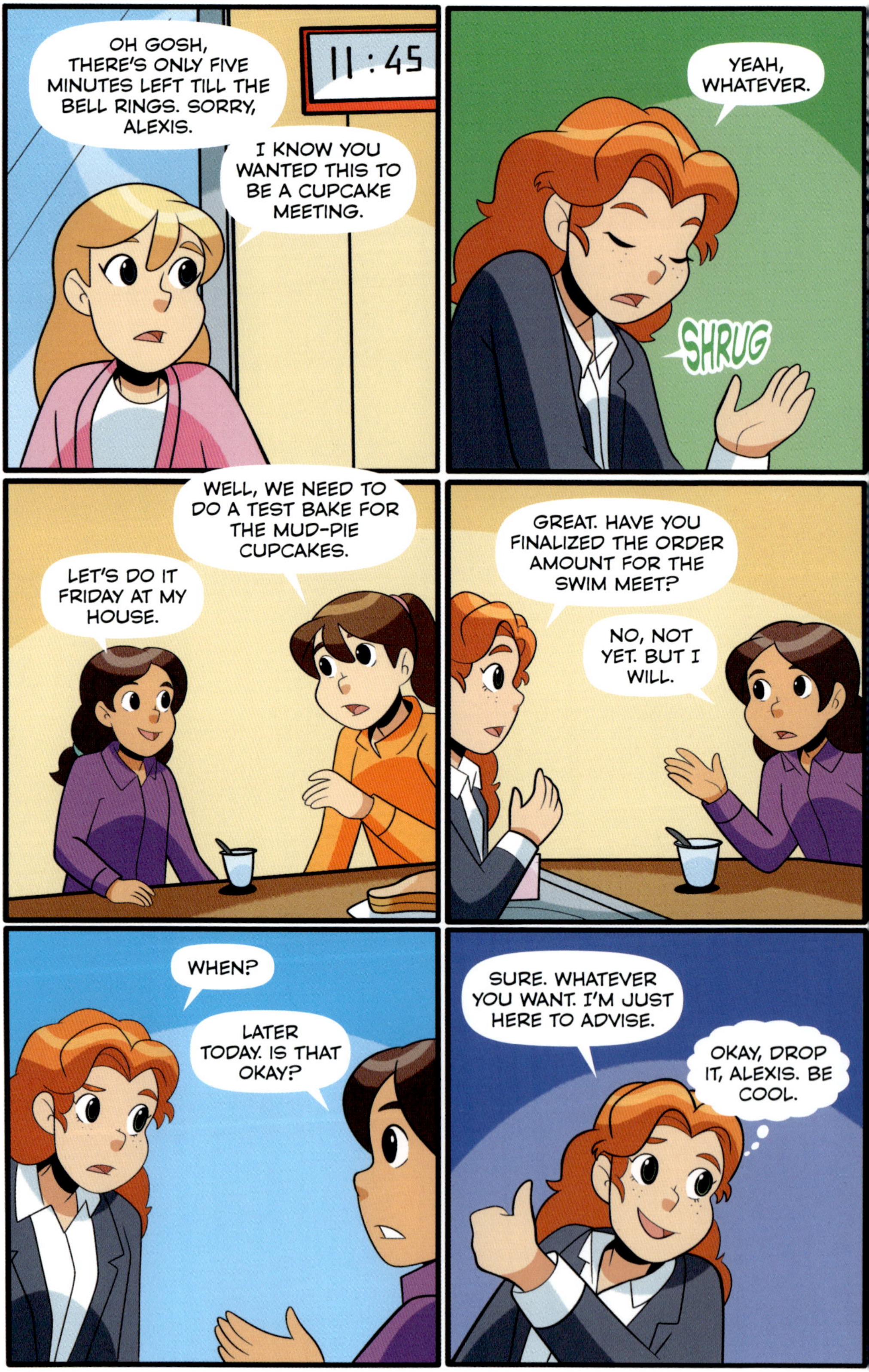
11:45
OH GOSH, THERE'S ONLY FIVE MINUTES LEFT TILL THE BELL RINGS. SORRY, ALEXIS.
I KNOW YOU WANTED THIS TO BE A CUPCAKE MEETING.
YEAH, WHATEVER.
SHRUG
WELL, WE NEED TO DO A TEST BAKE FOR THE MUD-PIE CUPCAKES.
LET'S DO IT FRIDAY AT MY HOUSE.
GREAT. HAVE YOU FINALIZED THE ORDER AMOUNT FOR THE SWIM MEET?
NO, NOT YET. BUT I WILL.
WHEN?
LATER TODAY. IS THAT OKAY?
SURE. WHATEVER YOU WANT. I'M JUST HERE TO ADVISE.
OKAY, DROP IT, ALEXIS. BE COOL.

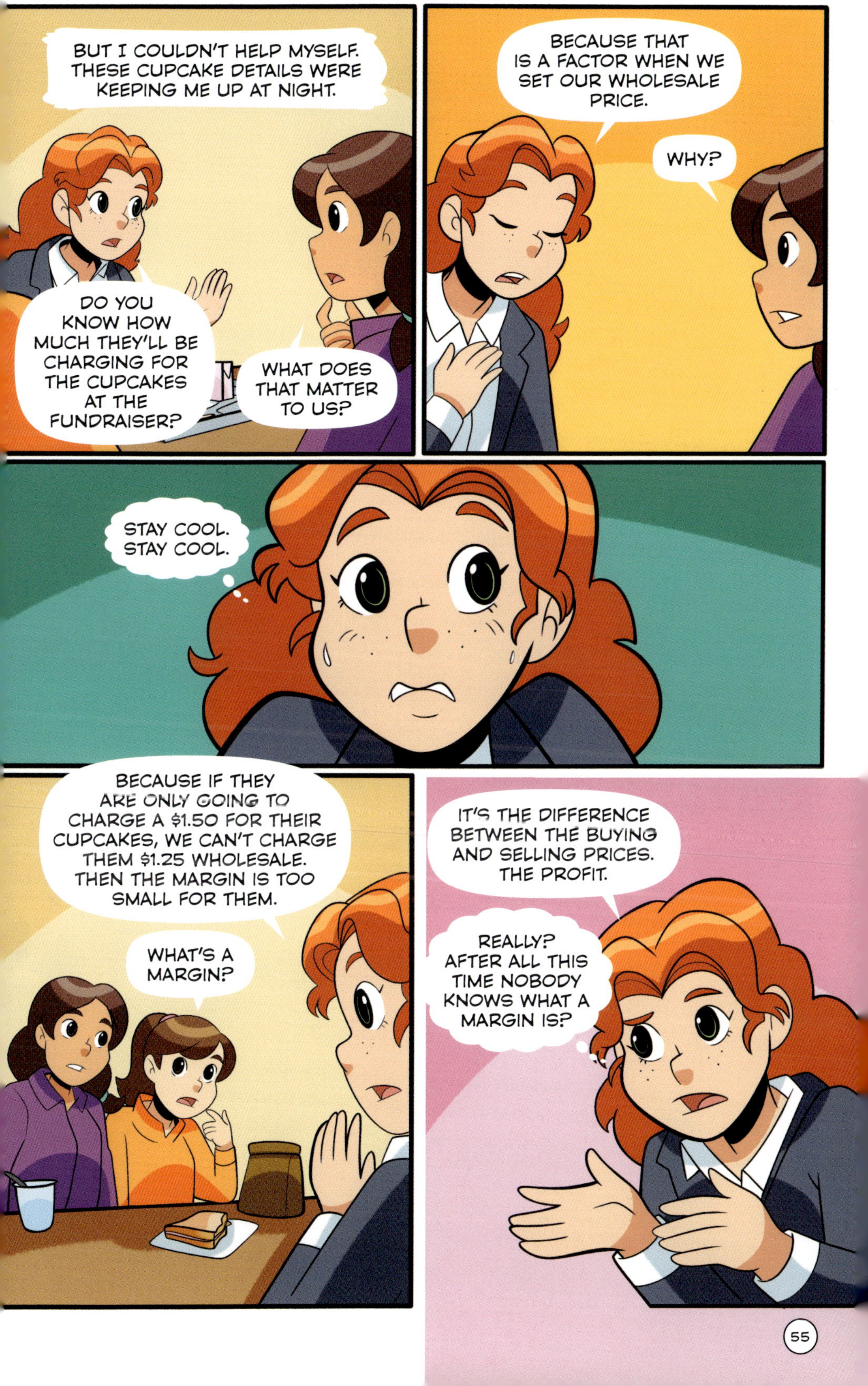

BUT I COULDN'T HELP MYSELF. THESE CUPCAKE DETAILS WERE KEEPING ME UP AT NIGHT.
DO YOU KNOW HOW MUCH THEY'LL BE CHARGING FOR THE CUPCAKES AT THE FUNDRAISER?
WHAT DOES THAT MATTER TO US?
BECAUSE THAT IS A FACTOR WHEN WE SET OUR WHOLESALE PRICE.
WHY?
STAY COOL. STAY COOL.
BECAUSE IF THEY ARE ONLY GOING TO CHARGE A $1.50 FOR THEIR CUPCAKES, WE CAN'T CHARGE THEM $1.25 WHOLESALE. THEN THE MARGIN IS TOO SMALL FOR THEM.
WHAT'S A MARGIN?
IT'S THE DIFFERENCE BETWEEN THE BUYING AND SELLING PRICES. THE PROFIT.
REALLY? AFTER ALL THIS TIME NOBODY KNOWS WHAT A MARGIN IS?

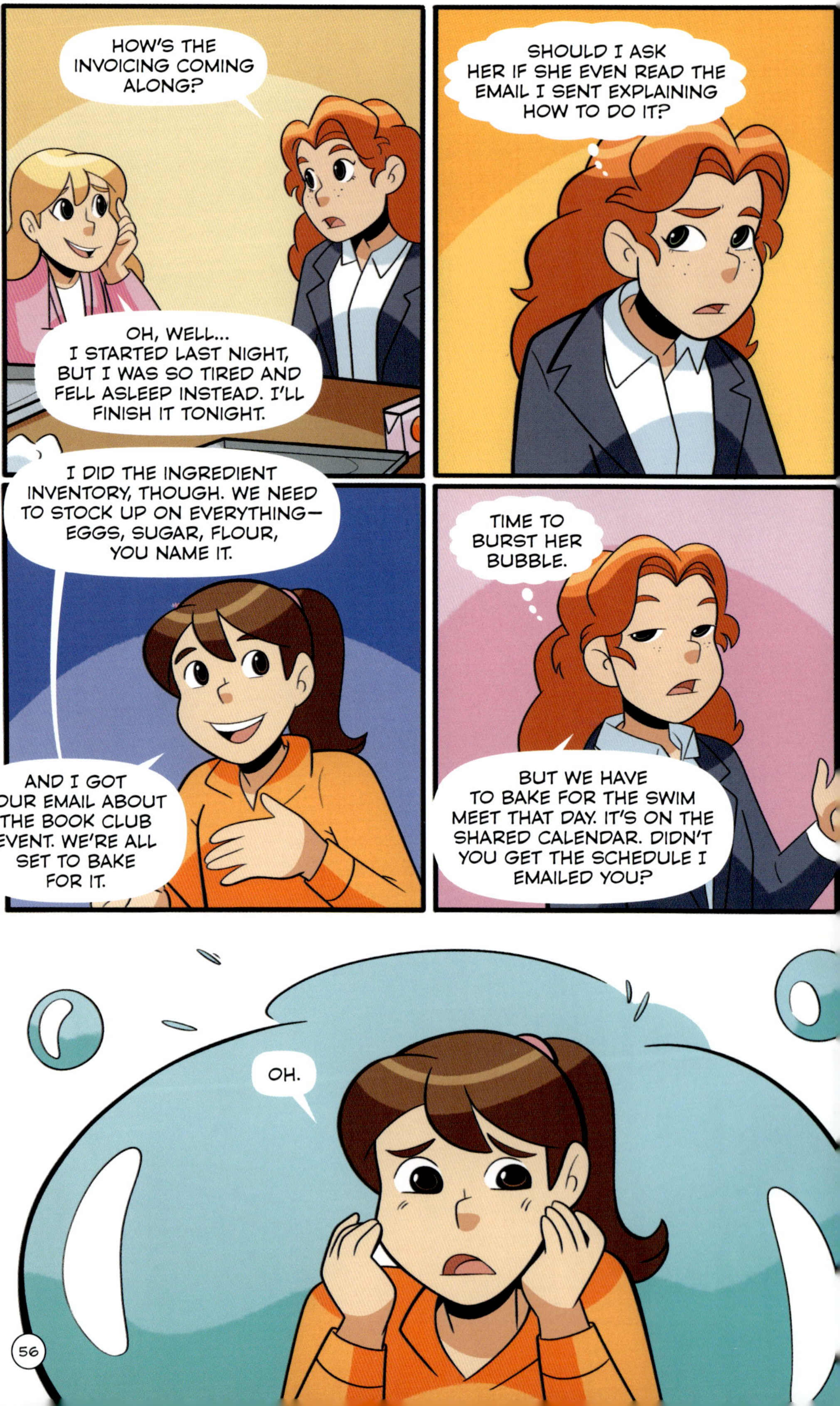

HOW'S THE INVOICING COMING ALONG?
OH, WELL... I STARTED LAST NIGHT, BUT I WAS SO TIRED AND FELL ASLEEP INSTEAD. I'LL FINISH IT TONIGHT.
SHOULD I ASK HER IF SHE EVEN READ THE EMAIL I SENT EXPLAINING HOW TO DO IT?
I DID THE INGREDIENT INVENTORY, THOUGH. WE NEED TO STOCK UP ON EVERYTHING—EGGS, SUGAR, FLOUR, YOU NAME IT.
AND I GOT YOUR EMAIL ABOUT THE BOOK CLUB EVENT. WE'RE ALL SET TO BAKE FOR IT.
TIME TO BURST HER BUBBLE.
BUT WE HAVE TO BAKE FOR THE SWIM MEET THAT DAY. IT'S ON THE SHARED CALENDAR. DIDN'T YOU GET THE SCHEDULE I EMAILED YOU?
OH.

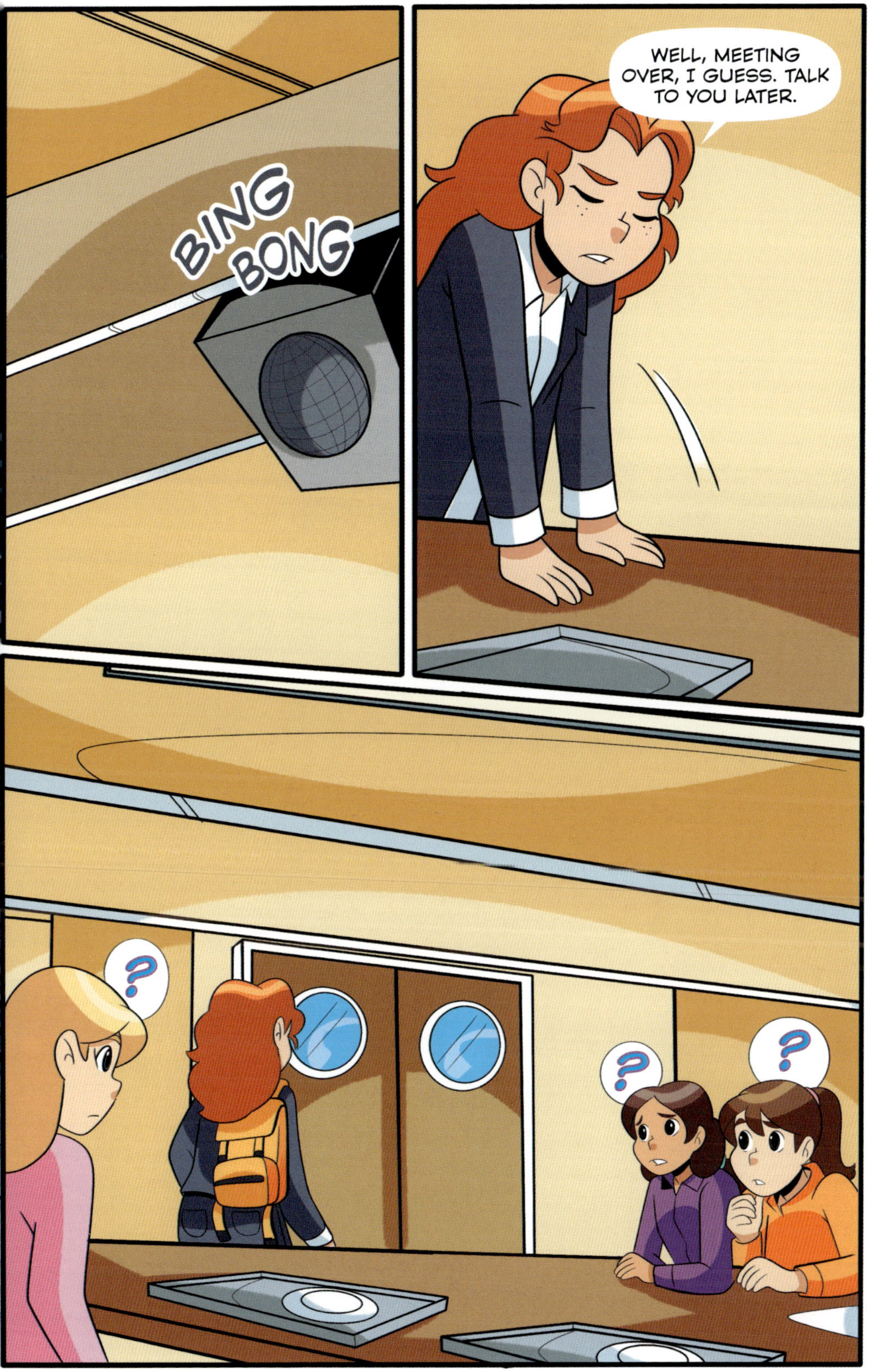
BING
BONG
WELL, MEETING OVER, I GUESS. TALK TO YOU LATER.
?
?
?

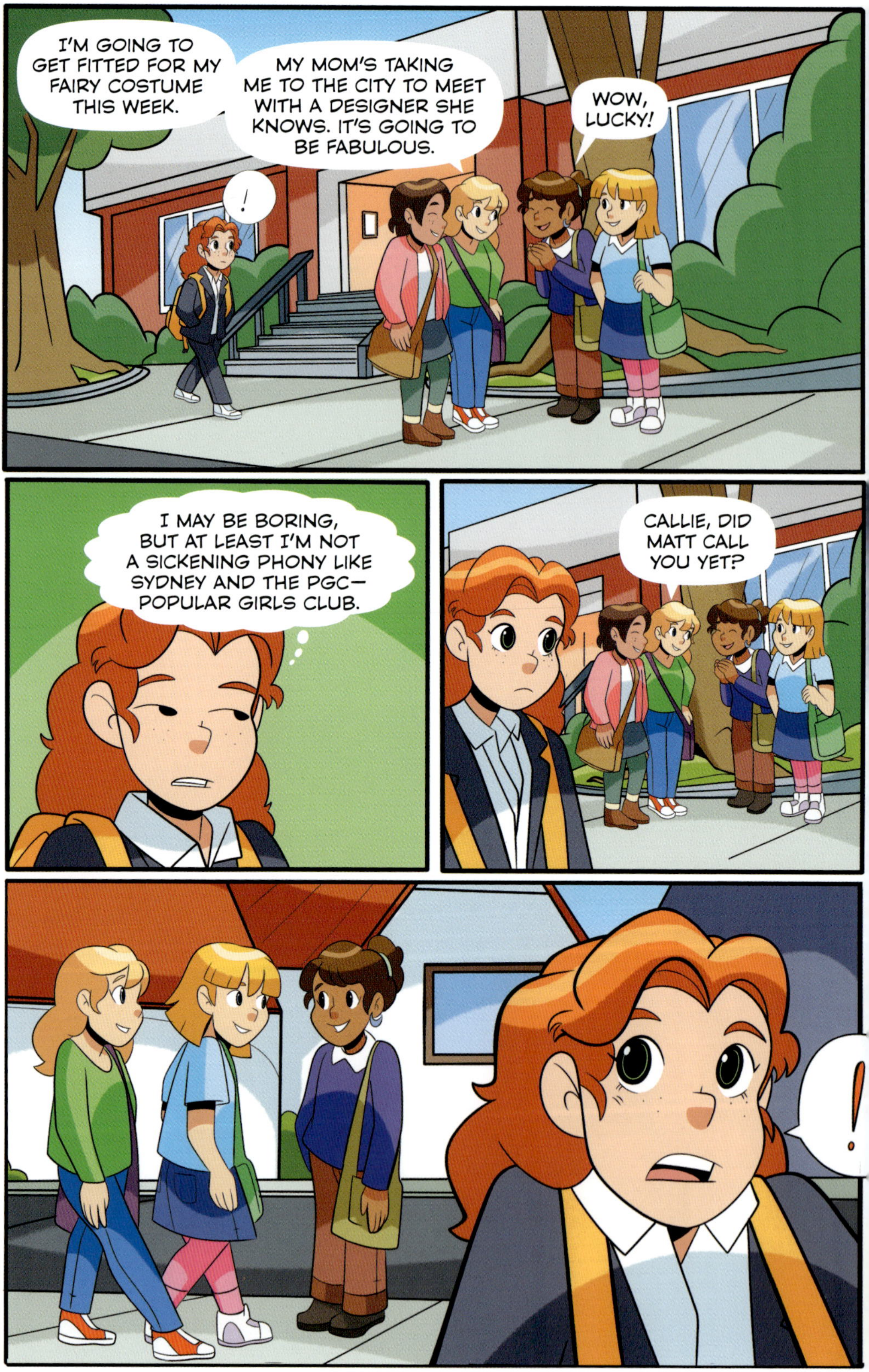
I'M GOING TO GET FITTED FOR MY FAIRY COSTUME THIS WEEK.
MY MOM'S TAKING ME TO THE CITY TO MEET WITH A DESIGNER SHE KNOWS. IT'S GOING TO BE FABULOUS.
WOW, LUCKY!
!
I MAY BE BORING, BUT AT LEAST I'M NOT A SICKENING PHONY LIKE SYDNEY AND THE PGC— POPULAR GIRLS CLUB.
CALLIE, DID MATT CALL YOU YET?
!

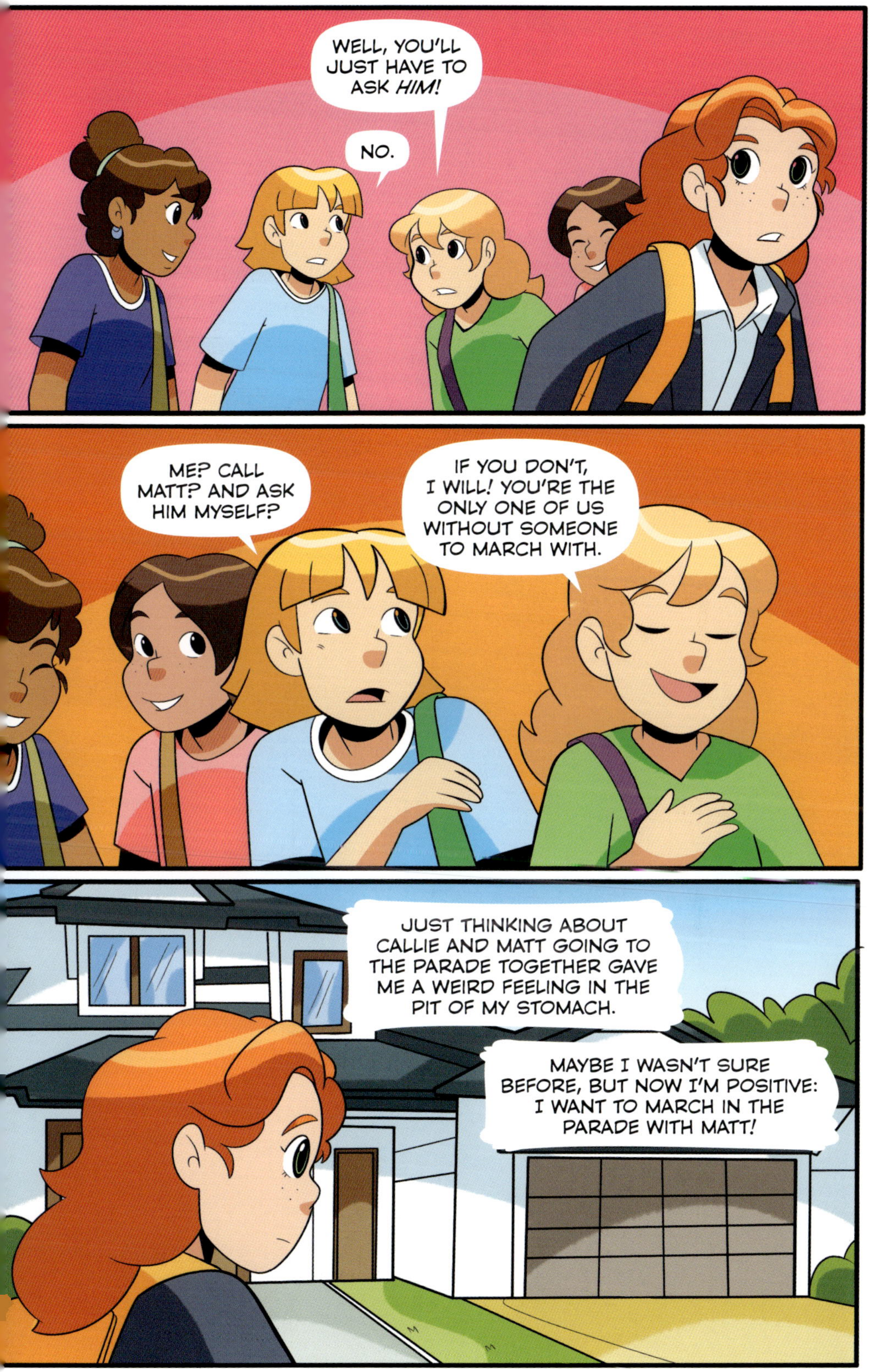

WELL, YOU'LL JUST HAVE TO ASK *HIM*!
NO.
ME? CALL MATT? AND ASK HIM MYSELF?
IF YOU DON'T, I WILL! YOU'RE THE ONLY ONE OF US WITHOUT SOMEONE TO MARCH WITH.
JUST THINKING ABOUT CALLIE AND MATT GOING TO THE PARADE TOGETHER GAVE ME A WEIRD FEELING IN THE PIT OF MY STOMACH.
MAYBE I WASN'T SURE BEFORE, BUT NOW I'M POSITIVE: I WANT TO MARCH IN THE PARADE WITH MATT!

Chapter 6

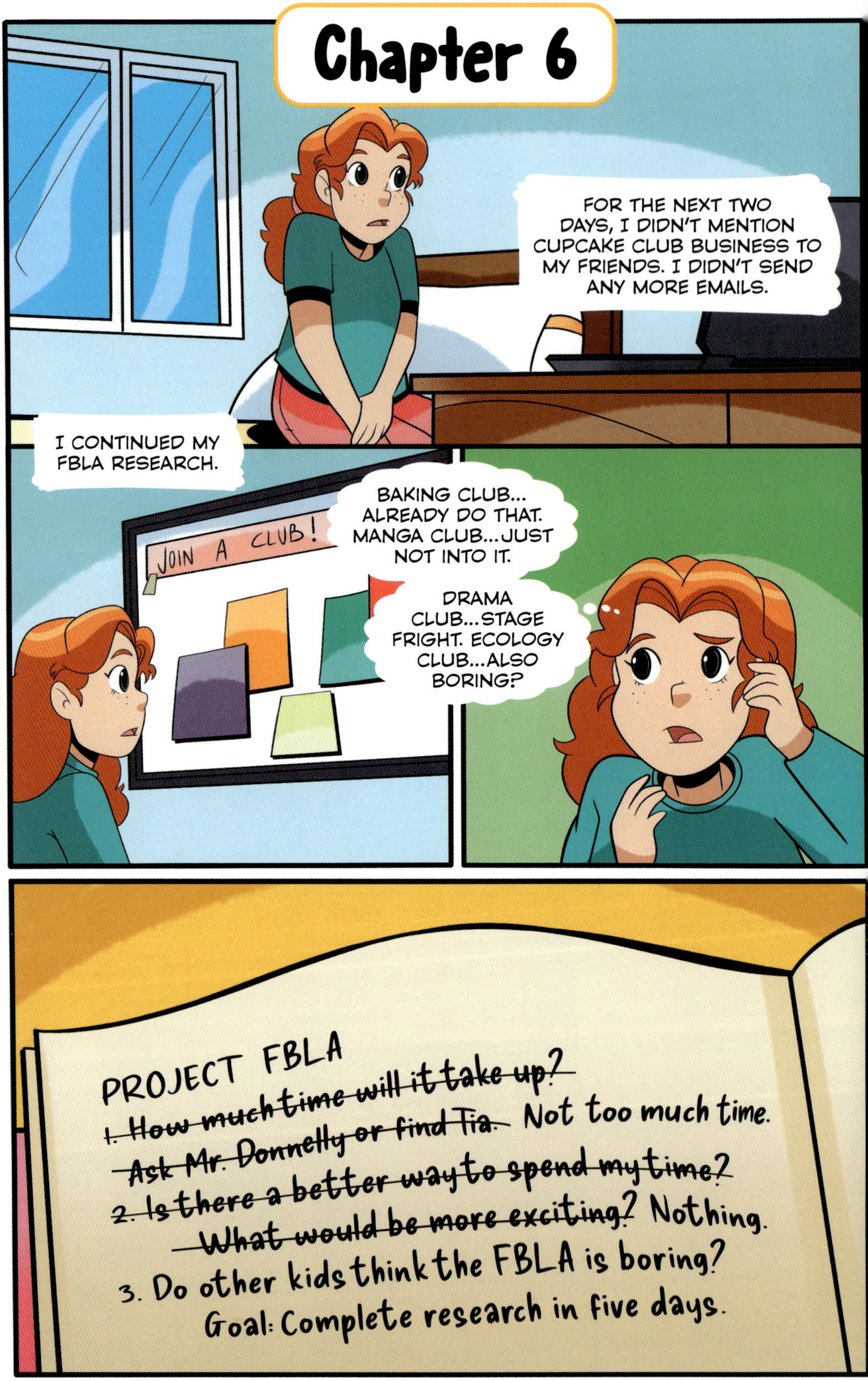
FOR THE NEXT TWO DAYS, I DIDN'T MENTION CUPCAKE CLUB BUSINESS TO MY FRIENDS. I DIDN'T SEND ANY MORE EMAILS.
I CONTINUED MY FBLA RESEARCH.
JOIN A CLUB!
BAKING CLUB... ALREADY DO THAT. MANGA CLUB...JUST NOT INTO IT.
DRAMA CLUB...STAGE FRIGHT. ECOLOGY CLUB...ALSO BORING?
PROJECT FBLA
~~1. How much time will it take up?~~
~~Ask Mr. Donnelly or find Tia.~~ Not too much time.
~~2. Is there a better way to spend my time?~~
~~What would be more exciting?~~ Nothing.
3. Do other kids think the FBLA is boring?
Goal: Complete research in five days.

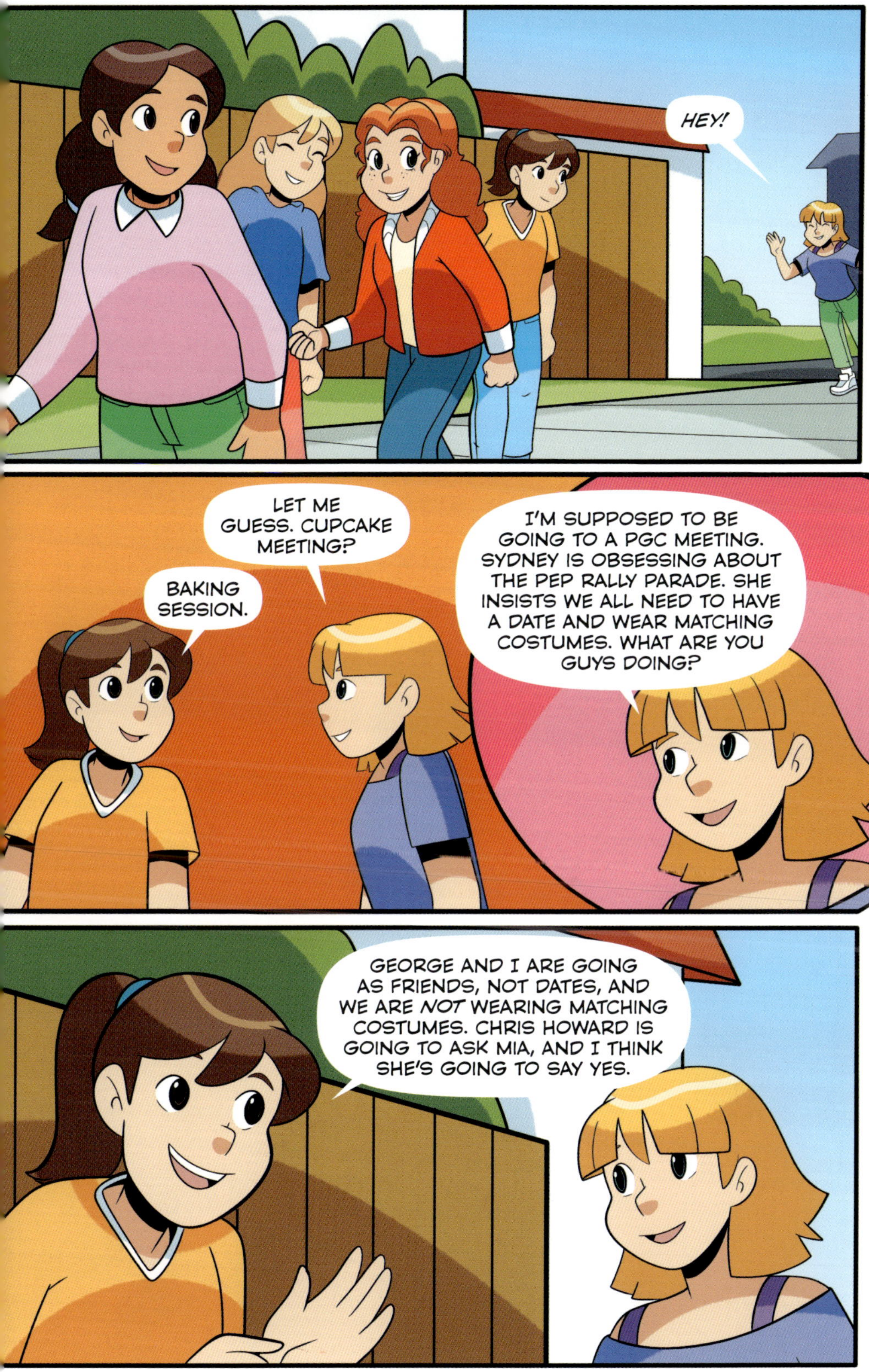
HEY!
LET ME GUESS. CUPCAKE MEETING?
BAKING SESSION.
I'M SUPPOSED TO BE GOING TO A PGC MEETING. SYDNEY IS OBSESSING ABOUT THE PEP RALLY PARADE. SHE INSISTS WE ALL NEED TO HAVE A DATE AND WEAR MATCHING COSTUMES. WHAT ARE YOU GUYS DOING?
GEORGE AND I ARE GOING AS FRIENDS, NOT DATES, AND WE ARE *NOT* WEARING MATCHING COSTUMES. CHRIS HOWARD IS GOING TO ASK MIA, AND I THINK SHE'S GOING TO SAY YES.

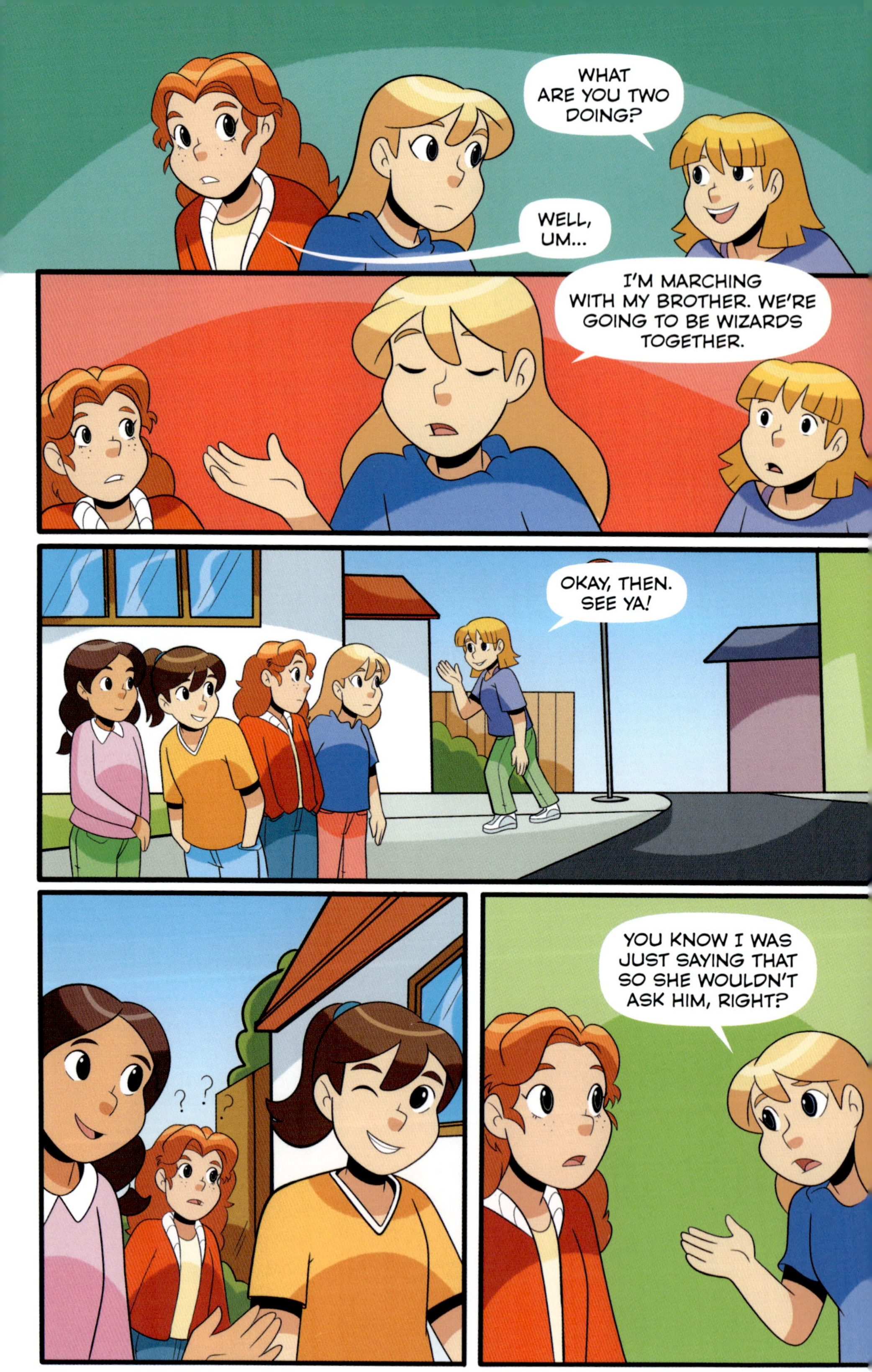
WHAT ARE YOU TWO DOING?
WELL, UM...
I'M MARCHING WITH MY BROTHER. WE'RE GOING TO BE WIZARDS TOGETHER.
OKAY, THEN. SEE YA!
? ? ?
YOU KNOW I WAS JUST SAYING THAT SO SHE WOULDN'T ASK HIM, RIGHT?

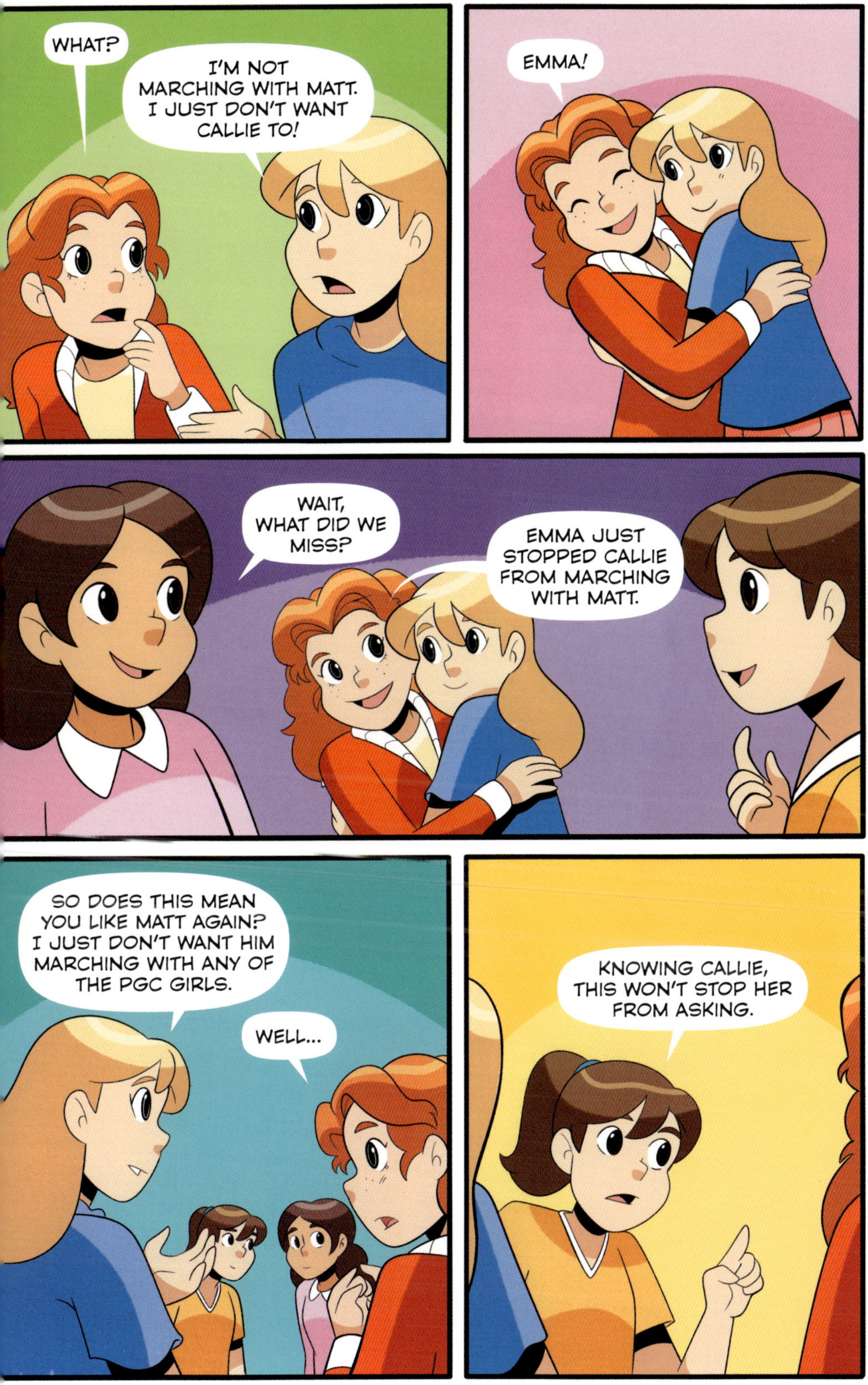
WHAT?
I'M NOT MARCHING WITH MATT. I JUST DON'T WANT CALLIE TO!
EMMA!
WAIT, WHAT DID WE MISS?
EMMA JUST STOPPED CALLIE FROM MARCHING WITH MATT.
SO DOES THIS MEAN YOU LIKE MATT AGAIN?
I JUST DON'T WANT HIM MARCHING WITH ANY OF THE PGC GIRLS.
WELL...
KNOWING CALLIE, THIS WON'T STOP HER FROM ASKING.

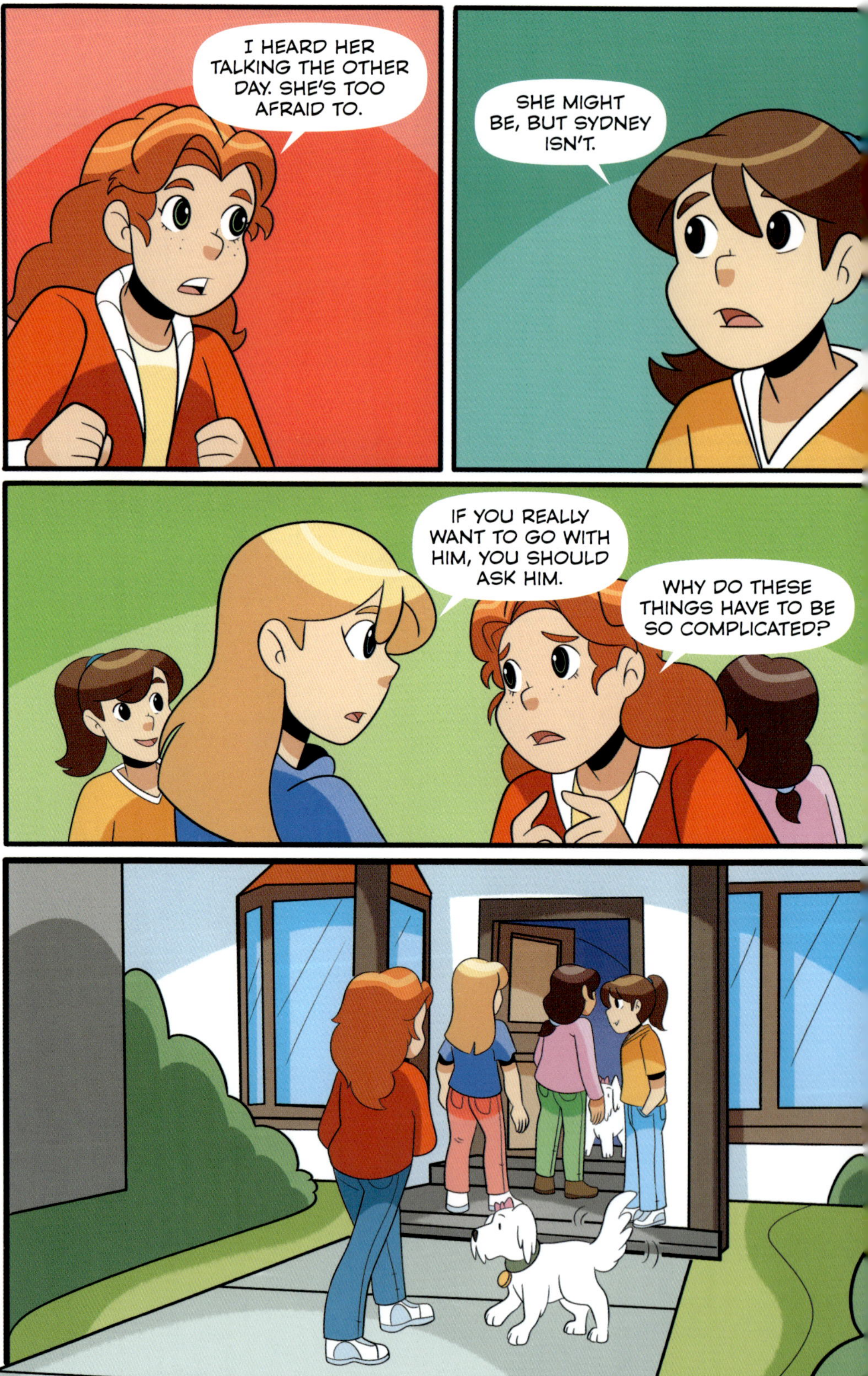
I HEARD HER TALKING THE OTHER DAY. SHE'S TOO AFRAID TO.
SHE MIGHT BE, BUT SYDNEY ISN'T.
IF YOU REALLY WANT TO GO WITH HIM, YOU SHOULD ASK HIM.
WHY DO THESE THINGS HAVE TO BE SO COMPLICATED?

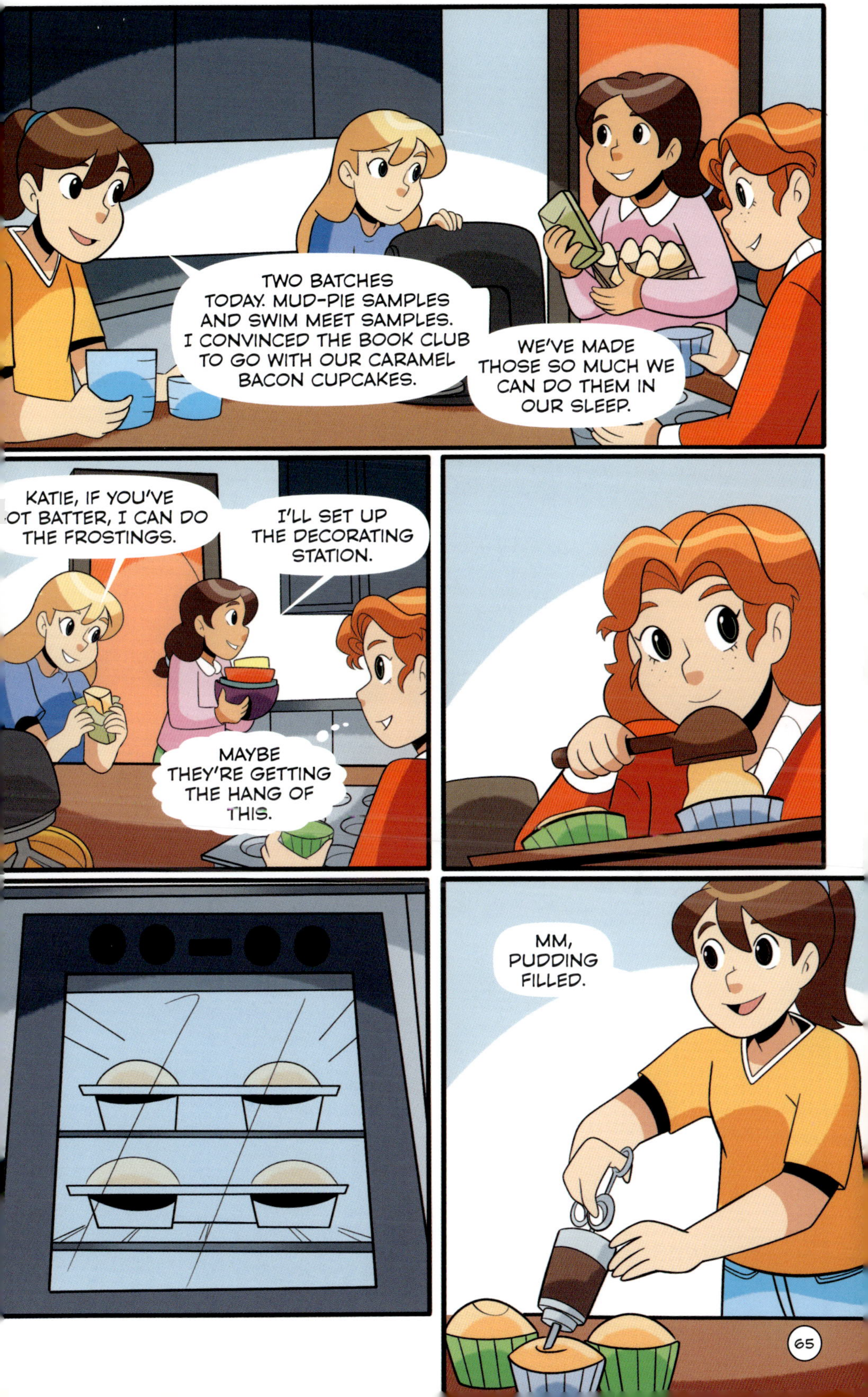
TWO BATCHES TODAY. MUD-PIE SAMPLES AND SWIM MEET SAMPLES. I CONVINCED THE BOOK CLUB TO GO WITH OUR CARAMEL BACON CUPCAKES.
WE'VE MADE THOSE SO MUCH WE CAN DO THEM IN OUR SLEEP.
KATIE, IF YOU'VE OT BATTER, I CAN DO THE FROSTINGS.
I'LL SET UP THE DECORATING STATION.
MAYBE THEY'RE GETTING THE HANG OF THIS.
MM, PUDDING FILLED.

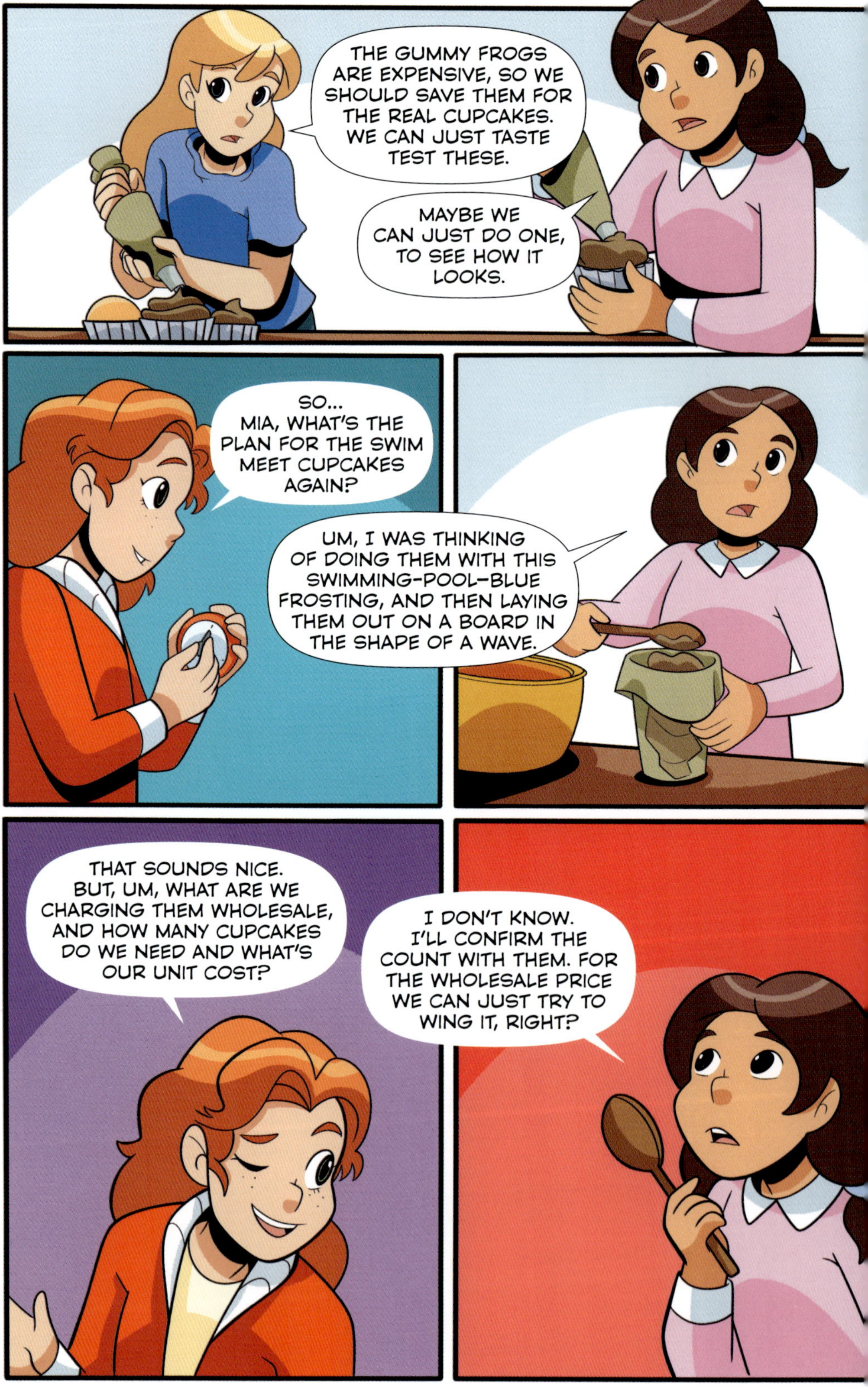
THE GUMMY FROGS ARE EXPENSIVE, SO WE SHOULD SAVE THEM FOR THE REAL CUPCAKES. WE CAN JUST TASTE TEST THESE.
MAYBE WE CAN JUST DO ONE, TO SEE HOW IT LOOKS.
SO... MIA, WHAT'S THE PLAN FOR THE SWIM MEET CUPCAKES AGAIN?
UM, I WAS THINKING OF DOING THEM WITH THIS SWIMMING-POOL-BLUE FROSTING, AND THEN LAYING THEM OUT ON A BOARD IN THE SHAPE OF A WAVE.
THAT SOUNDS NICE. BUT, UM, WHAT ARE WE CHARGING THEM WHOLESALE, AND HOW MANY CUPCAKES DO WE NEED AND WHAT'S OUR UNIT COST?
I DON'T KNOW. I'LL CONFIRM THE COUNT WITH THEM. FOR THE WHOLESALE PRICE WE CAN JUST TRY TO WING IT, RIGHT?

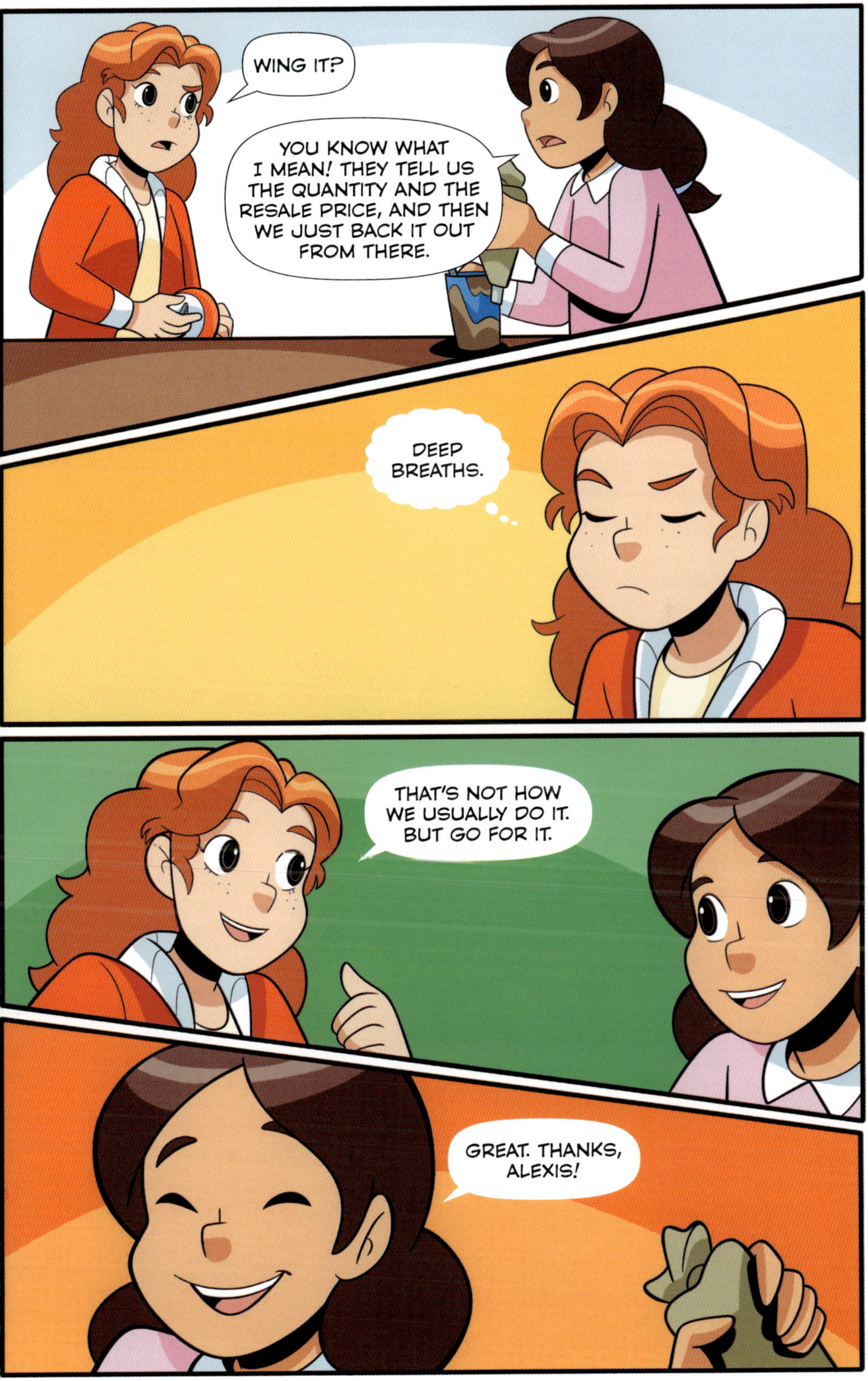
WING IT?
YOU KNOW WHAT I MEAN! THEY TELL US THE QUANTITY AND THE RESALE PRICE, AND THEN WE JUST BACK IT OUT FROM THERE.
DEEP BREATHS.
THAT'S NOT HOW WE USUALLY DO IT. BUT GO FOR IT.
GREAT. THANKS, ALEXIS!

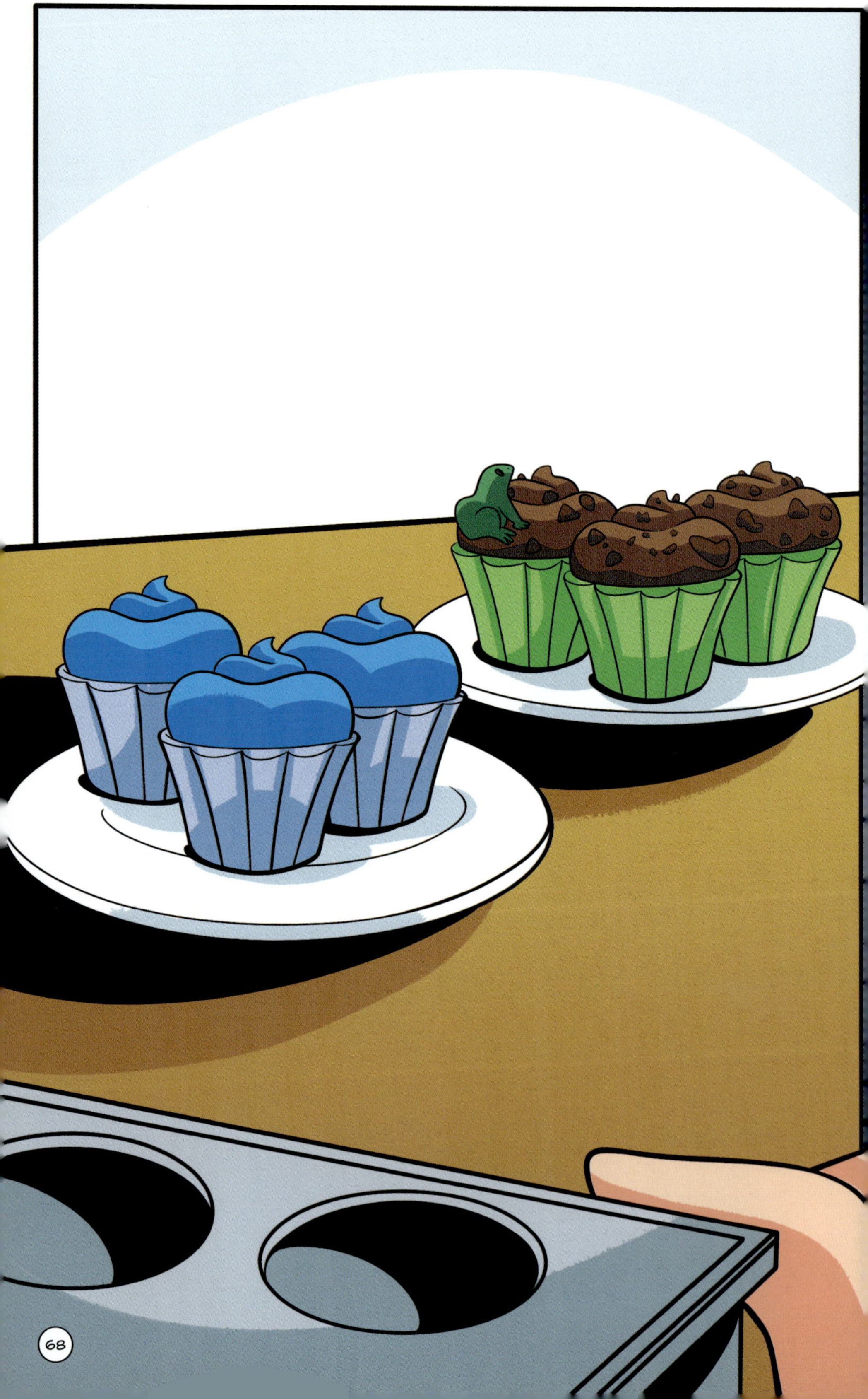

Chapter 7

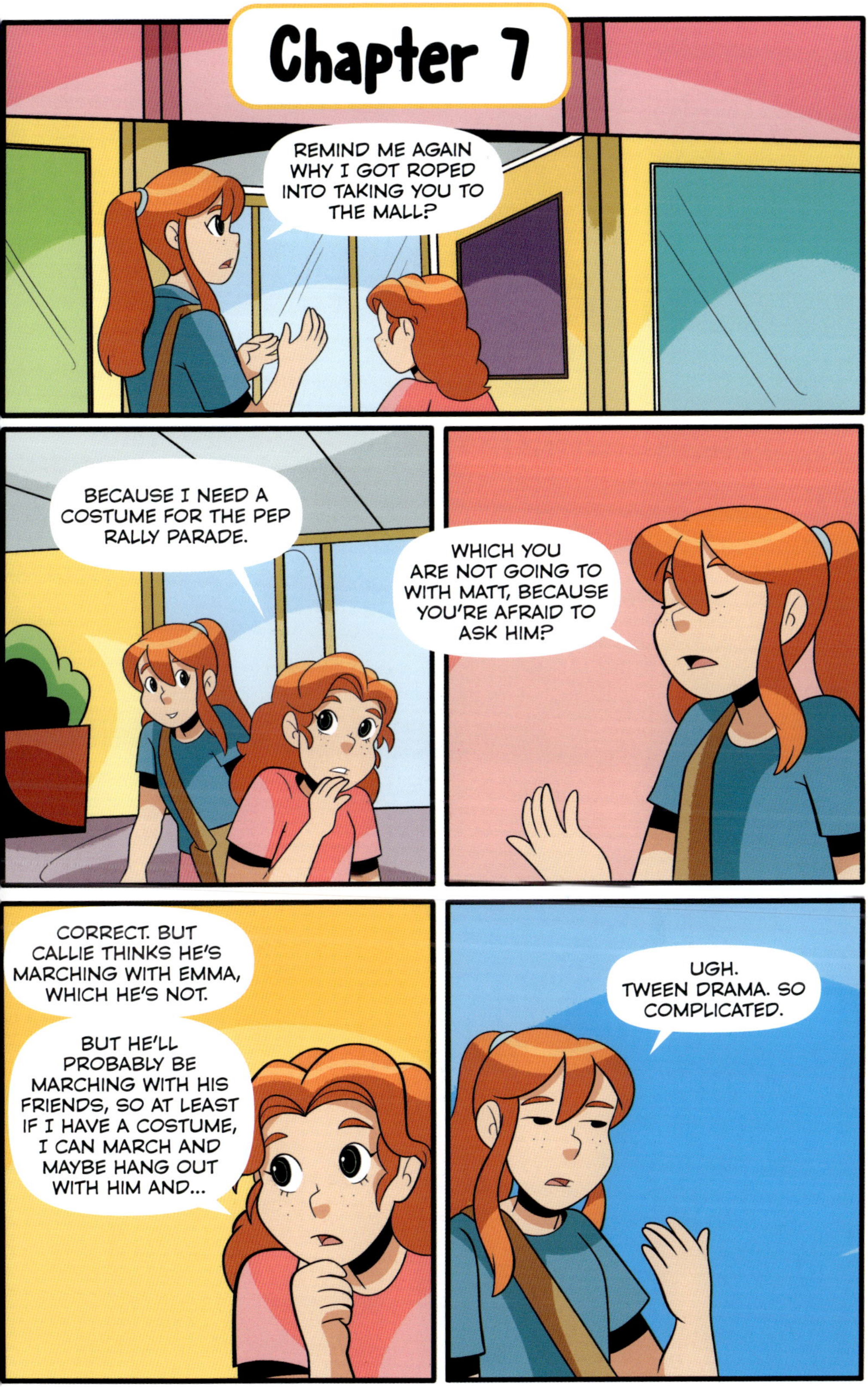
REMIND ME AGAIN WHY I GOT ROPED INTO TAKING YOU TO THE MALL?
BECAUSE I NEED A COSTUME FOR THE PEP RALLY PARADE.
WHICH YOU ARE NOT GOING TO WITH MATT, BECAUSE YOU'RE AFRAID TO ASK HIM?
CORRECT. BUT CALLIE THINKS HE'S MARCHING WITH EMMA, WHICH HE'S NOT.
BUT HE'LL PROBABLY BE MARCHING WITH HIS FRIENDS, SO AT LEAST IF I HAVE A COSTUME, I CAN MARCH AND MAYBE HANG OUT WITH HIM AND...
UGH. TWEEN DRAMA. SO COMPLICATED.

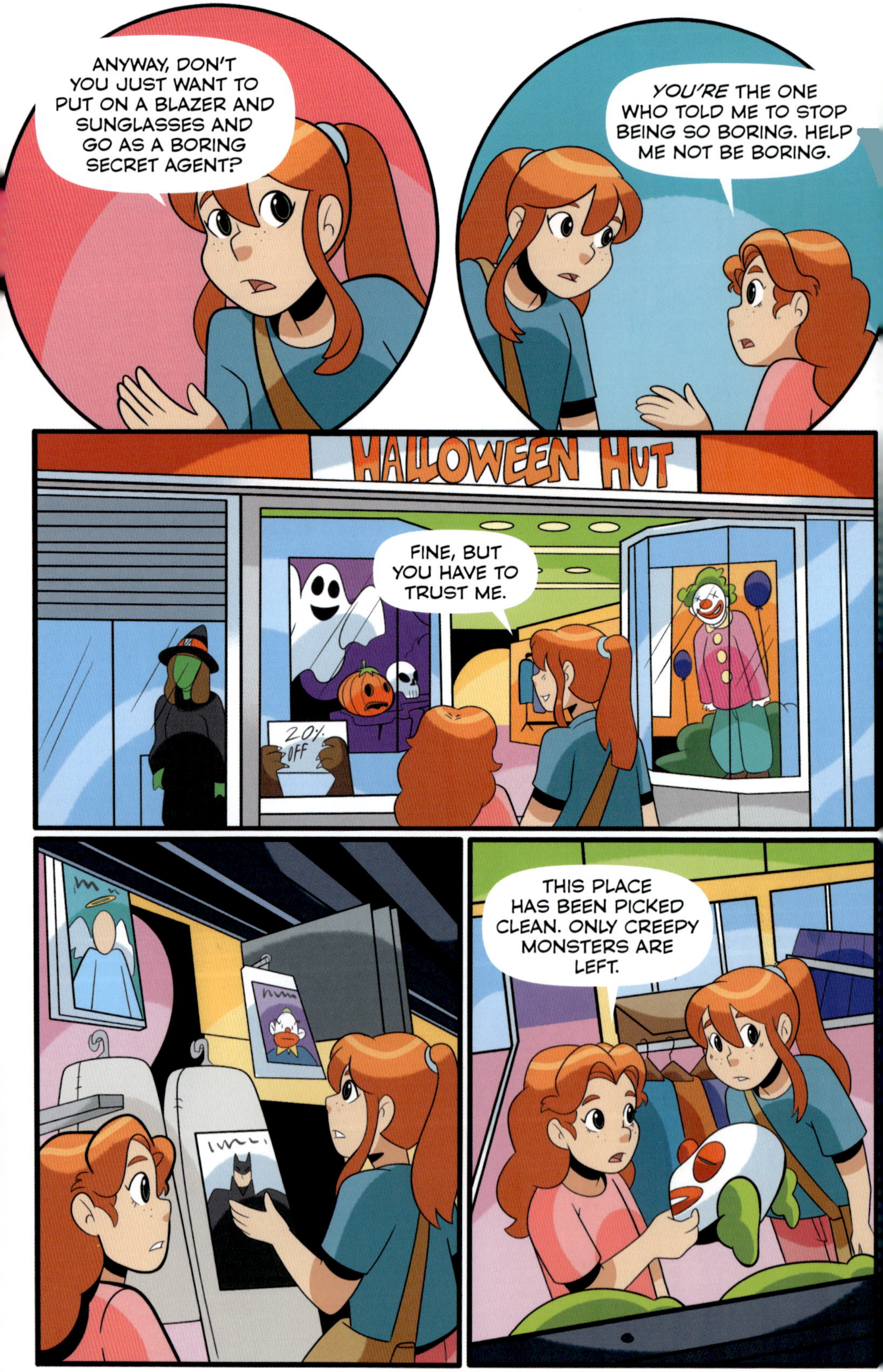
ANYWAY, DON'T YOU JUST WANT TO PUT ON A BLAZER AND SUNGLASSES AND GO AS A BORING SECRET AGENT?
YOU'RE THE ONE WHO TOLD ME TO STOP BEING SO BORING. HELP ME NOT BE BORING.
HALLOWEEN HUT
FINE, BUT YOU HAVE TO TRUST ME.
20% OFF
THIS PLACE HAS BEEN PICKED CLEAN. ONLY CREEPY MONSTERS ARE LEFT.

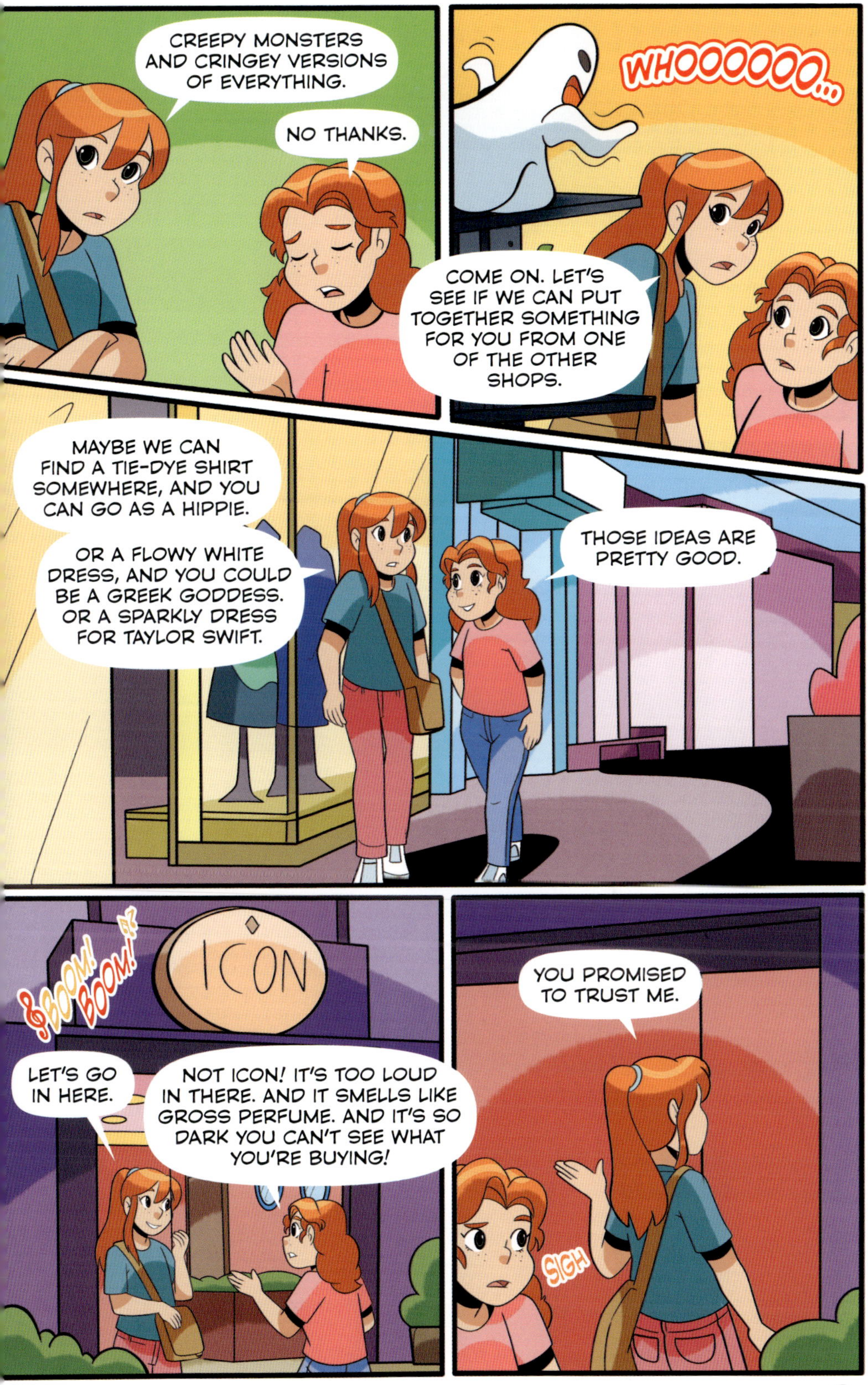
CREEPY MONSTERS AND CRINGEY VERSIONS OF EVERYTHING.
NO THANKS.
WHOOOOOO...
COME ON. LET'S SEE IF WE CAN PUT TOGETHER SOMETHING FOR YOU FROM ONE OF THE OTHER SHOPS.
MAYBE WE CAN FIND A TIE-DYE SHIRT SOMEWHERE, AND YOU CAN GO AS A HIPPIE.
OR A FLOWY WHITE DRESS, AND YOU COULD BE A GREEK GODDESS. OR A SPARKLY DRESS FOR TAYLOR SWIFT.
THOSE IDEAS ARE PRETTY GOOD.
BOOM! BOOM!
ICON
LET'S GO IN HERE.
NOT ICON! IT'S TOO LOUD IN THERE. AND IT SMELLS LIKE GROSS PERFUME. AND IT'S SO DARK YOU CAN'T SEE WHAT YOU'RE BUYING!
YOU PROMISED TO TRUST ME.
SIGH

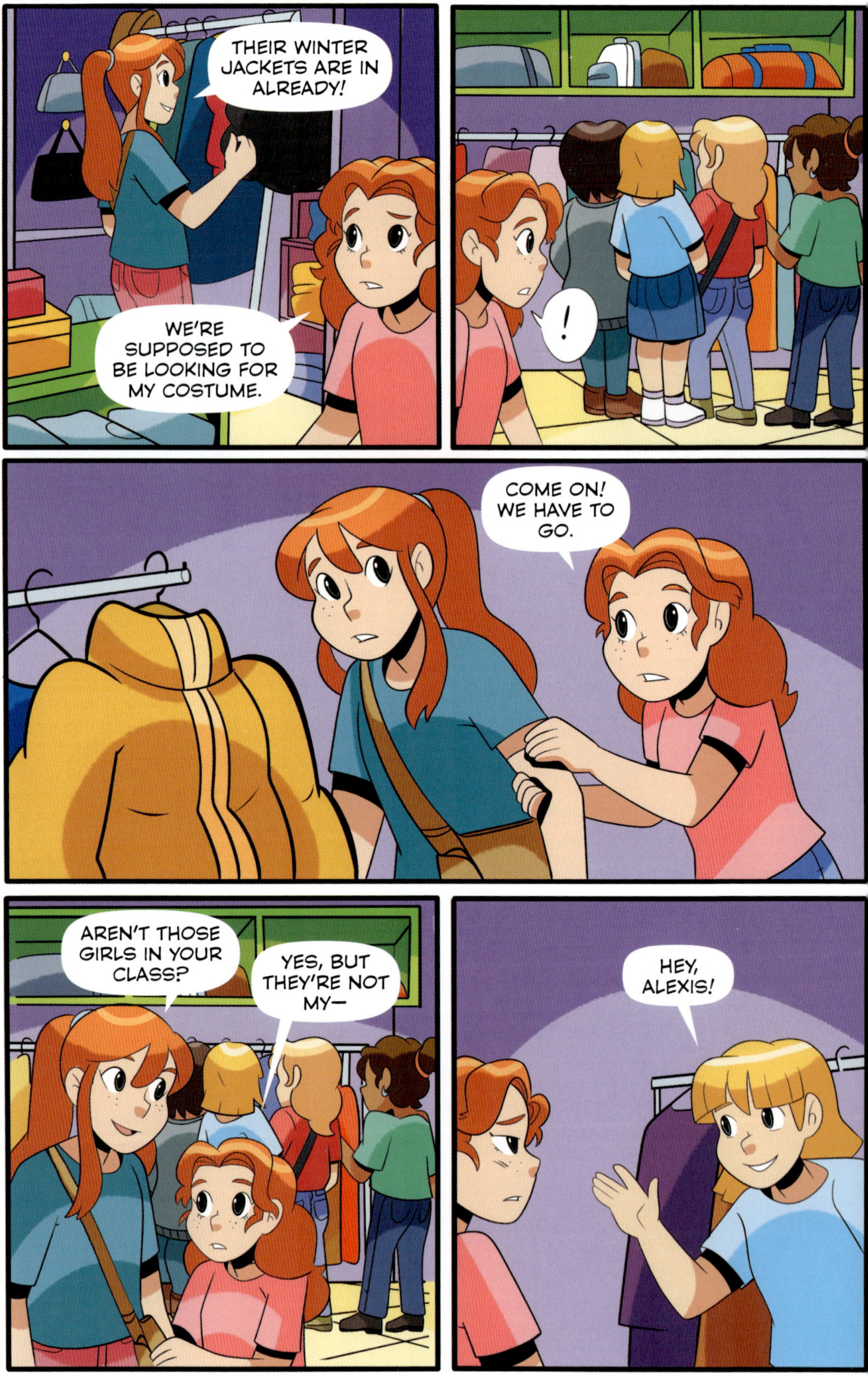
THEIR WINTER JACKETS ARE IN ALREADY!
WE'RE SUPPOSED TO BE LOOKING FOR MY COSTUME.
!
COME ON! WE HAVE TO GO.
AREN'T THOSE GIRLS IN YOUR CLASS?
YES, BUT THEY'RE NOT MY—
HEY, ALEXIS!

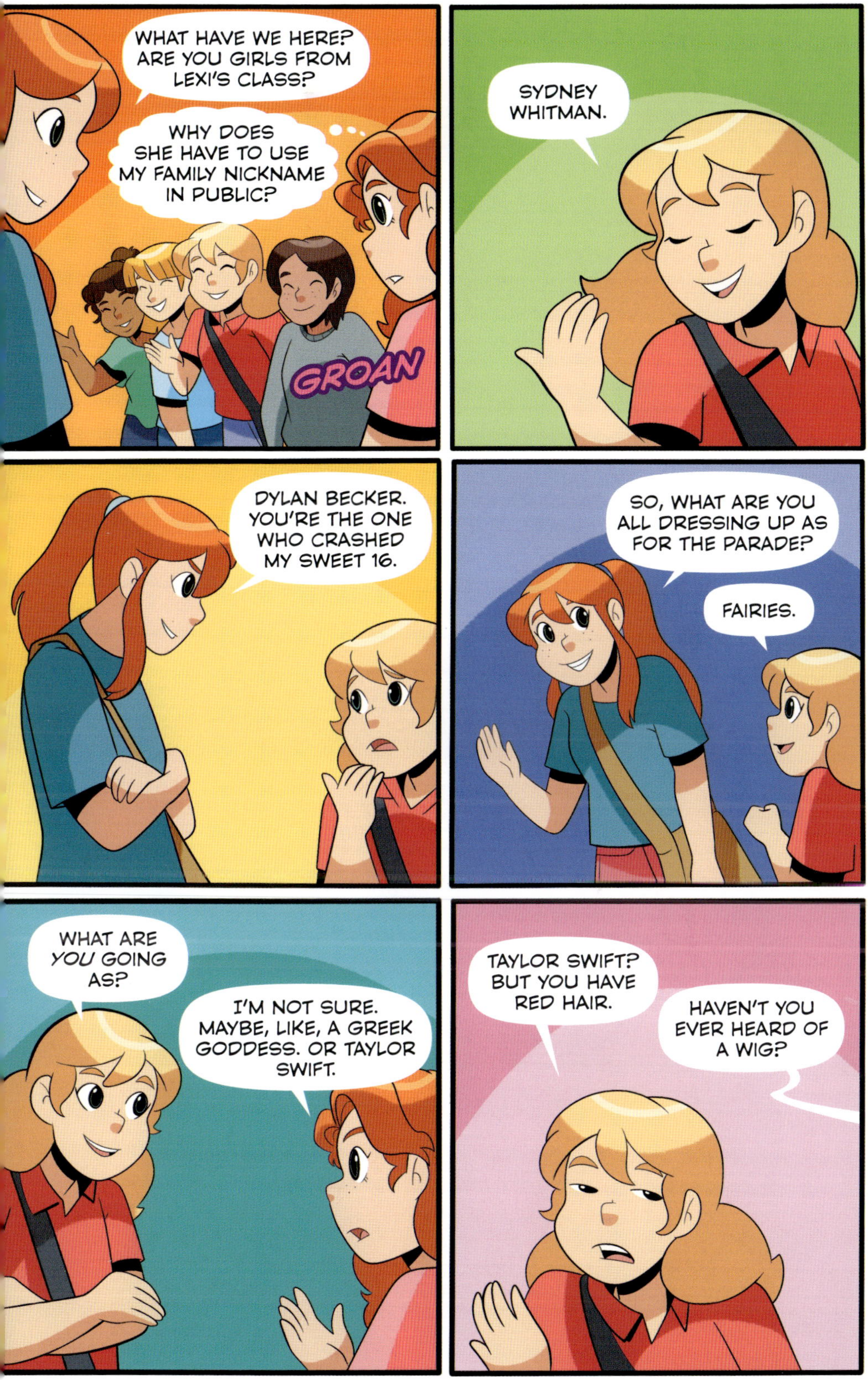
WHAT HAVE WE HERE? ARE YOU GIRLS FROM LEXI'S CLASS?
WHY DOES SHE HAVE TO USE MY FAMILY NICKNAME IN PUBLIC?
GROAN
SYDNEY WHITMAN.
DYLAN BECKER. YOU'RE THE ONE WHO CRASHED MY SWEET 16.
SO, WHAT ARE YOU ALL DRESSING UP AS FOR THE PARADE?
FAIRIES.
WHAT ARE *YOU* GOING AS?
I'M NOT SURE. MAYBE, LIKE, A GREEK GODDESS. OR TAYLOR SWIFT.
TAYLOR SWIFT? BUT YOU HAVE RED HAIR.
HAVEN'T YOU EVER HEARD OF A WIG?

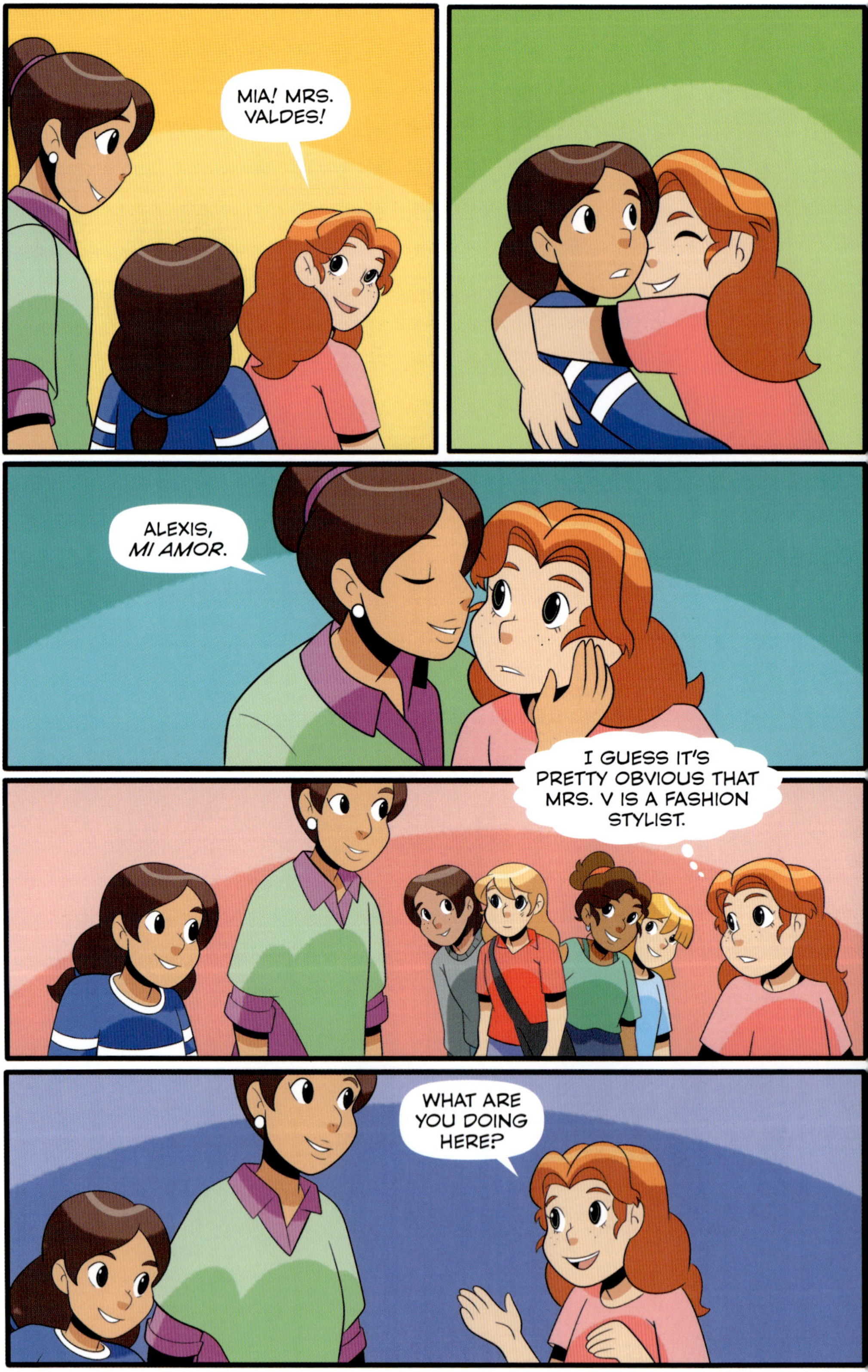
MIA! MRS. VALDES!
ALEXIS, *MI AMOR.*
I GUESS IT'S PRETTY OBVIOUS THAT MRS. V IS A FASHION STYLIST.
WHAT ARE YOU DOING HERE?

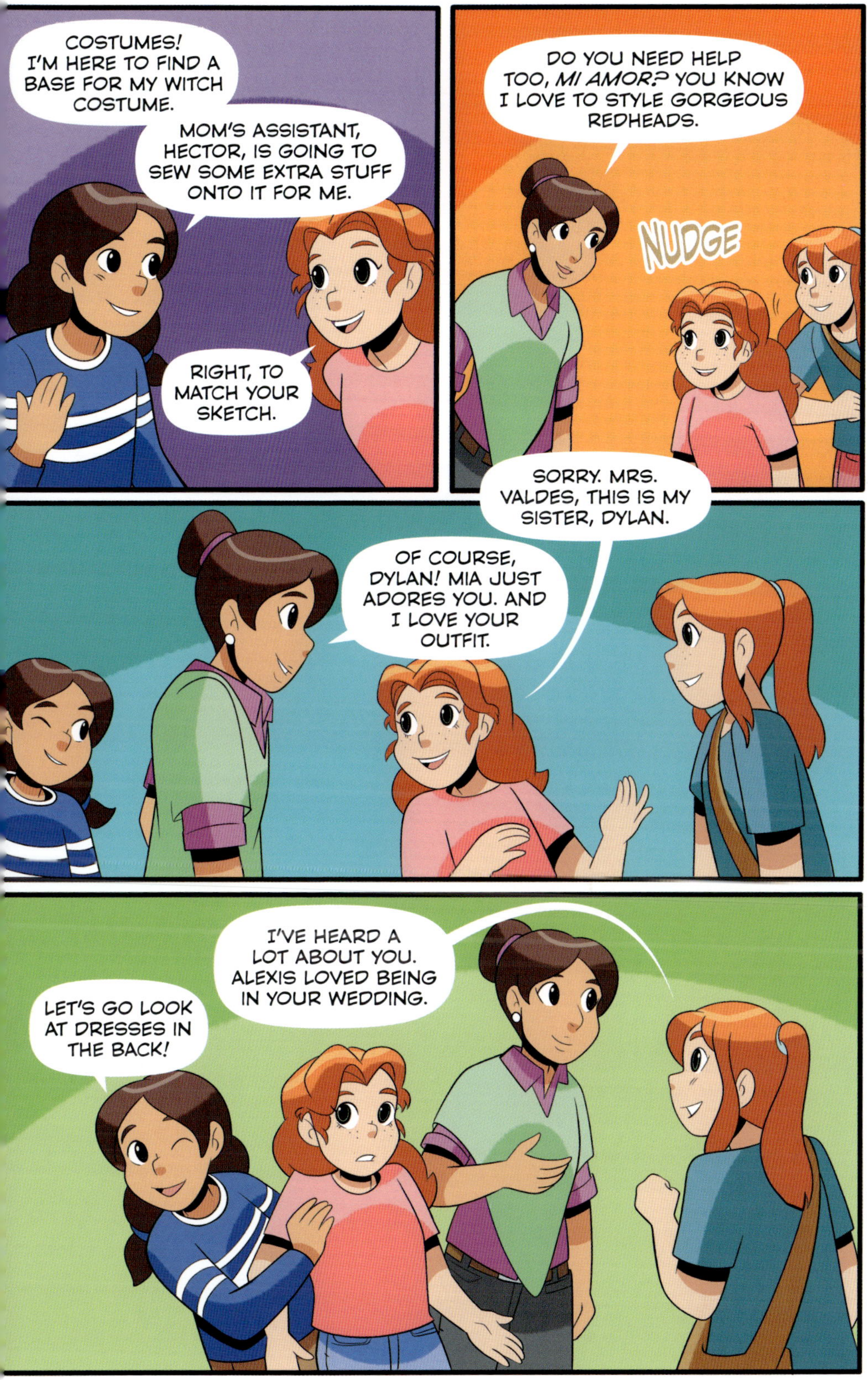
COSTUMES! I'M HERE TO FIND A BASE FOR MY WITCH COSTUME.
MOM'S ASSISTANT, HECTOR, IS GOING TO SEW SOME EXTRA STUFF ONTO IT FOR ME.
RIGHT, TO MATCH YOUR SKETCH.
DO YOU NEED HELP TOO, *MI AMOR*? YOU KNOW I LOVE TO STYLE GORGEOUS REDHEADS.
NUDGE
SORRY. MRS. VALDES, THIS IS MY SISTER, DYLAN.
OF COURSE, DYLAN! MIA JUST ADORES YOU. AND I LOVE YOUR OUTFIT.
LET'S GO LOOK AT DRESSES IN THE BACK!
I'VE HEARD A LOT ABOUT YOU. ALEXIS LOVED BEING IN YOUR WEDDING.

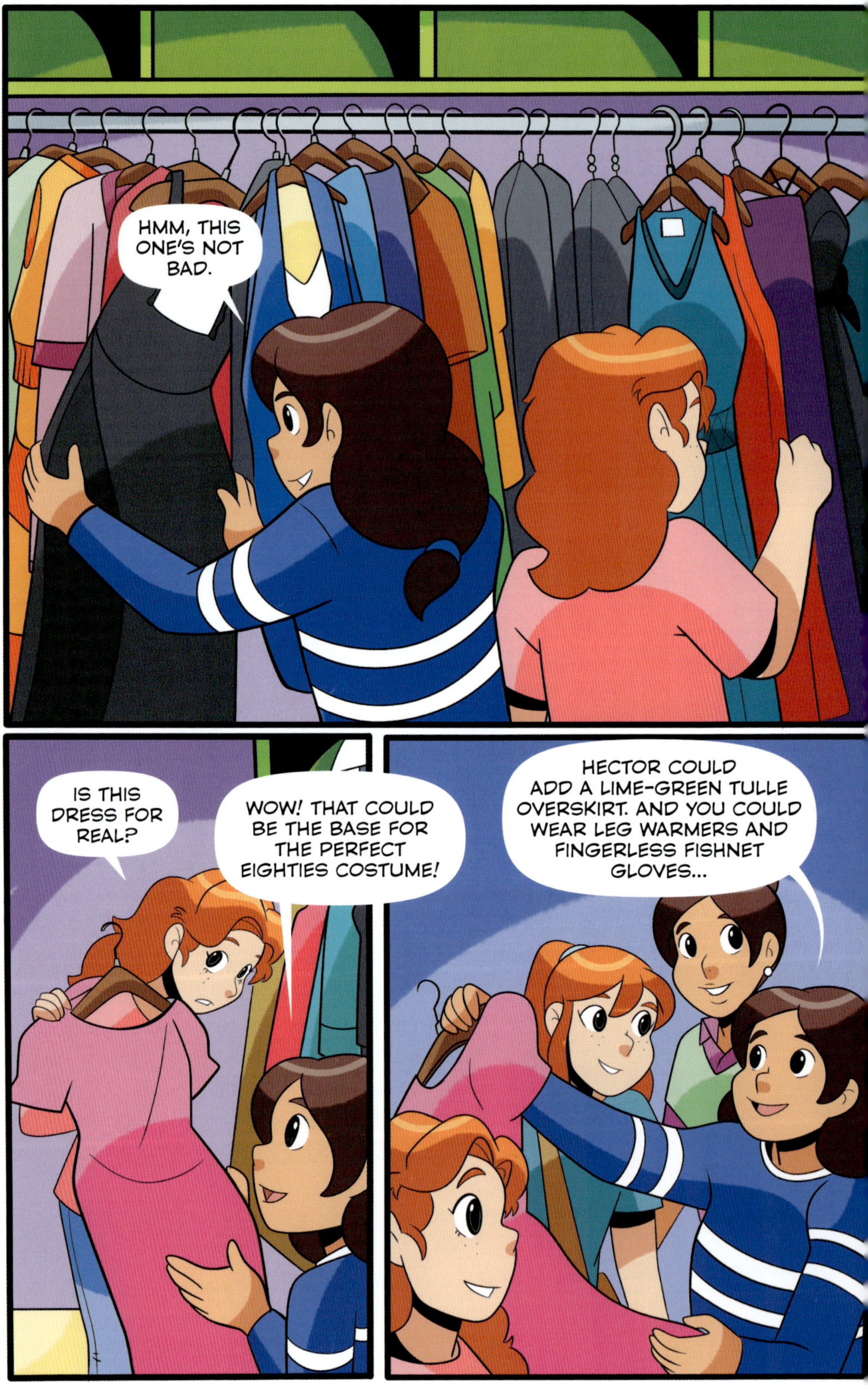
HMM, THIS ONE'S NOT BAD.
IS THIS DRESS FOR REAL?
WOW! THAT COULD BE THE BASE FOR THE PERFECT EIGHTIES COSTUME!
HECTOR COULD ADD A LIME-GREEN TULLE OVERSKIRT. AND YOU COULD WEAR LEG WARMERS AND FINGERLESS FISHNET GLOVES...

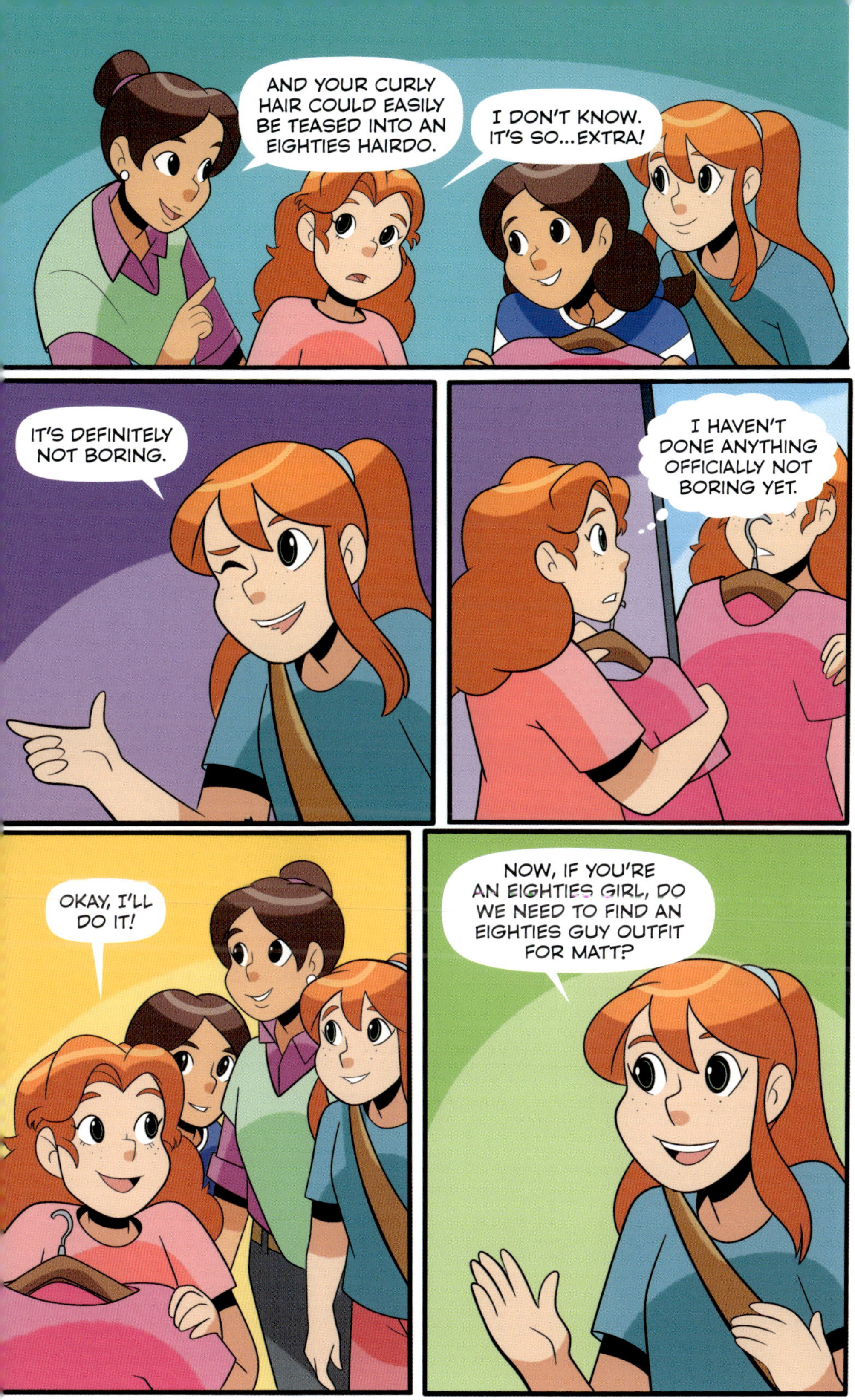

AND YOUR CURLY HAIR COULD EASILY BE TEASED INTO AN EIGHTIES HAIRDO.
I DON'T KNOW. IT'S SO...EXTRA!
IT'S DEFINITELY NOT BORING.
I HAVEN'T DONE ANYTHING OFFICIALLY NOT BORING YET.
OKAY, I'LL DO IT!
NOW, IF YOU'RE AN EIGHTIES GIRL, DO WE NEED TO FIND AN EIGHTIES GUY OUTFIT FOR MATT?

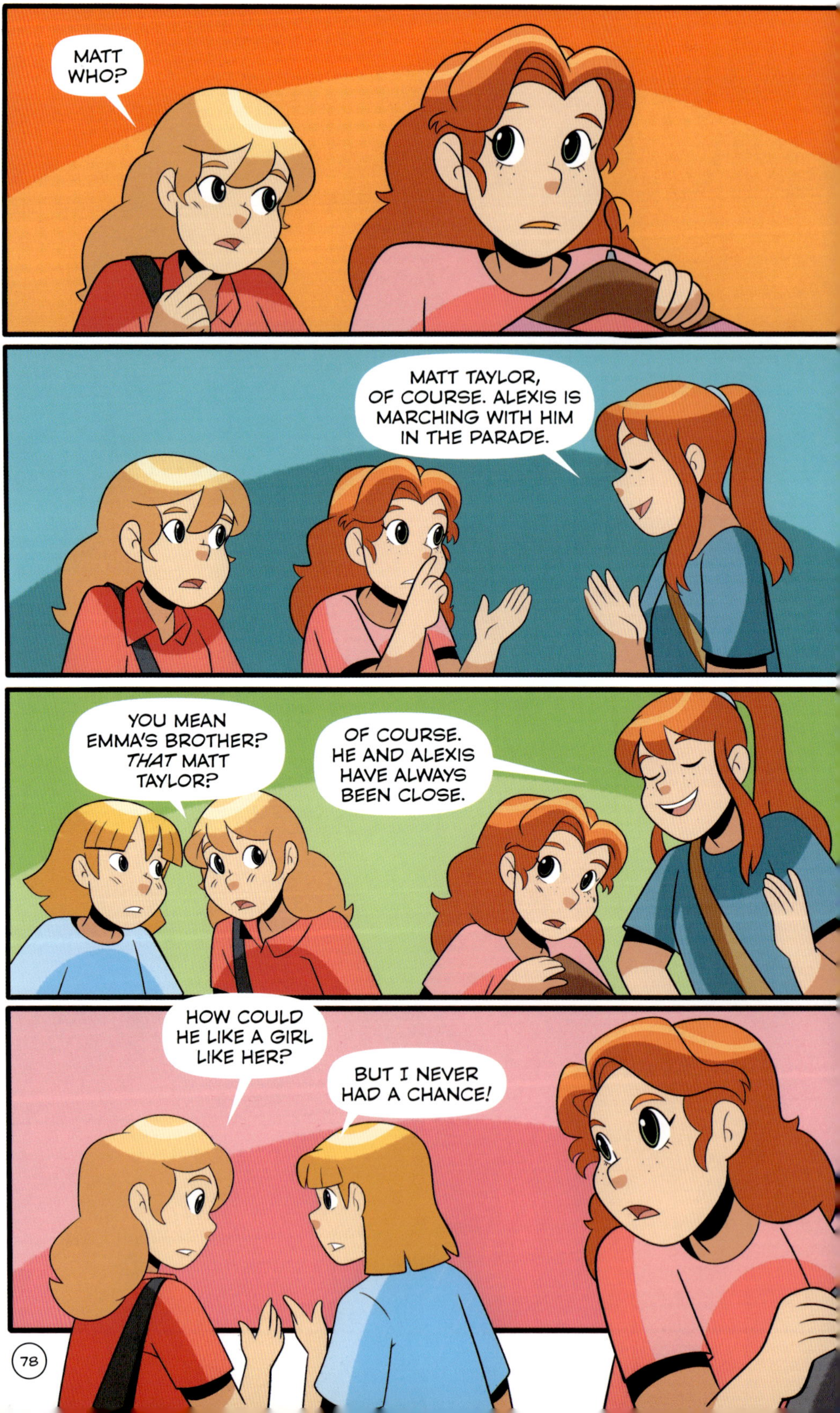
MATT WHO?
MATT TAYLOR, OF COURSE. ALEXIS IS MARCHING WITH HIM IN THE PARADE.
YOU MEAN EMMA'S BROTHER? *THAT* MATT TAYLOR?
OF COURSE. HE AND ALEXIS HAVE ALWAYS BEEN CLOSE.
HOW COULD HE LIKE A GIRL LIKE HER?
BUT I NEVER HAD A CHANCE!

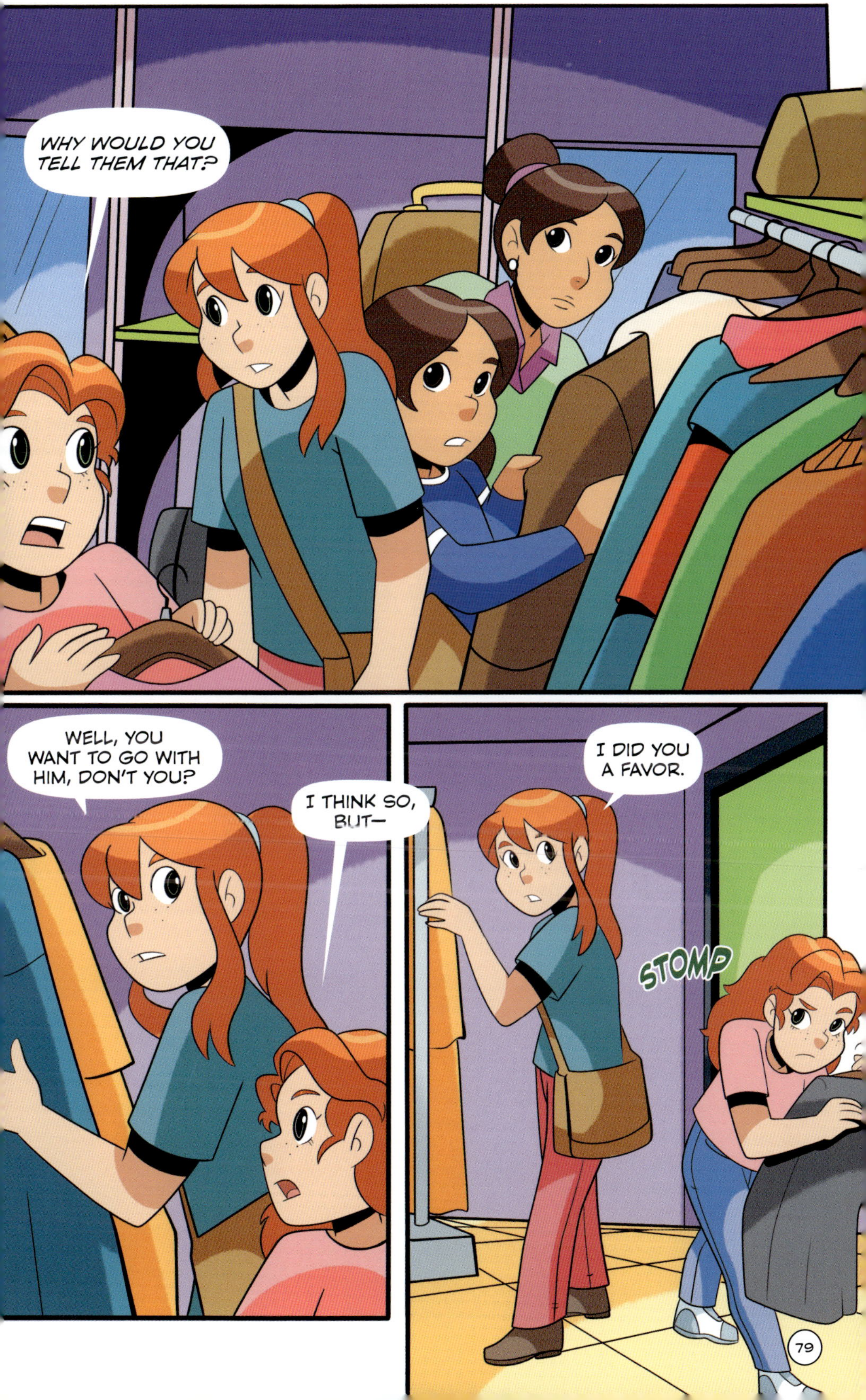
WHY WOULD YOU TELL THEM THAT?
WELL, YOU WANT TO GO WITH HIM, DON'T YOU?
I THINK SO, BUT—
I DID YOU A FAVOR.
STOMP

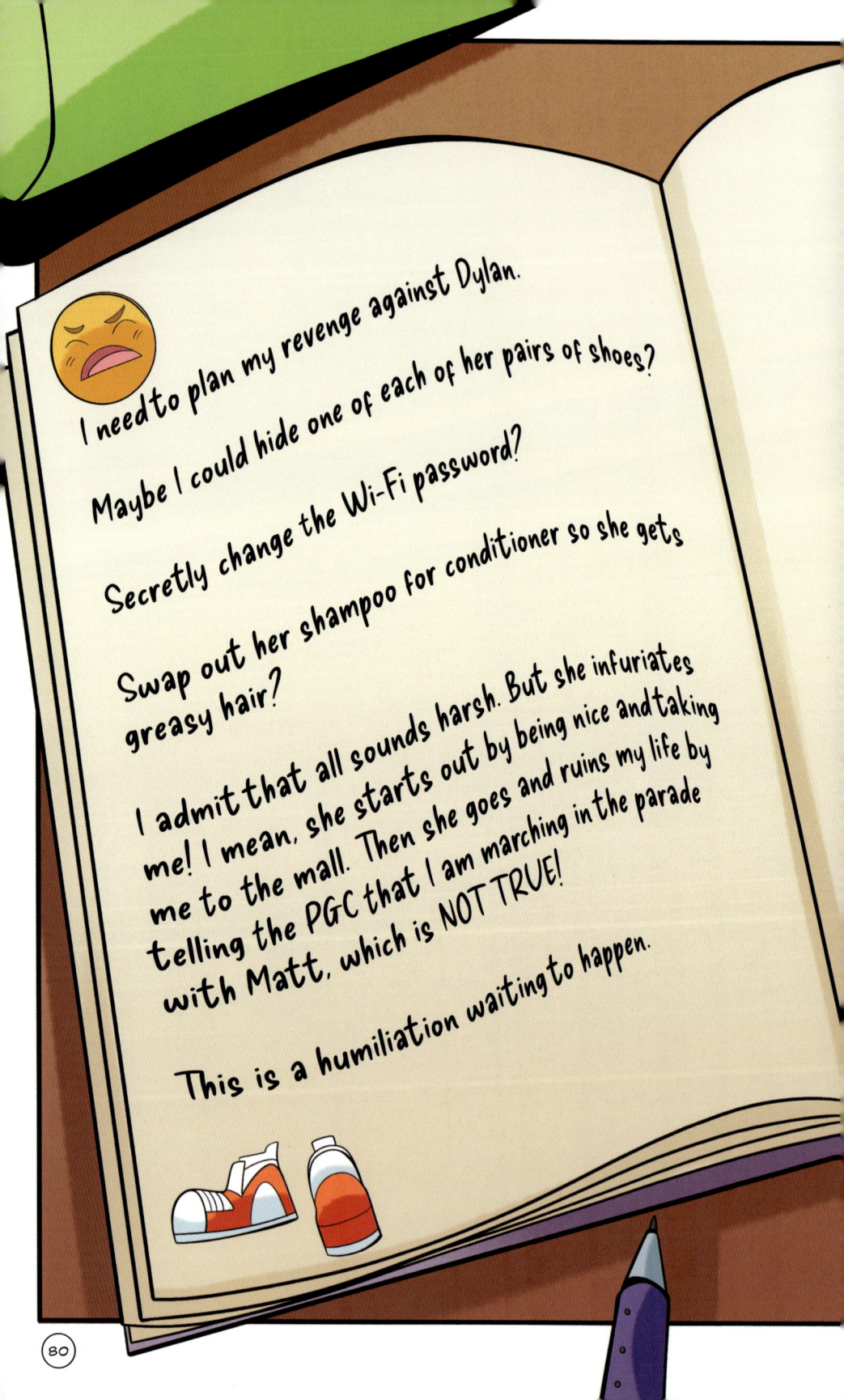

I need to plan my revenge against Dylan.

Maybe I could hide one of each of her pairs of shoes?

Secretly change the Wi-Fi password?

Swap out her shampoo for conditioner so she gets greasy hair?

I admit that all sounds harsh. But she infuriates me! I mean, she starts out by being nice and taking me to the mall. Then she goes and ruins my life by telling the PGC that I am marching in the parade with Matt, which is NOT TRUE!

This is a humiliation waiting to happen.

Chapter 8

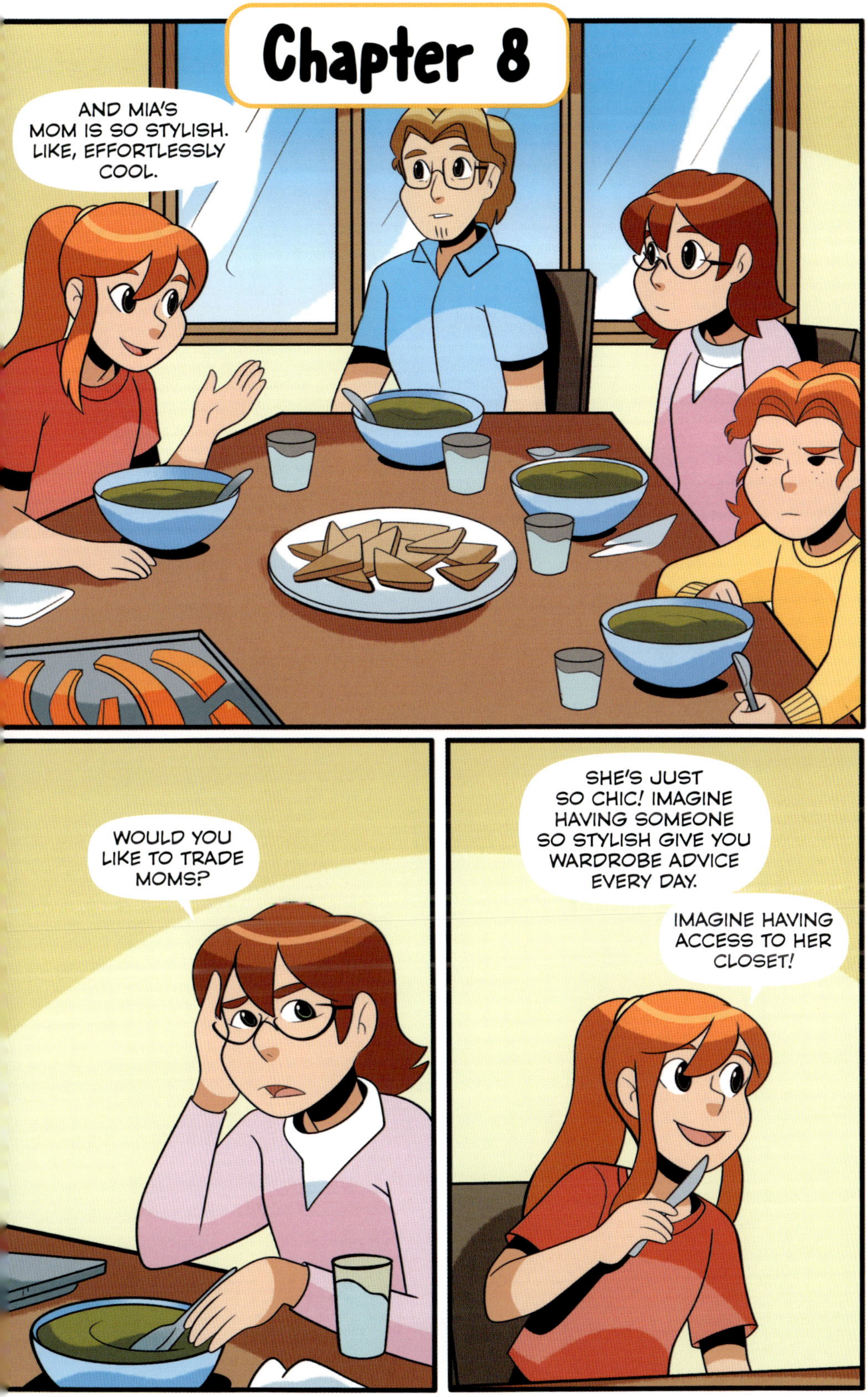
AND MIA'S MOM IS SO STYLISH. LIKE, EFFORTLESSLY COOL.
WOULD YOU LIKE TO TRADE MOMS?
SHE'S JUST SO CHIC! IMAGINE HAVING SOMEONE SO STYLISH GIVE YOU WARDROBE ADVICE EVERY DAY.
IMAGINE HAVING ACCESS TO HER CLOSET!

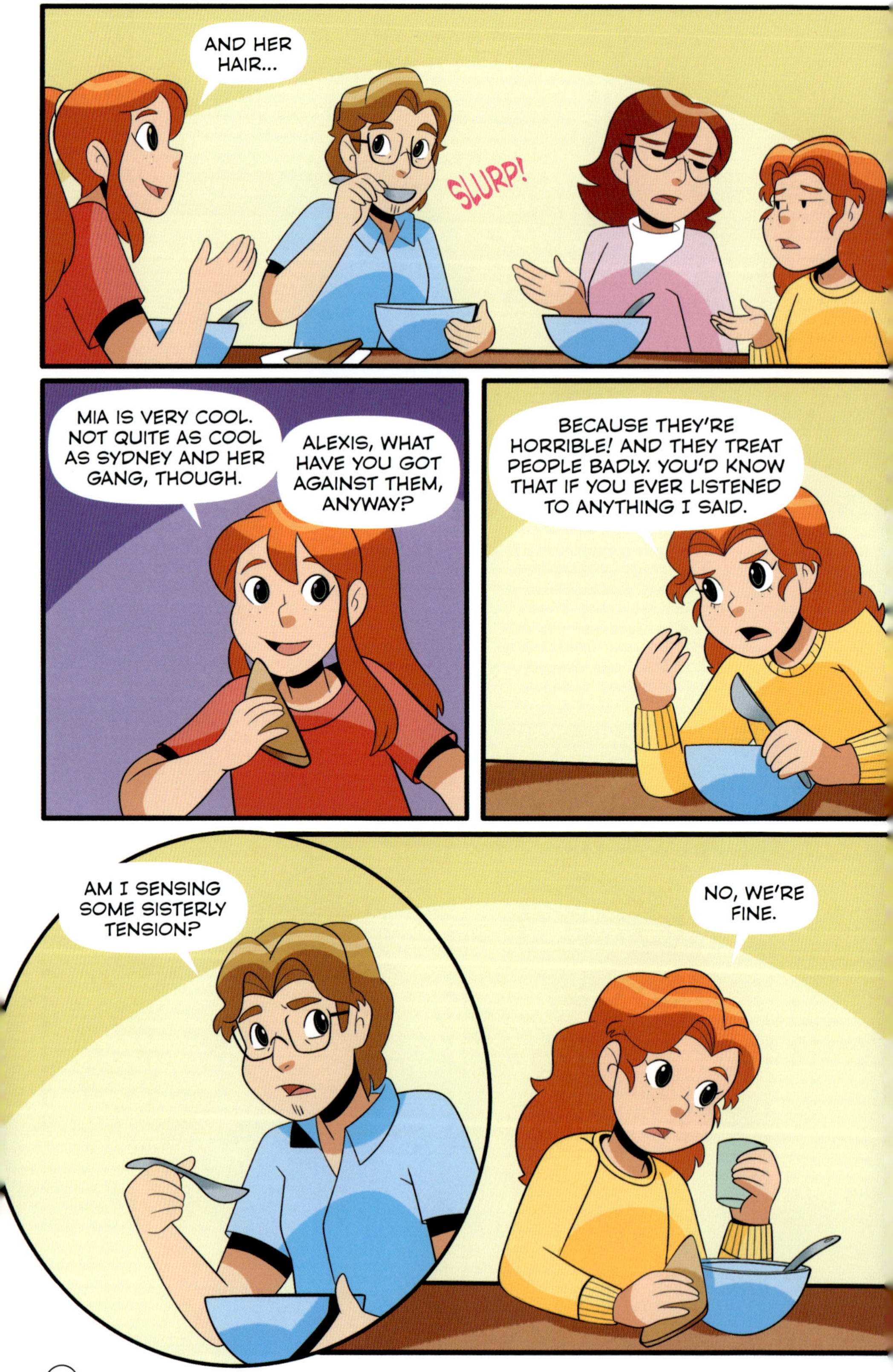
AND HER HAIR...
SLURP!
MIA IS VERY COOL. NOT QUITE AS COOL AS SYDNEY AND HER GANG, THOUGH.
ALEXIS, WHAT HAVE YOU GOT AGAINST THEM, ANYWAY?
BECAUSE THEY'RE HORRIBLE! AND THEY TREAT PEOPLE BADLY. YOU'D KNOW THAT IF YOU EVER LISTENED TO ANYTHING I SAID.
AM I SENSING SOME SISTERLY TENSION?
NO, WE'RE FINE.

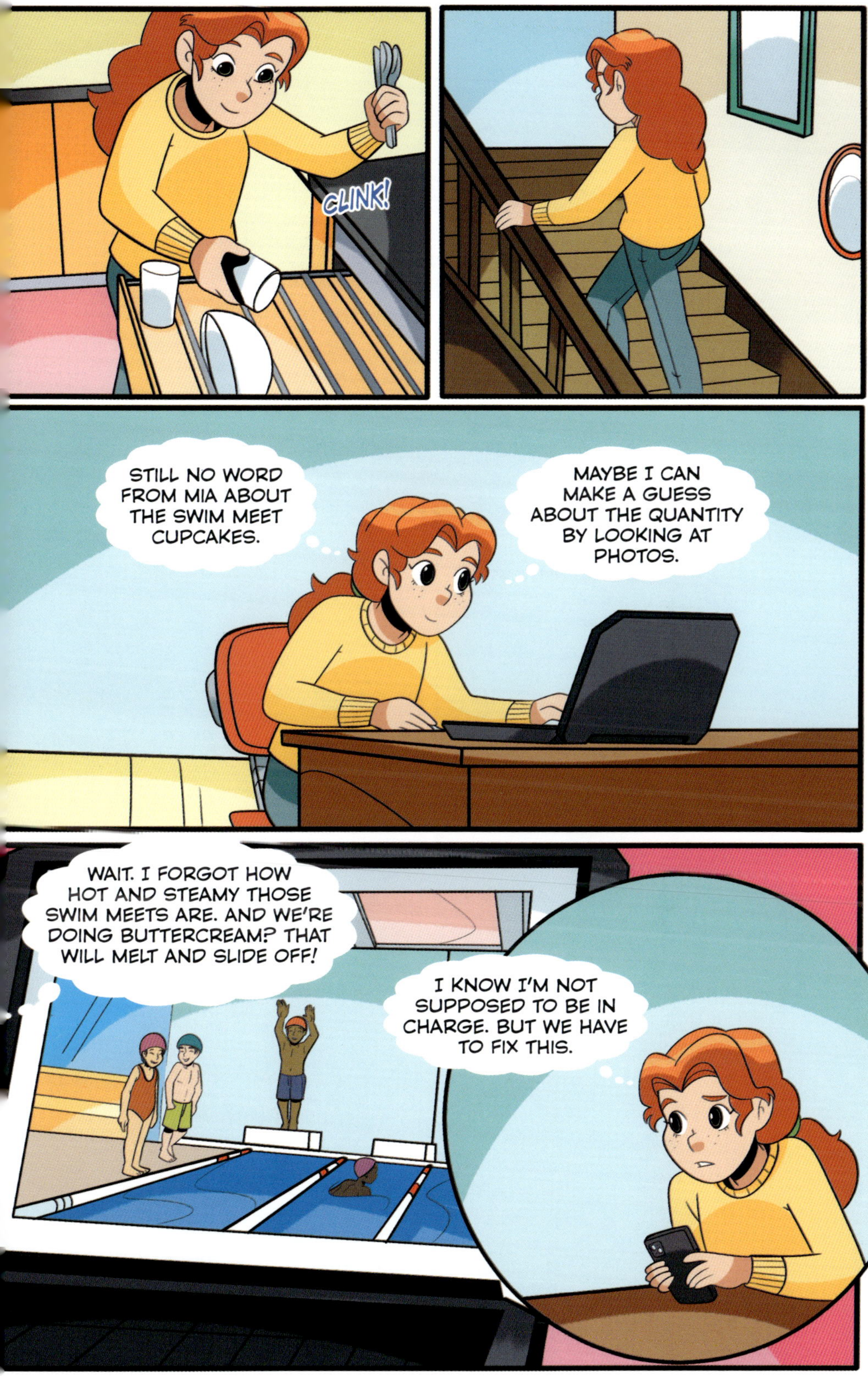
CLINK!
STILL NO WORD FROM MIA ABOUT THE SWIM MEET CUPCAKES.
MAYBE I CAN MAKE A GUESS ABOUT THE QUANTITY BY LOOKING AT PHOTOS.
WAIT. I FORGOT HOW HOT AND STEAMY THOSE SWIM MEETS ARE. AND WE'RE DOING BUTTERCREAM? THAT WILL MELT AND SLIDE OFF!
I KNOW I'M NOT SUPPOSED TO BE IN CHARGE. BUT WE HAVE TO FIX THIS.

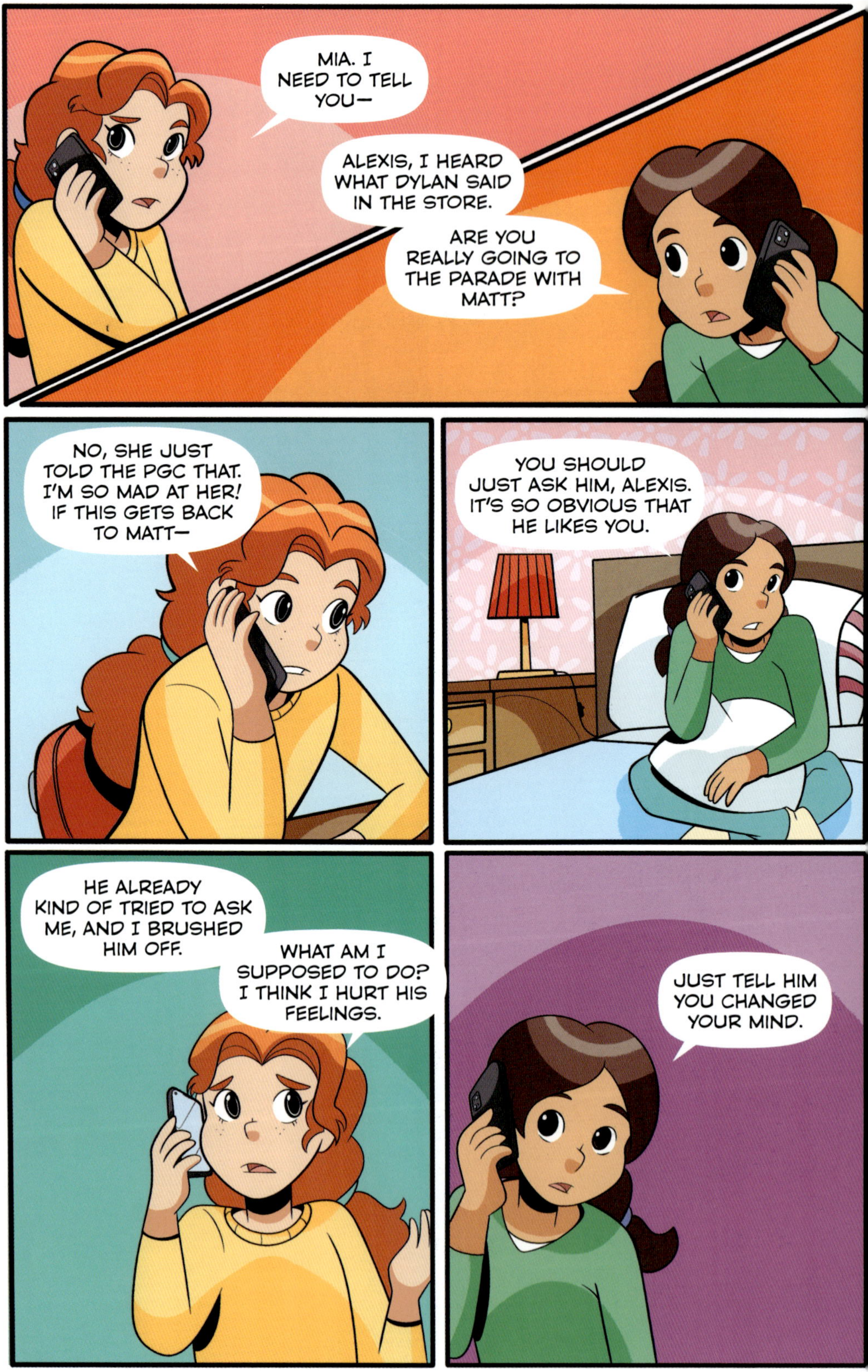

MIA. I NEED TO TELL YOU—
ALEXIS, I HEARD WHAT DYLAN SAID IN THE STORE.
ARE YOU REALLY GOING TO THE PARADE WITH MATT?
NO, SHE JUST TOLD THE PGC THAT. I'M SO MAD AT HER! IF THIS GETS BACK TO MATT—
YOU SHOULD JUST ASK HIM, ALEXIS. IT'S SO OBVIOUS THAT HE LIKES YOU.
HE ALREADY KIND OF TRIED TO ASK ME, AND I BRUSHED HIM OFF.
WHAT AM I SUPPOSED TO DO? I THINK I HURT HIS FEELINGS.
JUST TELL HIM YOU CHANGED YOUR MIND.

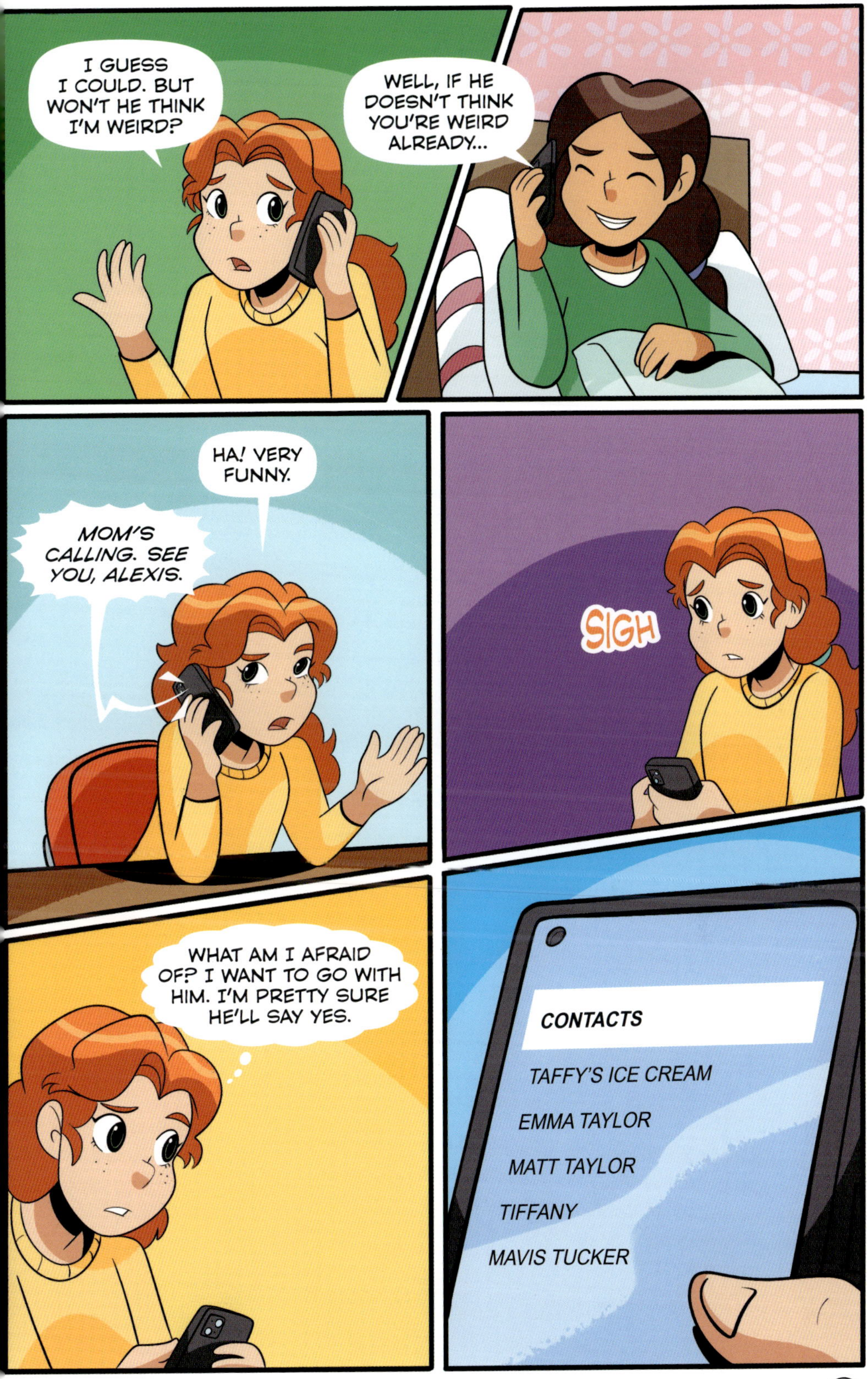
I GUESS I COULD. BUT WON'T HE THINK I'M WEIRD?
WELL, IF HE DOESN'T THINK YOU'RE WEIRD ALREADY...
HA! VERY FUNNY.
MOM'S CALLING. SEE YOU, ALEXIS.
SIGH
WHAT AM I AFRAID OF? I WANT TO GO WITH HIM. I'M PRETTY SURE HE'LL SAY YES.
CONTACTS
TAFFY'S ICE CREAM
EMMA TAYLOR
MATT TAYLOR
TIFFANY
MAVIS TUCKER

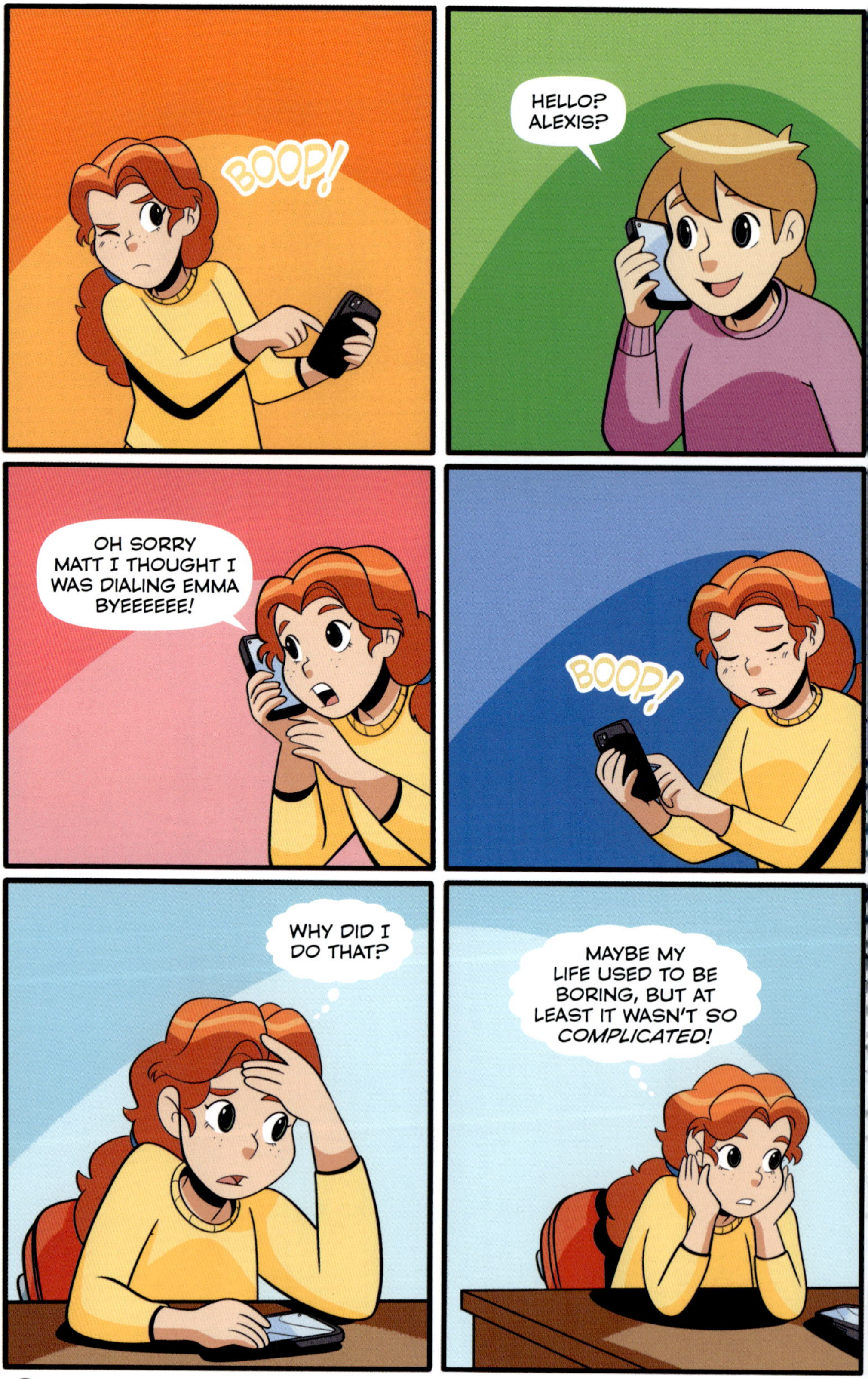
BOOP!
HELLO? ALEXIS?
OH SORRY MATT I THOUGHT I WAS DIALING EMMA BYEEEEEE!
BOOP!
WHY DID I DO THAT?
MAYBE MY LIFE USED TO BE BORING, BUT AT LEAST IT WASN'T SO *COMPLICATED*!

Chapter 9

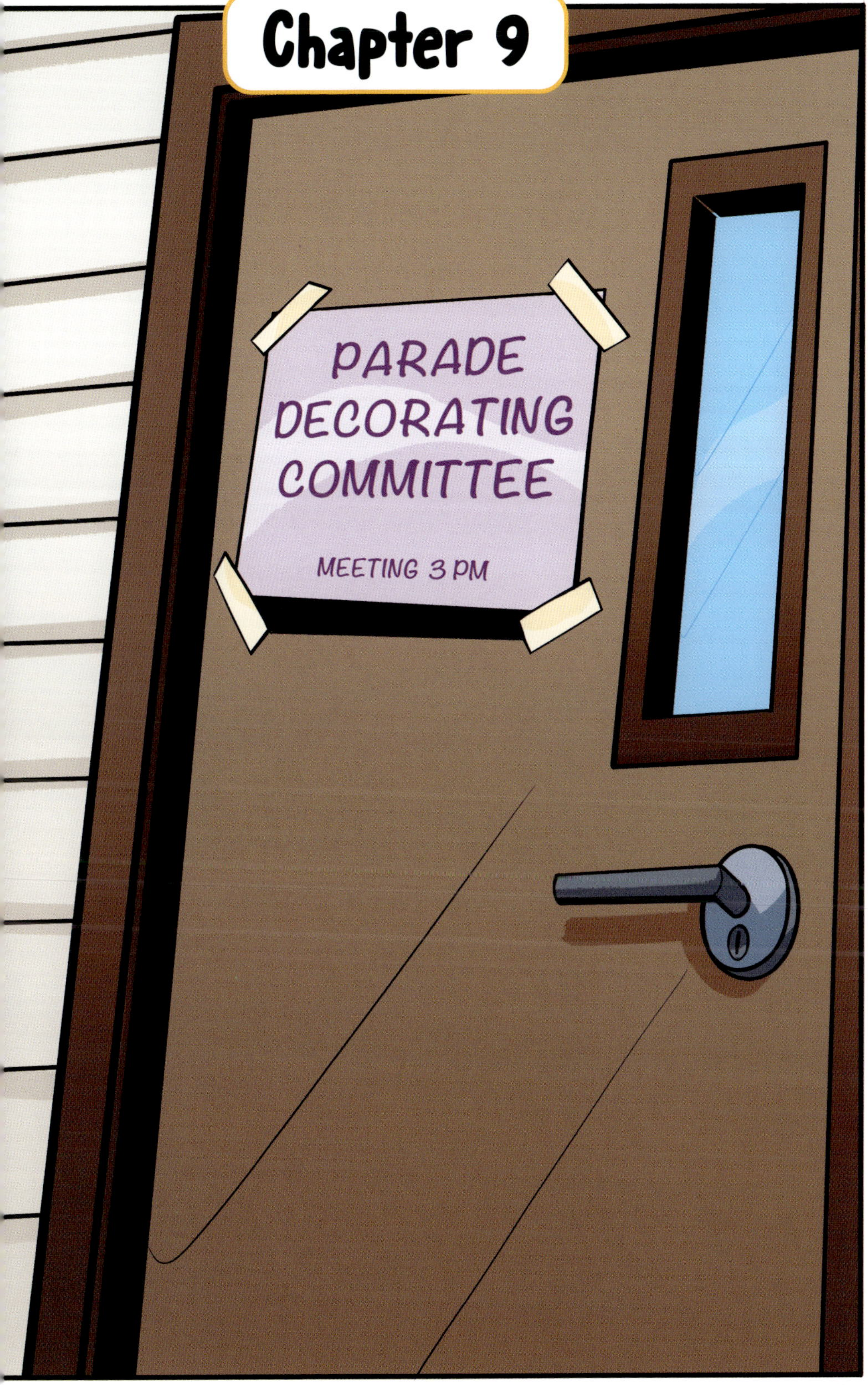
PARADE DECORATING COMMITTEE
MEETING 3 PM

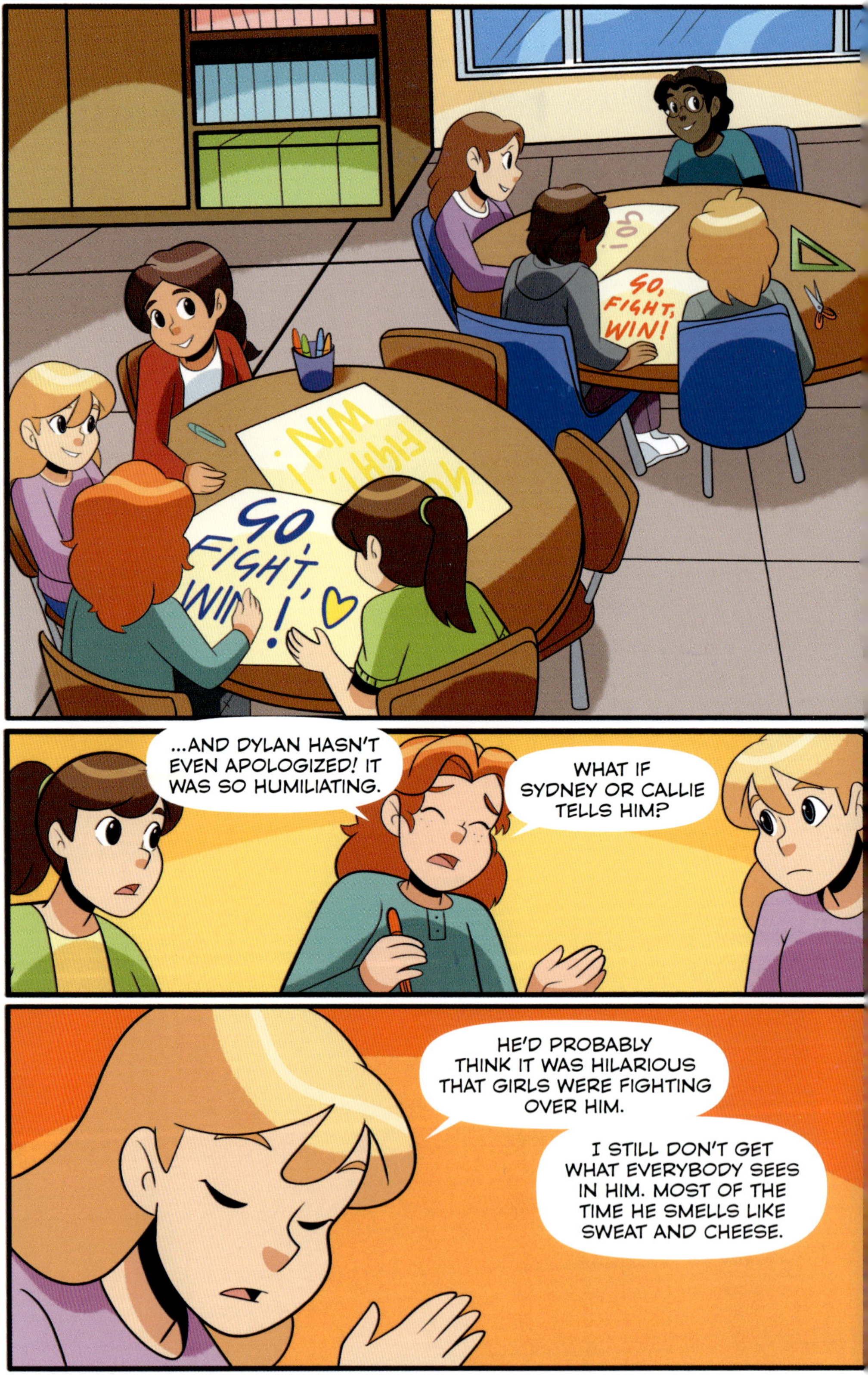
SO, FIGHT, WIN!
SO, FIGHT, WIN!
SO, FIGHT, WIN!
SO!
...AND DYLAN HASN'T EVEN APOLOGIZED! IT WAS SO HUMILIATING.
WHAT IF SYDNEY OR CALLIE TELLS HIM?
HE'D PROBABLY THINK IT WAS HILARIOUS THAT GIRLS WERE FIGHTING OVER HIM.
I STILL DON'T GET WHAT EVERYBODY SEES IN HIM. MOST OF THE TIME HE SMELLS LIKE SWEAT AND CHEESE.

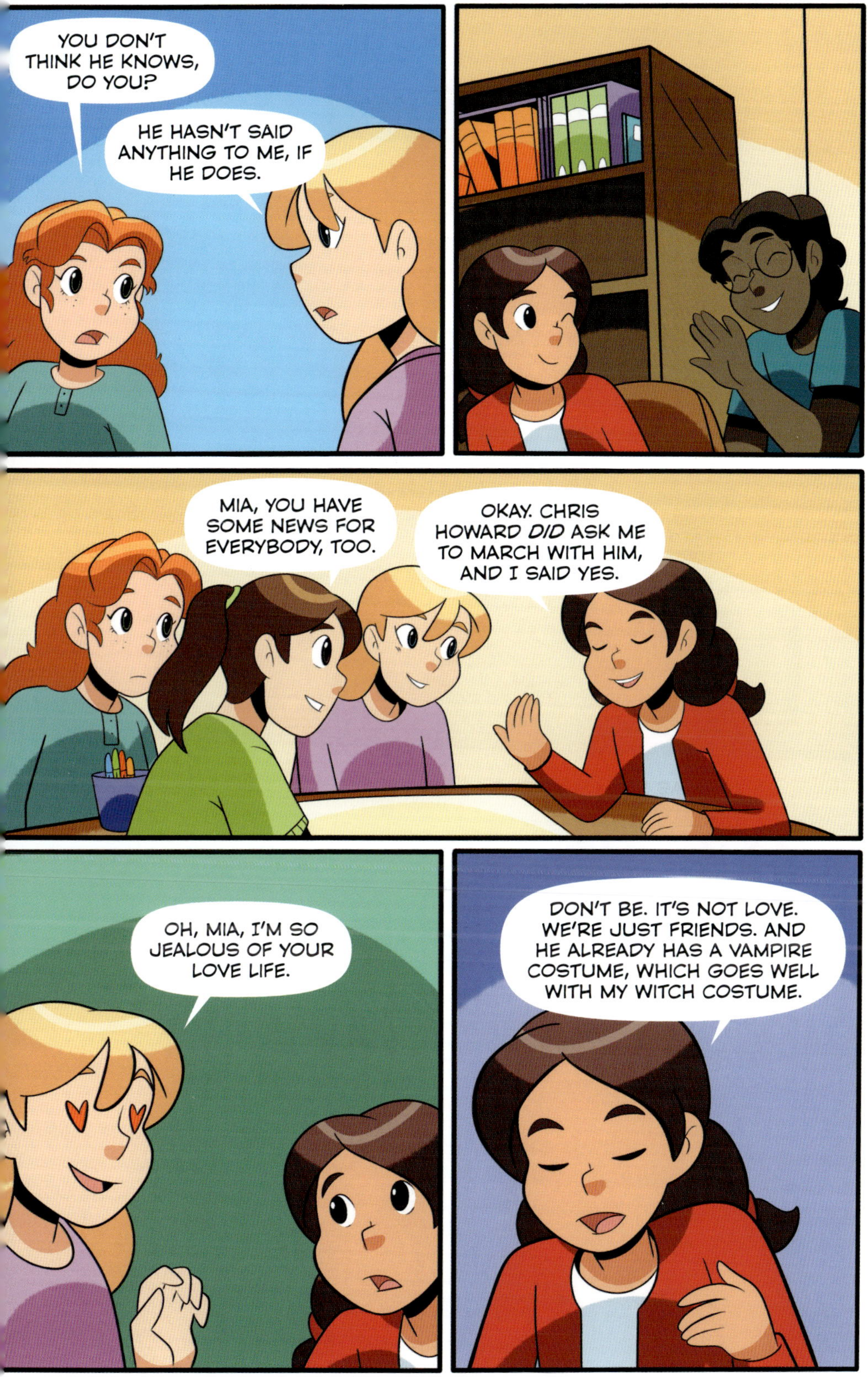
YOU DON'T THINK HE KNOWS, DO YOU?
HE HASN'T SAID ANYTHING TO ME, IF HE DOES.
MIA, YOU HAVE SOME NEWS FOR EVERYBODY, TOO.
OKAY. CHRIS HOWARD *DID* ASK ME TO MARCH WITH HIM, AND I SAID YES.
OH, MIA, I'M SO JEALOUS OF YOUR LOVE LIFE.
DON'T BE. IT'S NOT LOVE. WE'RE JUST FRIENDS. AND HE ALREADY HAS A VAMPIRE COSTUME, WHICH GOES WELL WITH MY WITCH COSTUME.

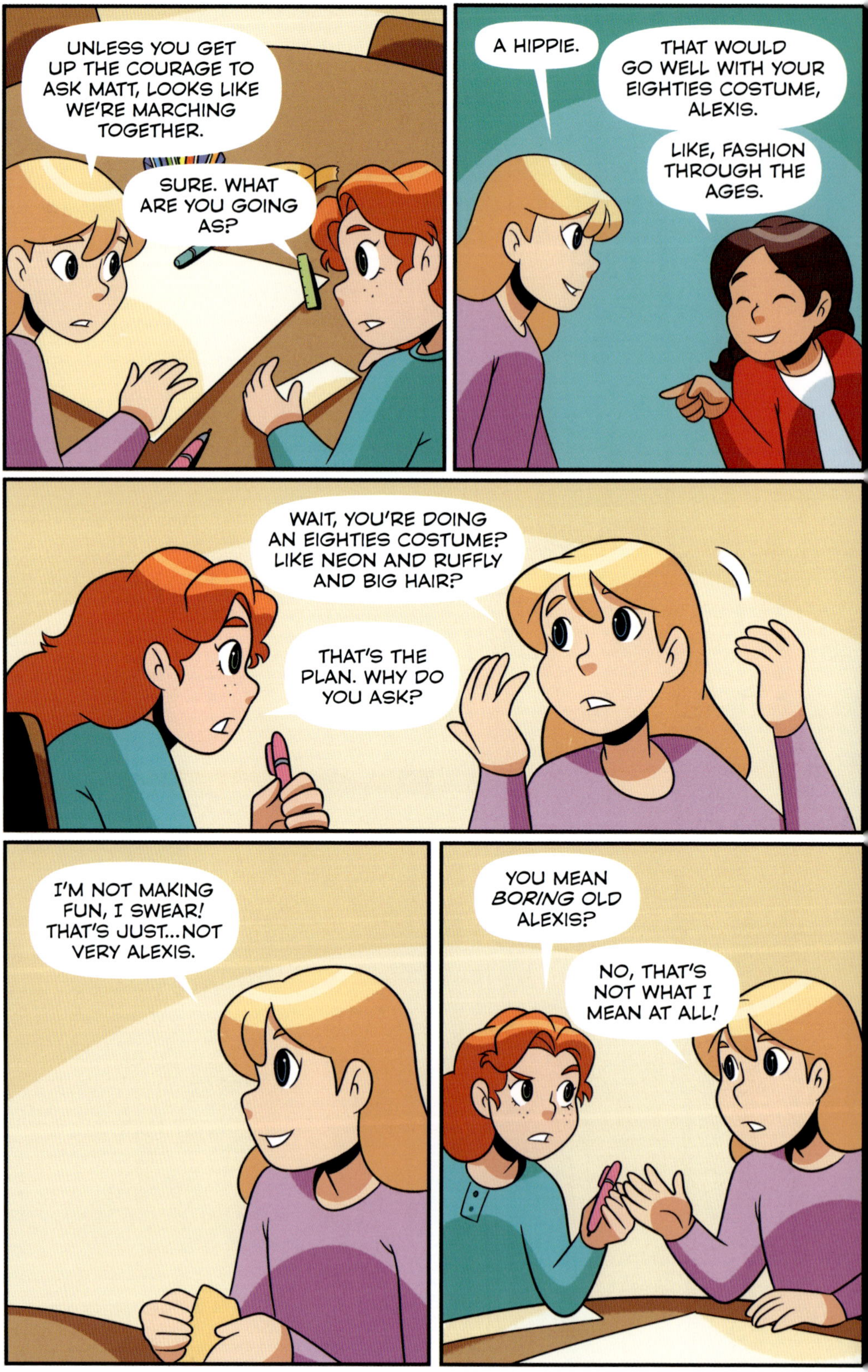
UNLESS YOU GET UP THE COURAGE TO ASK MATT, LOOKS LIKE WE'RE MARCHING TOGETHER.
SURE. WHAT ARE YOU GOING AS?
A HIPPIE.
THAT WOULD GO WELL WITH YOUR EIGHTIES COSTUME, ALEXIS.
LIKE, FASHION THROUGH THE AGES.
WAIT, YOU'RE DOING AN EIGHTIES COSTUME? LIKE NEON AND RUFFLY AND BIG HAIR?
THAT'S THE PLAN. WHY DO YOU ASK?
I'M NOT MAKING FUN, I SWEAR! THAT'S JUST...NOT VERY ALEXIS.
YOU MEAN *BORING* OLD ALEXIS?
NO, THAT'S NOT WHAT I MEAN AT ALL!

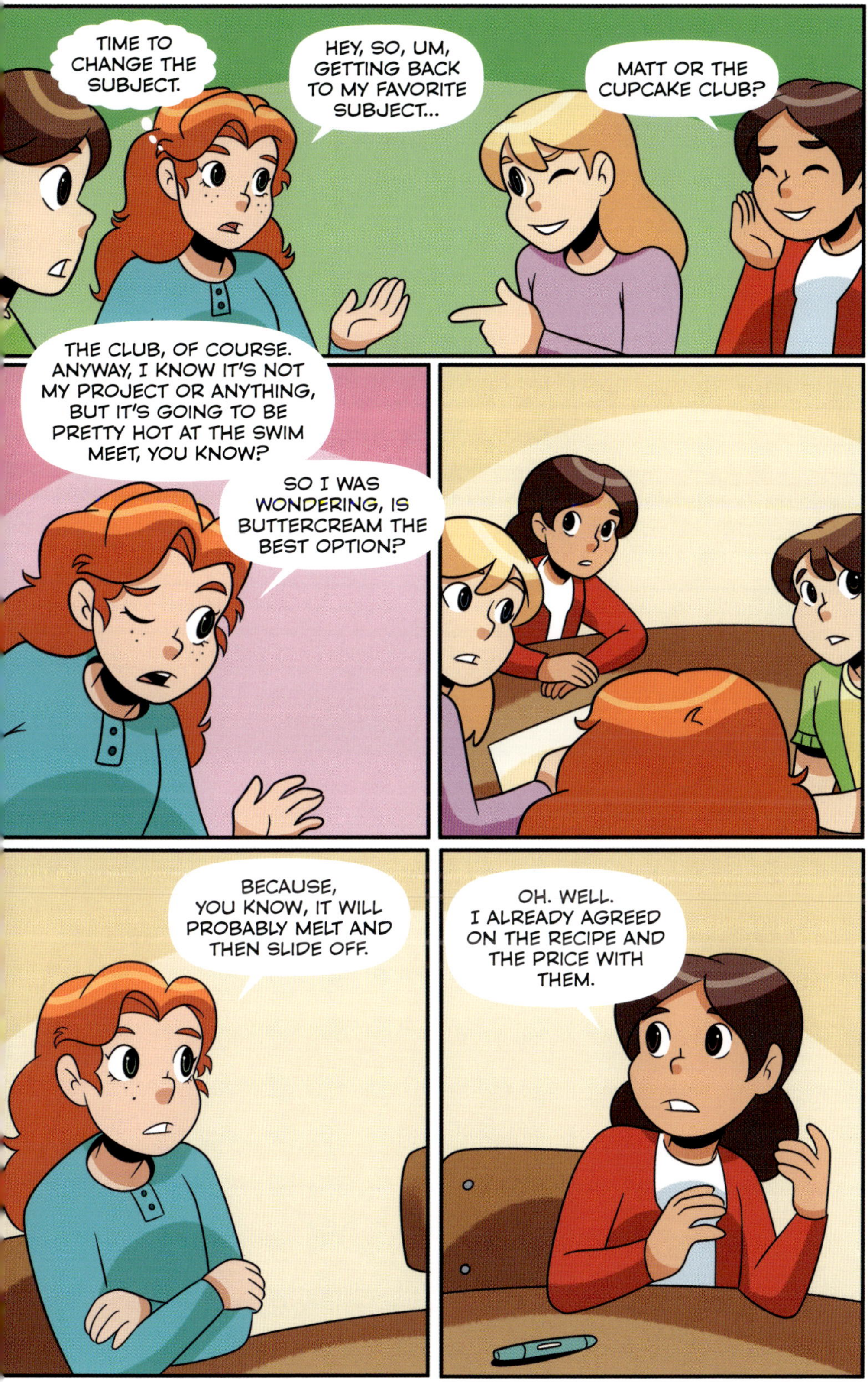
TIME TO CHANGE THE SUBJECT.
HEY, SO, UM, GETTING BACK TO MY FAVORITE SUBJECT...
MATT OR THE CUPCAKE CLUB?
THE CLUB, OF COURSE. ANYWAY, I KNOW IT'S NOT MY PROJECT OR ANYTHING, BUT IT'S GOING TO BE PRETTY HOT AT THE SWIM MEET, YOU KNOW?
SO I WAS WONDERING, IS BUTTERCREAM THE BEST OPTION?
BECAUSE, YOU KNOW, IT WILL PROBABLY MELT AND THEN SLIDE OFF.
OH. WELL. I ALREADY AGREED ON THE RECIPE AND THE PRICE WITH THEM.

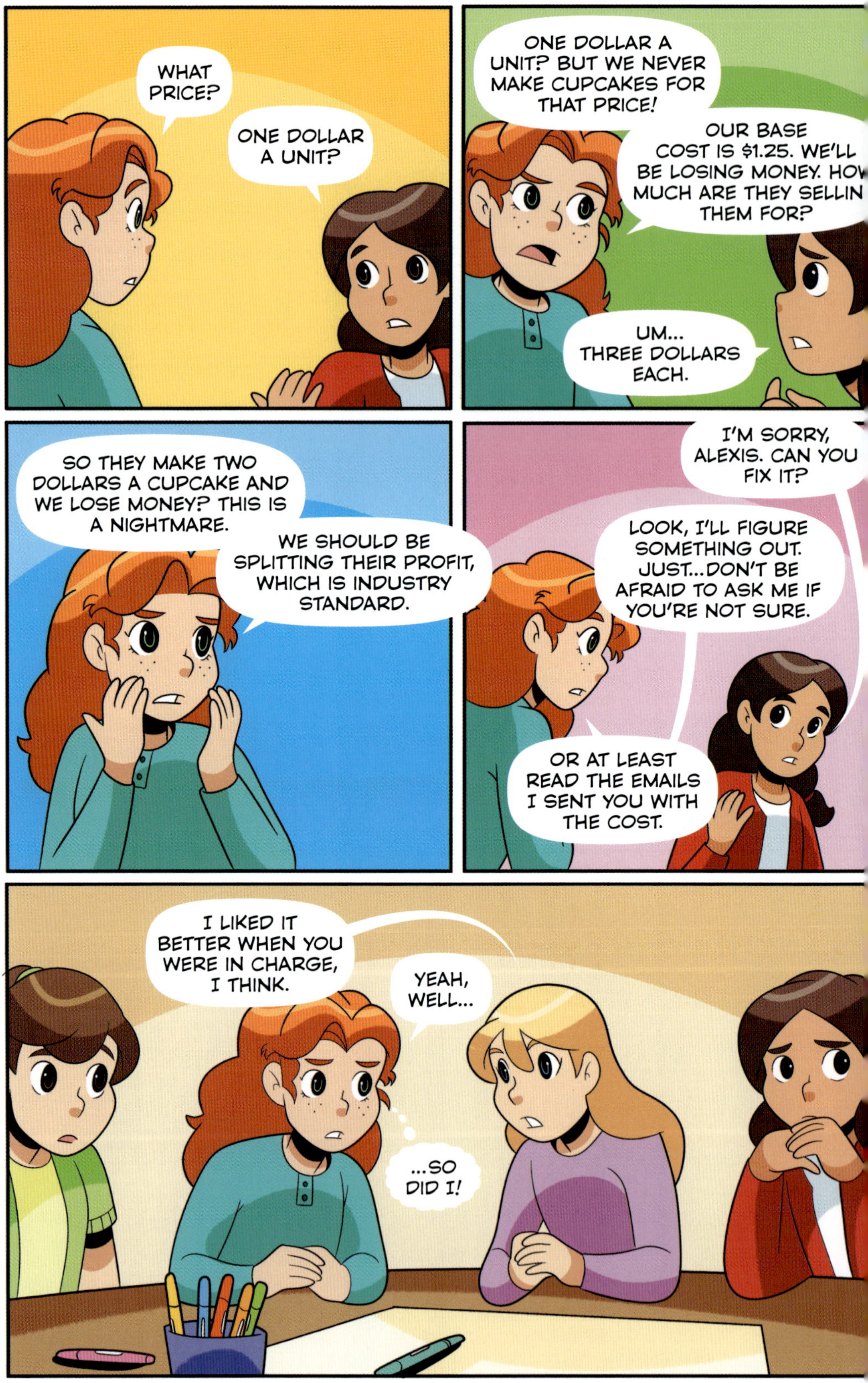
WHAT PRICE?
ONE DOLLAR A UNIT?
ONE DOLLAR A UNIT? BUT WE NEVER MAKE CUPCAKES FOR THAT PRICE!
OUR BASE COST IS $1.25. WE'LL BE LOSING MONEY. HOW MUCH ARE THEY SELLIN THEM FOR?
UM... THREE DOLLARS EACH.
SO THEY MAKE TWO DOLLARS A CUPCAKE AND WE LOSE MONEY? THIS IS A NIGHTMARE.
WE SHOULD BE SPLITTING THEIR PROFIT, WHICH IS INDUSTRY STANDARD.
I'M SORRY, ALEXIS. CAN YOU FIX IT?
LOOK, I'LL FIGURE SOMETHING OUT. JUST...DON'T BE AFRAID TO ASK ME IF YOU'RE NOT SURE.
OR AT LEAST READ THE EMAILS I SENT YOU WITH THE COST.
I LIKED IT BETTER WHEN YOU WERE IN CHARGE, I THINK.
YEAH, WELL...
...SO DID I!

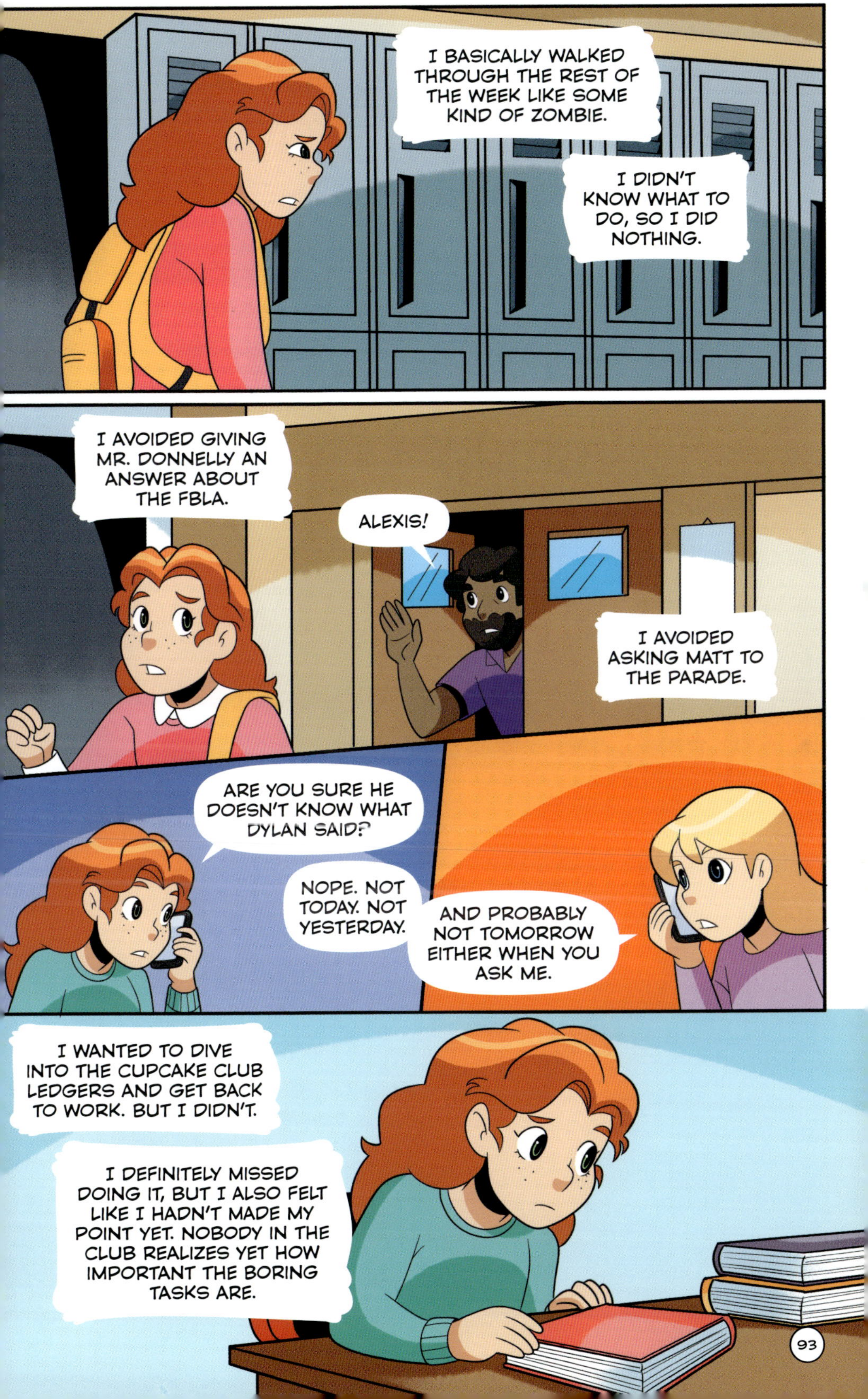
I BASICALLY WALKED THROUGH THE REST OF THE WEEK LIKE SOME KIND OF ZOMBIE.
I DIDN'T KNOW WHAT TO DO, SO I DID NOTHING.
I AVOIDED GIVING MR. DONNELLY AN ANSWER ABOUT THE FBLA.
ALEXIS!
I AVOIDED ASKING MATT TO THE PARADE.
ARE YOU SURE HE DOESN'T KNOW WHAT DYLAN SAID?
NOPE. NOT TODAY. NOT YESTERDAY.
AND PROBABLY NOT TOMORROW EITHER WHEN YOU ASK ME.
I WANTED TO DIVE INTO THE CUPCAKE CLUB LEDGERS AND GET BACK TO WORK. BUT I DIDN'T.
I DEFINITELY MISSED DOING IT, BUT I ALSO FELT LIKE I HADN'T MADE MY POINT YET. NOBODY IN THE CLUB REALIZES YET HOW IMPORTANT THE BORING TASKS ARE.

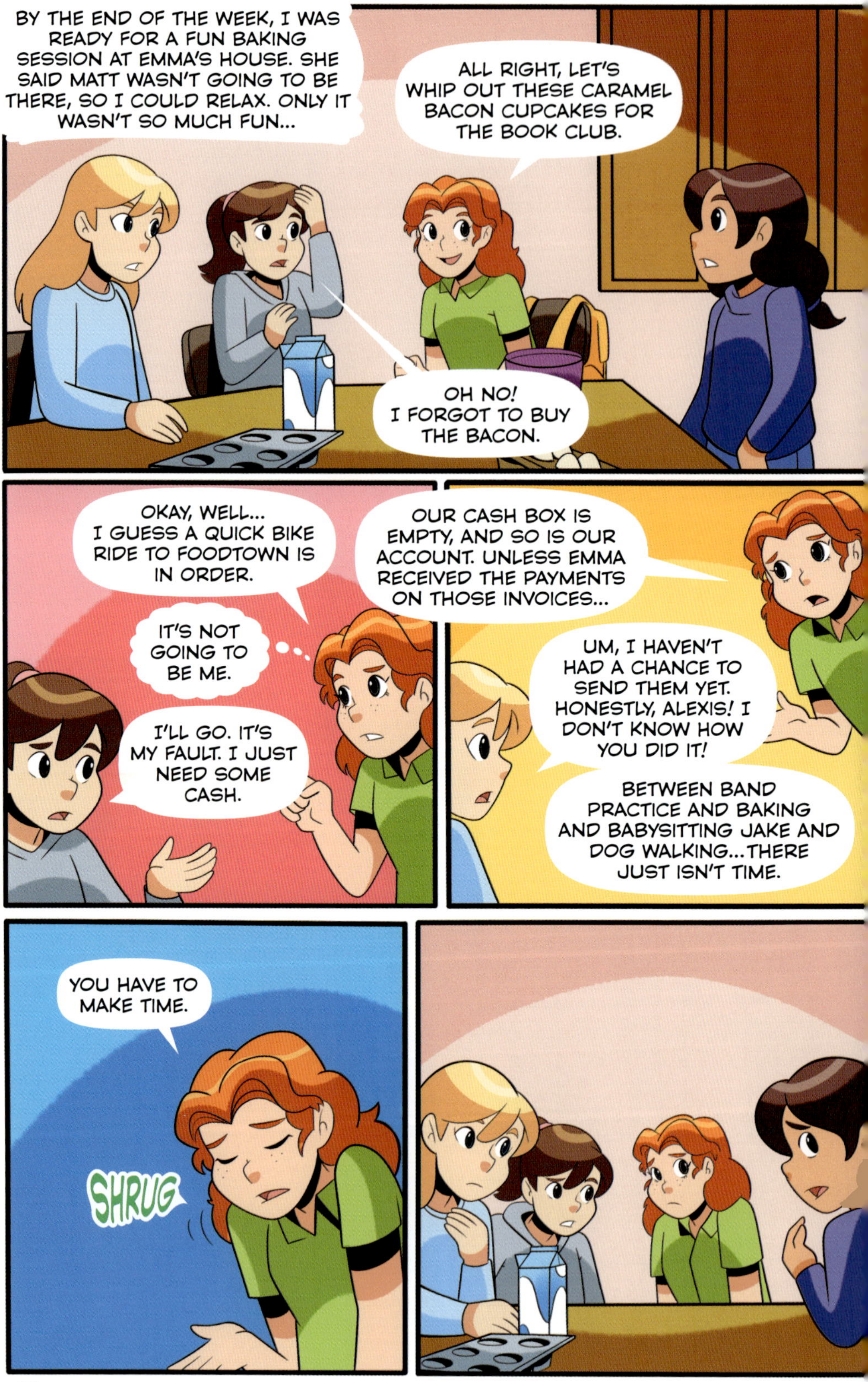
BY THE END OF THE WEEK, I WAS READY FOR A FUN BAKING SESSION AT EMMA'S HOUSE. SHE SAID MATT WASN'T GOING TO BE THERE, SO I COULD RELAX. ONLY IT WASN'T SO MUCH FUN...
ALL RIGHT, LET'S WHIP OUT THESE CARAMEL BACON CUPCAKES FOR THE BOOK CLUB.
OH NO! I FORGOT TO BUY THE BACON.
OKAY, WELL... I GUESS A QUICK BIKE RIDE TO FOODTOWN IS IN ORDER.
IT'S NOT GOING TO BE ME.
I'LL GO. IT'S MY FAULT. I JUST NEED SOME CASH.
OUR CASH BOX IS EMPTY, AND SO IS OUR ACCOUNT. UNLESS EMMA RECEIVED THE PAYMENTS ON THOSE INVOICES...
UM, I HAVEN'T HAD A CHANCE TO SEND THEM YET. HONESTLY, ALEXIS! I DON'T KNOW HOW YOU DID IT!
BETWEEN BAND PRACTICE AND BAKING AND BABYSITTING JAKE AND DOG WALKING...THERE JUST ISN'T TIME.
YOU HAVE TO MAKE TIME.
SHRUG

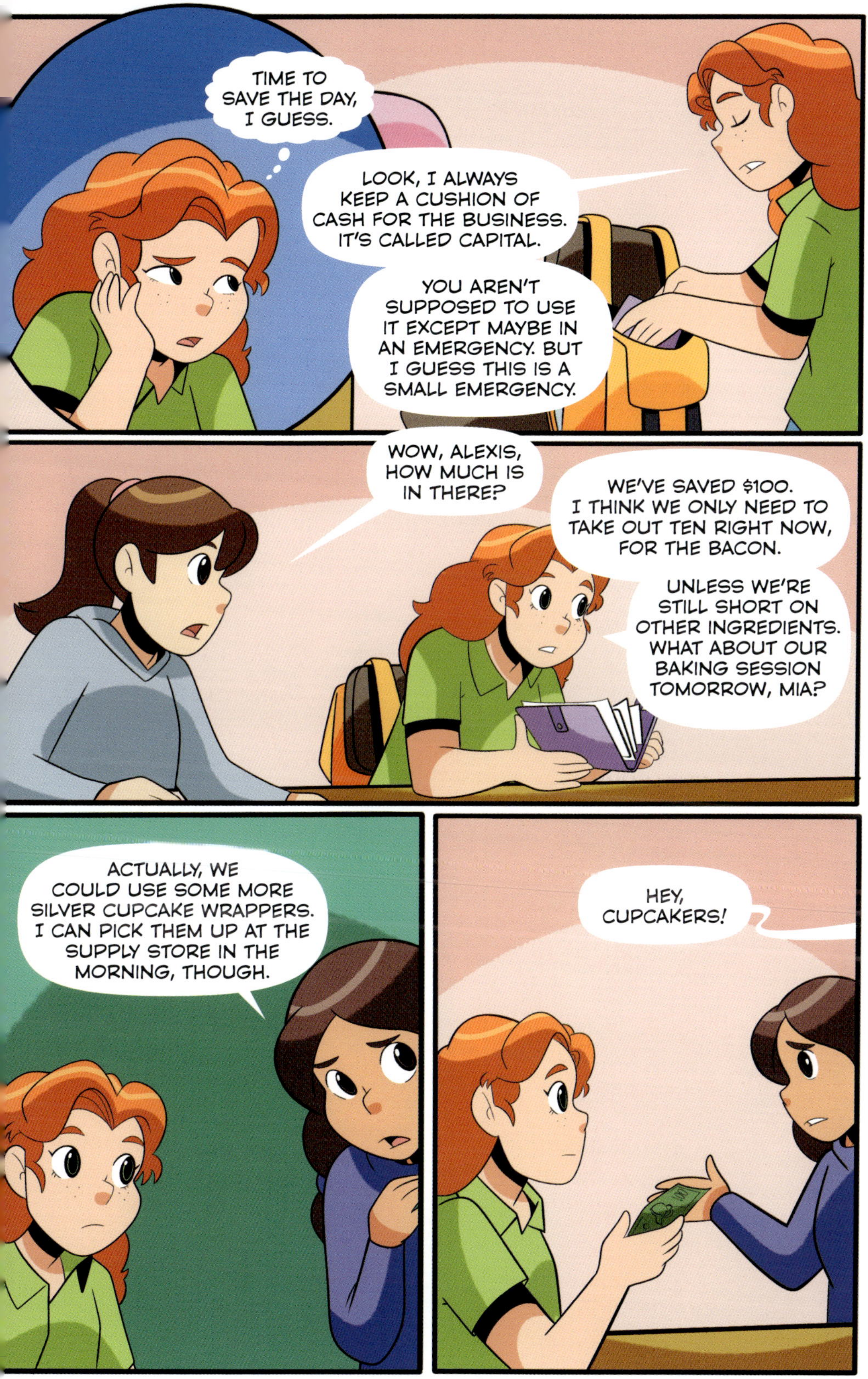
TIME TO SAVE THE DAY, I GUESS.
LOOK, I ALWAYS KEEP A CUSHION OF CASH FOR THE BUSINESS. IT'S CALLED CAPITAL.
YOU AREN'T SUPPOSED TO USE IT EXCEPT MAYBE IN AN EMERGENCY. BUT I GUESS THIS IS A SMALL EMERGENCY.
WOW, ALEXIS, HOW MUCH IS IN THERE?
WE'VE SAVED $100. I THINK WE ONLY NEED TO TAKE OUT TEN RIGHT NOW, FOR THE BACON.
UNLESS WE'RE STILL SHORT ON OTHER INGREDIENTS. WHAT ABOUT OUR BAKING SESSION TOMORROW, MIA?
ACTUALLY, WE COULD USE SOME MORE SILVER CUPCAKE WRAPPERS. I CAN PICK THEM UP AT THE SUPPLY STORE IN THE MORNING, THOUGH.
HEY, CUPCAKERS!

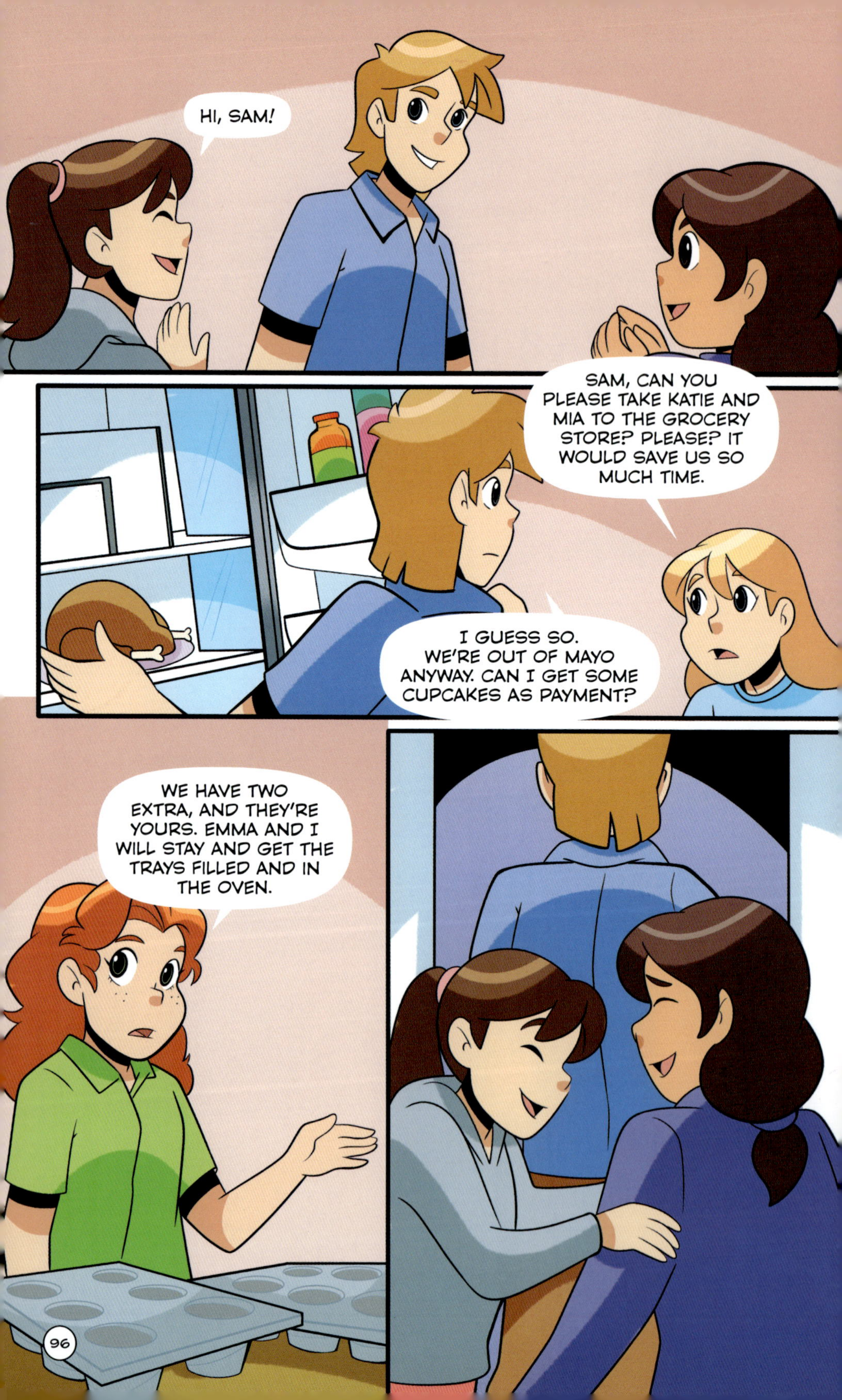
HI, SAM!
SAM, CAN YOU PLEASE TAKE KATIE AND MIA TO THE GROCERY STORE? PLEASE? IT WOULD SAVE US SO MUCH TIME.
I GUESS SO. WE'RE OUT OF MAYO ANYWAY. CAN I GET SOME CUPCAKES AS PAYMENT?
WE HAVE TWO EXTRA, AND THEY'RE YOURS. EMMA AND I WILL STAY AND GET THE TRAYS FILLED AND IN THE OVEN.

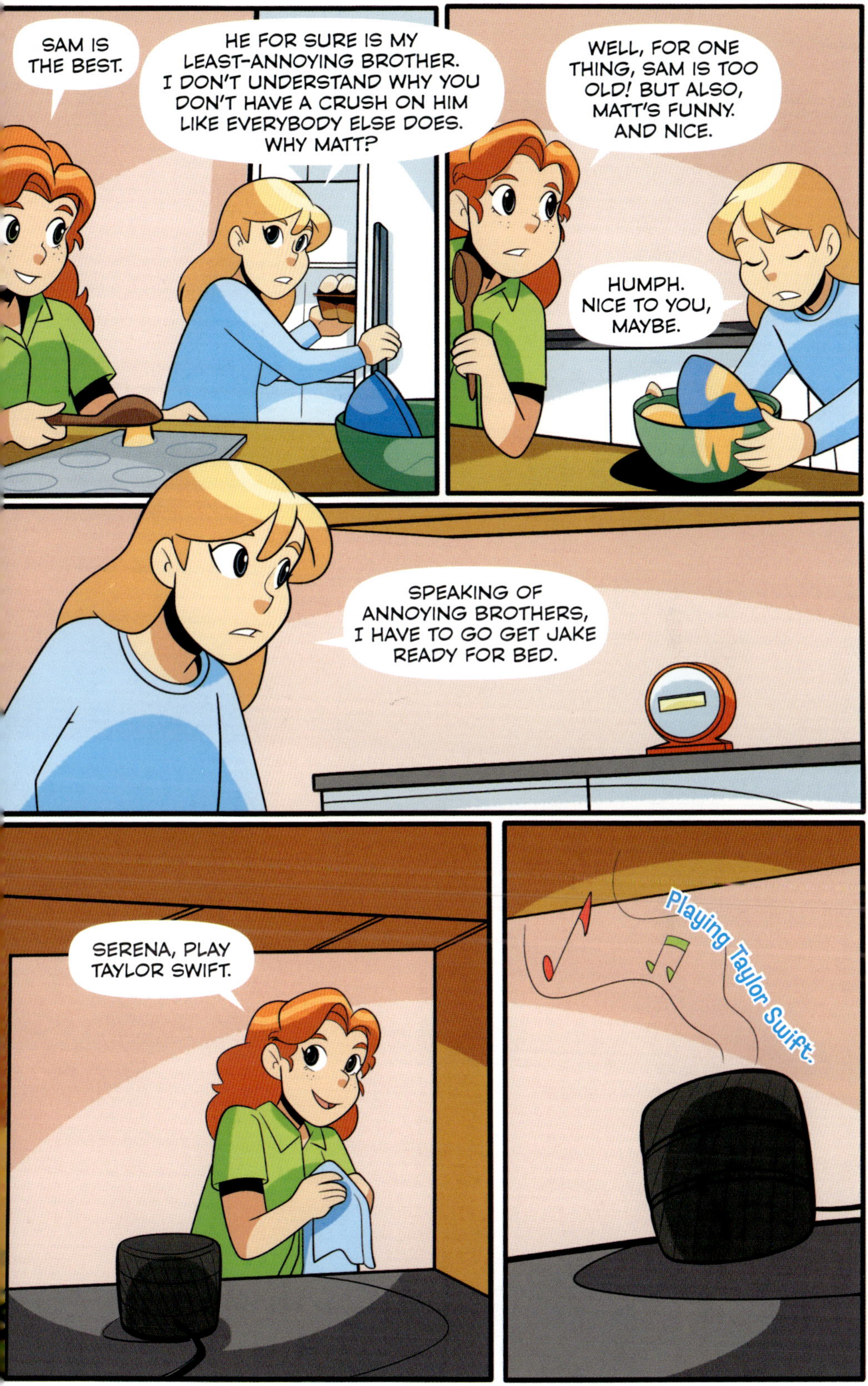
SAM IS THE BEST.
HE FOR SURE IS MY LEAST-ANNOYING BROTHER. I DON'T UNDERSTAND WHY YOU DON'T HAVE A CRUSH ON HIM LIKE EVERYBODY ELSE DOES. WHY MATT?
WELL, FOR ONE THING, SAM IS TOO OLD! BUT ALSO, MATT'S FUNNY. AND NICE.
HUMPH. NICE TO YOU, MAYBE.
SPEAKING OF ANNOYING BROTHERS, I HAVE TO GO GET JAKE READY FOR BED.
SERENA, PLAY TAYLOR SWIFT.
Playing Taylor Swift.

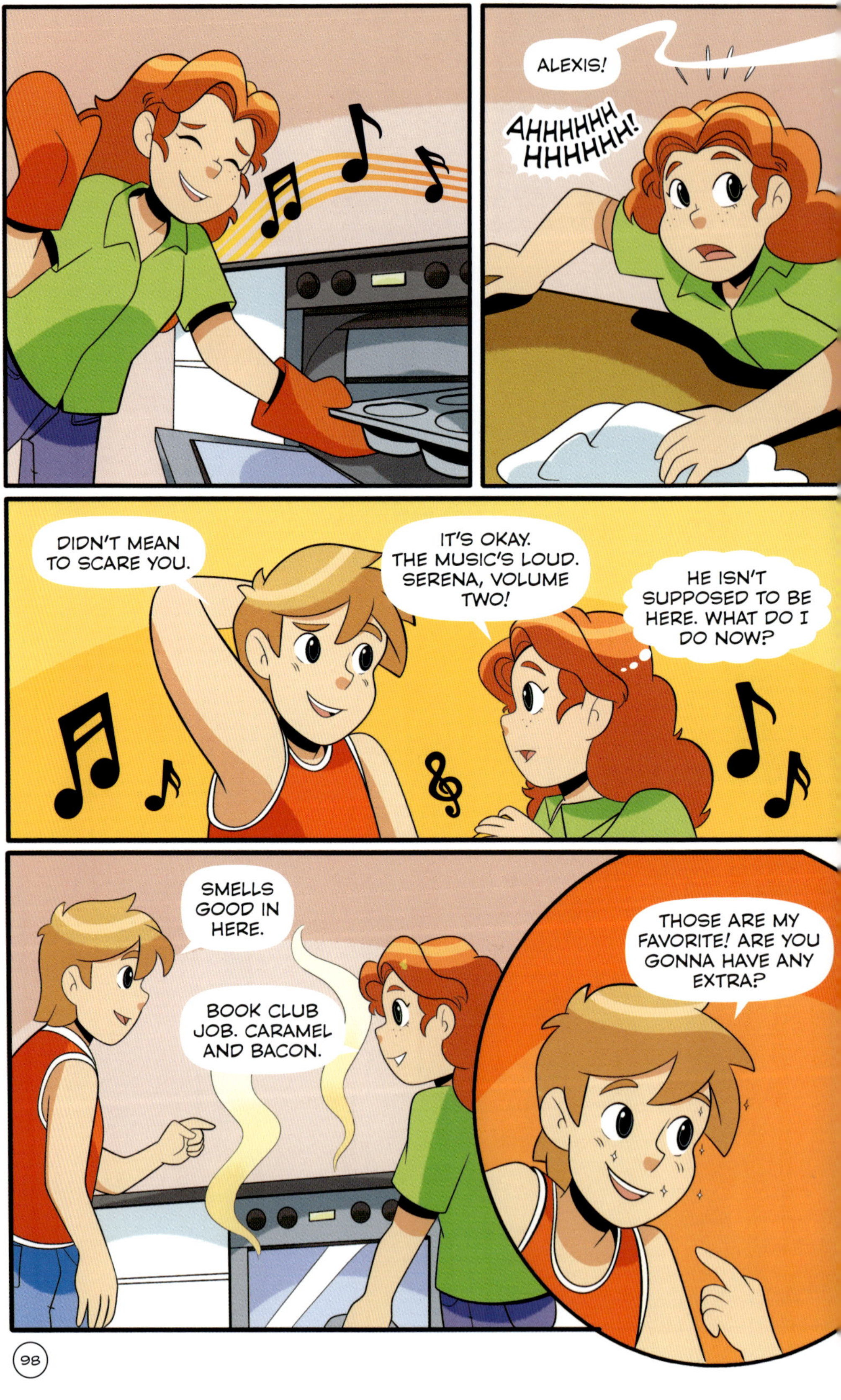
ALEXIS!
AHHHHHH HHHHHH!
DIDN'T MEAN TO SCARE YOU.
IT'S OKAY. THE MUSIC'S LOUD. SERENA, VOLUME TWO!
HE ISN'T SUPPOSED TO BE HERE. WHAT DO I DO NOW?
SMELLS GOOD IN HERE.
BOOK CLUB JOB. CARAMEL AND BACON.
THOSE ARE MY FAVORITE! ARE YOU GONNA HAVE ANY EXTRA?

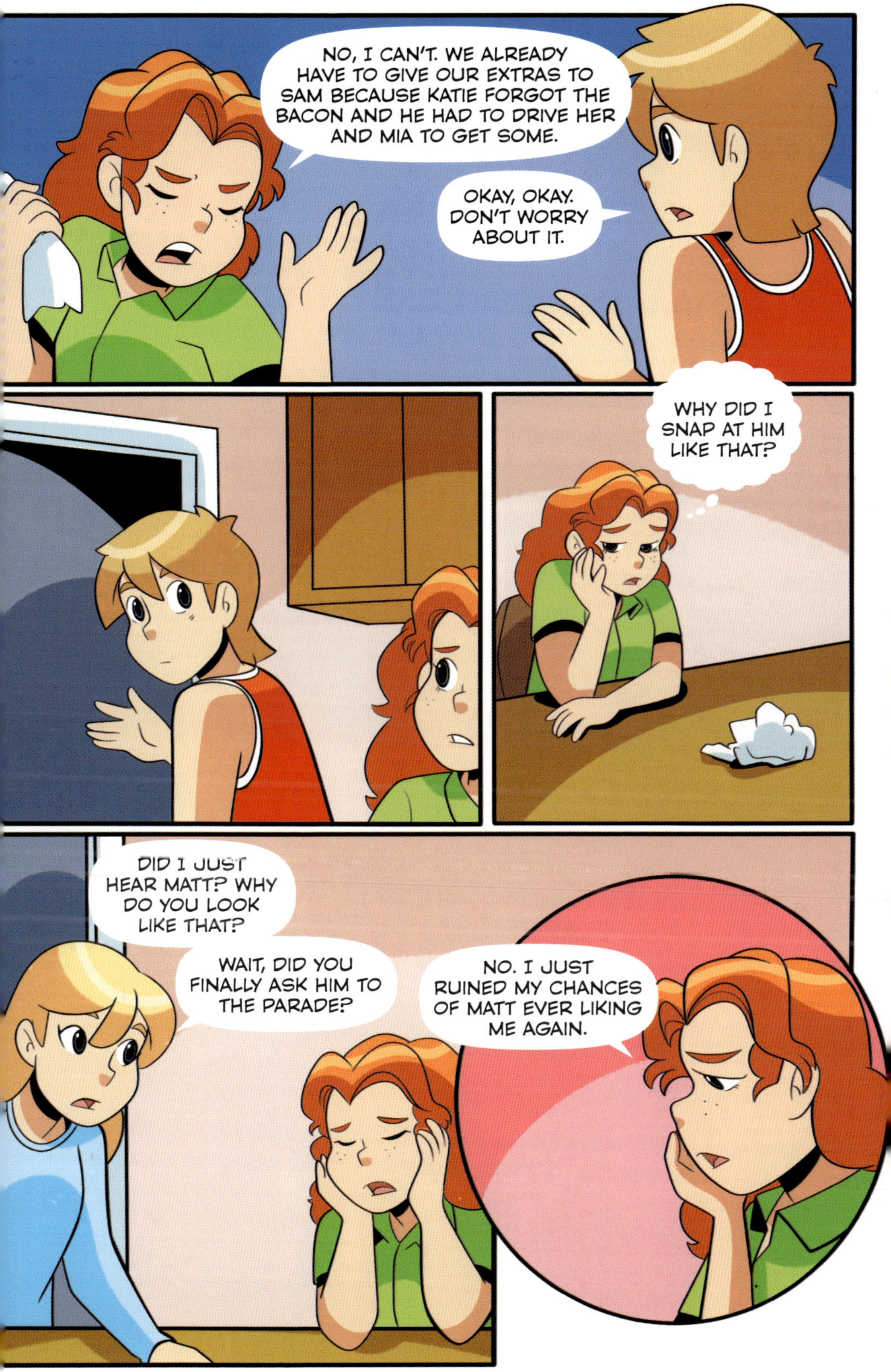
NO, I CAN'T. WE ALREADY HAVE TO GIVE OUR EXTRAS TO SAM BECAUSE KATIE FORGOT THE BACON AND HE HAD TO DRIVE HER AND MIA TO GET SOME.
OKAY, OKAY. DON'T WORRY ABOUT IT.
WHY DID I SNAP AT HIM LIKE THAT?
DID I JUST HEAR MATT? WHY DO YOU LOOK LIKE THAT?
WAIT, DID YOU FINALLY ASK HIM TO THE PARADE?
NO. I JUST RUINED MY CHANCES OF MATT EVER LIKING ME AGAIN.

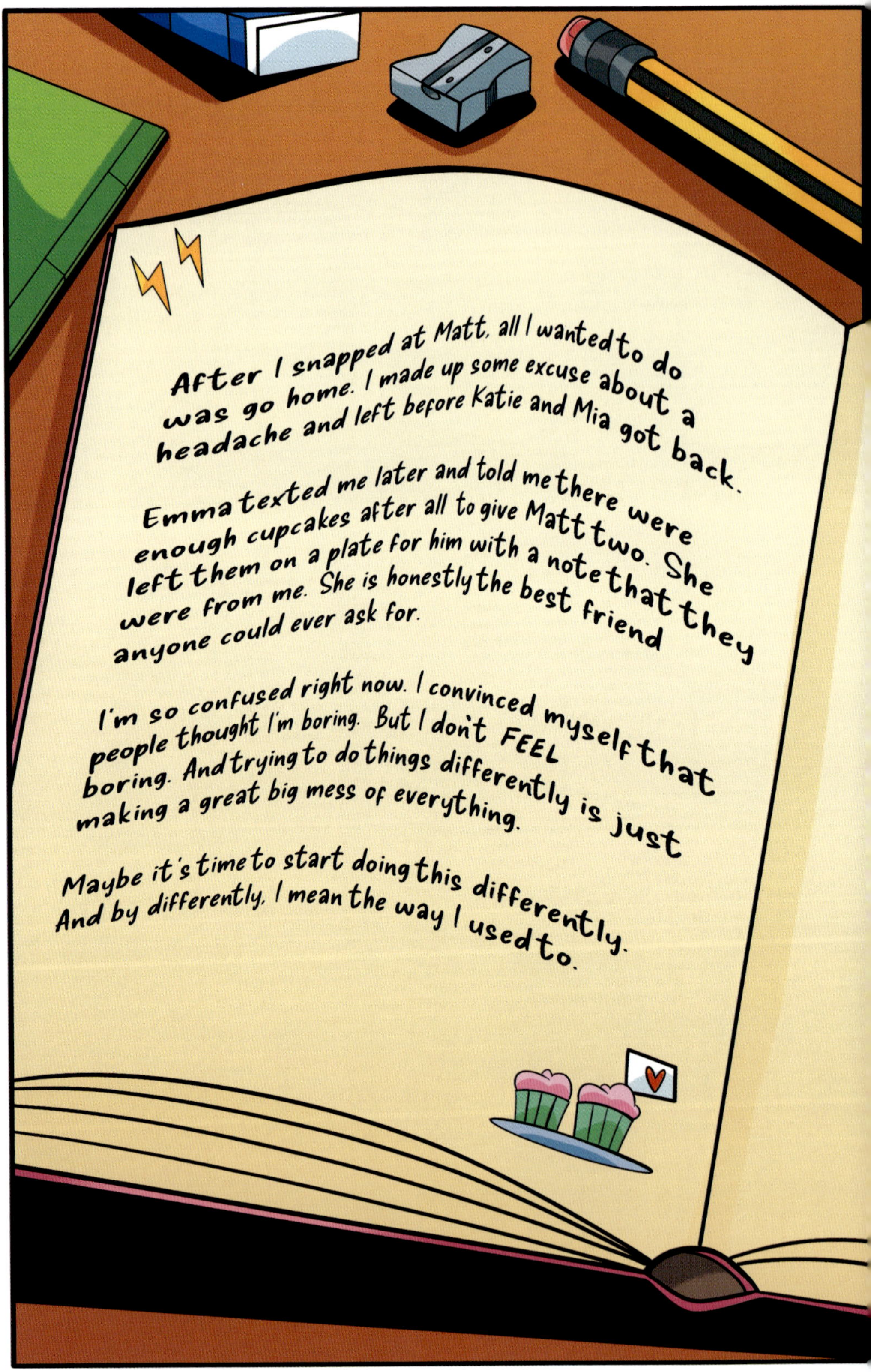
After I snapped at Matt, all I wanted to do was go home. I made up some excuse about a headache and left before Katie and Mia got back.
Emma texted me later and told me there were enough cupcakes after all to give Matt two. She left them on a plate for him with a note that they were from me. She is honestly the best friend anyone could ever ask for.
I'm so confused right now. I convinced myself that people thought I'm boring. But I don't FEEL boring. And trying to do things differently is just making a great big mess of everything.
Maybe it's time to start doing this differently. And by differently, I mean the way I used to.

Chapter 10

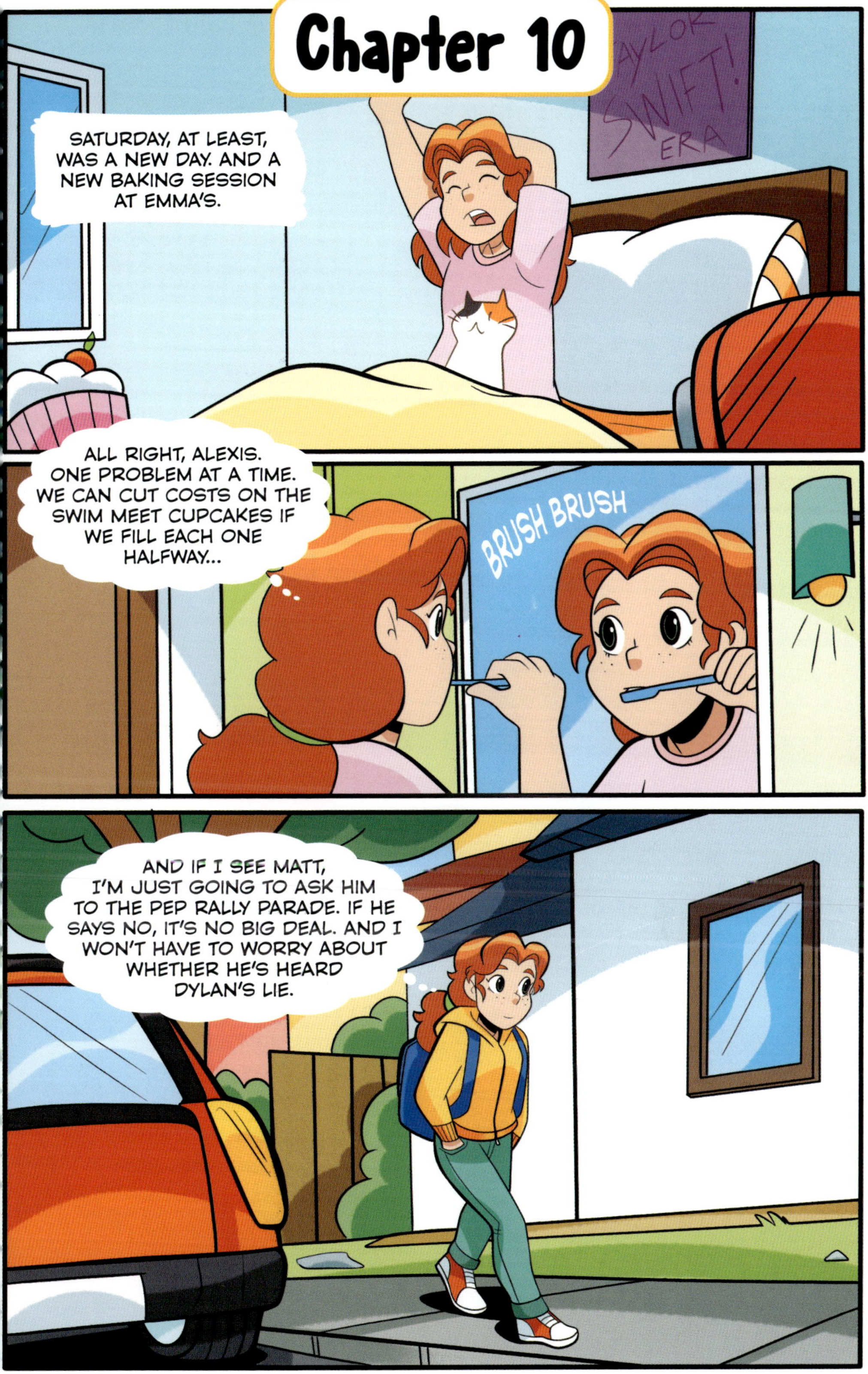
SATURDAY, AT LEAST, WAS A NEW DAY. AND A NEW BAKING SESSION AT EMMA'S.
SWIFT!
ERA
ALL RIGHT, ALEXIS. ONE PROBLEM AT A TIME. WE CAN CUT COSTS ON THE SWIM MEET CUPCAKES IF WE FILL EACH ONE HALFWAY...
BRUSH BRUSH
AND IF I SEE MATT, I'M JUST GOING TO ASK HIM TO THE PEP RALLY PARADE. IF HE SAYS NO, IT'S NO BIG DEAL. AND I WON'T HAVE TO WORRY ABOUT WHETHER HE'S HEARD DYLAN'S LIE.

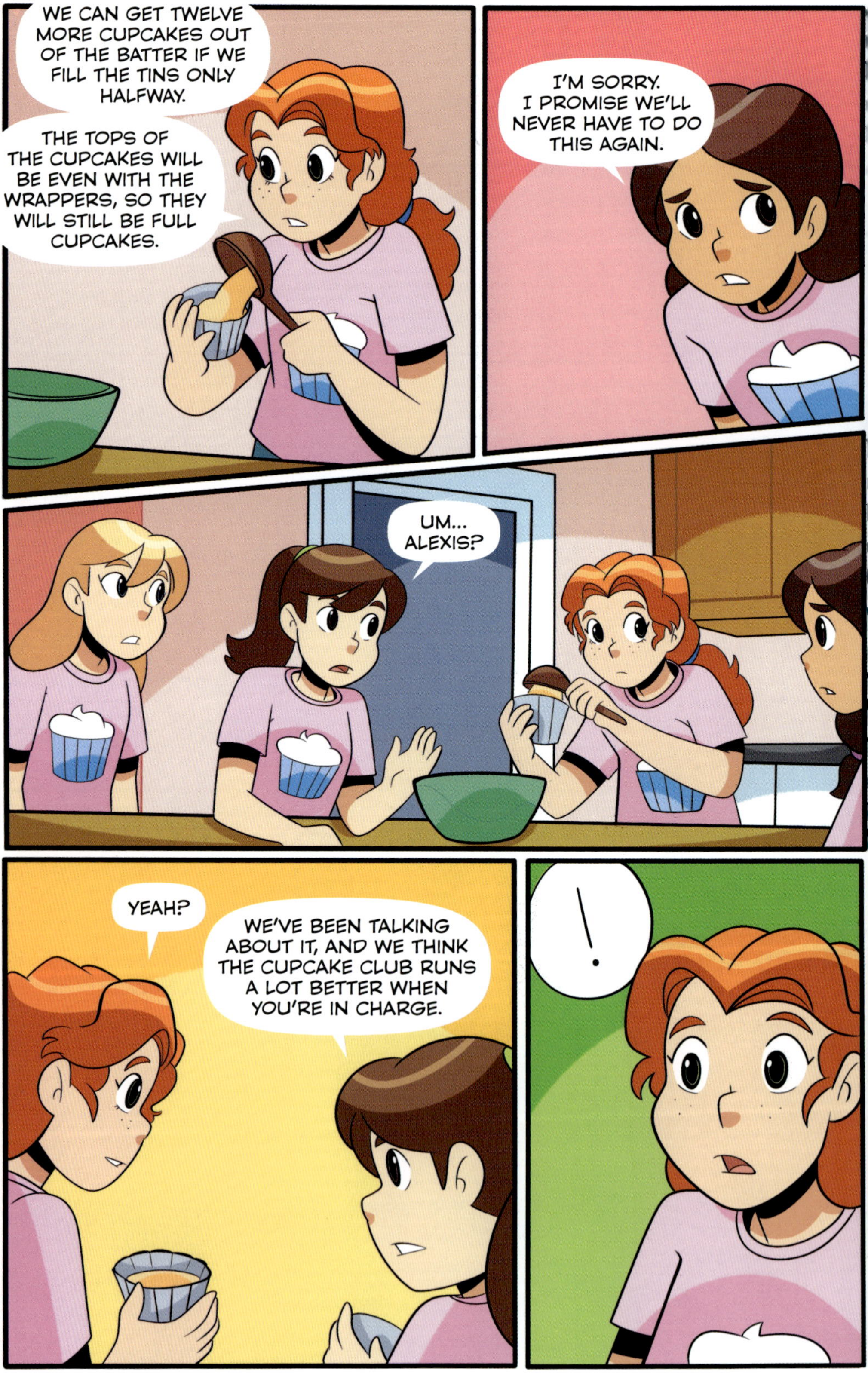
WE CAN GET TWELVE MORE CUPCAKES OUT OF THE BATTER IF WE FILL THE TINS ONLY HALFWAY.
THE TOPS OF THE CUPCAKES WILL BE EVEN WITH THE WRAPPERS, SO THEY WILL STILL BE FULL CUPCAKES.
I'M SORRY. I PROMISE WE'LL NEVER HAVE TO DO THIS AGAIN.
UM... ALEXIS?
YEAH?
WE'VE BEEN TALKING ABOUT IT, AND WE THINK THE CUPCAKE CLUB RUNS A LOT BETTER WHEN YOU'RE IN CHARGE.
!

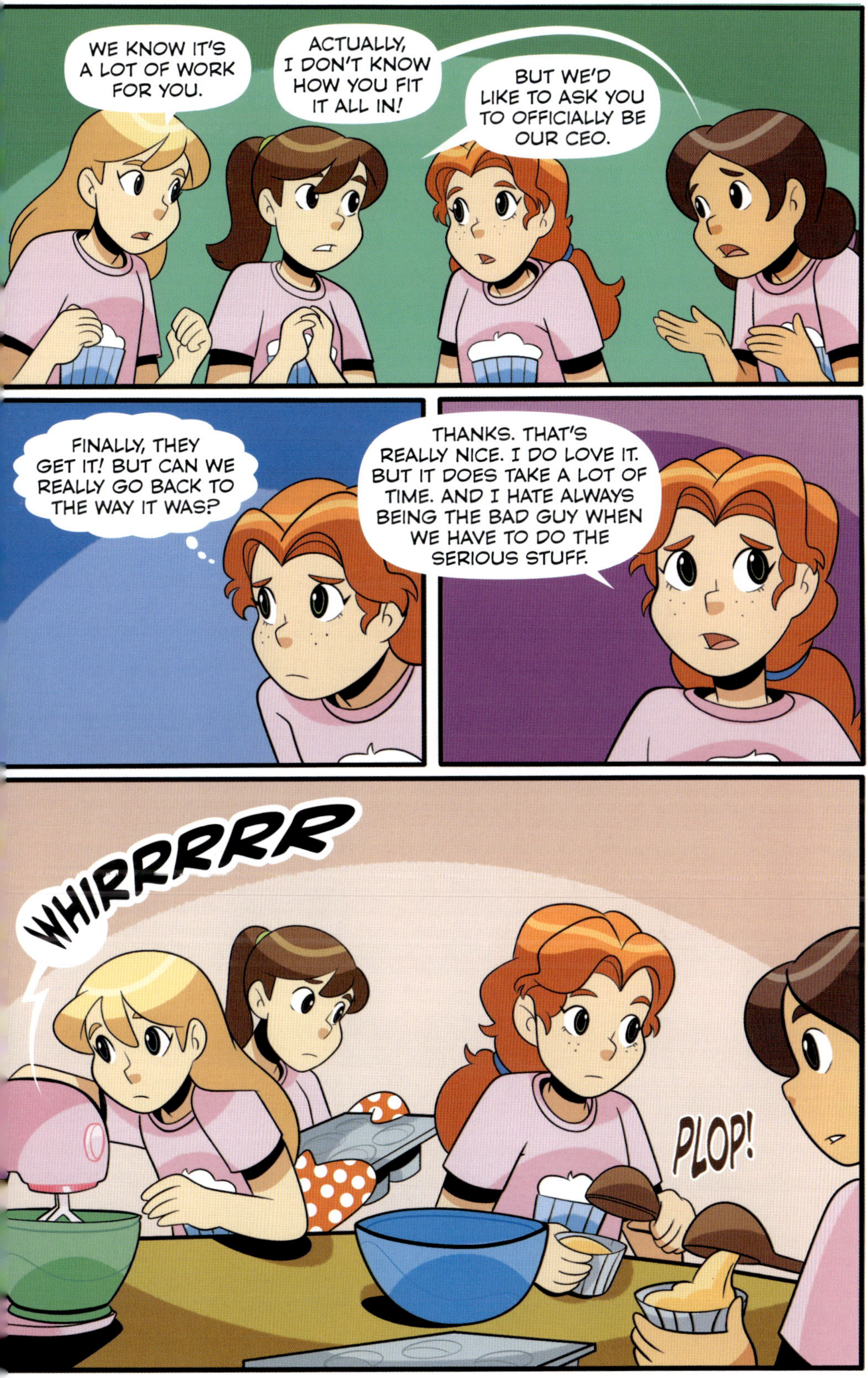
WE KNOW IT'S A LOT OF WORK FOR YOU.
ACTUALLY, I DON'T KNOW HOW YOU FIT IT ALL IN!
BUT WE'D LIKE TO ASK YOU TO OFFICIALLY BE OUR CEO.
FINALLY, THEY GET IT! BUT CAN WE REALLY GO BACK TO THE WAY IT WAS?
THANKS. THAT'S REALLY NICE. I DO LOVE IT. BUT IT DOES TAKE A LOT OF TIME. AND I HATE ALWAYS BEING THE BAD GUY WHEN WE HAVE TO DO THE SERIOUS STUFF.
WHIRRRRR
PLOP!

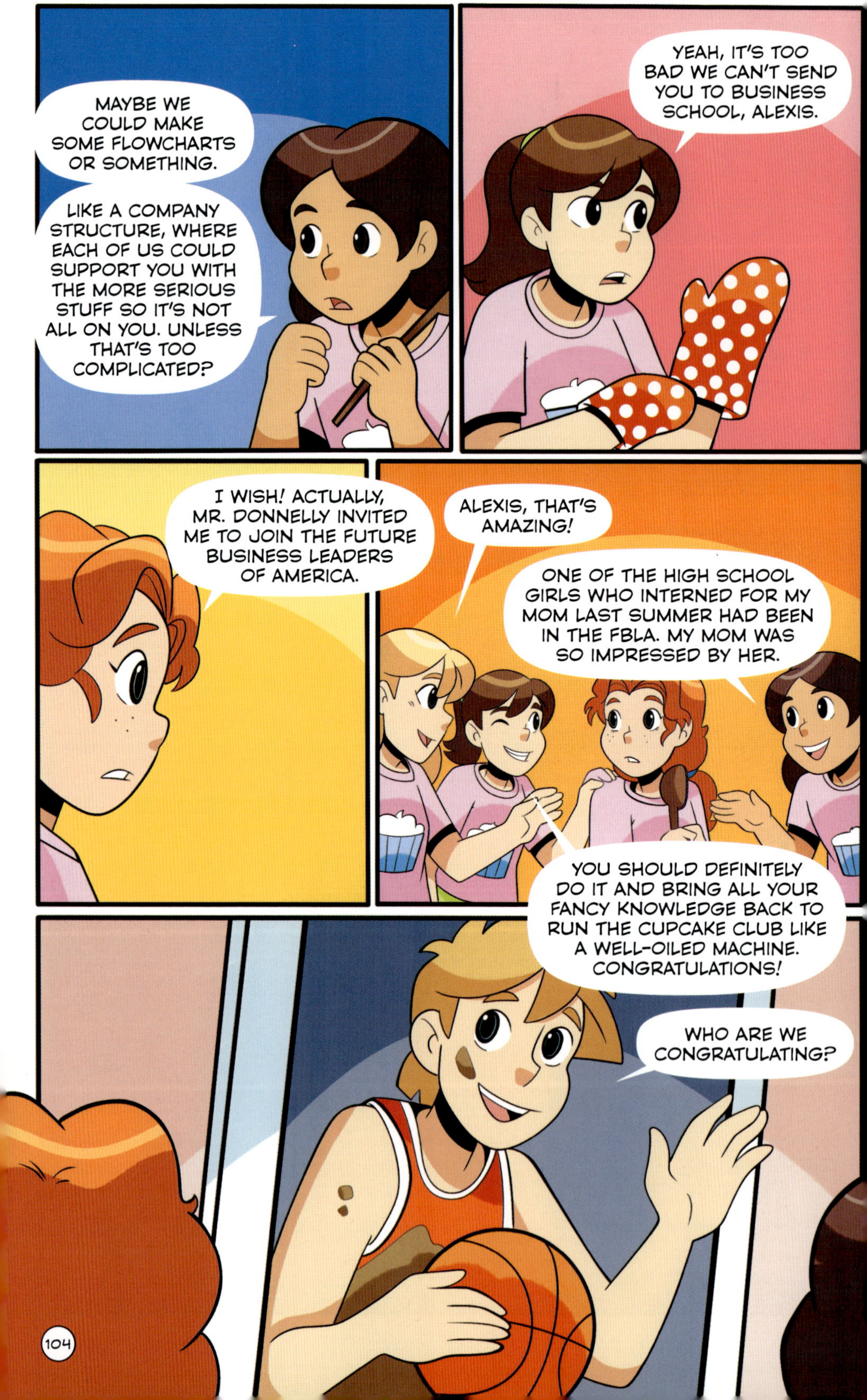
MAYBE WE COULD MAKE SOME FLOWCHARTS OR SOMETHING.
LIKE A COMPANY STRUCTURE, WHERE EACH OF US COULD SUPPORT YOU WITH THE MORE SERIOUS STUFF SO IT'S NOT ALL ON YOU. UNLESS THAT'S TOO COMPLICATED?
YEAH, IT'S TOO BAD WE CAN'T SEND YOU TO BUSINESS SCHOOL, ALEXIS.
I WISH! ACTUALLY, MR. DONNELLY INVITED ME TO JOIN THE FUTURE BUSINESS LEADERS OF AMERICA.
ALEXIS, THAT'S AMAZING!
ONE OF THE HIGH SCHOOL GIRLS WHO INTERNED FOR MY MOM LAST SUMMER HAD BEEN IN THE FBLA. MY MOM WAS SO IMPRESSED BY HER.
YOU SHOULD DEFINITELY DO IT AND BRING ALL YOUR FANCY KNOWLEDGE BACK TO RUN THE CUPCAKE CLUB LIKE A WELL-OILED MACHINE. CONGRATULATIONS!
WHO ARE WE CONGRATULATING?

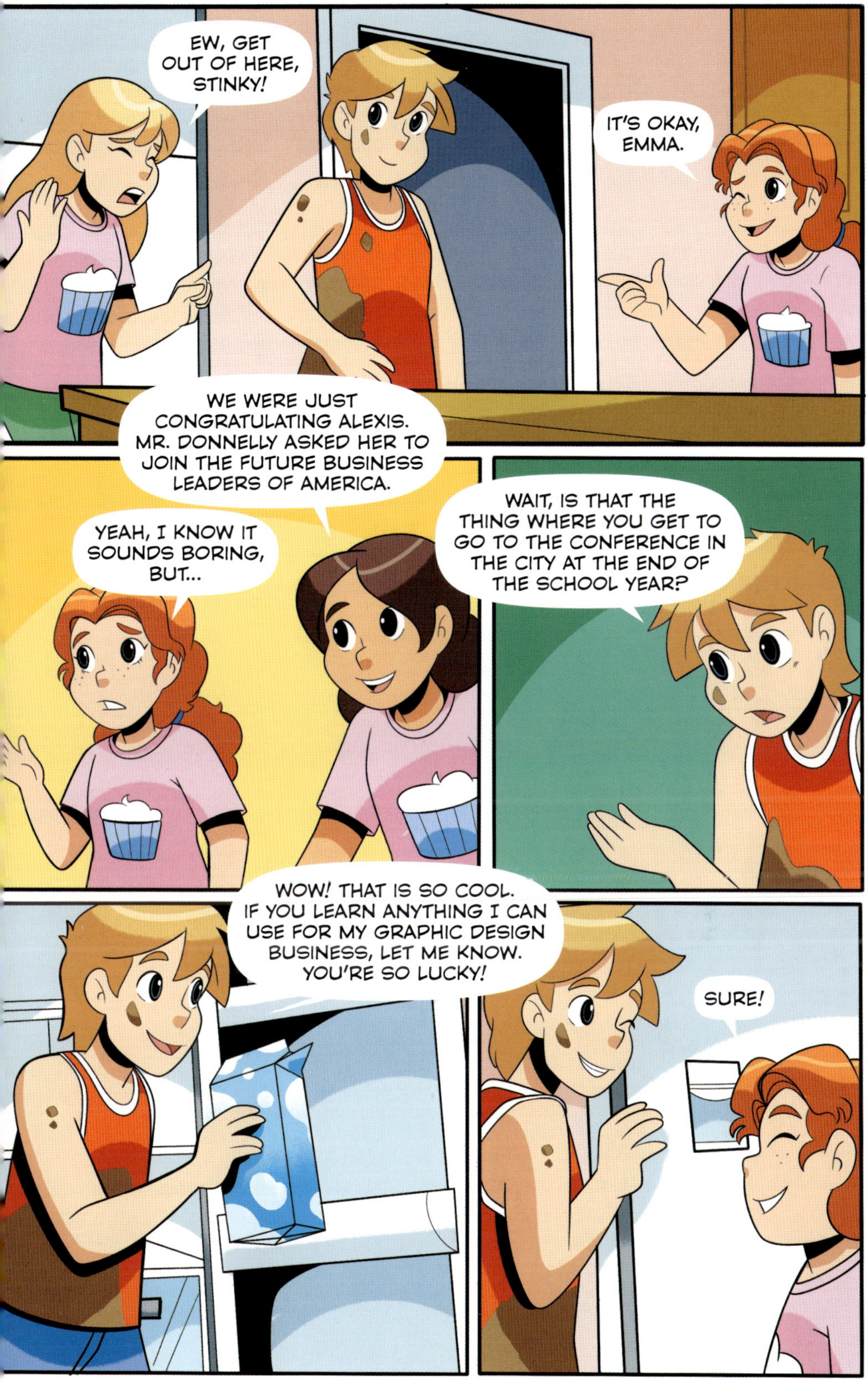
EW, GET OUT OF HERE, STINKY!
IT'S OKAY, EMMA.
WE WERE JUST CONGRATULATING ALEXIS. MR. DONNELLY ASKED HER TO JOIN THE FUTURE BUSINESS LEADERS OF AMERICA.
YEAH, I KNOW IT SOUNDS BORING, BUT...
WAIT, IS THAT THE THING WHERE YOU GET TO GO TO THE CONFERENCE IN THE CITY AT THE END OF THE SCHOOL YEAR?
WOW! THAT IS SO COOL. IF YOU LEARN ANYTHING I CAN USE FOR MY GRAPHIC DESIGN BUSINESS, LET ME KNOW. YOU'RE SO LUCKY!
SURE!

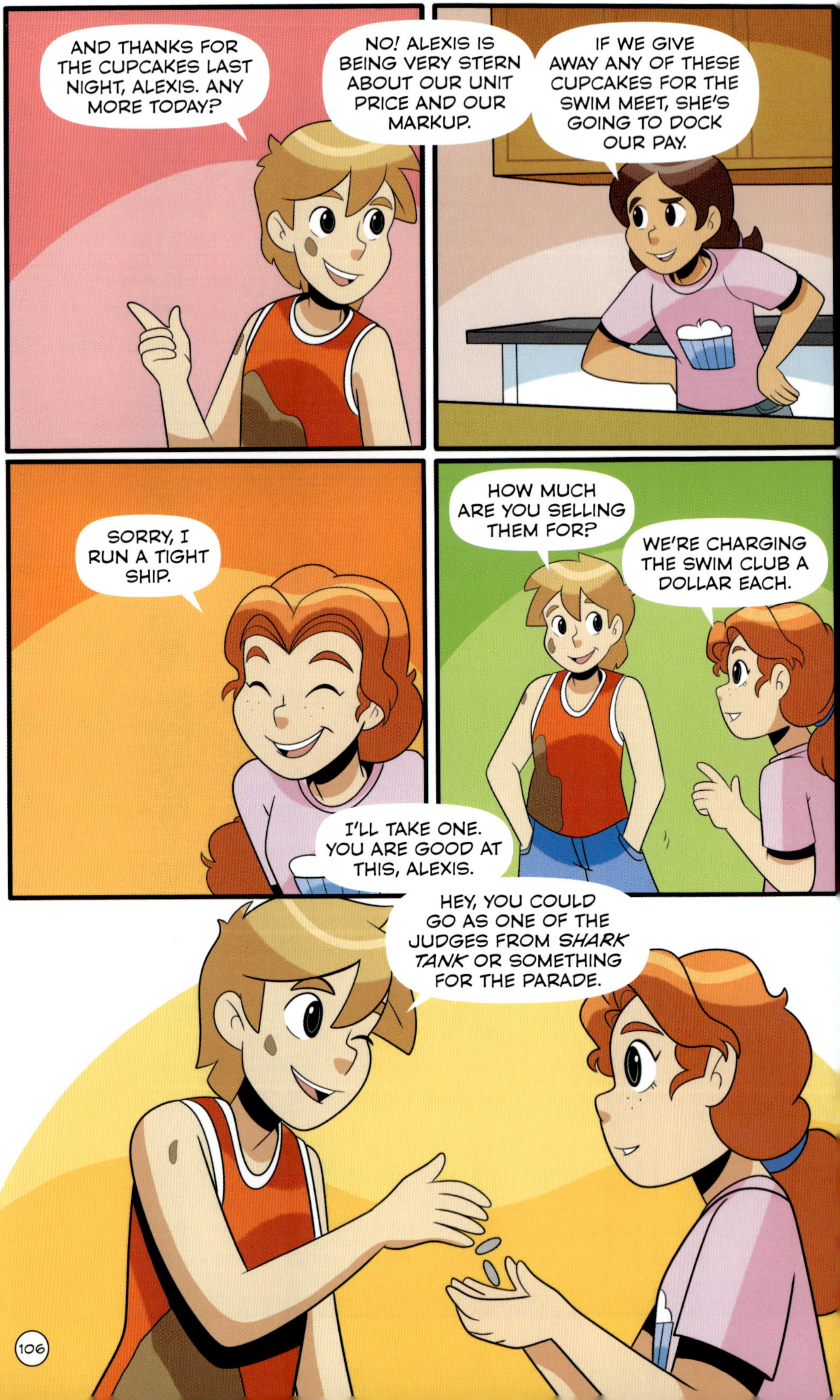
AND THANKS FOR THE CUPCAKES LAST NIGHT, ALEXIS. ANY MORE TODAY?
NO! ALEXIS IS BEING VERY STERN ABOUT OUR UNIT PRICE AND OUR MARKUP.
IF WE GIVE AWAY ANY OF THESE CUPCAKES FOR THE SWIM MEET, SHE'S GOING TO DOCK OUR PAY.
SORRY, I RUN A TIGHT SHIP.
HOW MUCH ARE YOU SELLING THEM FOR?
WE'RE CHARGING THE SWIM CLUB A DOLLAR EACH.
I'LL TAKE ONE. YOU ARE GOOD AT THIS, ALEXIS.
HEY, YOU COULD GO AS ONE OF THE JUDGES FROM *SHARK TANK* OR SOMETHING FOR THE PARADE.

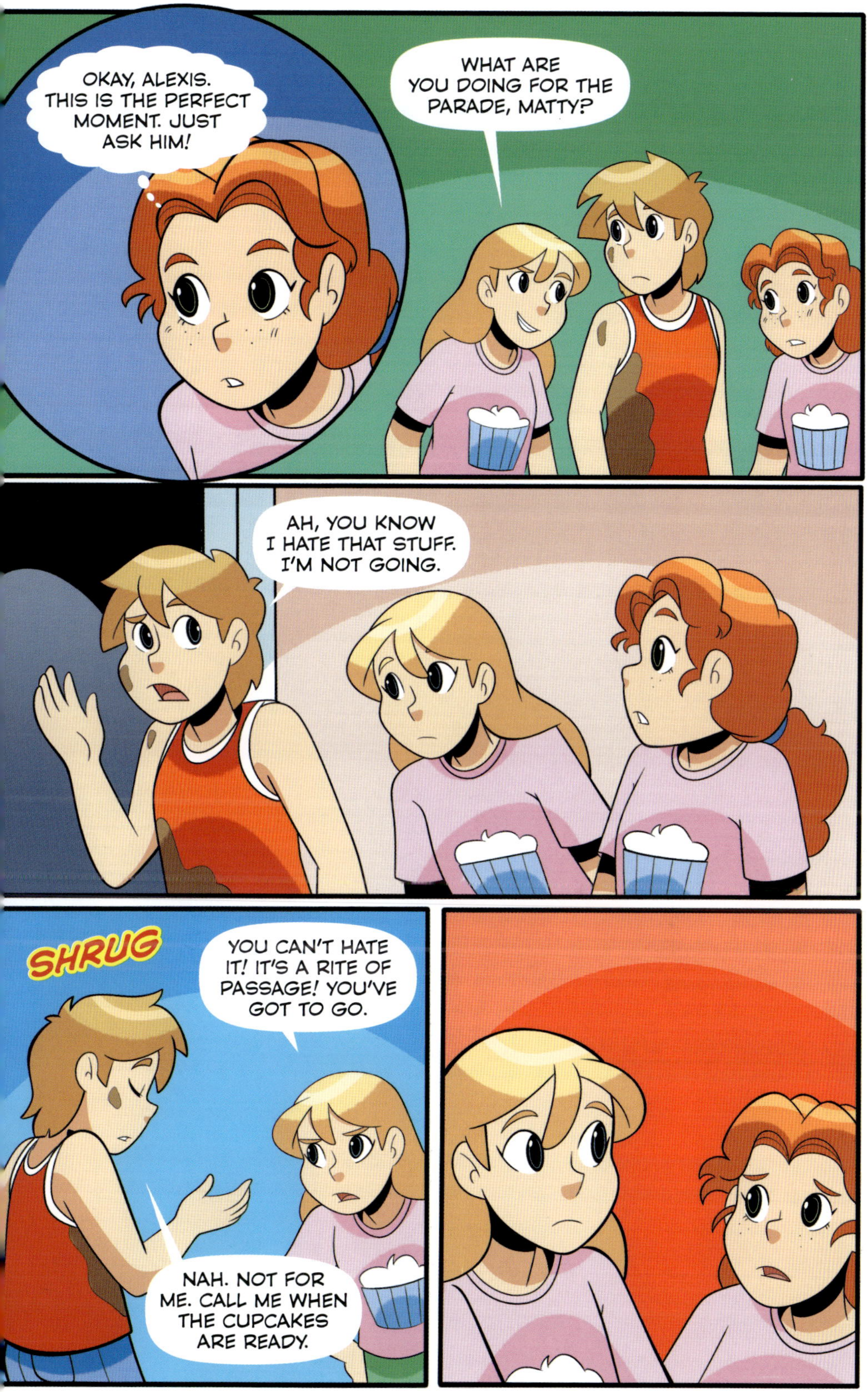
OKAY, ALEXIS. THIS IS THE PERFECT MOMENT. JUST ASK HIM!
WHAT ARE YOU DOING FOR THE PARADE, MATTY?
AH, YOU KNOW I HATE THAT STUFF. I'M NOT GOING.
SHRUG
YOU CAN'T HATE IT! IT'S A RITE OF PASSAGE! YOU'VE GOT TO GO.
NAH. NOT FOR ME. CALL ME WHEN THE CUPCAKES ARE READY.

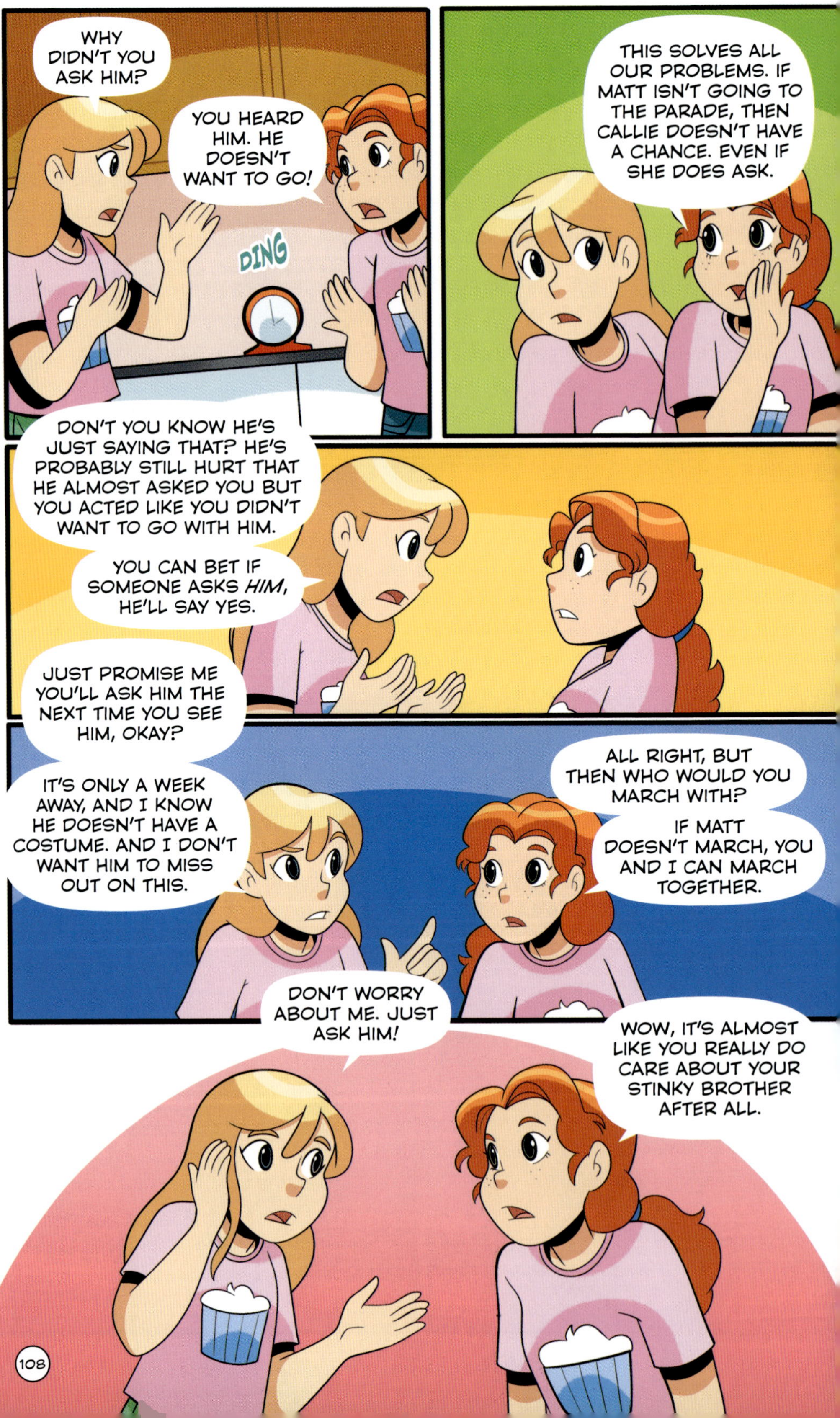
WHY DIDN'T YOU ASK HIM?
YOU HEARD HIM. HE DOESN'T WANT TO GO!
DING
THIS SOLVES ALL OUR PROBLEMS. IF MATT ISN'T GOING TO THE PARADE, THEN CALLIE DOESN'T HAVE A CHANCE. EVEN IF SHE DOES ASK.
DON'T YOU KNOW HE'S JUST SAYING THAT? HE'S PROBABLY STILL HURT THAT HE ALMOST ASKED YOU BUT YOU ACTED LIKE YOU DIDN'T WANT TO GO WITH HIM.
YOU CAN BET IF SOMEONE ASKS *HIM*, HE'LL SAY YES.
JUST PROMISE ME YOU'LL ASK HIM THE NEXT TIME YOU SEE HIM, OKAY?
IT'S ONLY A WEEK AWAY, AND I KNOW HE DOESN'T HAVE A COSTUME. AND I DON'T WANT HIM TO MISS OUT ON THIS.
ALL RIGHT, BUT THEN WHO WOULD YOU MARCH WITH?
IF MATT DOESN'T MARCH, YOU AND I CAN MARCH TOGETHER.
DON'T WORRY ABOUT ME. JUST ASK HIM!
WOW, IT'S ALMOST LIKE YOU REALLY DO CARE ABOUT YOUR STINKY BROTHER AFTER ALL.

Chapter 11

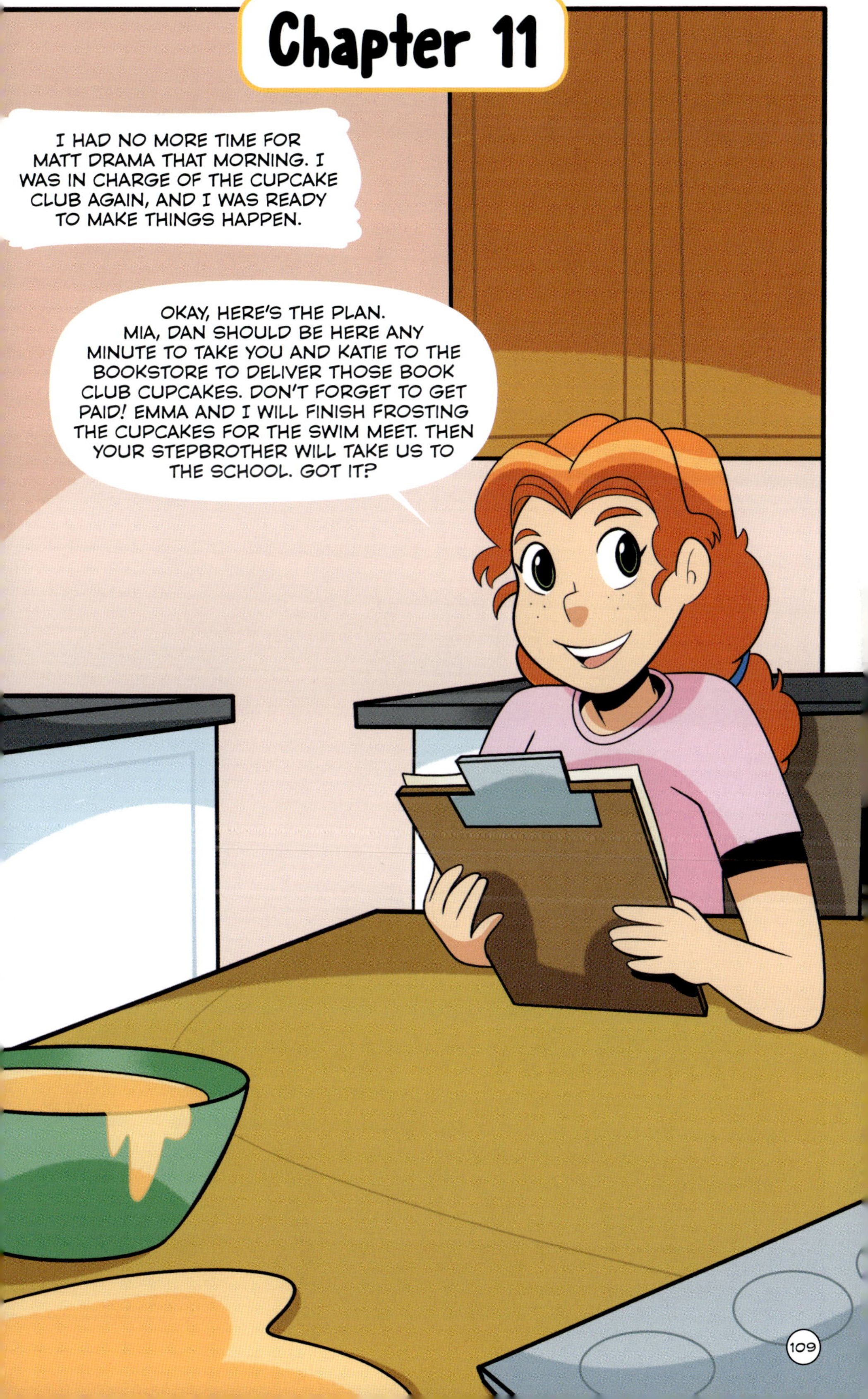
I HAD NO MORE TIME FOR MATT DRAMA THAT MORNING. I WAS IN CHARGE OF THE CUPCAKE CLUB AGAIN, AND I WAS READY TO MAKE THINGS HAPPEN.
OKAY, HERE'S THE PLAN. MIA, DAN SHOULD BE HERE ANY MINUTE TO TAKE YOU AND KATIE TO THE BOOKSTORE TO DELIVER THOSE BOOK CLUB CUPCAKES. DON'T FORGET TO GET PAID! EMMA AND I WILL FINISH FROSTING THE CUPCAKES FOR THE SWIM MEET. THEN YOUR STEPBROTHER WILL TAKE US TO THE SCHOOL. GOT IT?

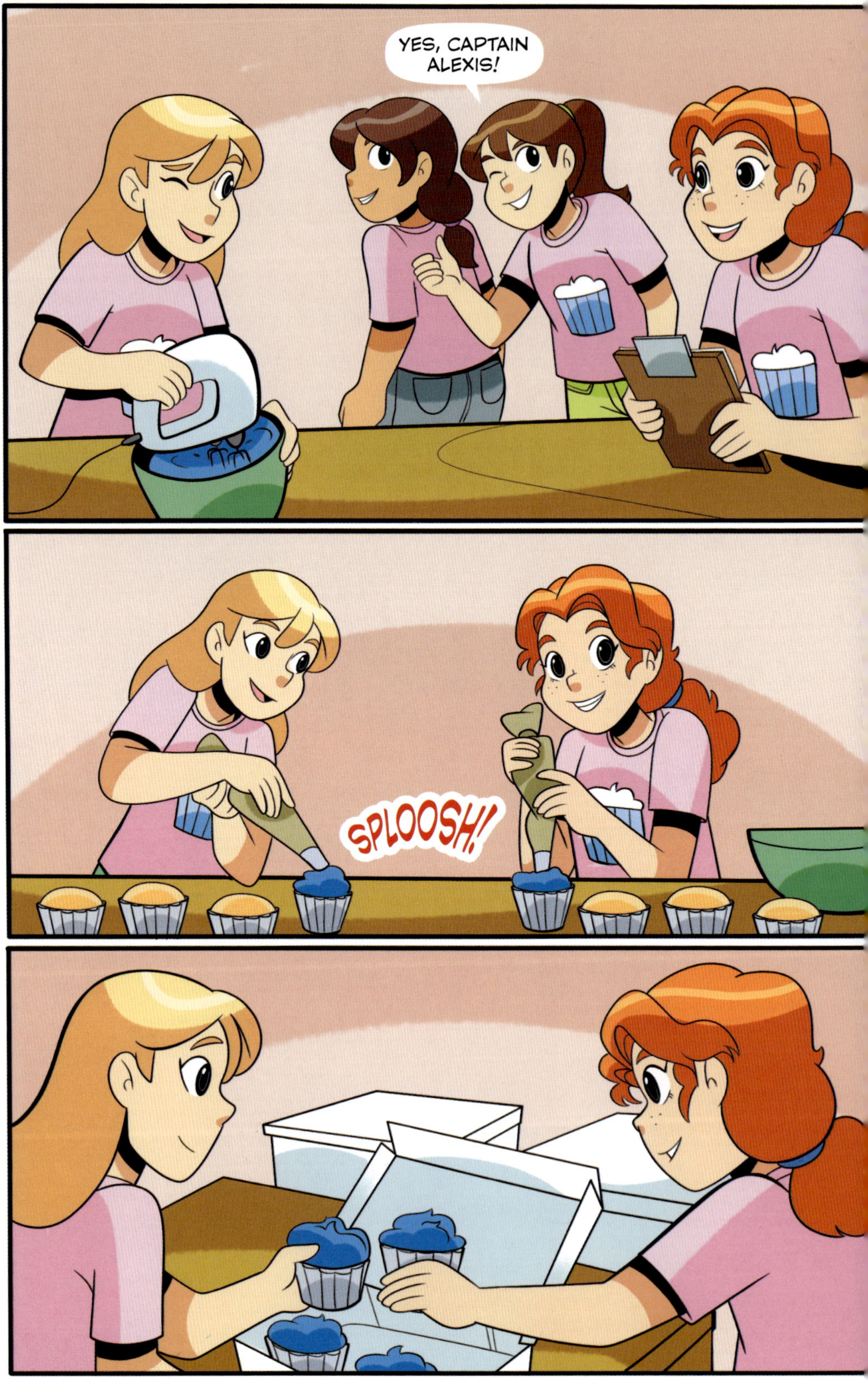
YES, CAPTAIN ALEXIS!
SPLOOSH!

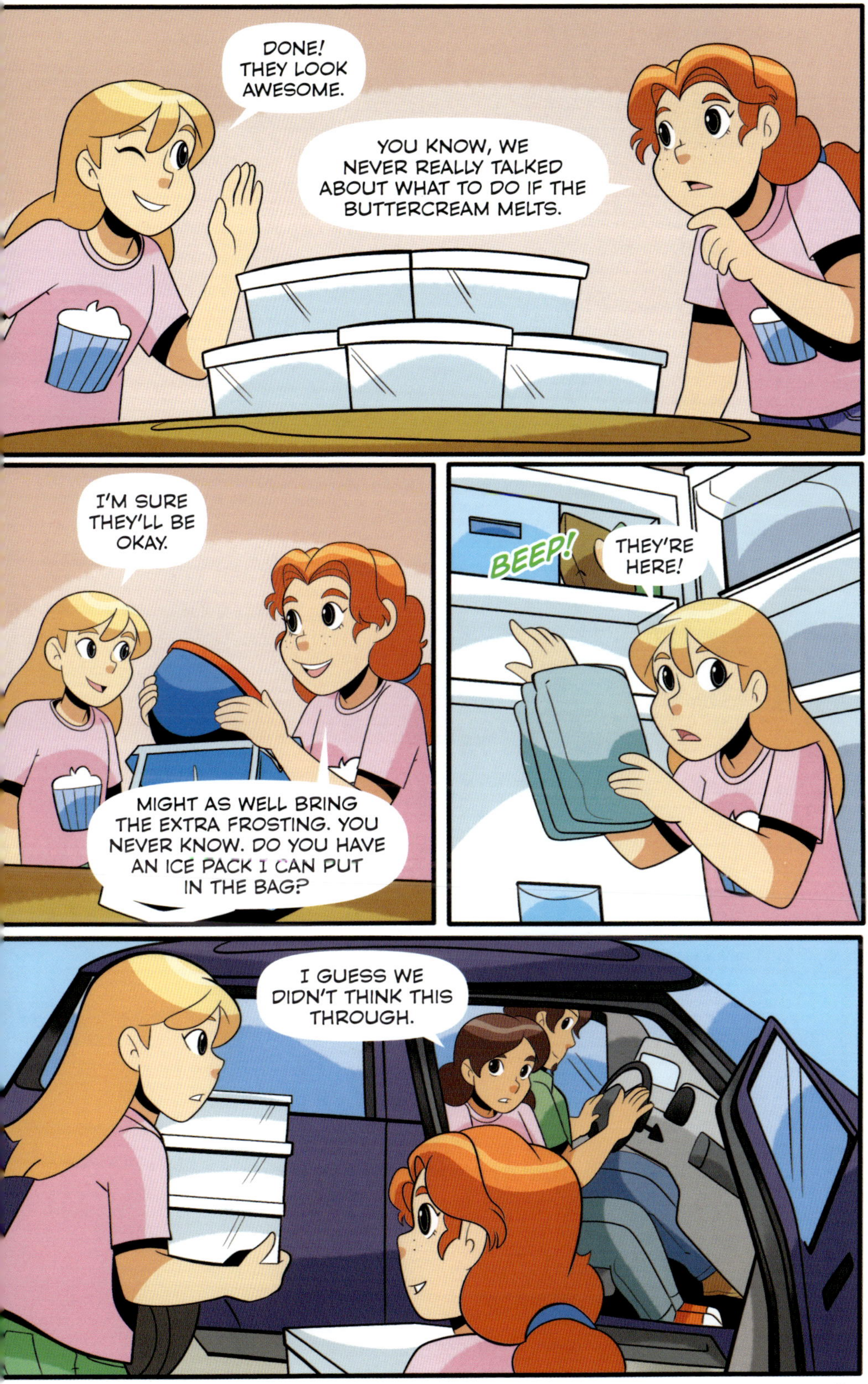
DONE! THEY LOOK AWESOME.
YOU KNOW, WE NEVER REALLY TALKED ABOUT WHAT TO DO IF THE BUTTERCREAM MELTS.
I'M SURE THEY'LL BE OKAY.
MIGHT AS WELL BRING THE EXTRA FROSTING. YOU NEVER KNOW. DO YOU HAVE AN ICE PACK I CAN PUT IN THE BAG?
BEEP!
THEY'RE HERE!
I GUESS WE DIDN'T THINK THIS THROUGH.

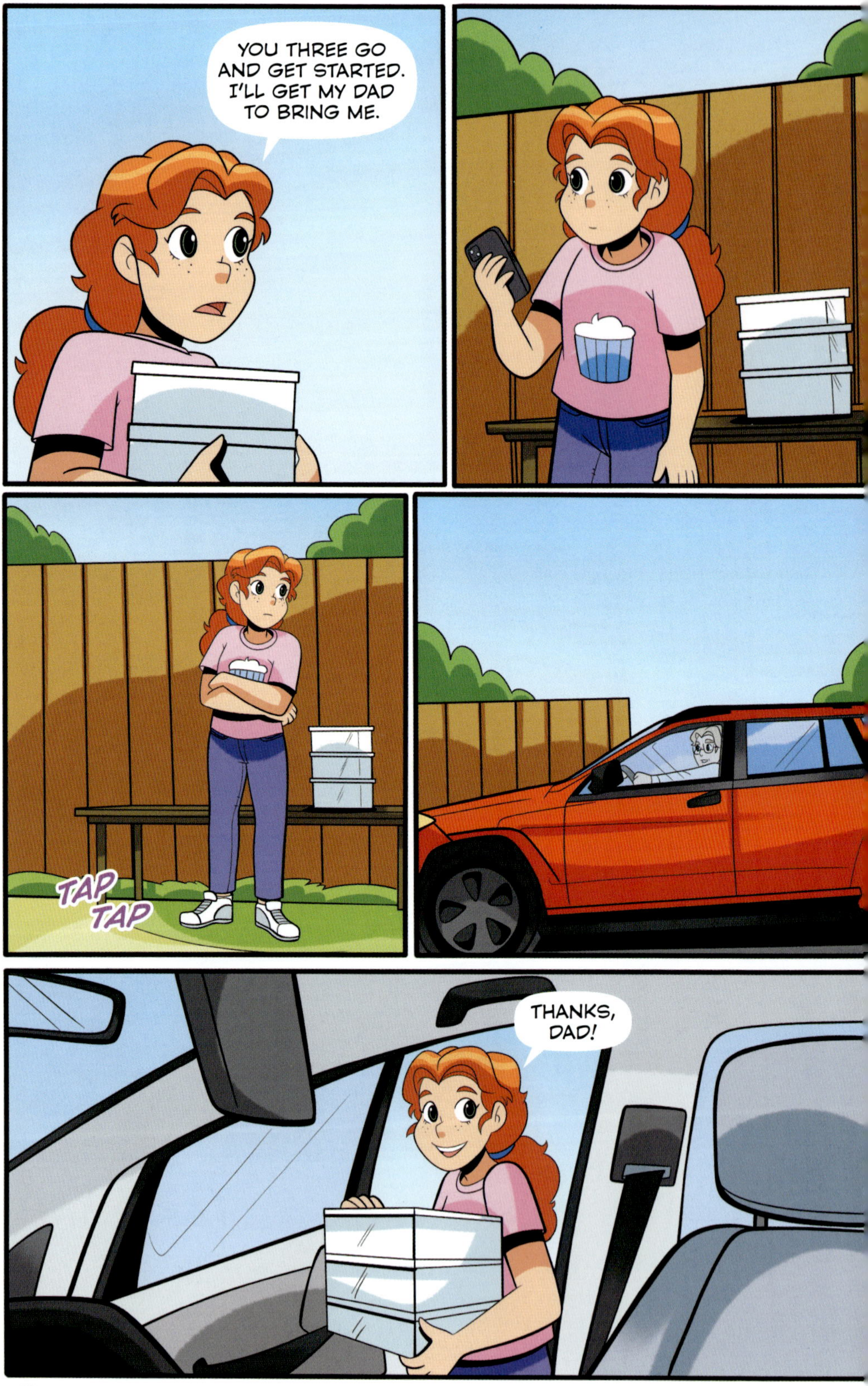
YOU THREE GO AND GET STARTED. I'LL GET MY DAD TO BRING ME.
TAP TAP
THANKS, DAD!

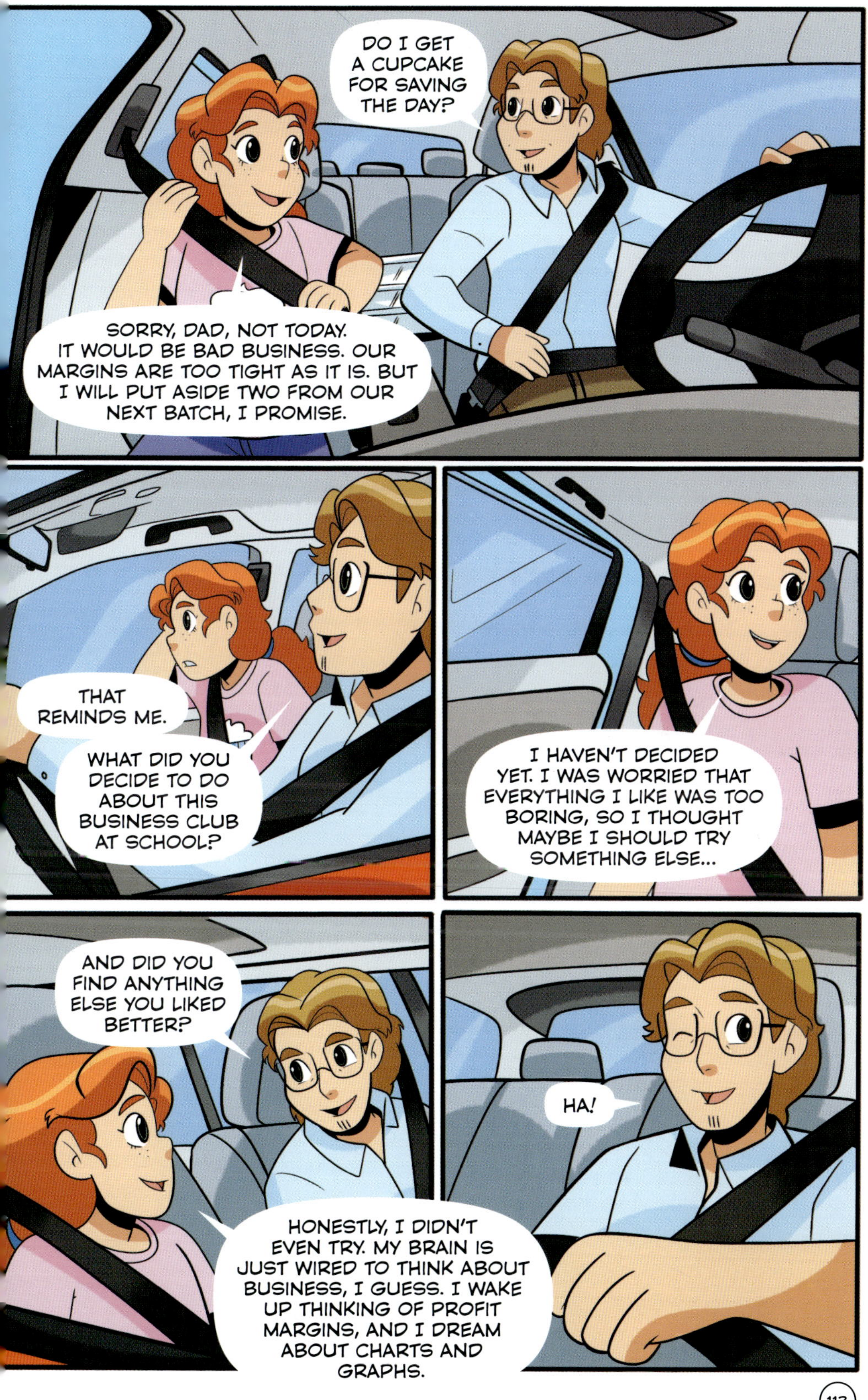
DO I GET A CUPCAKE FOR SAVING THE DAY?
SORRY, DAD, NOT TODAY. IT WOULD BE BAD BUSINESS. OUR MARGINS ARE TOO TIGHT AS IT IS. BUT I WILL PUT ASIDE TWO FROM OUR NEXT BATCH, I PROMISE.
THAT REMINDS ME.
WHAT DID YOU DECIDE TO DO ABOUT THIS BUSINESS CLUB AT SCHOOL?
I HAVEN'T DECIDED YET. I WAS WORRIED THAT EVERYTHING I LIKE WAS TOO BORING, SO I THOUGHT MAYBE I SHOULD TRY SOMETHING ELSE...
AND DID YOU FIND ANYTHING ELSE YOU LIKED BETTER?
HONESTLY, I DIDN'T EVEN TRY. MY BRAIN IS JUST WIRED TO THINK ABOUT BUSINESS, I GUESS. I WAKE UP THINKING OF PROFIT MARGINS, AND I DREAM ABOUT CHARTS AND GRAPHS.
HA!

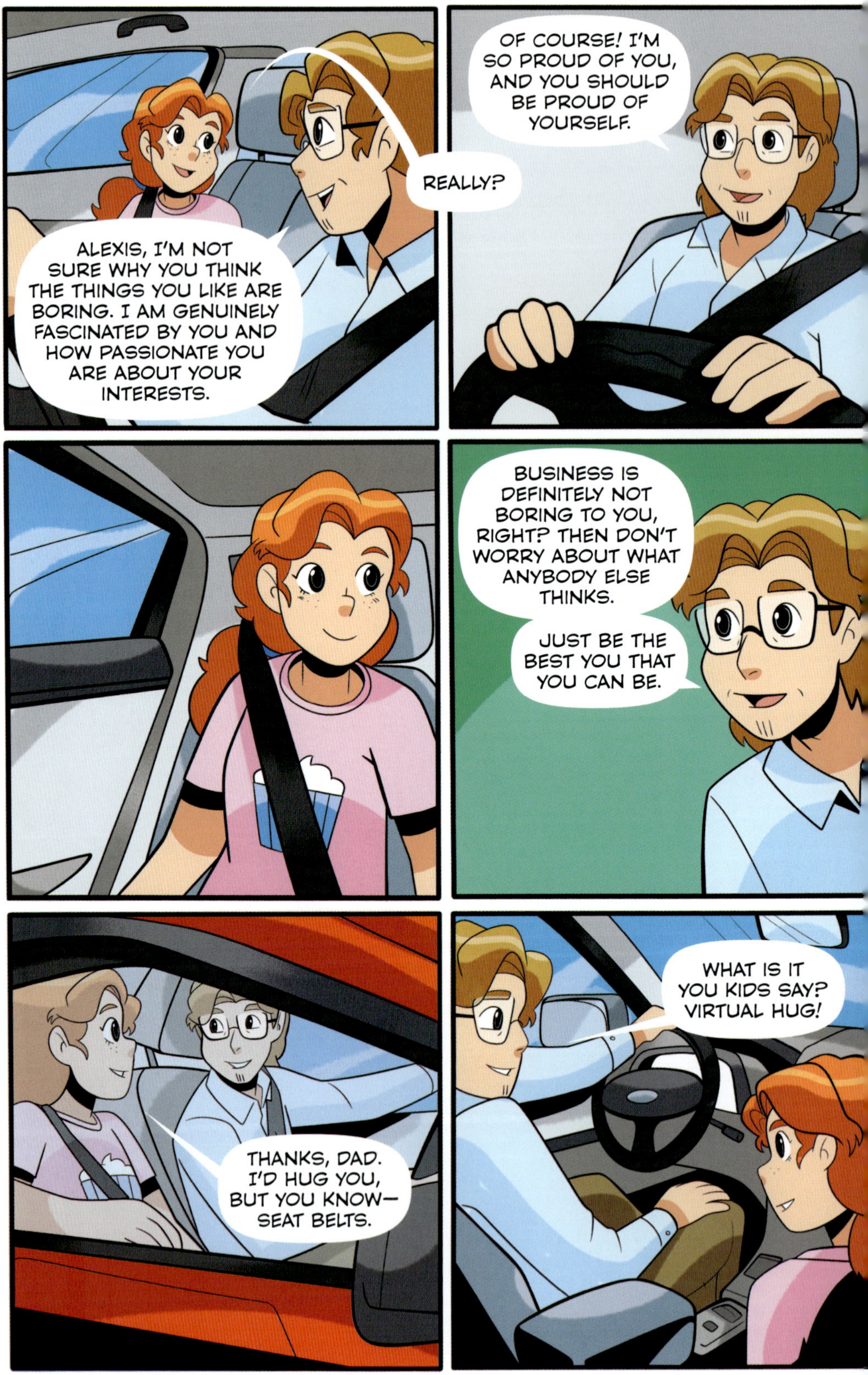
ALEXIS, I'M NOT SURE WHY YOU THINK THE THINGS YOU LIKE ARE BORING. I AM GENUINELY FASCINATED BY YOU AND HOW PASSIONATE YOU ARE ABOUT YOUR INTERESTS.
REALLY?
OF COURSE! I'M SO PROUD OF YOU, AND YOU SHOULD BE PROUD OF YOURSELF.
BUSINESS IS DEFINITELY NOT BORING TO YOU, RIGHT? THEN DON'T WORRY ABOUT WHAT ANYBODY ELSE THINKS.
JUST BE THE BEST YOU THAT YOU CAN BE.
THANKS, DAD. I'D HUG YOU, BUT YOU KNOW— SEAT BELTS.
WHAT IS IT YOU KIDS SAY? VIRTUAL HUG!

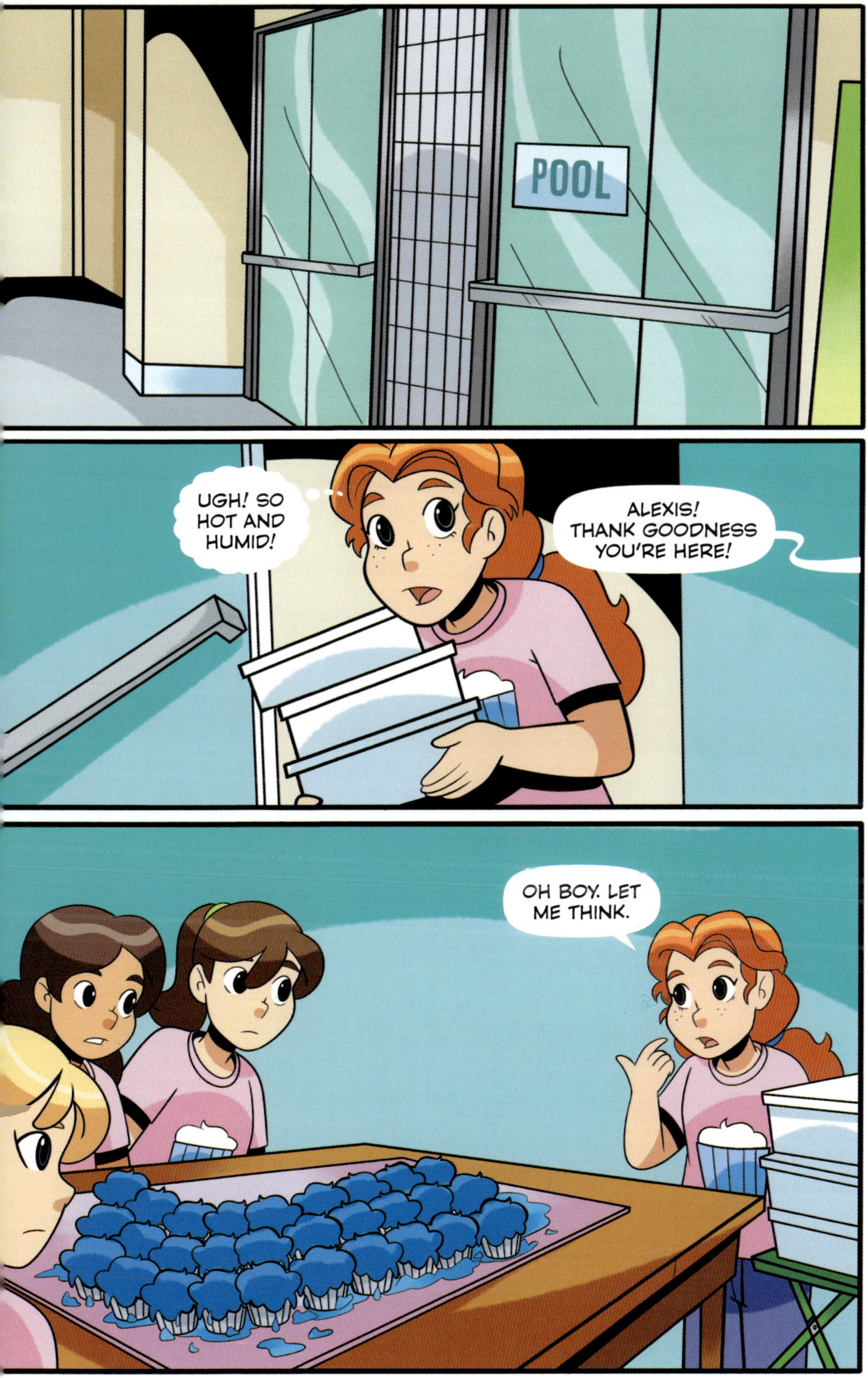
POOL
UGH! SO HOT AND HUMID!
ALEXIS! THANK GOODNESS YOU'RE HERE!
OH BOY. LET ME THINK.

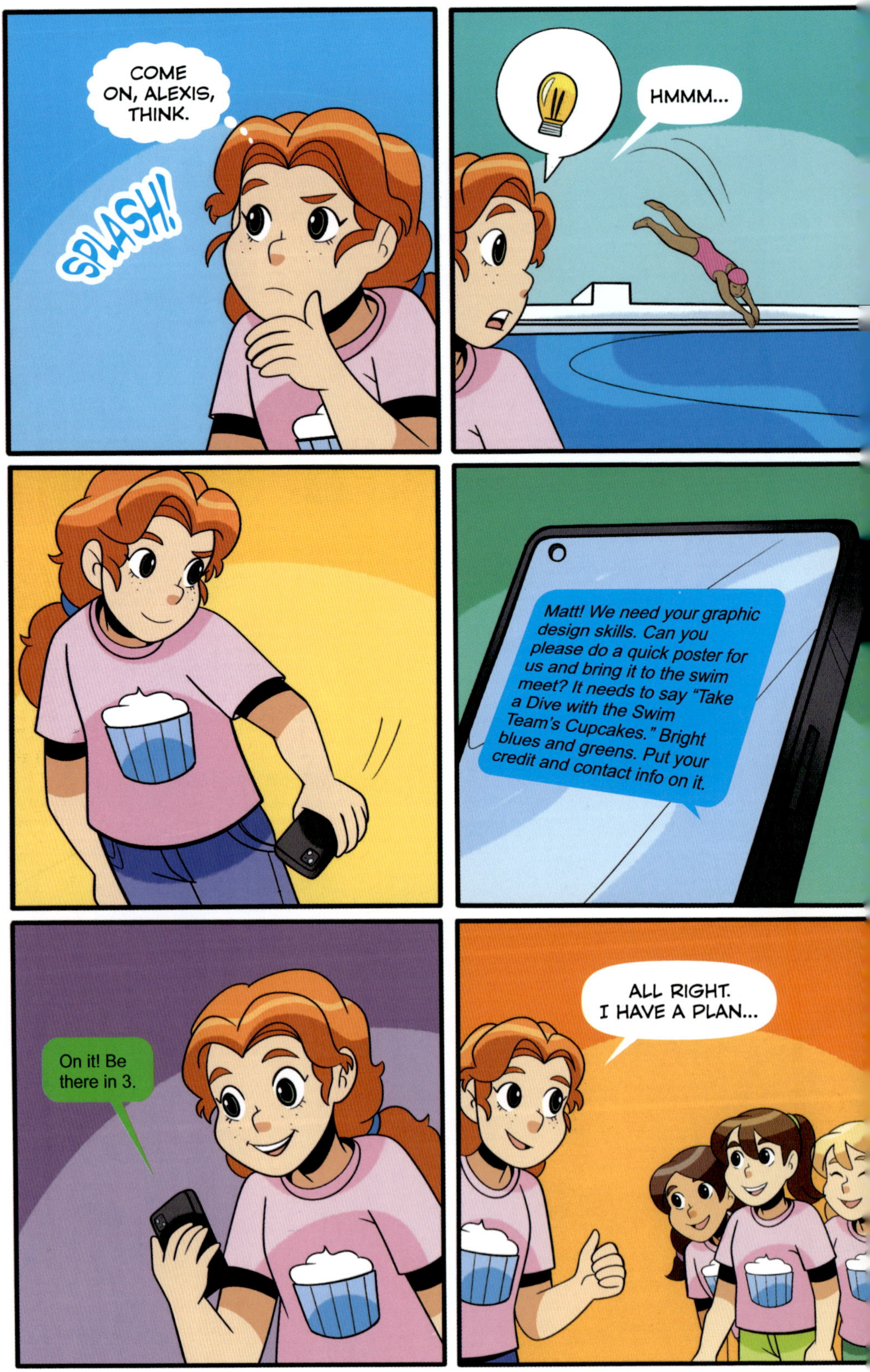
COME ON, ALEXIS, THINK.
SPLASH!
HMMM...
Matt! We need your graphic design skills. Can you please do a quick poster for us and bring it to the swim meet? It needs to say "Take a Dive with the Swim Team's Cupcakes." Bright blues and greens. Put your credit and contact info on it.
On it! Be there in 3.
ALL RIGHT. I HAVE A PLAN...

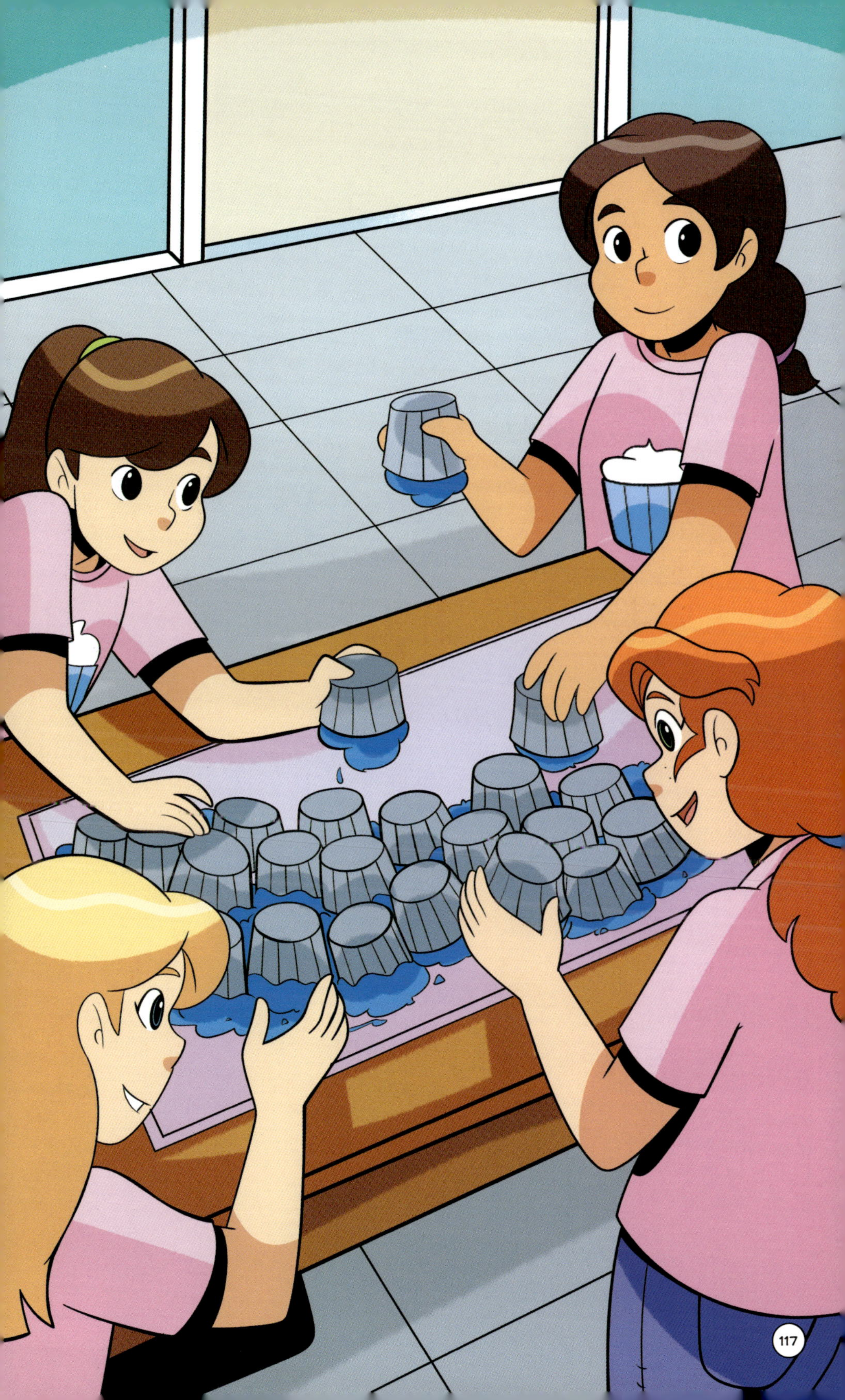

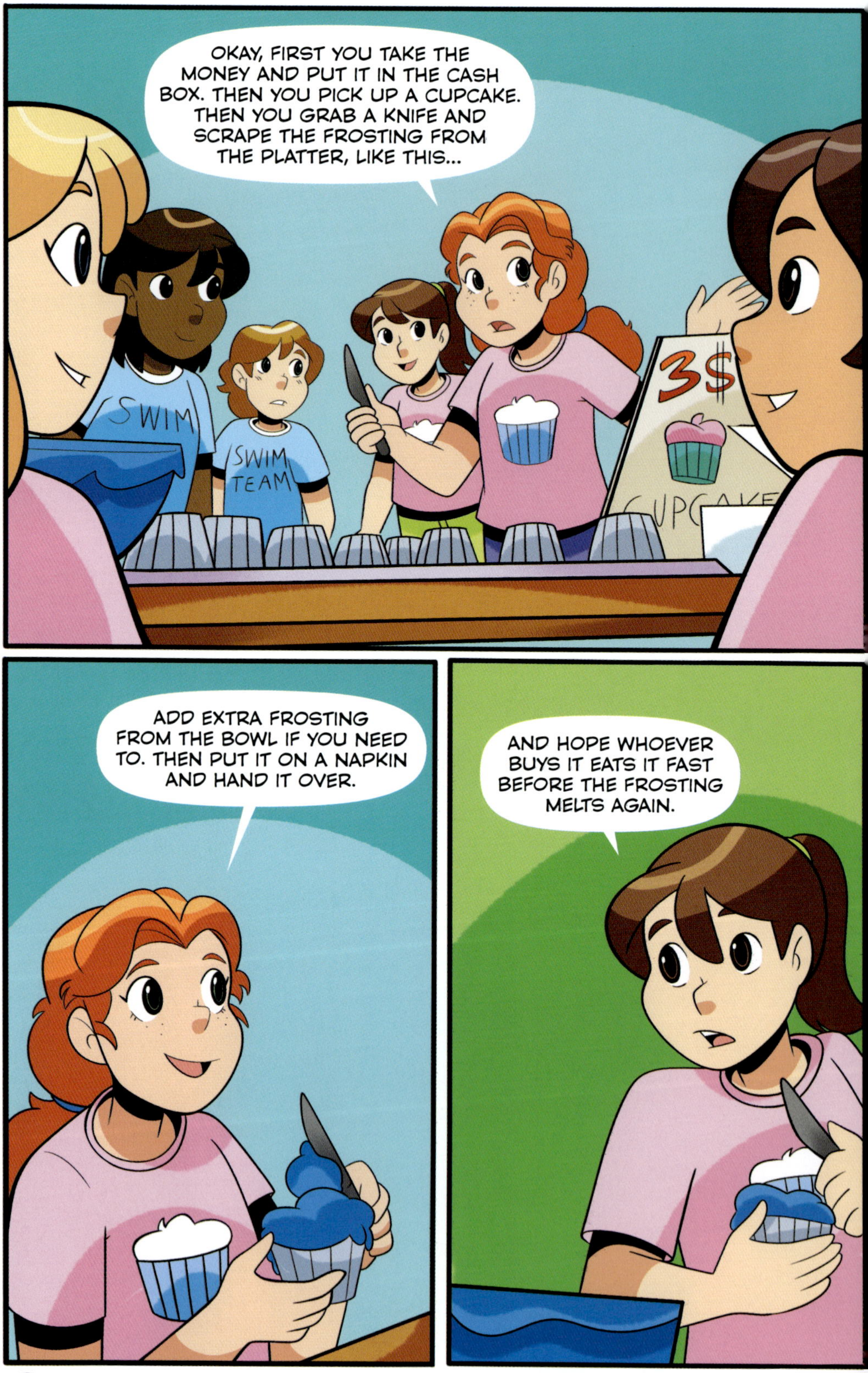
OKAY, FIRST YOU TAKE THE MONEY AND PUT IT IN THE CASH BOX. THEN YOU PICK UP A CUPCAKE. THEN YOU GRAB A KNIFE AND SCRAPE THE FROSTING FROM THE PLATTER, LIKE THIS...
SWIM
SWIM TEAM
3$
ADD EXTRA FROSTING FROM THE BOWL IF YOU NEED TO. THEN PUT IT ON A NAPKIN AND HAND IT OVER.
AND HOPE WHOEVER BUYS IT EATS IT FAST BEFORE THE FROSTING MELTS AGAIN.

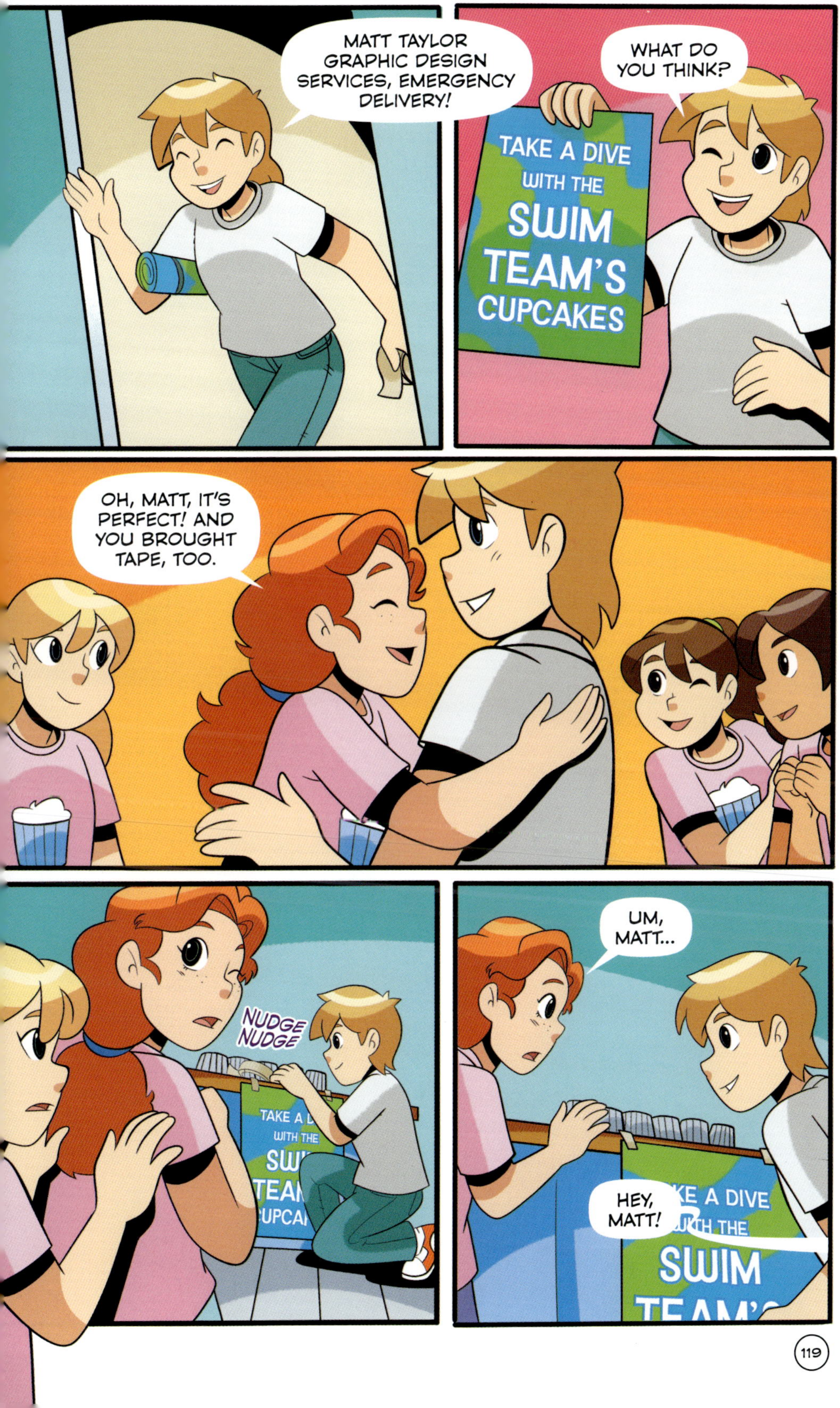
MATT TAYLOR GRAPHIC DESIGN SERVICES, EMERGENCY DELIVERY!
WHAT DO YOU THINK?
TAKE A DIVE WITH THE SWIM TEAM'S CUPCAKES
OH, MATT, IT'S PERFECT! AND YOU BROUGHT TAPE, TOO.
NUDGE NUDGE
UM, MATT...
HEY, MATT!

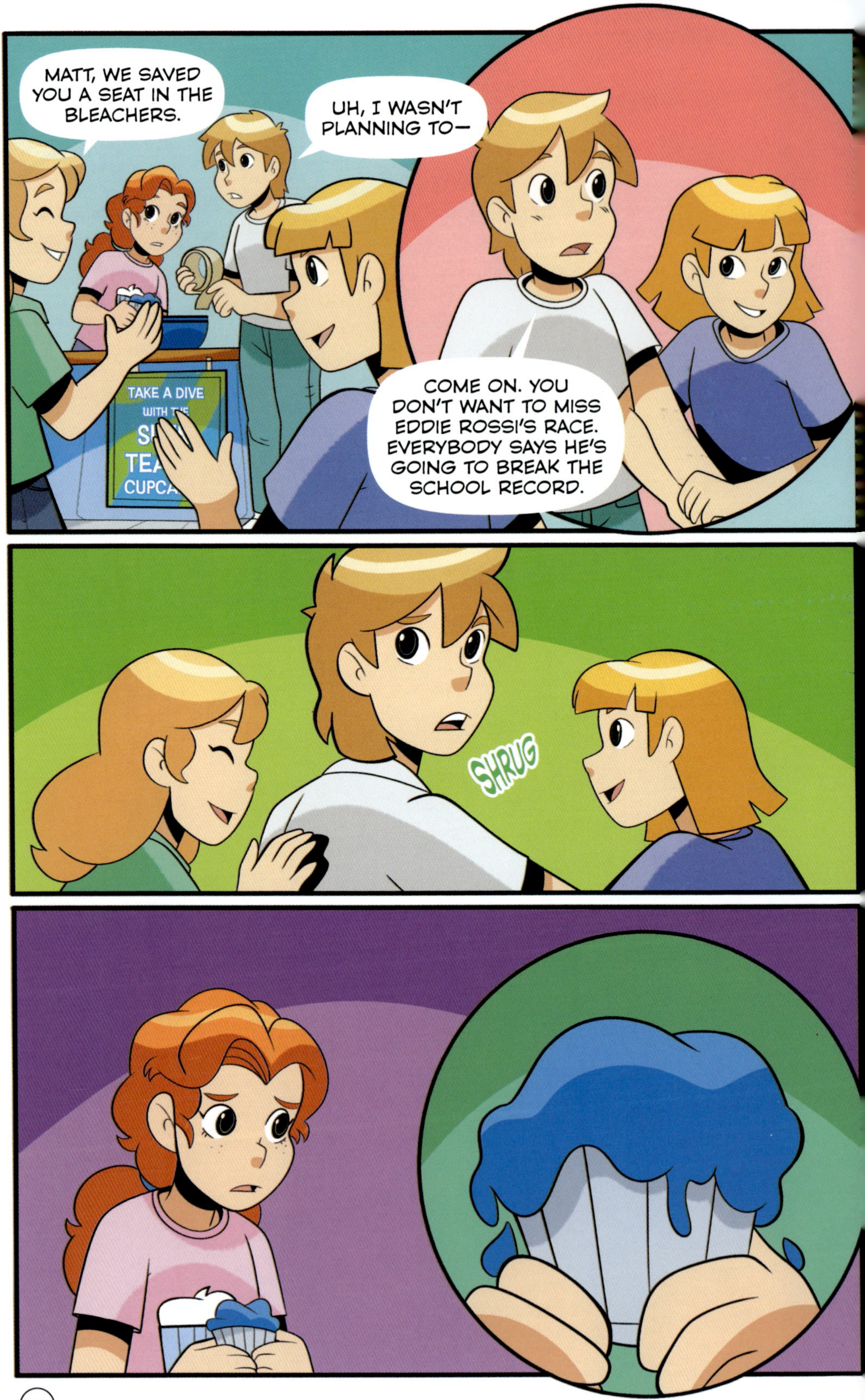
MATT, WE SAVED YOU A SEAT IN THE BLEACHERS.
UH, I WASN'T PLANNING TO—
COME ON. YOU DON'T WANT TO MISS EDDIE ROSSI'S RACE. EVERYBODY SAYS HE'S GOING TO BREAK THE SCHOOL RECORD.
TAKE A DIVE WITH THE
SHRUG

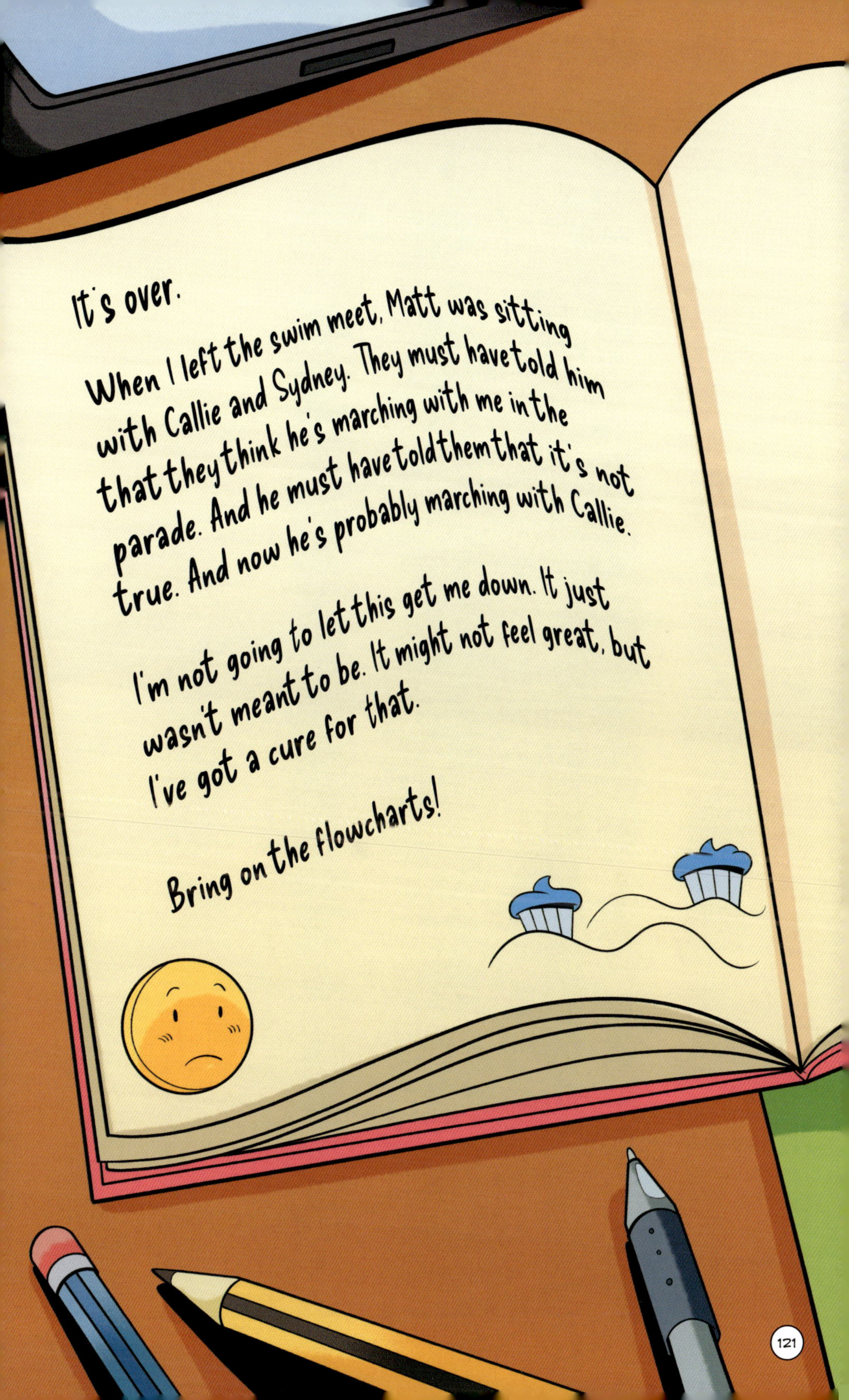
It's over.
When I left the swim meet, Matt was sitting with Callie and Sydney. They must have told him that they think he's marching with me in the parade. And he must have told them that it's not true. And now he's probably marching with Callie.
I'm not going to let this get me down. It just wasn't meant to be. It might not feel great, but I've got a cure for that.
Bring on the flowcharts!

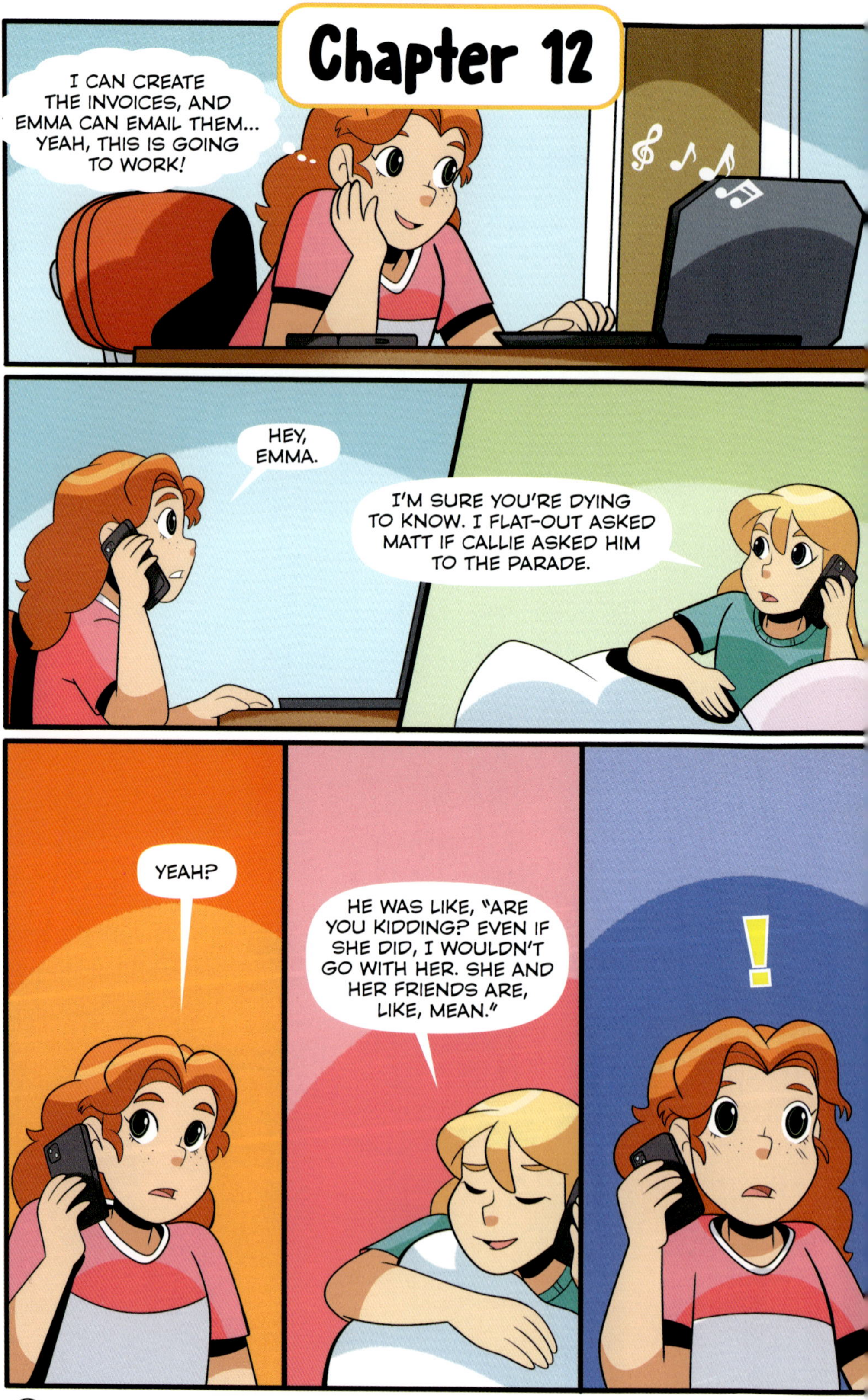
Chapter 12
I CAN CREATE THE INVOICES, AND EMMA CAN EMAIL THEM... YEAH, THIS IS GOING TO WORK!
HEY, EMMA.
I'M SURE YOU'RE DYING TO KNOW. I FLAT-OUT ASKED MATT IF CALLIE ASKED HIM TO THE PARADE.
YEAH?
HE WAS LIKE, "ARE YOU KIDDING? EVEN IF SHE DID, I WOULDN'T GO WITH HER. SHE AND HER FRIENDS ARE, LIKE, MEAN."
!

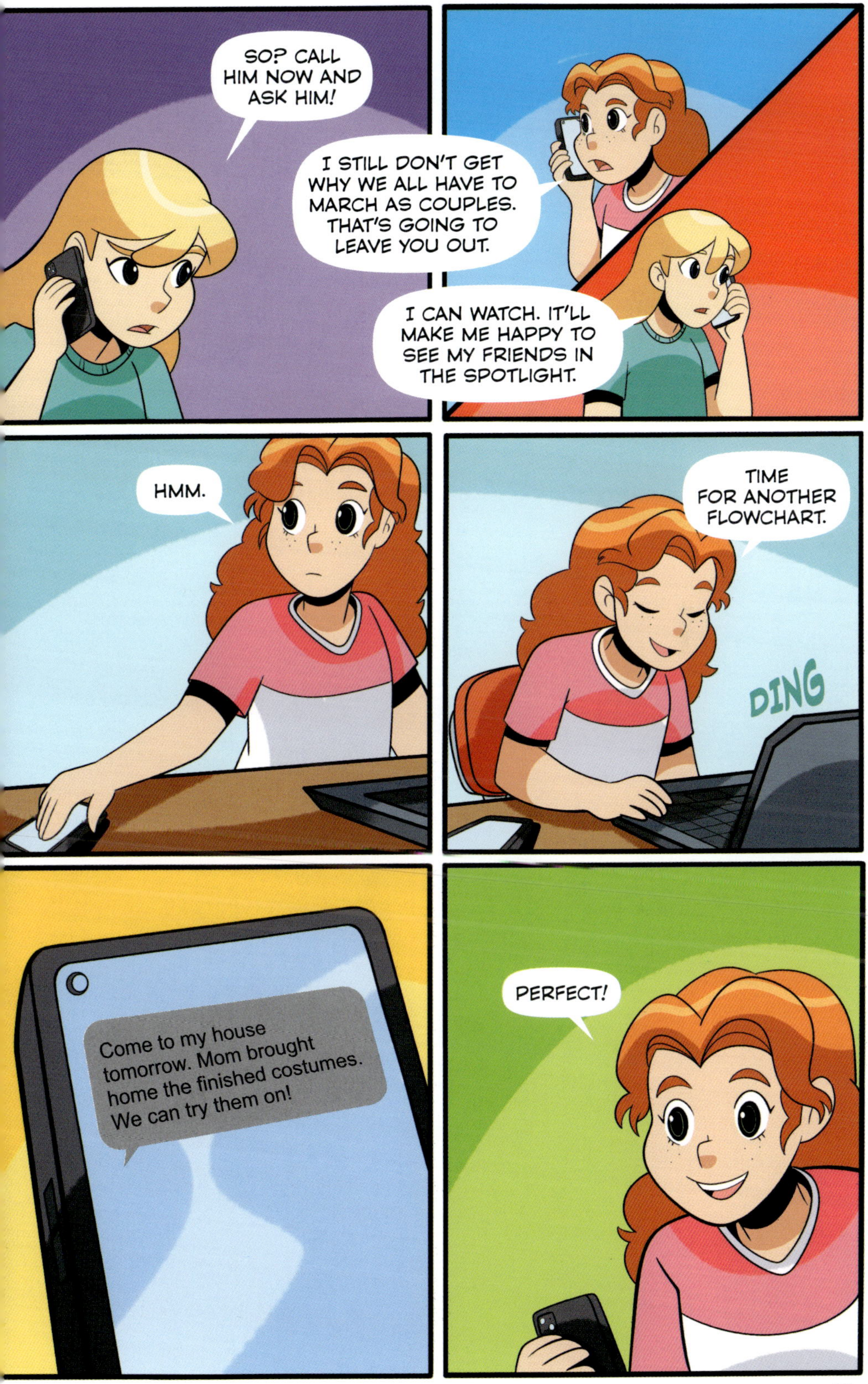
SO? CALL HIM NOW AND ASK HIM!
I STILL DON'T GET WHY WE ALL HAVE TO MARCH AS COUPLES. THAT'S GOING TO LEAVE YOU OUT.
I CAN WATCH. IT'LL MAKE ME HAPPY TO SEE MY FRIENDS IN THE SPOTLIGHT.
HMM.
TIME FOR ANOTHER FLOWCHART.
DING
Come to my house tomorrow. Mom brought home the finished costumes. We can try them on!
PERFECT!

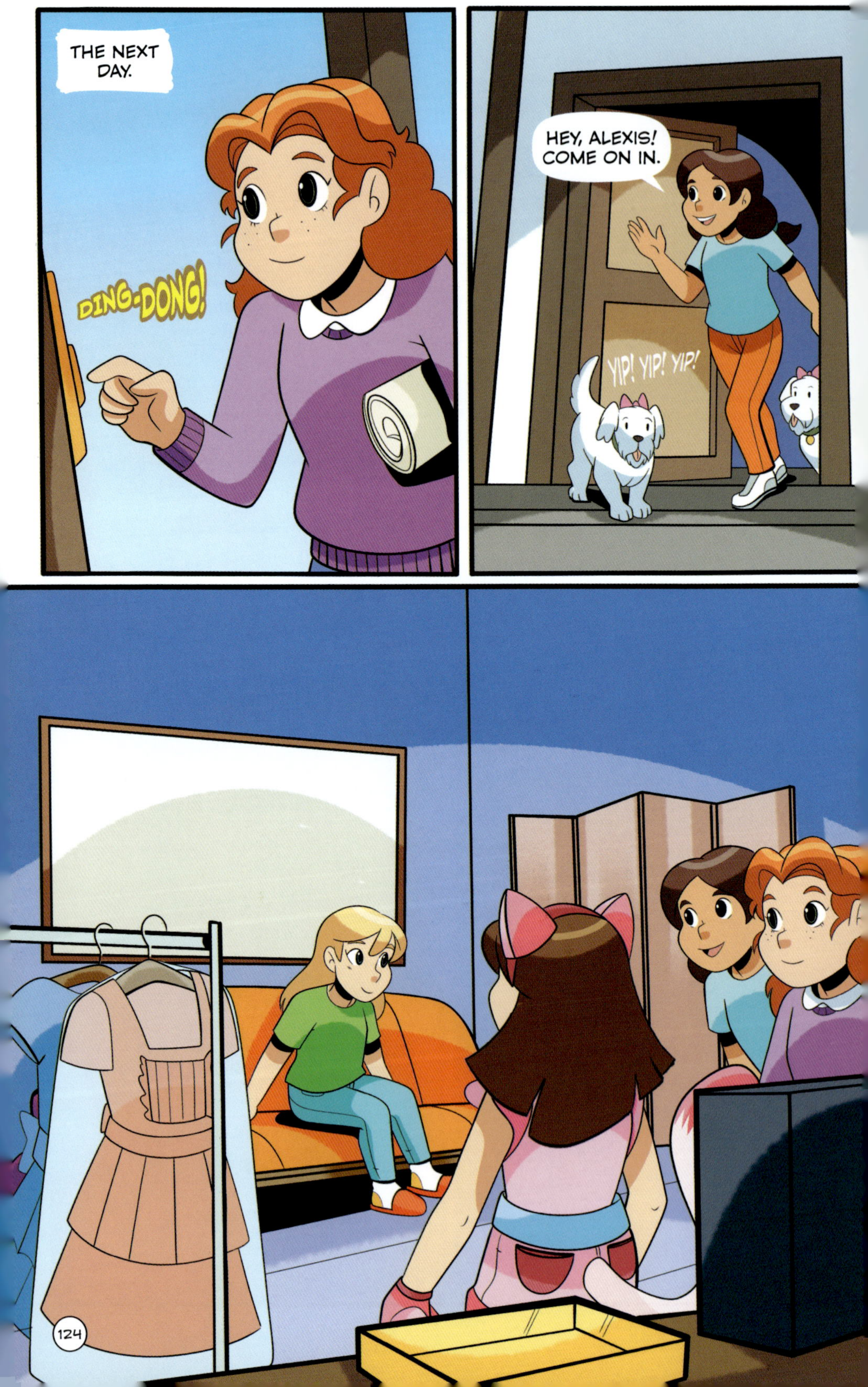
THE NEXT DAY.
DING-DONG!
HEY, ALEXIS! COME ON IN.
YIP! YIP! YIP!

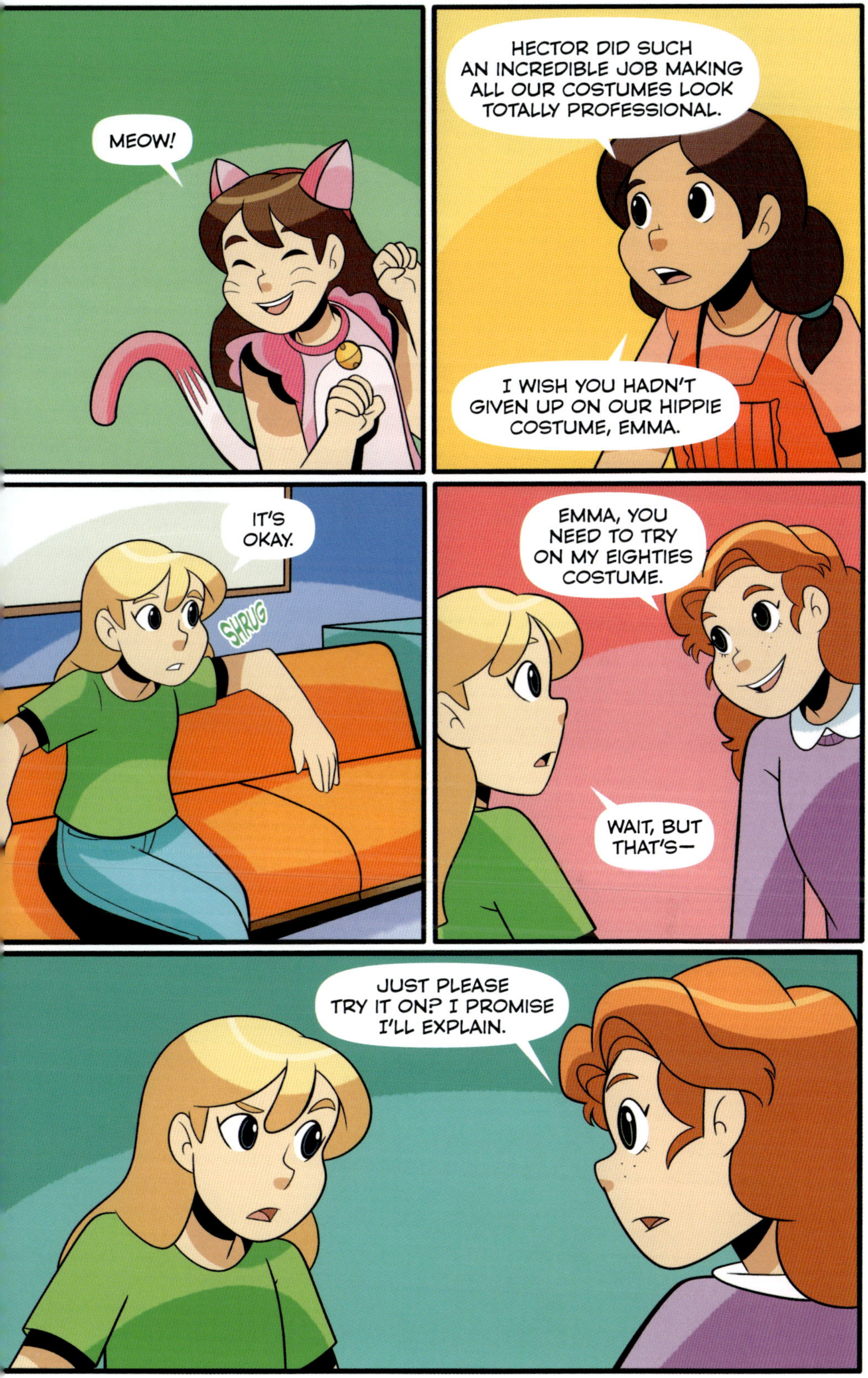
MEOW!
HECTOR DID SUCH AN INCREDIBLE JOB MAKING ALL OUR COSTUMES LOOK TOTALLY PROFESSIONAL.
I WISH YOU HADN'T GIVEN UP ON OUR HIPPIE COSTUME, EMMA.
IT'S OKAY.
SHRUG
EMMA, YOU NEED TO TRY ON MY EIGHTIES COSTUME.
WAIT, BUT THAT'S—
JUST PLEASE TRY IT ON? I PROMISE I'LL EXPLAIN.

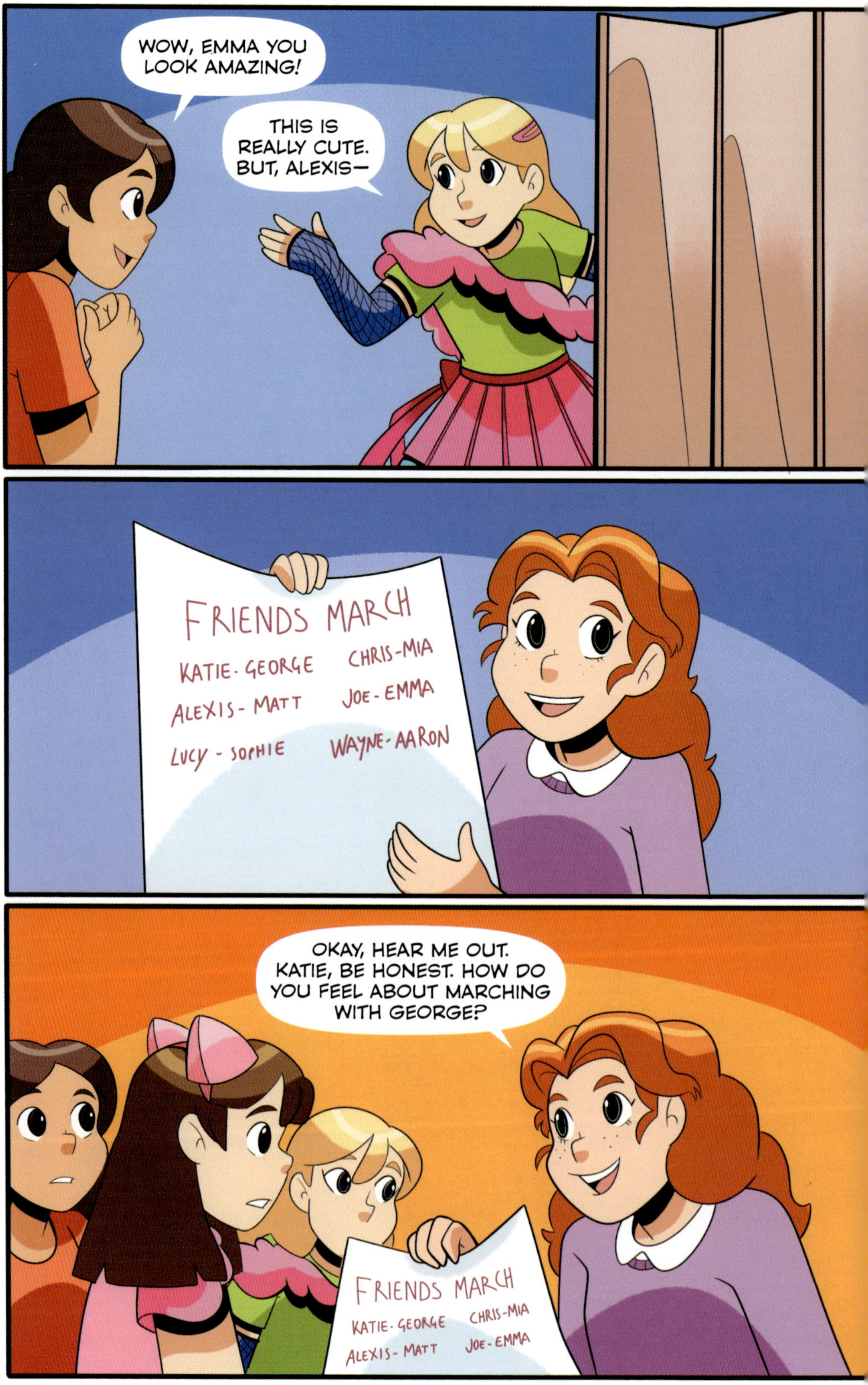
WOW, EMMA YOU LOOK AMAZING!
THIS IS REALLY CUTE. BUT, ALEXIS—
FRIENDS MARCH
KATIE - GEORGE
ALEXIS - MATT
LUCY - SOPHIE
CHRIS - MIA
JOE - EMMA
WAYNE - AARON
OKAY, HEAR ME OUT. KATIE, BE HONEST. HOW DO YOU FEEL ABOUT MARCHING WITH GEORGE?
FRIENDS MARCH
KATIE - GEORGE
CHRIS - MIA
ALEXIS - MATT
JOE - EMMA

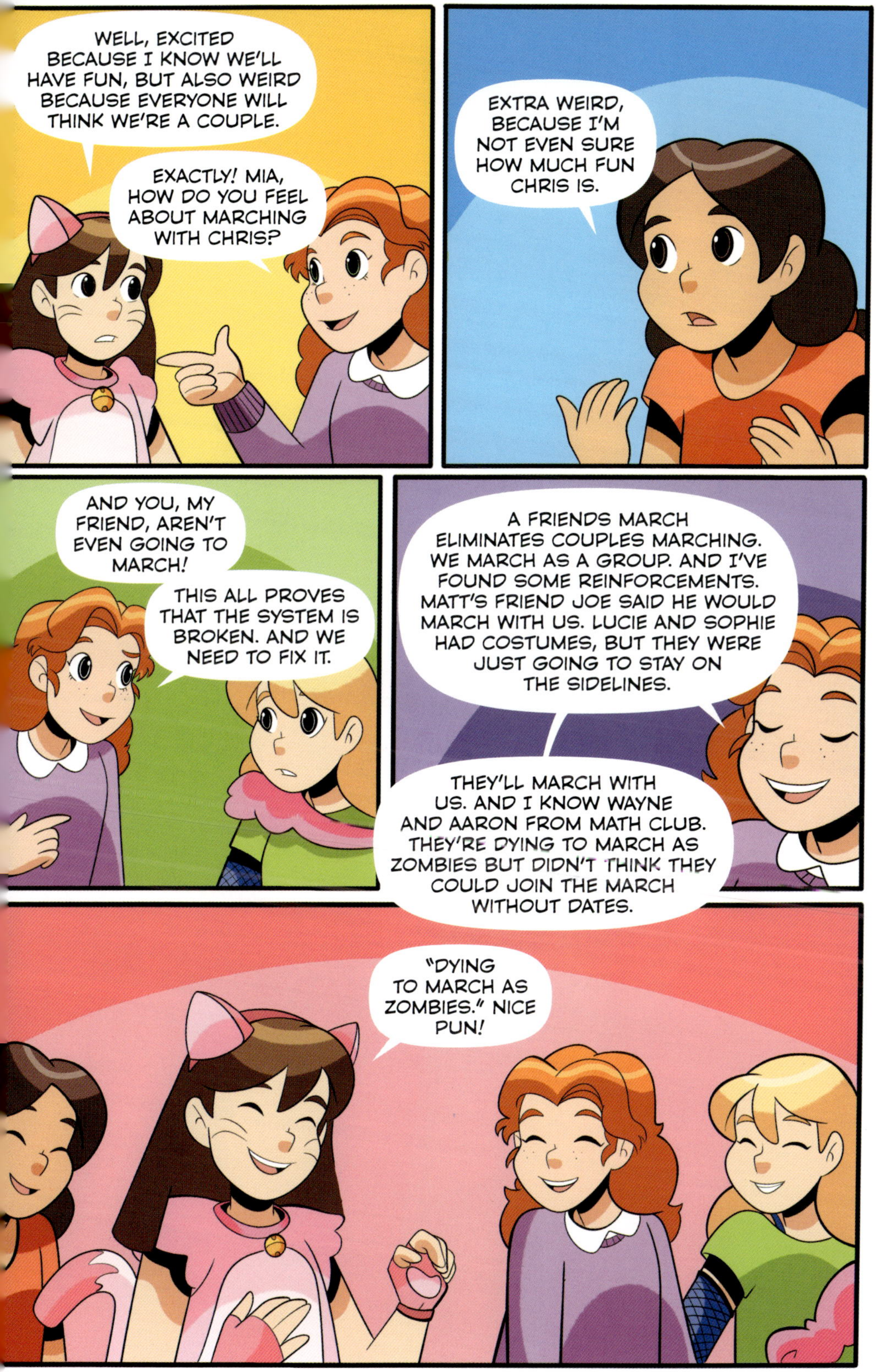
WELL, EXCITED BECAUSE I KNOW WE'LL HAVE FUN, BUT ALSO WEIRD BECAUSE EVERYONE WILL THINK WE'RE A COUPLE.
EXACTLY! MIA, HOW DO YOU FEEL ABOUT MARCHING WITH CHRIS?
EXTRA WEIRD, BECAUSE I'M NOT EVEN SURE HOW MUCH FUN CHRIS IS.
AND YOU, MY FRIEND, AREN'T EVEN GOING TO MARCH!
THIS ALL PROVES THAT THE SYSTEM IS BROKEN. AND WE NEED TO FIX IT.
A FRIENDS MARCH ELIMINATES COUPLES MARCHING. WE MARCH AS A GROUP. AND I'VE FOUND SOME REINFORCEMENTS. MATT'S FRIEND JOE SAID HE WOULD MARCH WITH US. LUCIE AND SOPHIE HAD COSTUMES, BUT THEY WERE JUST GOING TO STAY ON THE SIDELINES.
THEY'LL MARCH WITH US. AND I KNOW WAYNE AND AARON FROM MATH CLUB. THEY'RE DYING TO MARCH AS ZOMBIES BUT DIDN'T THINK THEY COULD JOIN THE MARCH WITHOUT DATES.
"DYING TO MARCH AS ZOMBIES." NICE PUN!

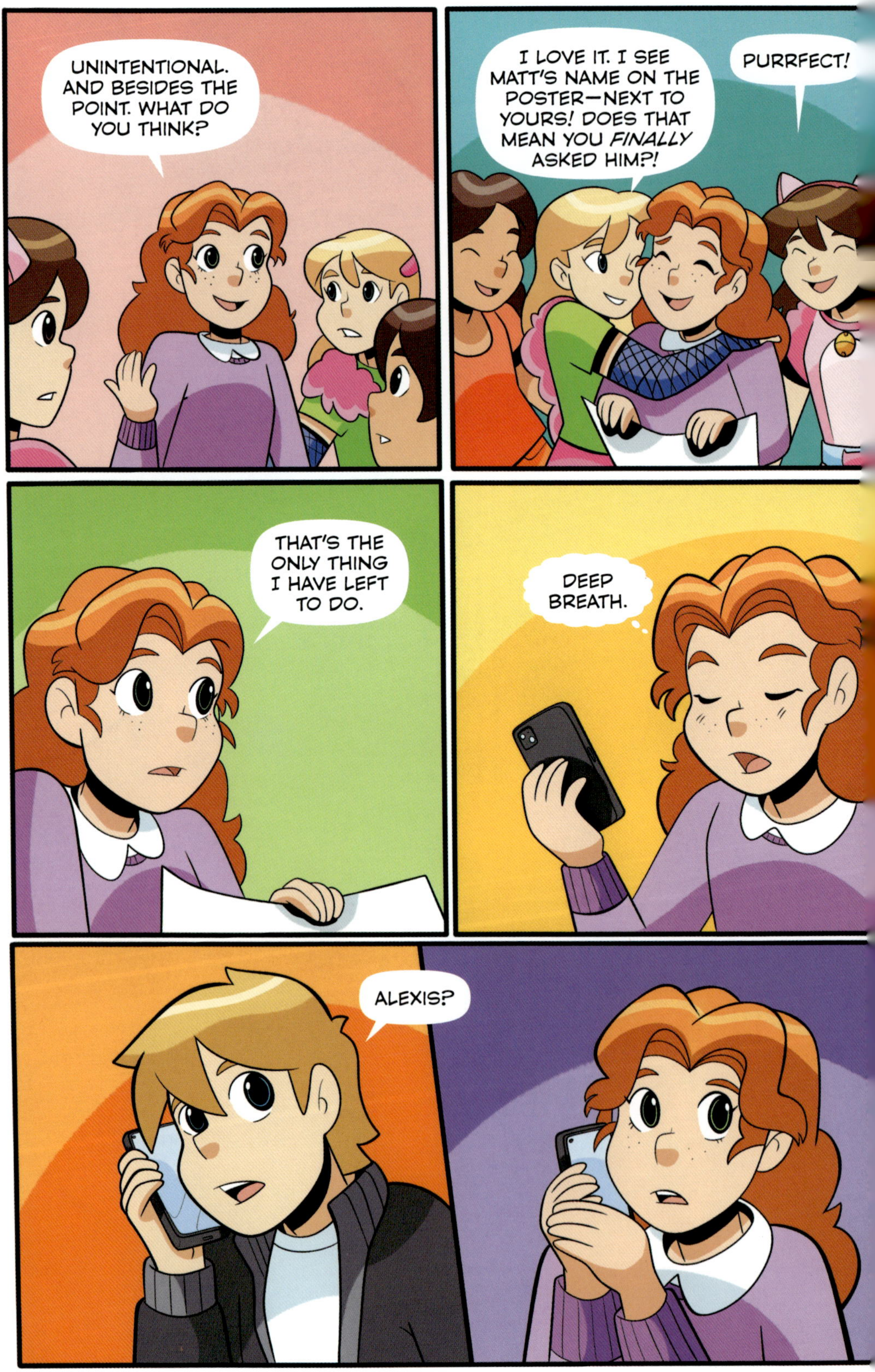
UNINTENTIONAL. AND BESIDES THE POINT. WHAT DO YOU THINK?
I LOVE IT. I SEE MATT'S NAME ON THE POSTER—NEXT TO YOURS! DOES THAT MEAN YOU *FINALLY* ASKED HIM?!
PURRFECT!
THAT'S THE ONLY THING I HAVE LEFT TO DO.
DEEP BREATH.
ALEXIS?

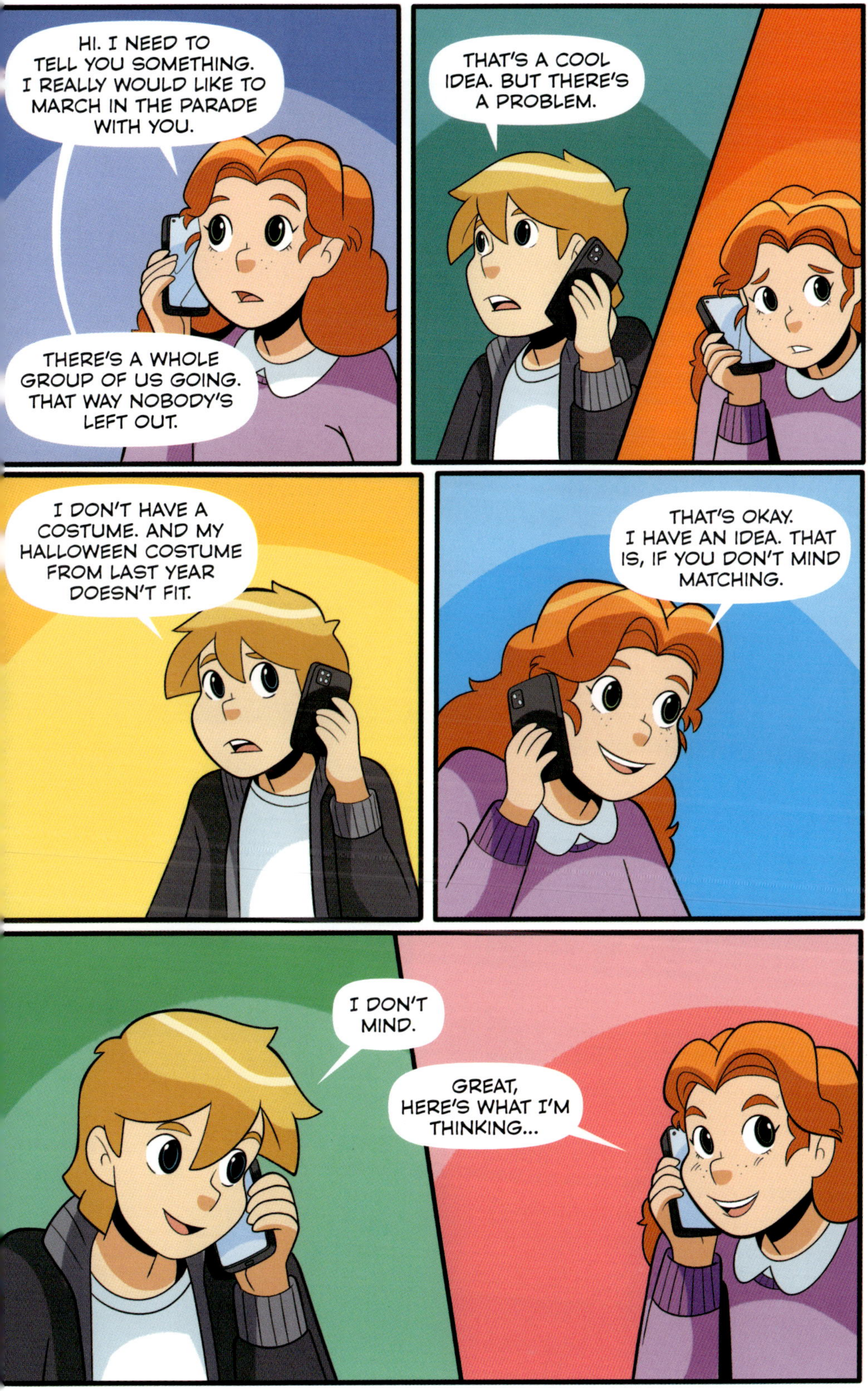
HI. I NEED TO TELL YOU SOMETHING. I REALLY WOULD LIKE TO MARCH IN THE PARADE WITH YOU.
THERE'S A WHOLE GROUP OF US GOING. THAT WAY NOBODY'S LEFT OUT.
THAT'S A COOL IDEA. BUT THERE'S A PROBLEM.
I DON'T HAVE A COSTUME. AND MY HALLOWEEN COSTUME FROM LAST YEAR DOESN'T FIT.
THAT'S OKAY. I HAVE AN IDEA. THAT IS, IF YOU DON'T MIND MATCHING.
I DON'T MIND.
GREAT, HERE'S WHAT I'M THINKING...

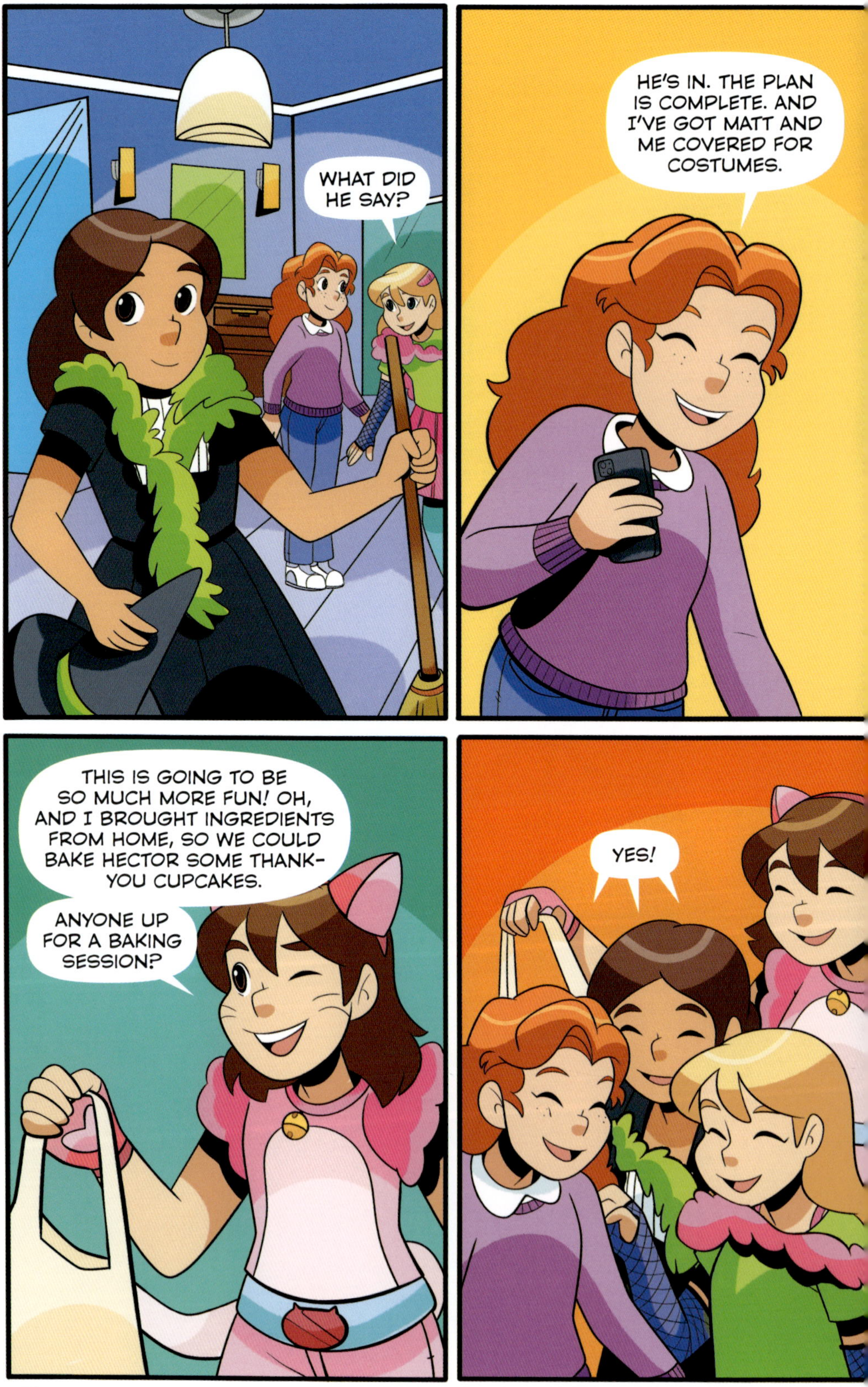
WHAT DID HE SAY?
HE'S IN. THE PLAN IS COMPLETE. AND I'VE GOT MATT AND ME COVERED FOR COSTUMES.
THIS IS GOING TO BE SO MUCH MORE FUN! OH, AND I BROUGHT INGREDIENTS FROM HOME, SO WE COULD BAKE HECTOR SOME THANK-YOU CUPCAKES.
ANYONE UP FOR A BAKING SESSION?
YES!

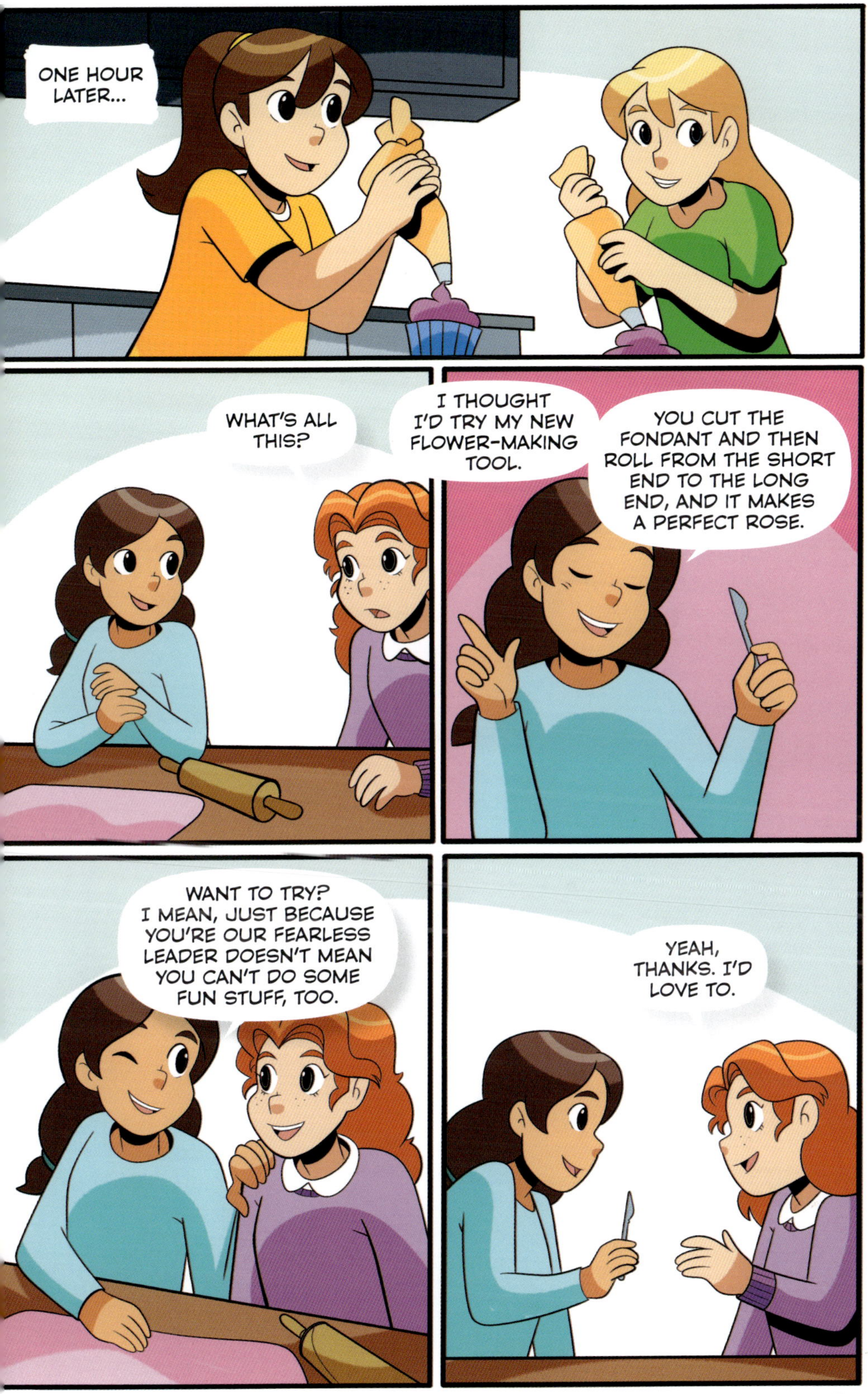
ONE HOUR LATER...
WHAT'S ALL THIS?
I THOUGHT I'D TRY MY NEW FLOWER-MAKING TOOL.
YOU CUT THE FONDANT AND THEN ROLL FROM THE SHORT END TO THE LONG END, AND IT MAKES A PERFECT ROSE.
WANT TO TRY? I MEAN, JUST BECAUSE YOU'RE OUR FEARLESS LEADER DOESN'T MEAN YOU CAN'T DO SOME FUN STUFF, TOO.
YEAH, THANKS. I'D LOVE TO.

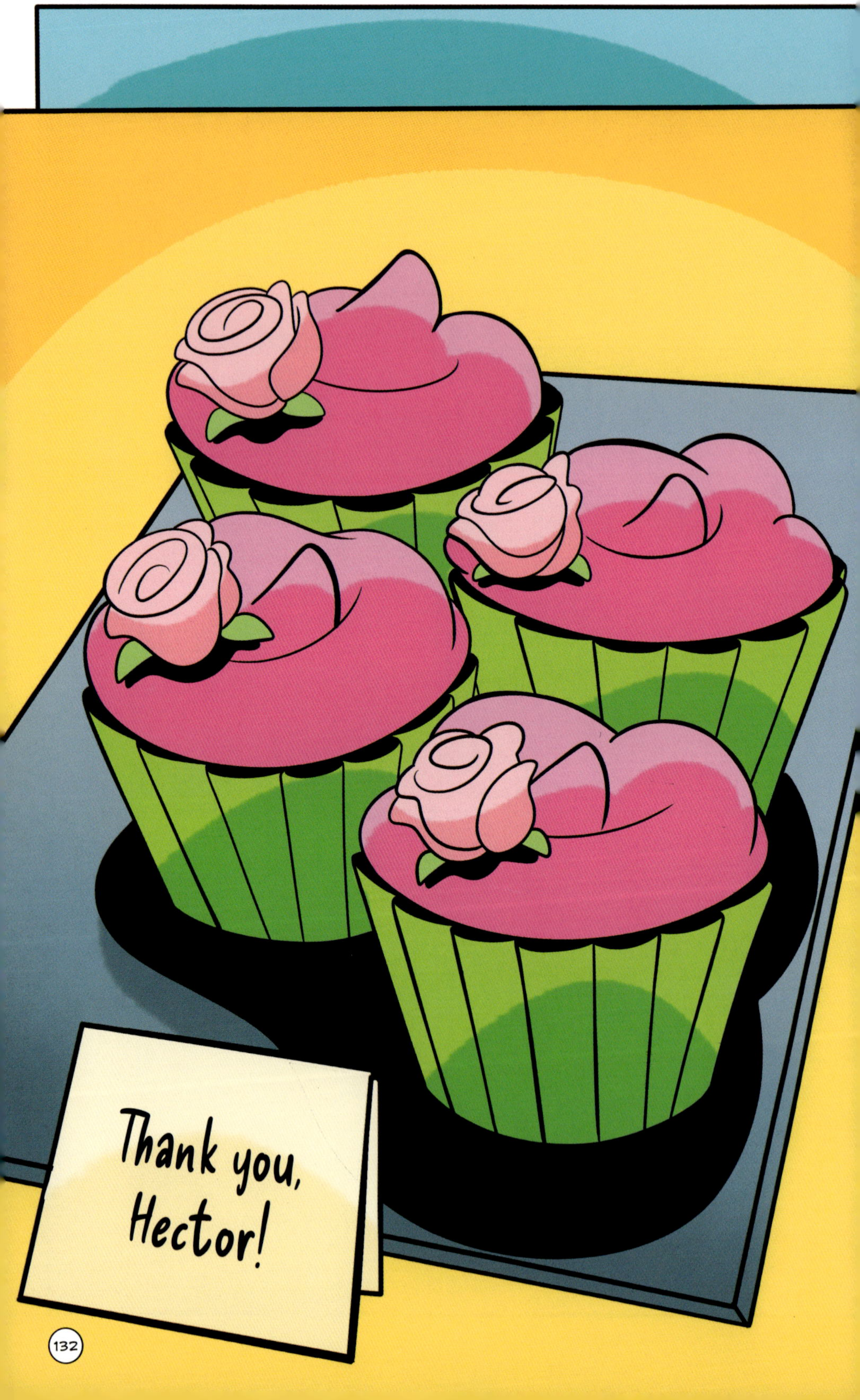
Thank you,
Hector!

Chapter 13

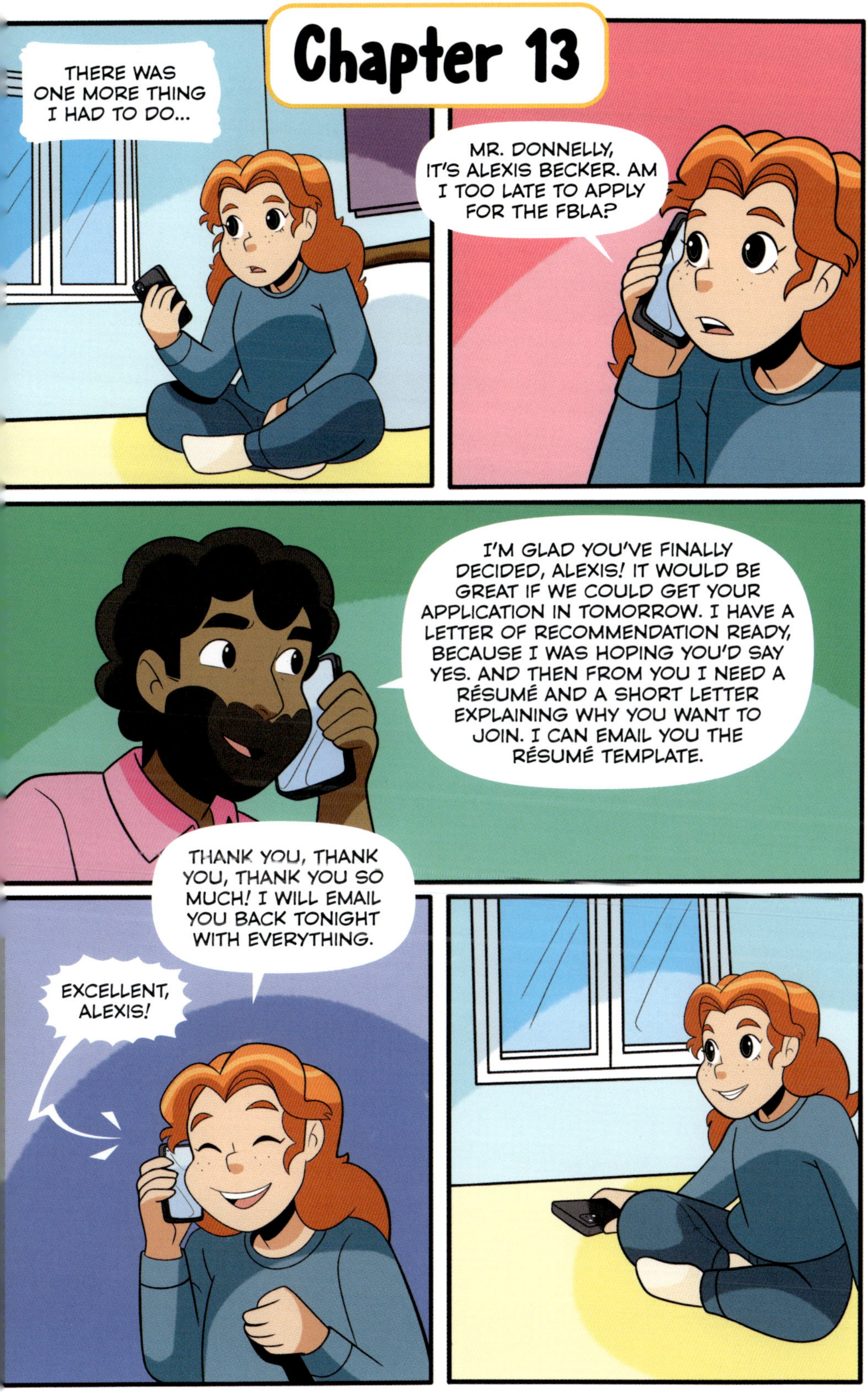

THERE WAS ONE MORE THING I HAD TO DO...
MR. DONNELLY, IT'S ALEXIS BECKER. AM I TOO LATE TO APPLY FOR THE FBLA?
I'M GLAD YOU'VE FINALLY DECIDED, ALEXIS! IT WOULD BE GREAT IF WE COULD GET YOUR APPLICATION IN TOMORROW. I HAVE A LETTER OF RECOMMENDATION READY, BECAUSE I WAS HOPING YOU'D SAY YES. AND THEN FROM YOU I NEED A RÉSUMÉ AND A SHORT LETTER EXPLAINING WHY YOU WANT TO JOIN. I CAN EMAIL YOU THE RÉSUMÉ TEMPLATE.
THANK YOU, THANK YOU, THANK YOU SO MUCH! I WILL EMAIL YOU BACK TONIGHT WITH EVERYTHING.
EXCELLENT, ALEXIS!

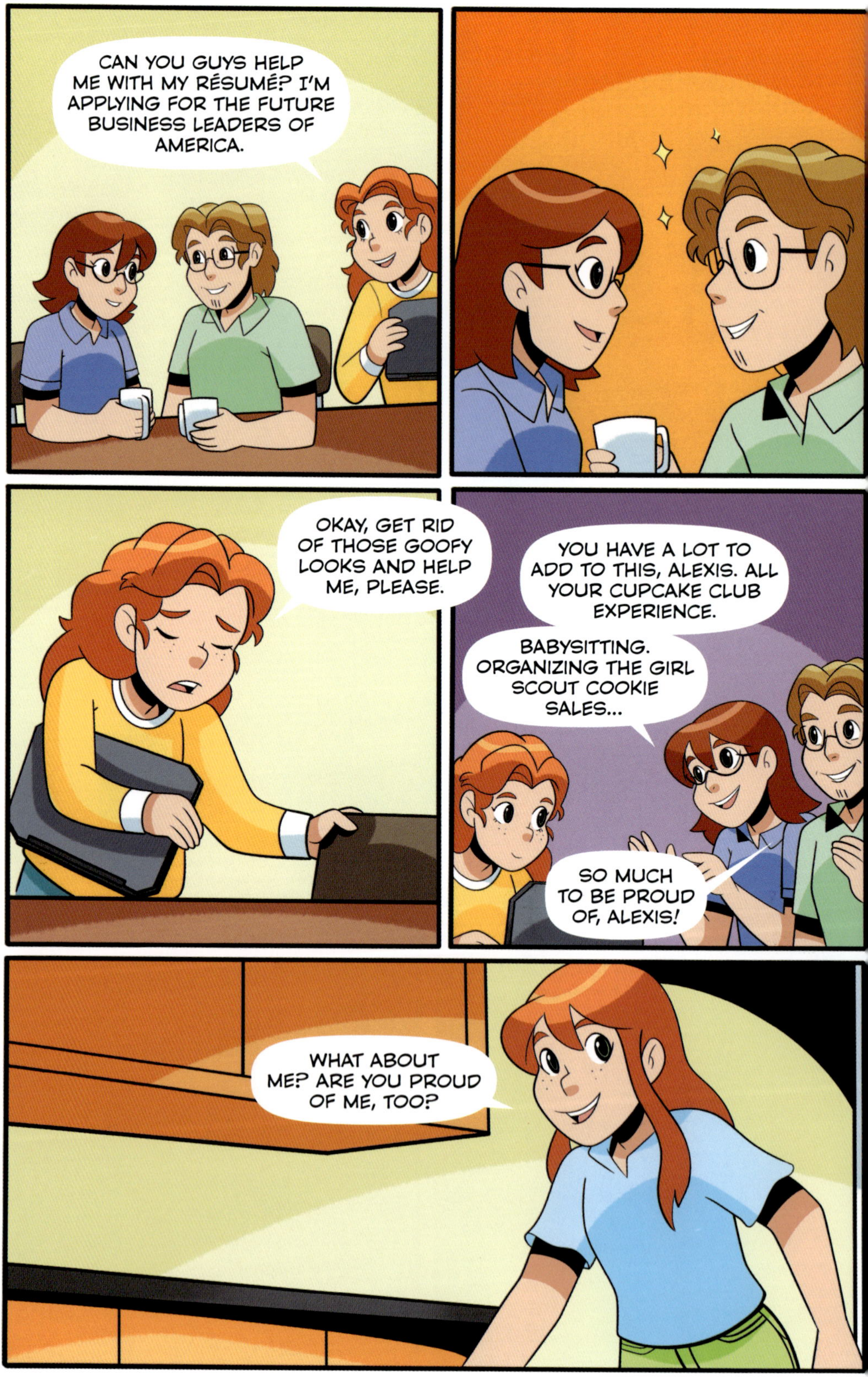
CAN YOU GUYS HELP ME WITH MY RÉSUMÉ? I'M APPLYING FOR THE FUTURE BUSINESS LEADERS OF AMERICA.
OKAY, GET RID OF THOSE GOOFY LOOKS AND HELP ME, PLEASE.
YOU HAVE A LOT TO ADD TO THIS, ALEXIS. ALL YOUR CUPCAKE CLUB EXPERIENCE.
BABYSITTING. ORGANIZING THE GIRL SCOUT COOKIE SALES...
SO MUCH TO BE PROUD OF, ALEXIS!
WHAT ABOUT ME? ARE YOU PROUD OF ME, TOO?

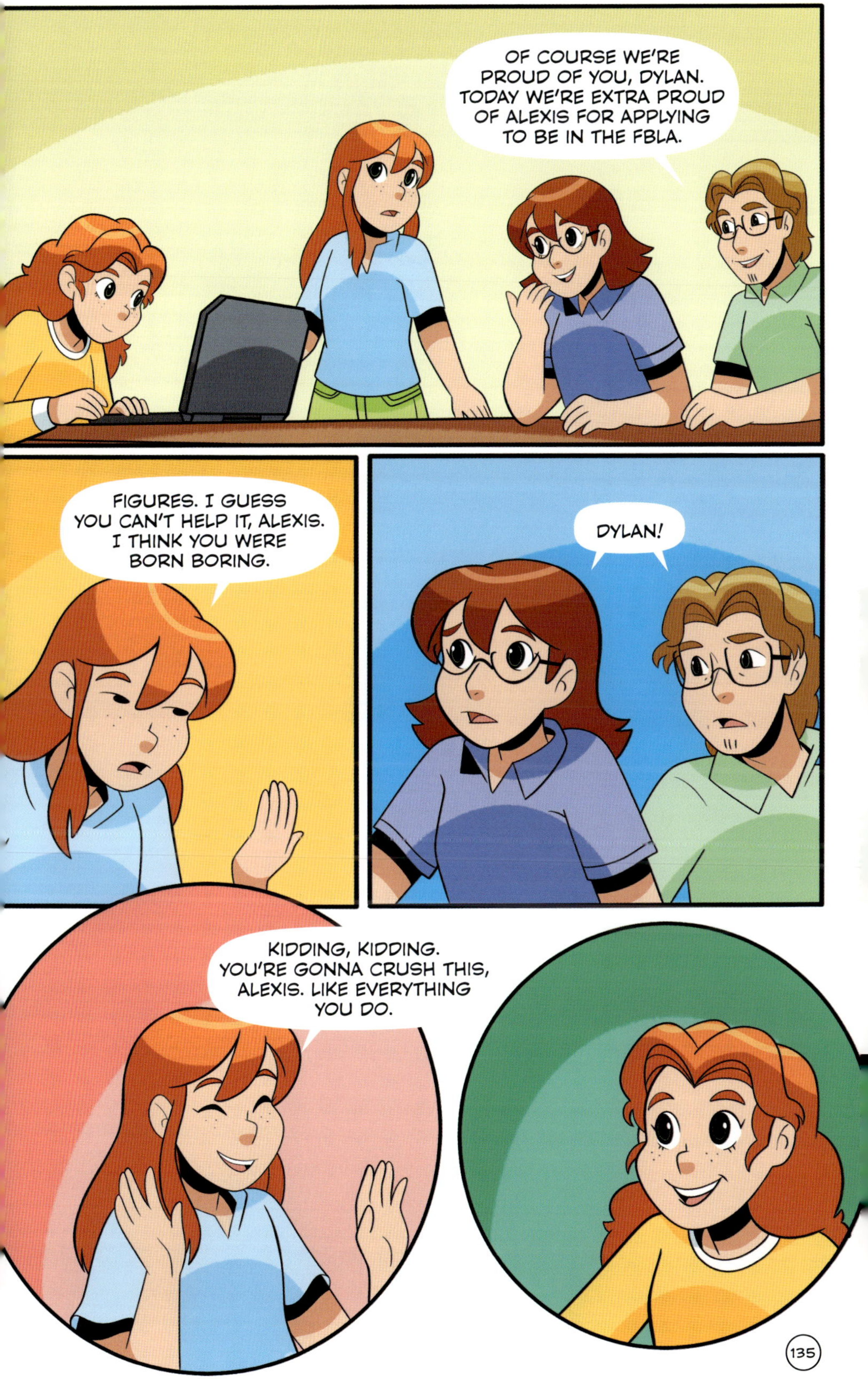
OF COURSE WE'RE PROUD OF YOU, DYLAN. TODAY WE'RE EXTRA PROUD OF ALEXIS FOR APPLYING TO BE IN THE FBLA.
FIGURES. I GUESS YOU CAN'T HELP IT, ALEXIS. I THINK YOU WERE BORN BORING.
DYLAN!
KIDDING, KIDDING. YOU'RE GONNA CRUSH THIS, ALEXIS. LIKE EVERYTHING YOU DO.

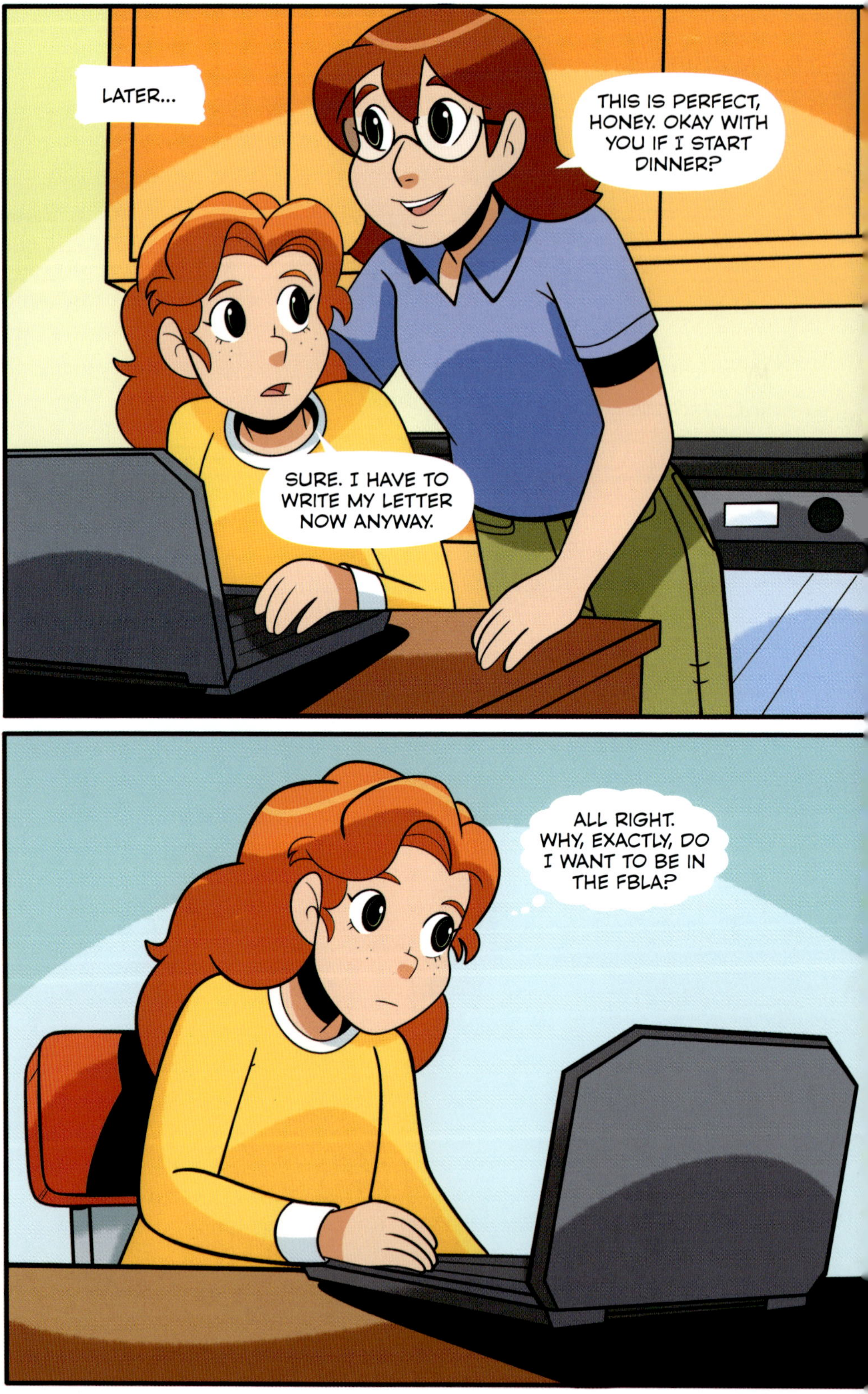
LATER...
THIS IS PERFECT, HONEY. OKAY WITH YOU IF I START DINNER?
SURE. I HAVE TO WRITE MY LETTER NOW ANYWAY.
ALL RIGHT. WHY, EXACTLY, DO I WANT TO BE IN THE FBLA?

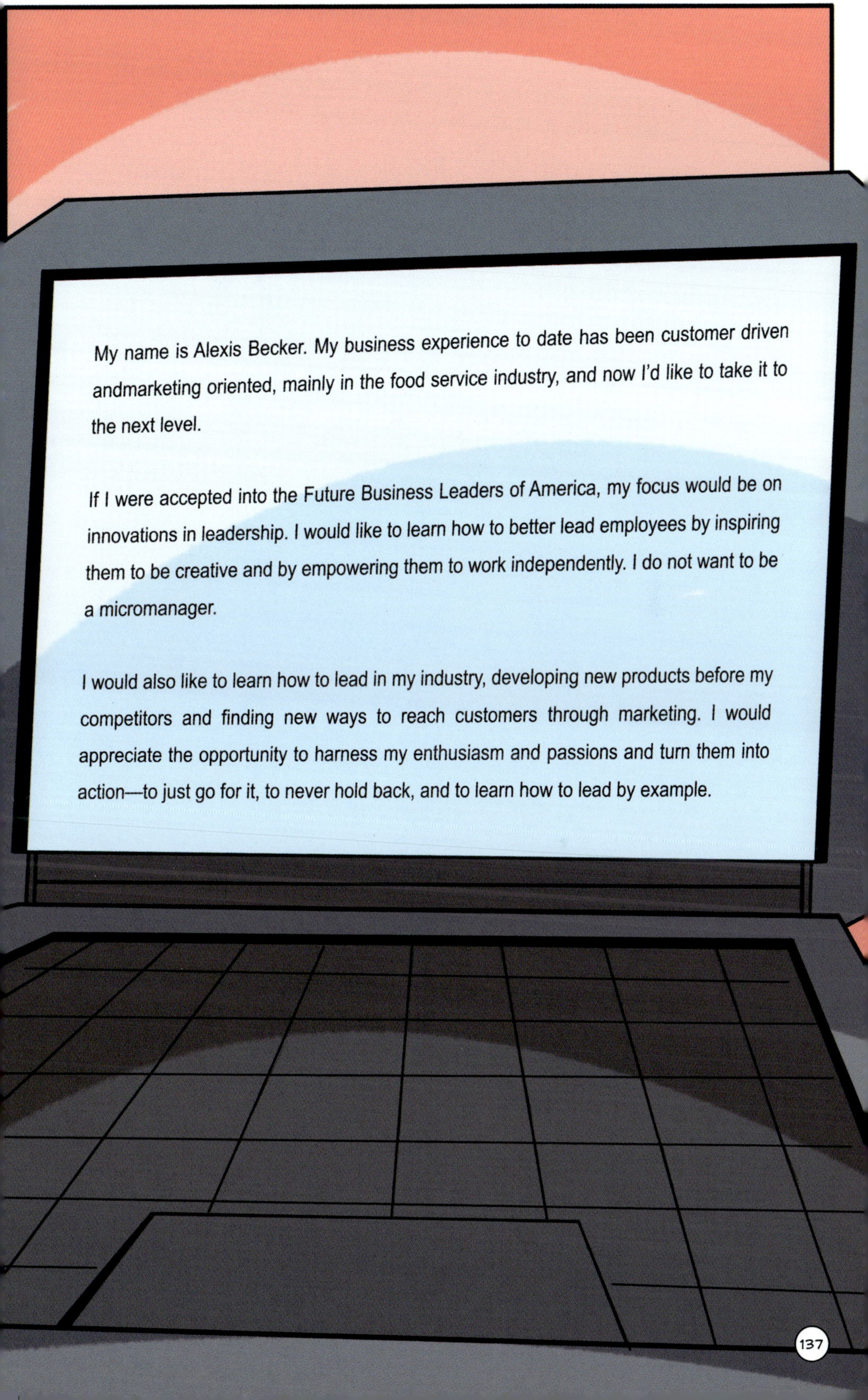
My name is Alexis Becker. My business experience to date has been customer driven andmarketing oriented, mainly in the food service industry, and now I'd like to take it to the next level.
If I were accepted into the Future Business Leaders of America, my focus would be on innovations in leadership. I would like to learn how to better lead employees by inspiring them to be creative and by empowering them to work independently. I do not want to be a micromanager.
I would also like to learn how to lead in my industry, developing new products before my competitors and finding new ways to reach customers through marketing. I would appreciate the opportunity to harness my enthusiasm and passions and turn them into action—to just go for it, to never hold back, and to learn how to lead by example.

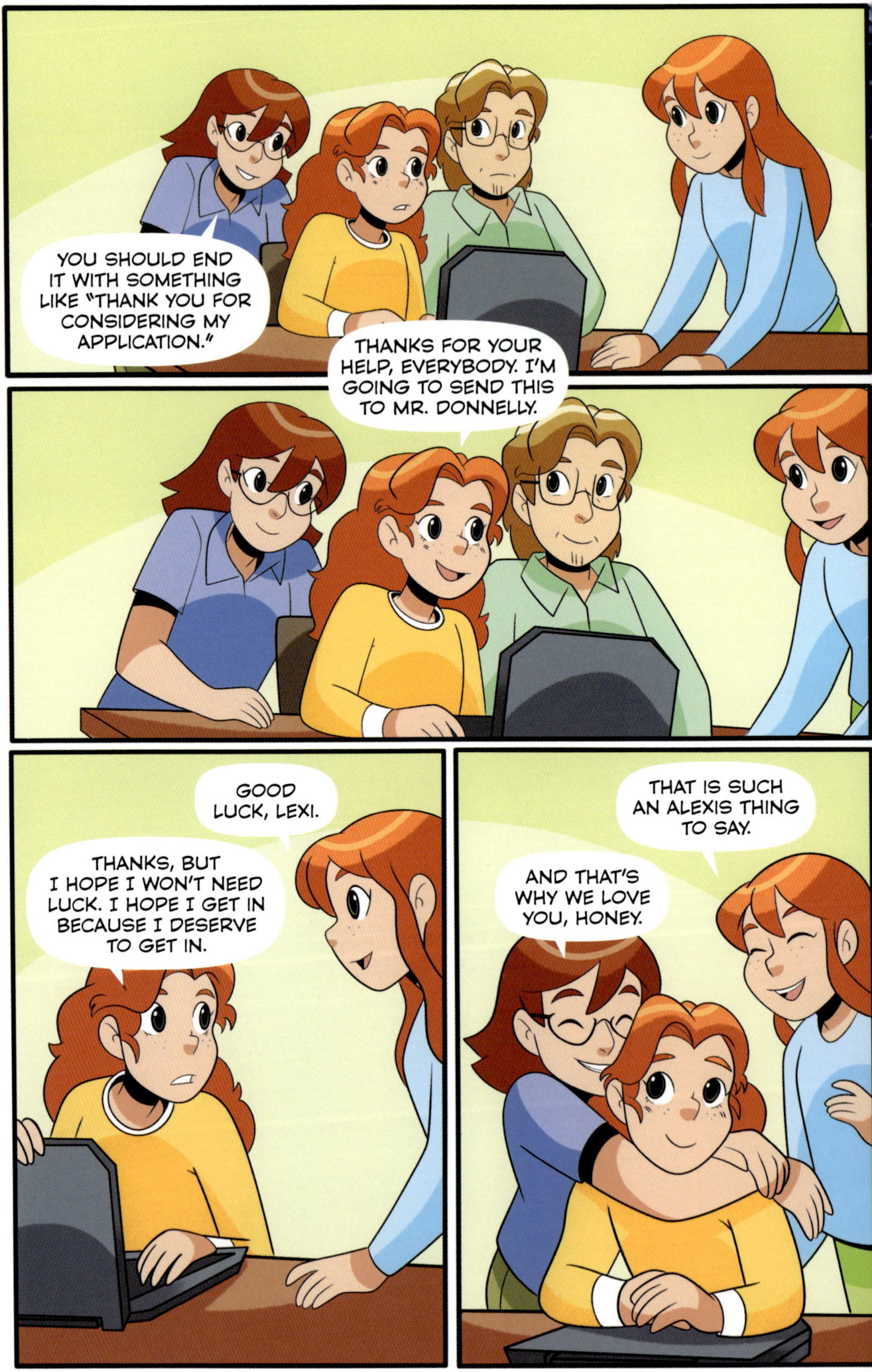
YOU SHOULD END IT WITH SOMETHING LIKE "THANK YOU FOR CONSIDERING MY APPLICATION."
THANKS FOR YOUR HELP, EVERYBODY. I'M GOING TO SEND THIS TO MR. DONNELLY.
GOOD LUCK, LEXI.
THANKS, BUT I HOPE I WON'T NEED LUCK. I HOPE I GET IN BECAUSE I DESERVE TO GET IN.
THAT IS SUCH AN ALEXIS THING TO SAY.
AND THAT'S WHY WE LOVE YOU, HONEY.

Chapter 14

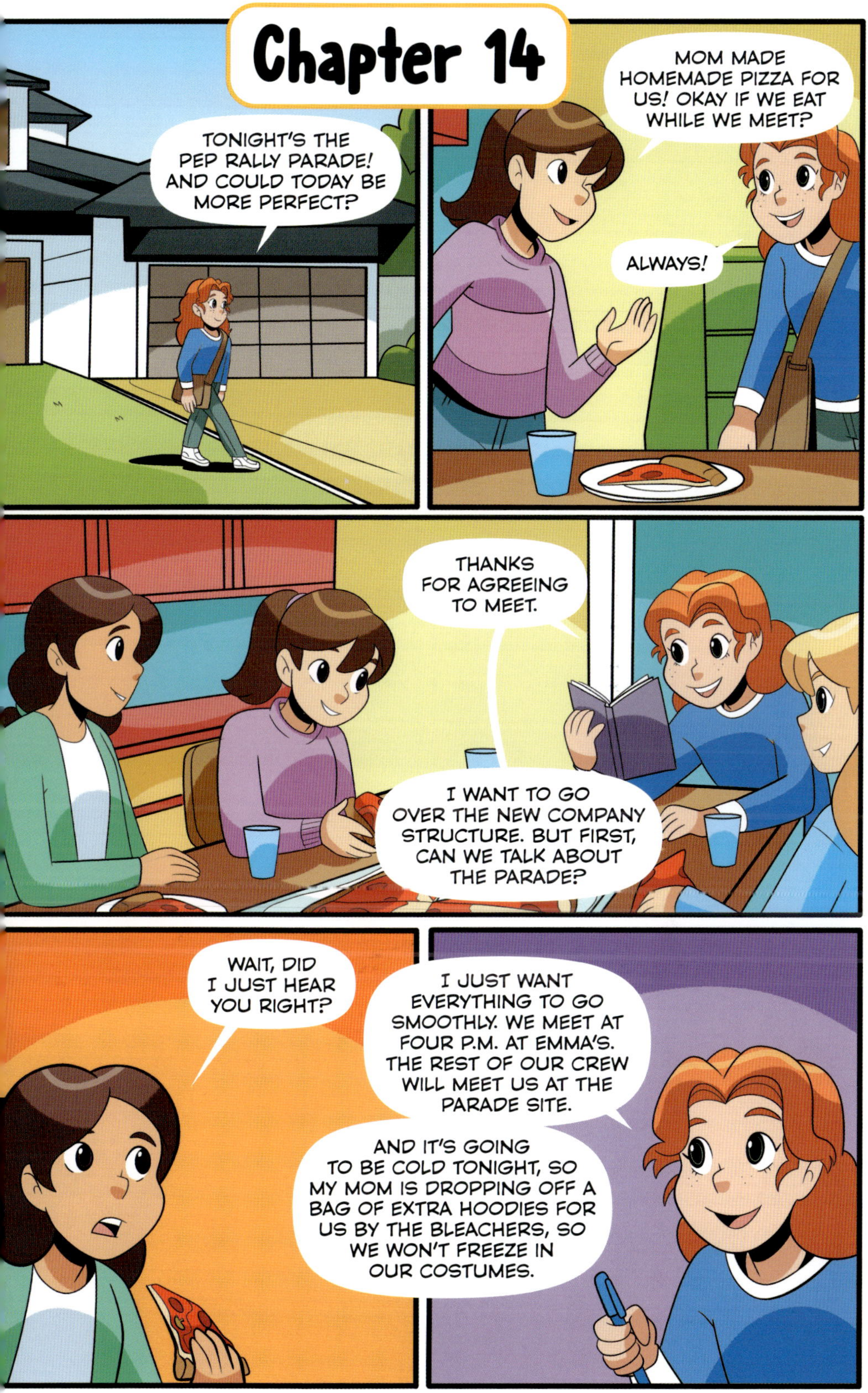
TONIGHT'S THE PEP RALLY PARADE! AND COULD TODAY BE MORE PERFECT?
MOM MADE HOMEMADE PIZZA FOR US! OKAY IF WE EAT WHILE WE MEET?
ALWAYS!
THANKS FOR AGREEING TO MEET.
I WANT TO GO OVER THE NEW COMPANY STRUCTURE. BUT FIRST, CAN WE TALK ABOUT THE PARADE?
WAIT, DID I JUST HEAR YOU RIGHT?
I JUST WANT EVERYTHING TO GO SMOOTHLY. WE MEET AT FOUR P.M. AT EMMA'S. THE REST OF OUR CREW WILL MEET US AT THE PARADE SITE.
AND IT'S GOING TO BE COLD TONIGHT, SO MY MOM IS DROPPING OFF A BAG OF EXTRA HOODIES FOR US BY THE BLEACHERS, SO WE WON'T FREEZE IN OUR COSTUMES.

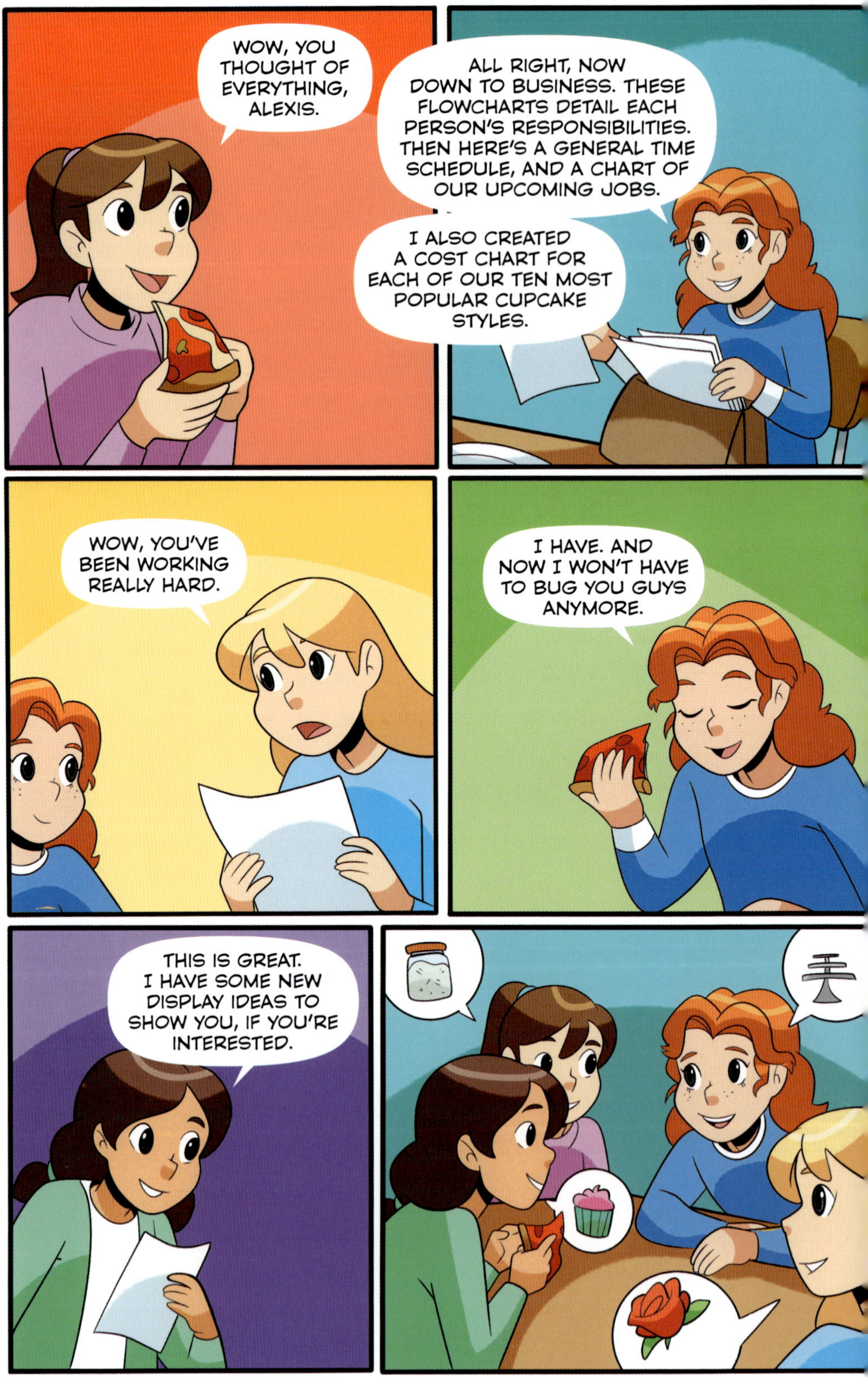
WOW, YOU THOUGHT OF EVERYTHING, ALEXIS.
ALL RIGHT, NOW DOWN TO BUSINESS. THESE FLOWCHARTS DETAIL EACH PERSON'S RESPONSIBILITIES. THEN HERE'S A GENERAL TIME SCHEDULE, AND A CHART OF OUR UPCOMING JOBS.
I ALSO CREATED A COST CHART FOR EACH OF OUR TEN MOST POPULAR CUPCAKE STYLES.
WOW, YOU'VE BEEN WORKING REALLY HARD.
I HAVE. AND NOW I WON'T HAVE TO BUG YOU GUYS ANYMORE.
THIS IS GREAT. I HAVE SOME NEW DISPLAY IDEAS TO SHOW YOU, IF YOU'RE INTERESTED.

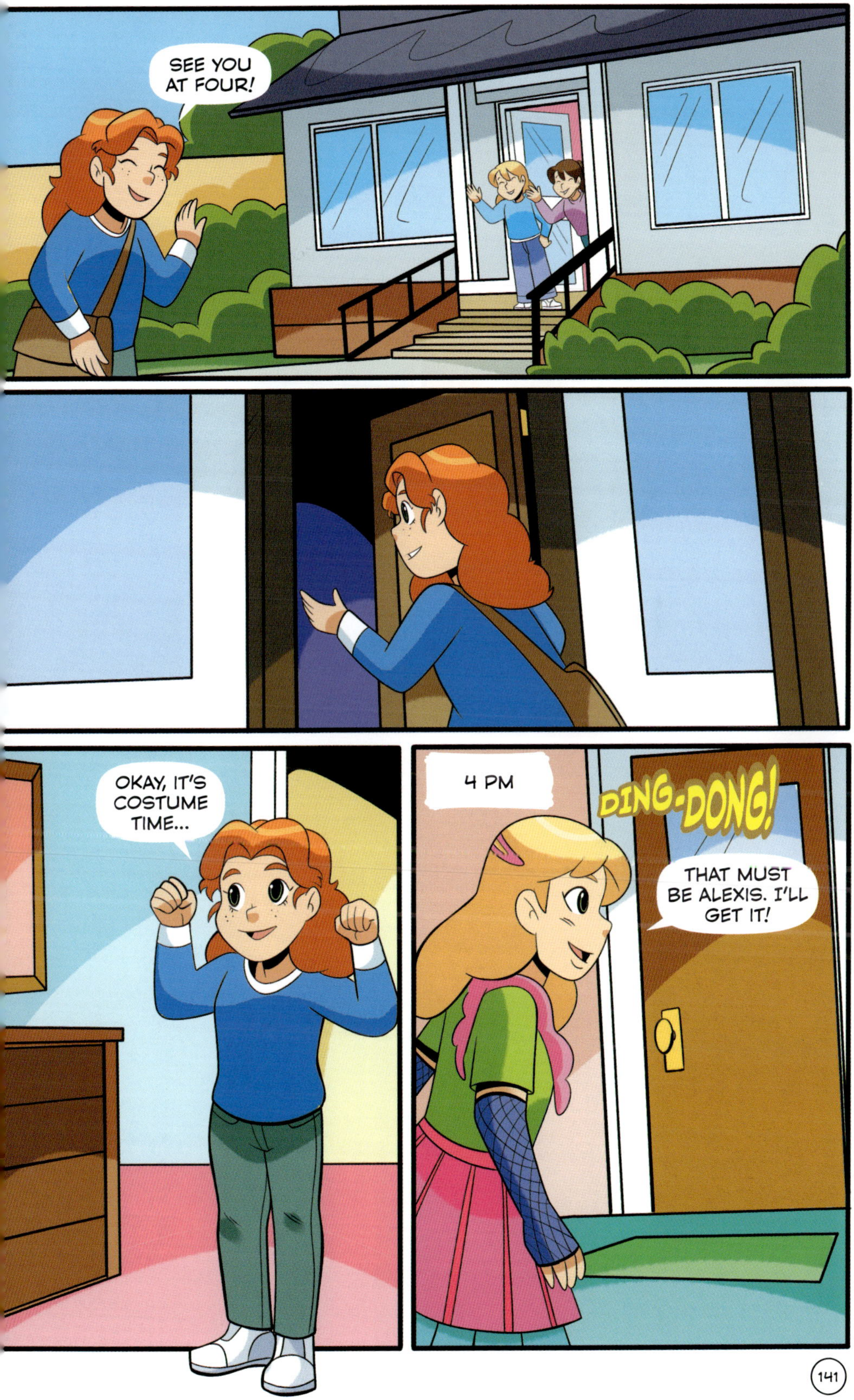
SEE YOU AT FOUR!
OKAY, IT'S COSTUME TIME...
4 PM
DING-DONG!
THAT MUST BE ALEXIS. I'LL GET IT!

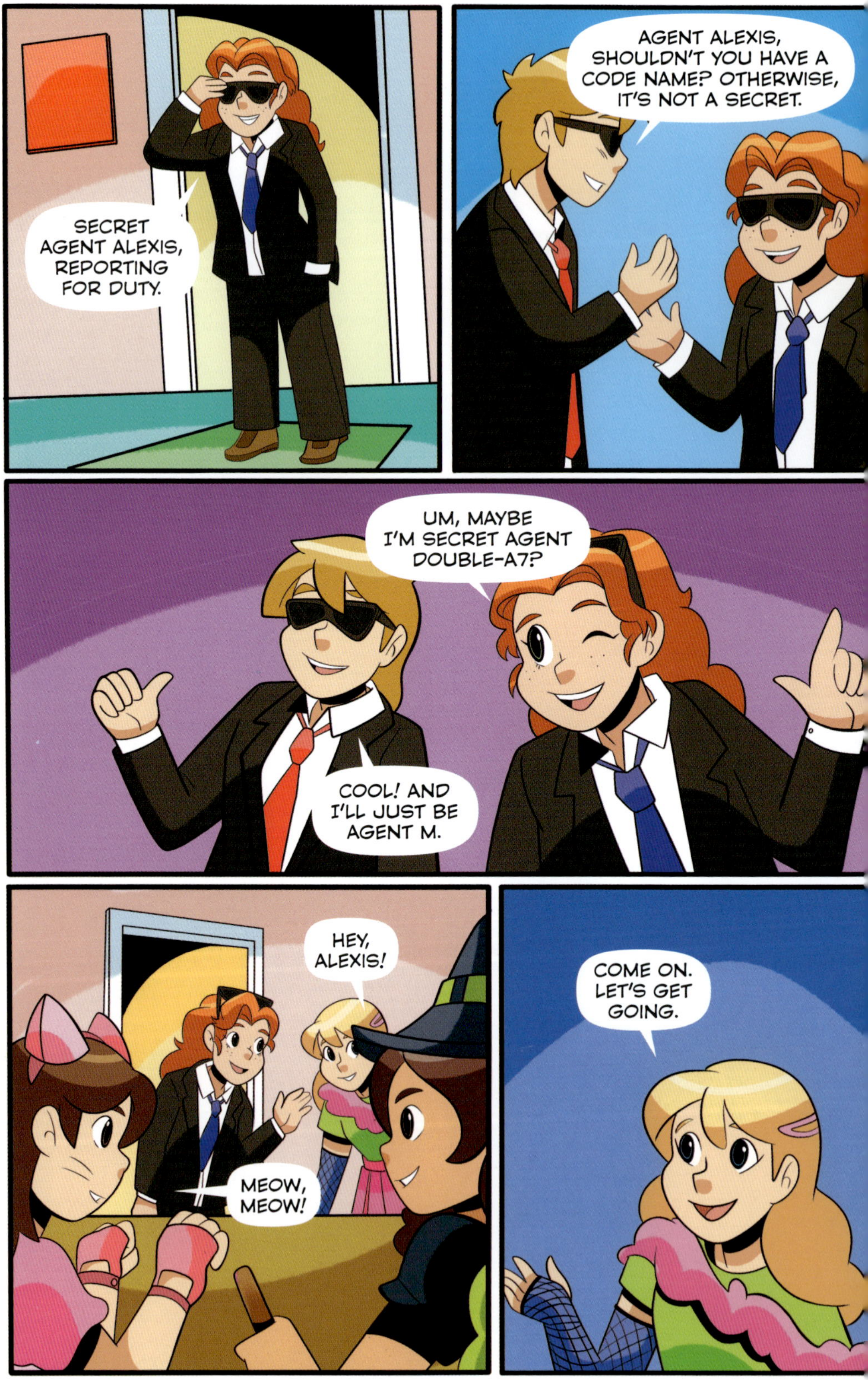
SECRET AGENT ALEXIS, REPORTING FOR DUTY.
AGENT ALEXIS, SHOULDN'T YOU HAVE A CODE NAME? OTHERWISE, IT'S NOT A SECRET.
UM, MAYBE I'M SECRET AGENT DOUBLE-A7?
COOL! AND I'LL JUST BE AGENT M.
HEY, ALEXIS!
MEOW, MEOW!
COME ON. LET'S GET GOING.

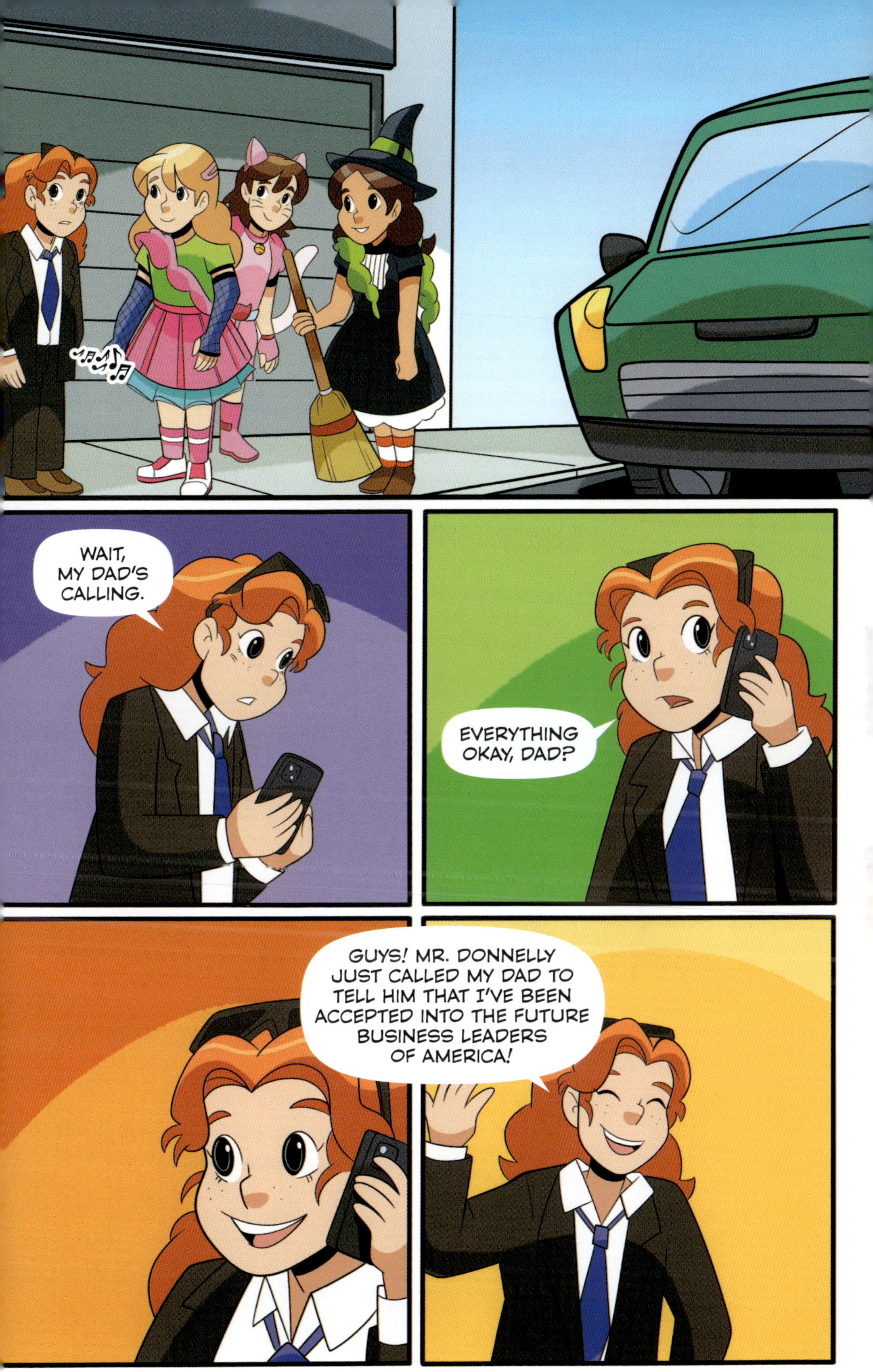
WAIT, MY DAD'S CALLING.
EVERYTHING OKAY, DAD?
GUYS! MR. DONNELLY JUST CALLED MY DAD TO TELL HIM THAT I'VE BEEN ACCEPTED INTO THE FUTURE BUSINESS LEADERS OF AMERICA!

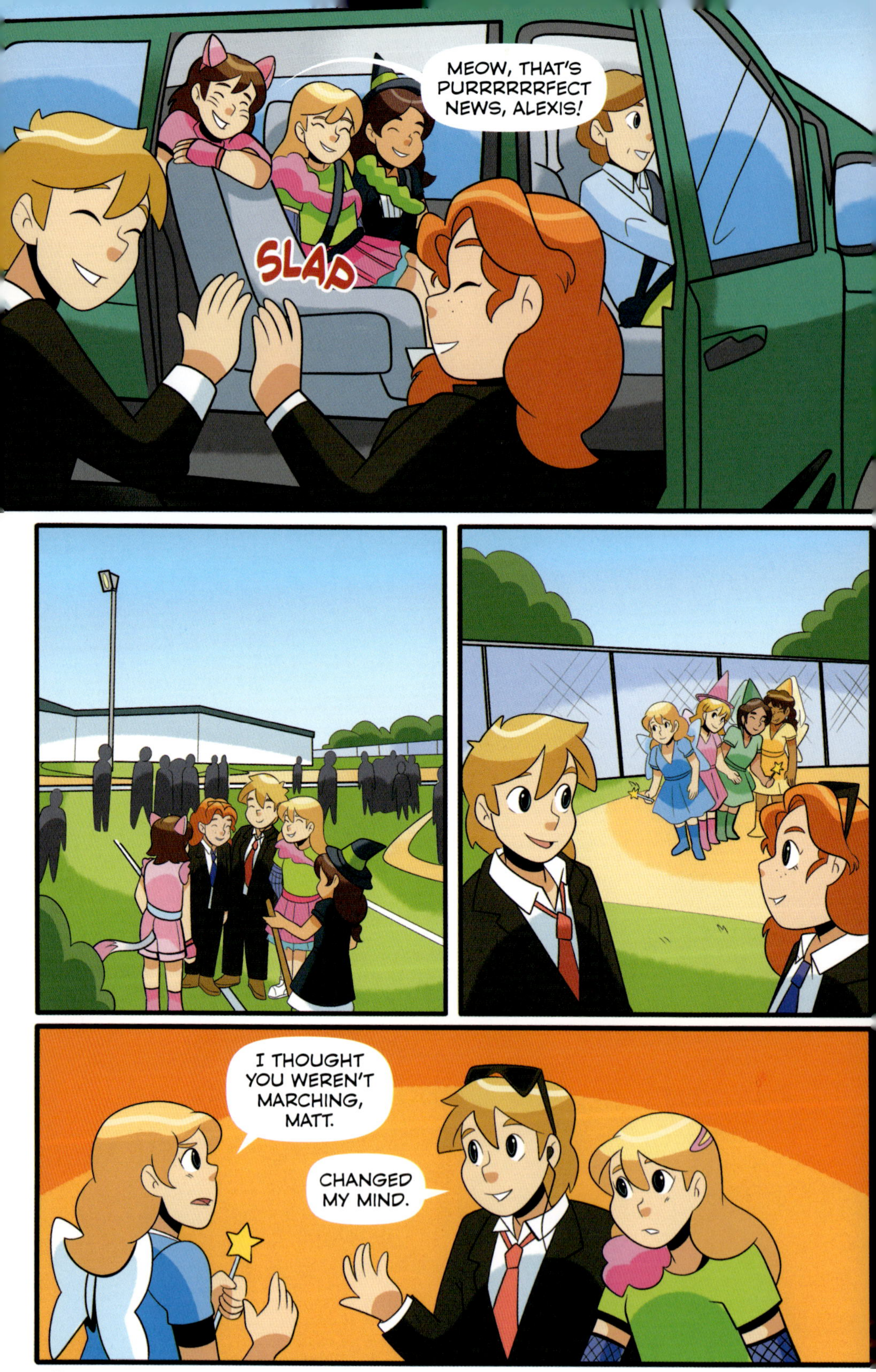
MEOW, THAT'S PURRRRRRFECT NEWS, ALEXIS!
SLAP
I THOUGHT YOU WEREN'T MARCHING, MATT.
CHANGED MY MIND.

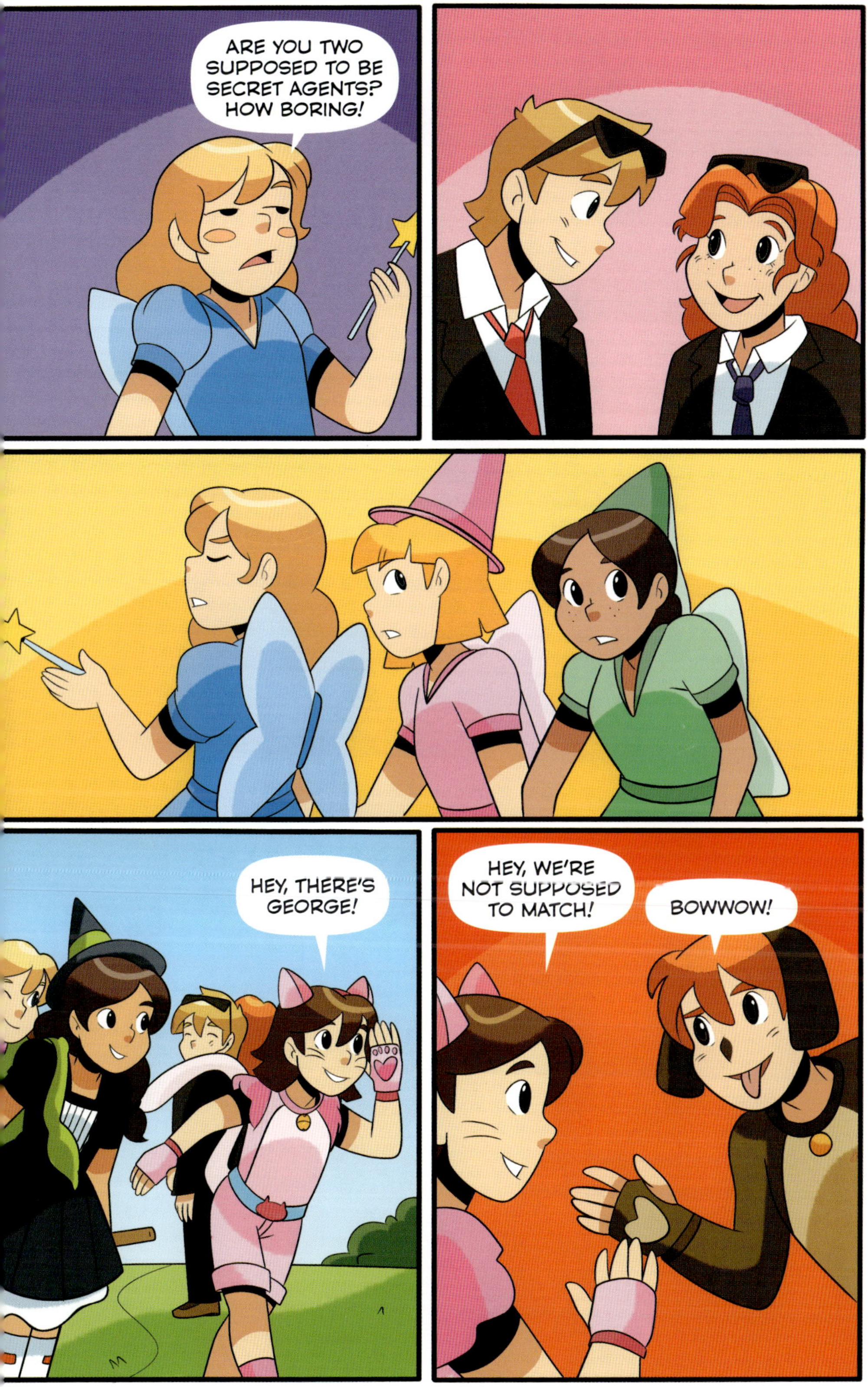
ARE YOU TWO SUPPOSED TO BE SECRET AGENTS? HOW BORING!
HEY, THERE'S GEORGE!
HEY, WE'RE NOT SUPPOSED TO MATCH!
BOWWOW!

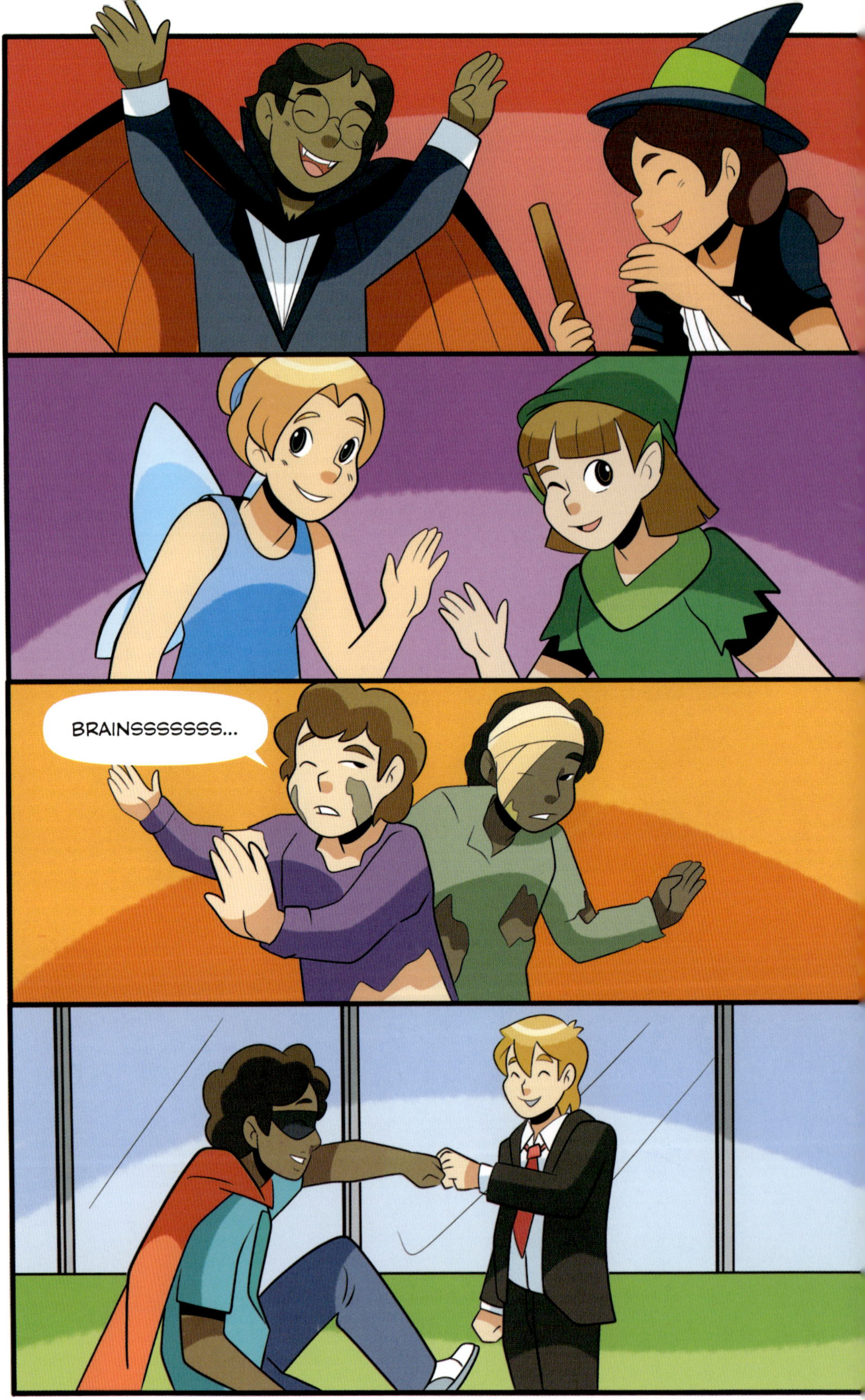
BRAINSSSSSSS...

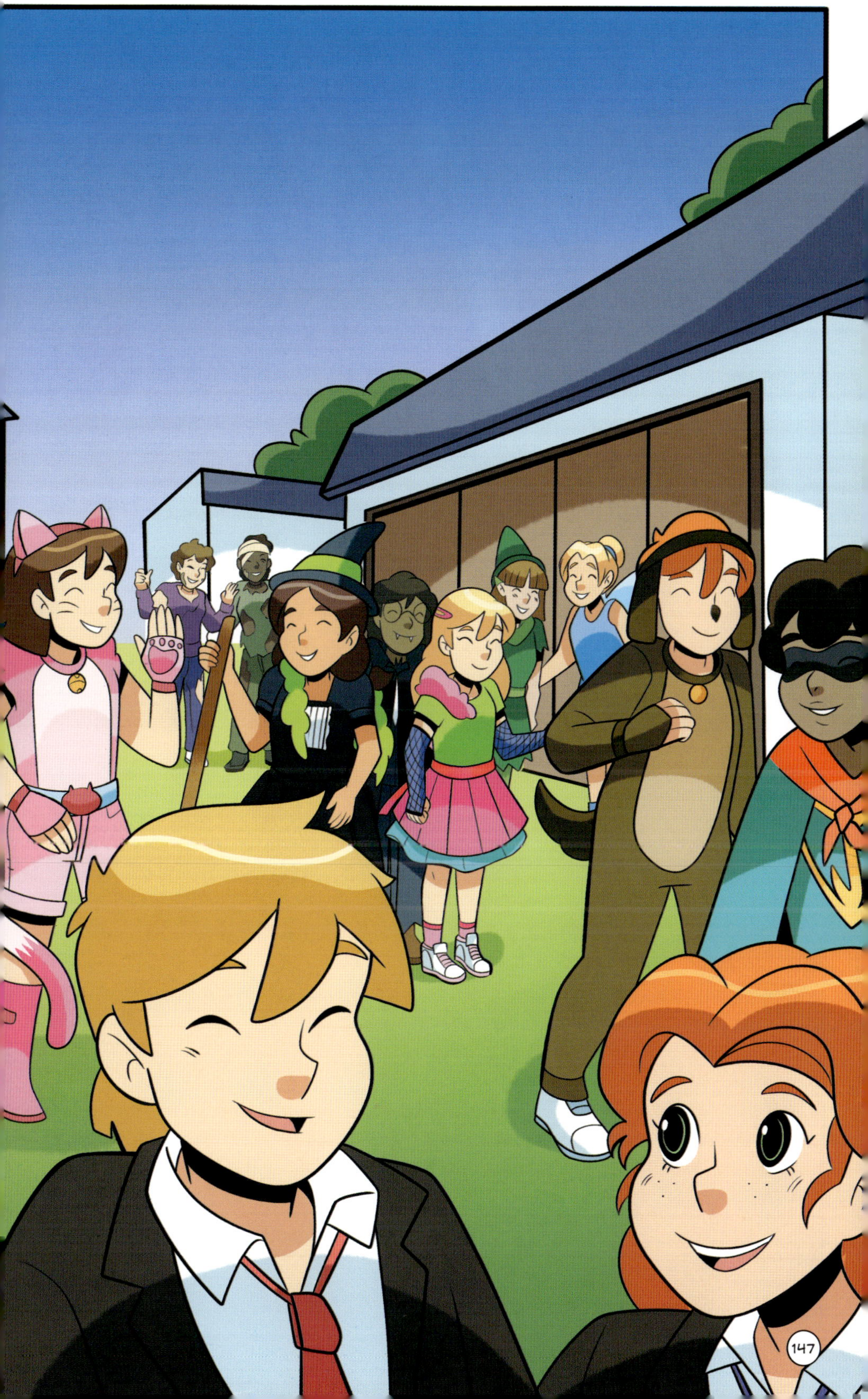

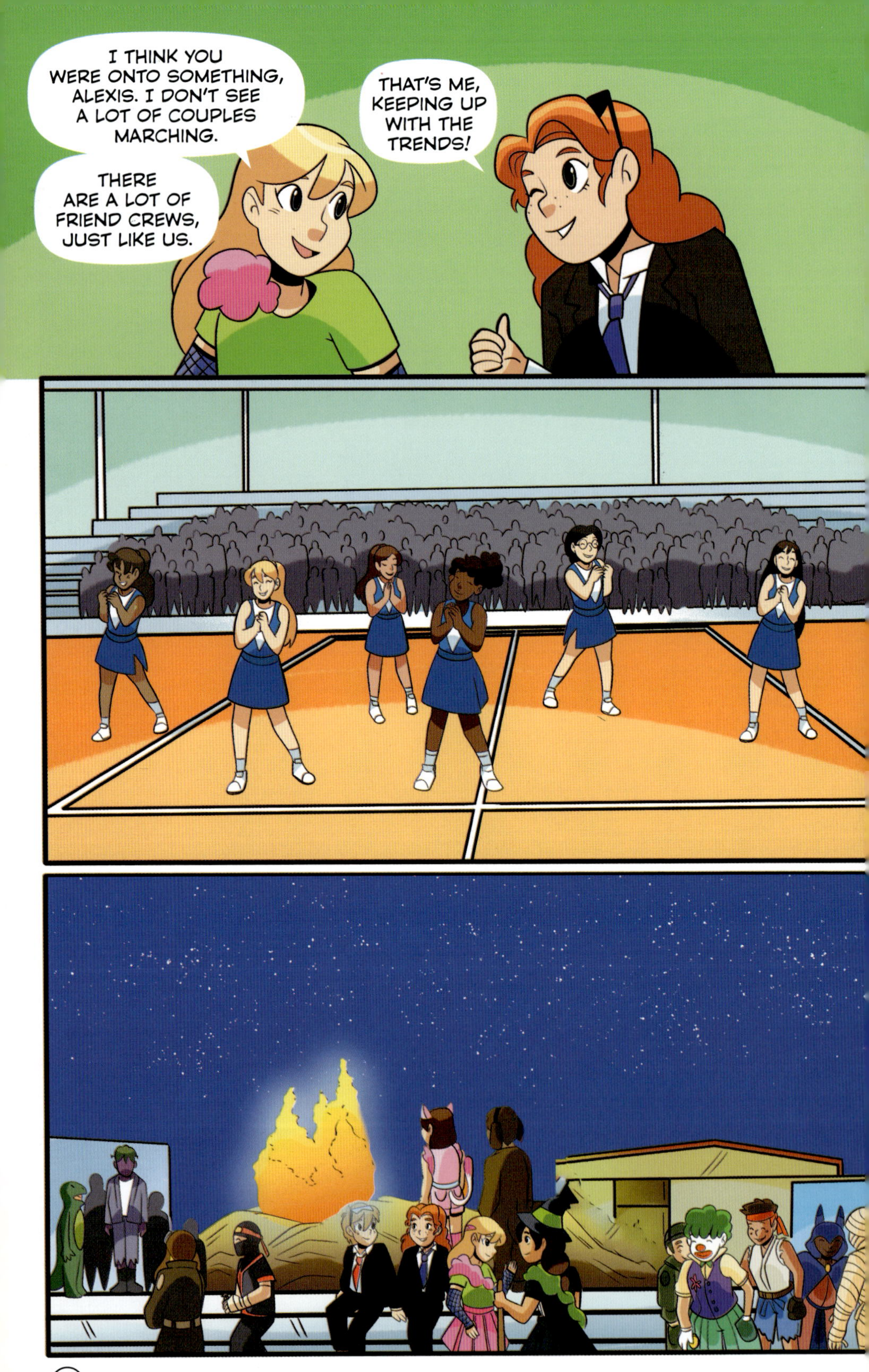
I THINK YOU WERE ONTO SOMETHING, ALEXIS. I DON'T SEE A LOT OF COUPLES MARCHING.
THERE ARE A LOT OF FRIEND CREWS, JUST LIKE US.
THAT'S ME, KEEPING UP WITH THE TRENDS!

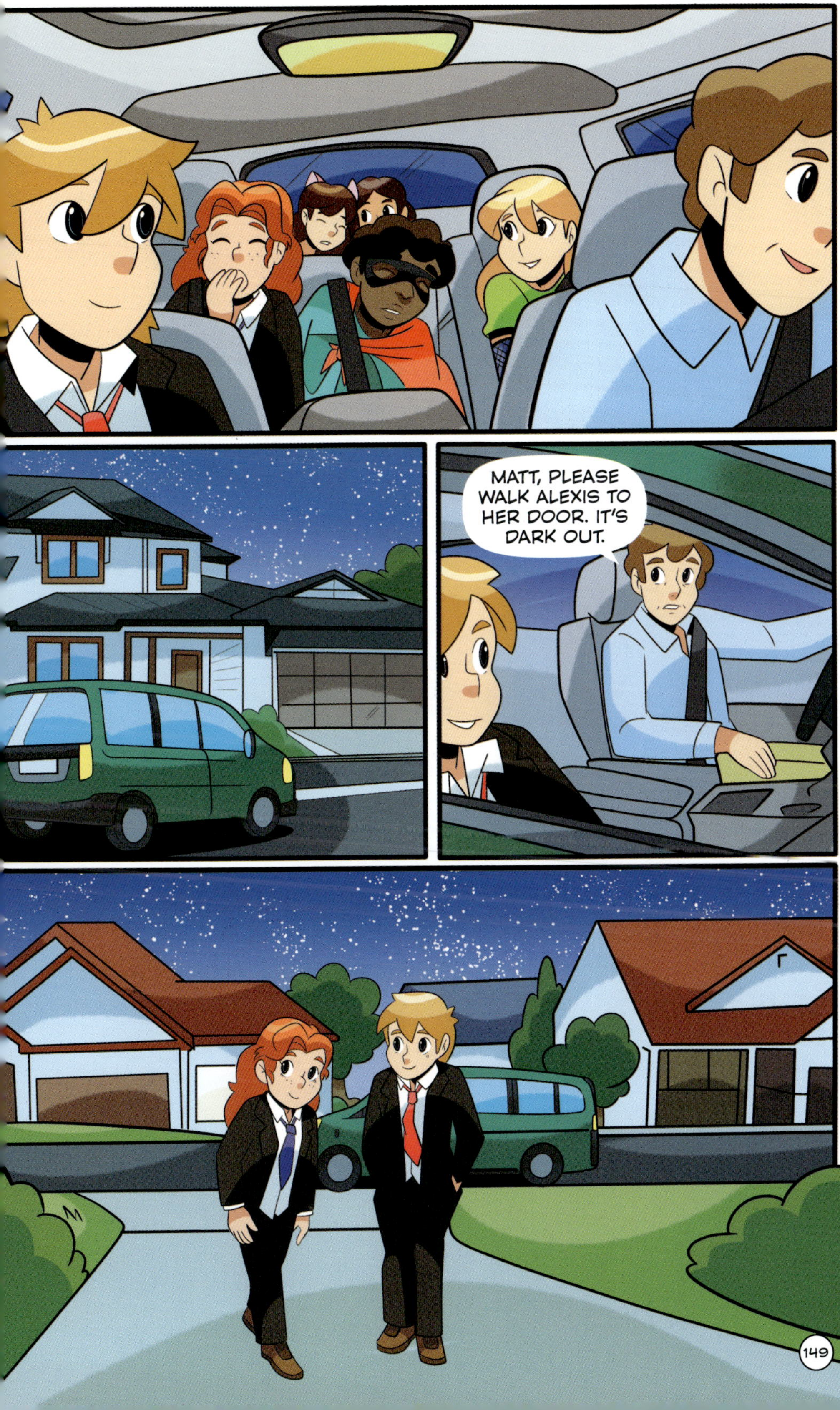
MATT, PLEASE WALK ALEXIS TO HER DOOR. IT'S DARK OUT.

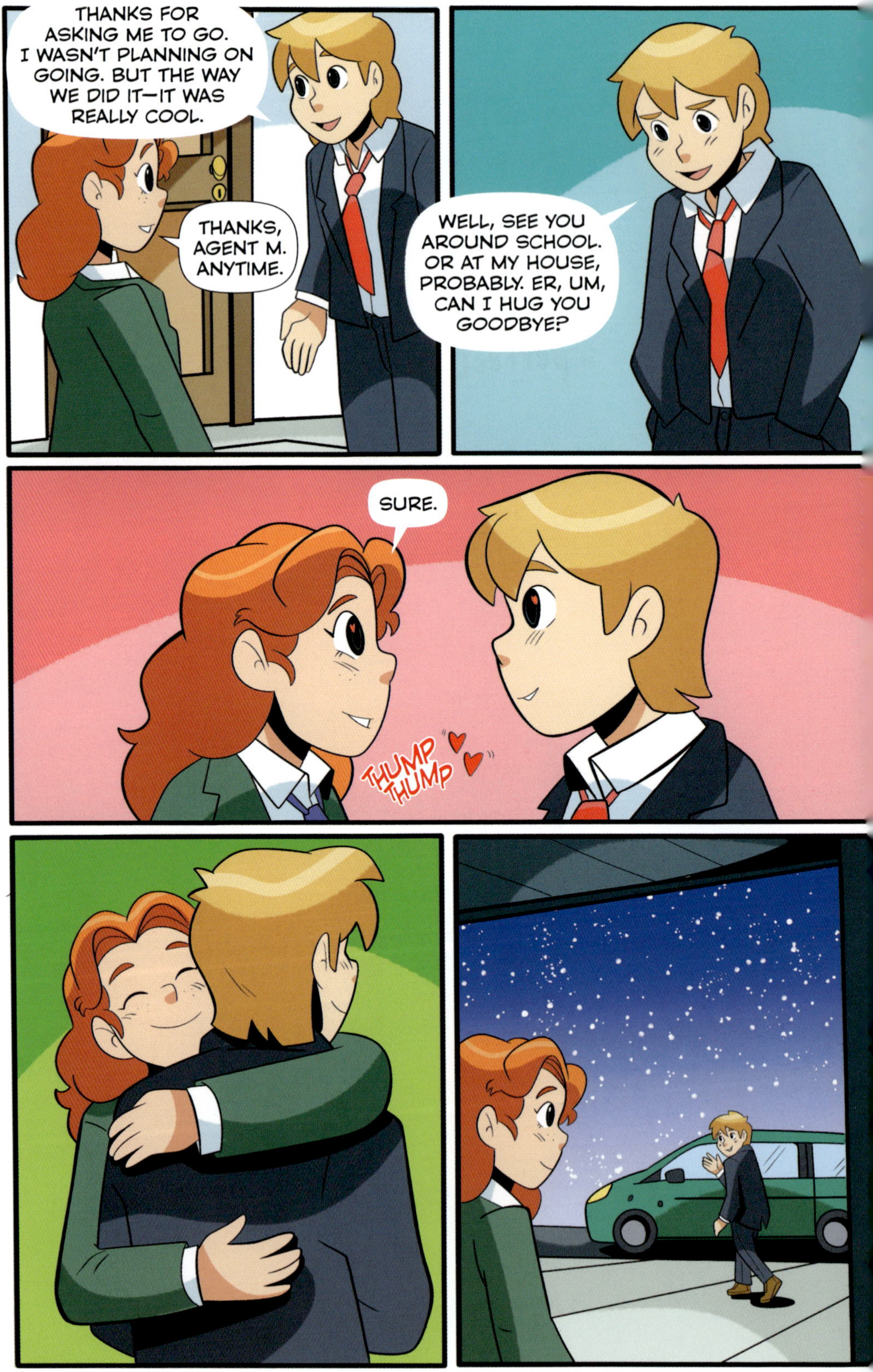
THANKS FOR ASKING ME TO GO. I WASN'T PLANNING ON GOING. BUT THE WAY WE DID IT—IT WAS REALLY COOL.
THANKS, AGENT M. ANYTIME.
WELL, SEE YOU AROUND SCHOOL. OR AT MY HOUSE, PROBABLY. ER, UM, CAN I HUG YOU GOODBYE?
SURE.
THUMP THUMP

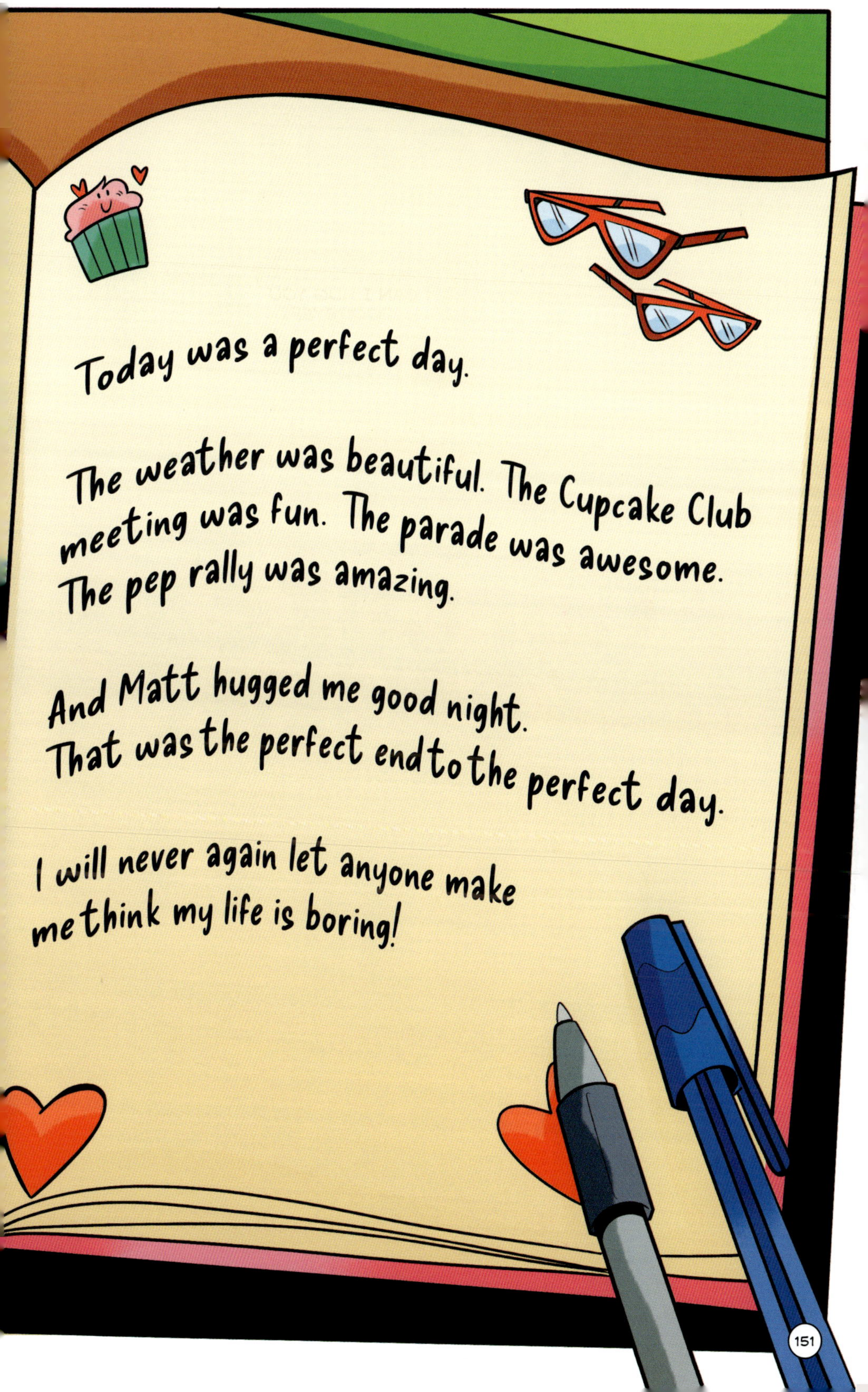
Today was a perfect day.
The weather was beautiful. The Cupcake Club meeting was fun. The parade was awesome. The pep rally was amazing.
And Matt hugged me good night. That was the perfect end to the perfect day.
I will never again let anyone make me think my life is boring!

Make sure you read them all!

CUPCAKE DIARIES

Emma All Stirred Up!

From the bestselling author of Cupcake Diaries Coco Simon
CUPCAKE DIARIES
#7
THE GRAPHIC NOVEL
Emma All Stirred Up!

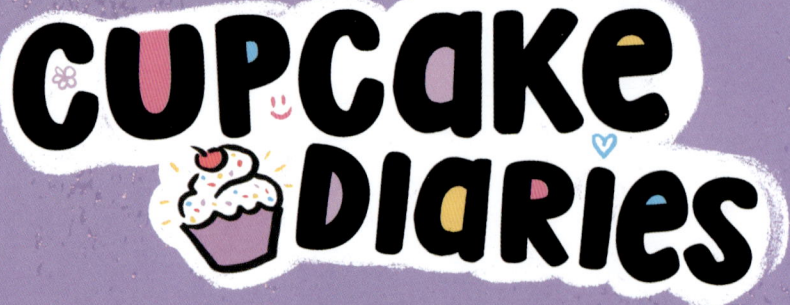

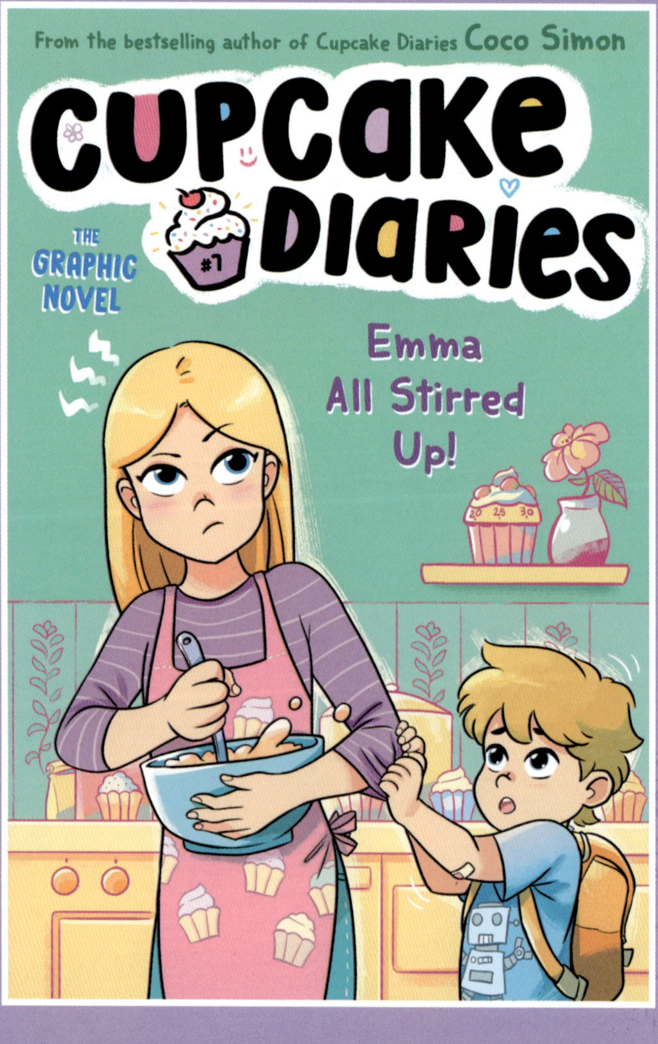

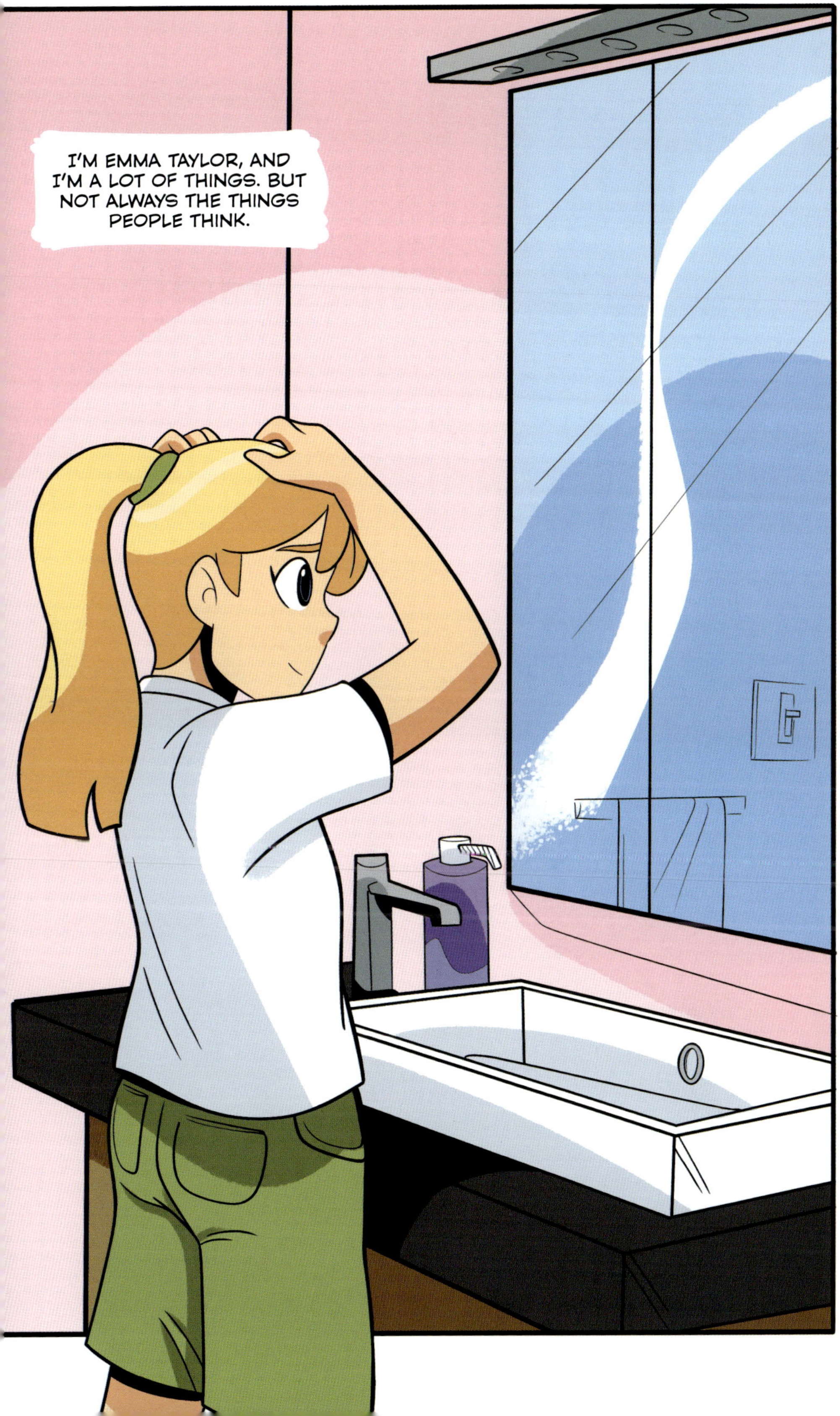
I'M EMMA TAYLOR, AND I'M A LOT OF THINGS. BUT NOT ALWAYS THE THINGS PEOPLE THINK.

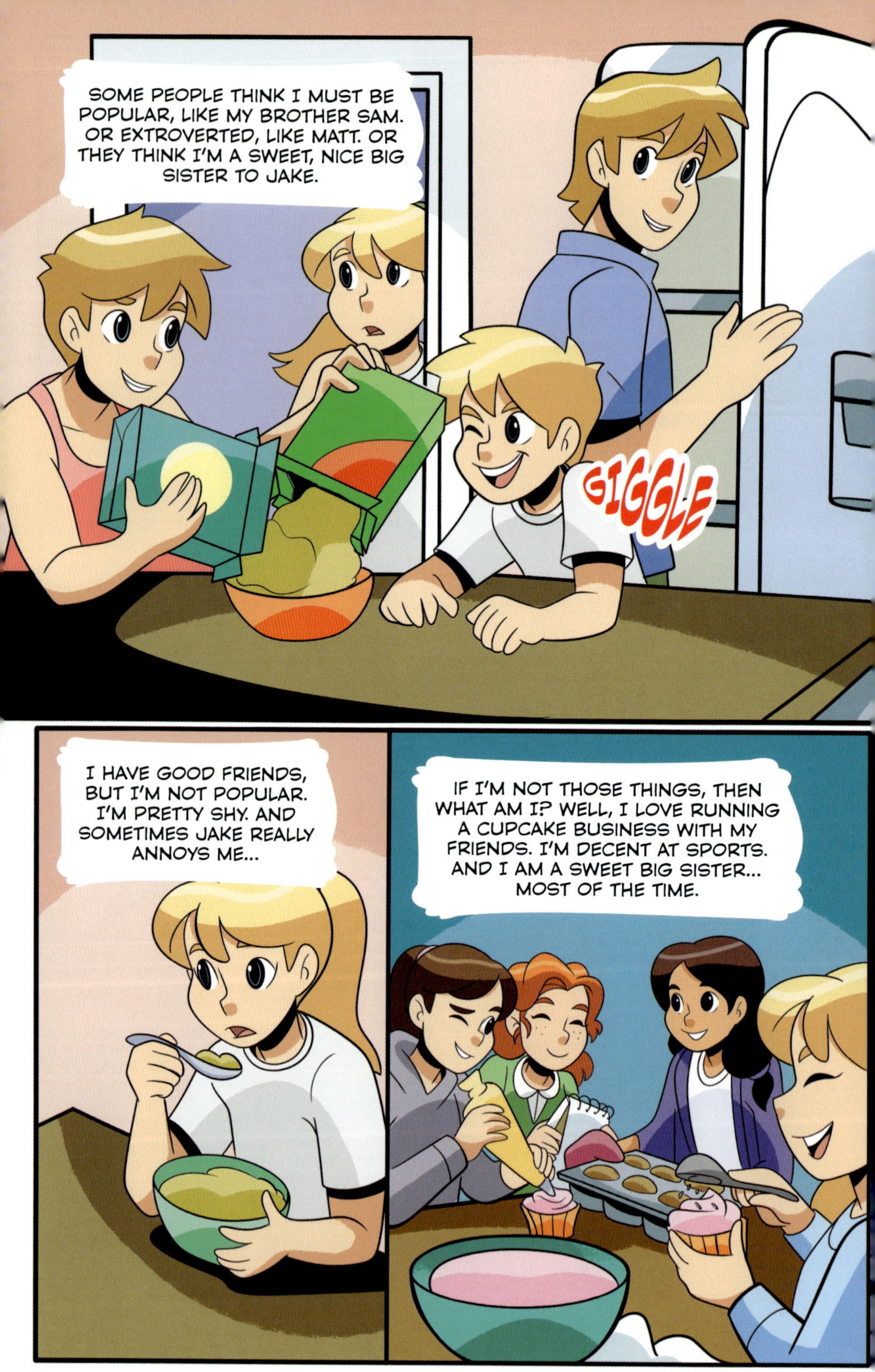
SOME PEOPLE THINK I MUST BE POPULAR, LIKE MY BROTHER SAM. OR EXTROVERTED, LIKE MATT. OR THEY THINK I'M A SWEET, NICE BIG SISTER TO JAKE.
GIGGLE
I HAVE GOOD FRIENDS, BUT I'M NOT POPULAR. I'M PRETTY SHY. AND SOMETIMES JAKE REALLY ANNOYS ME...
IF I'M NOT THOSE THINGS, THEN WHAT AM I? WELL, I LOVE RUNNING A CUPCAKE BUSINESS WITH MY FRIENDS. I'M DECENT AT SPORTS. AND I AM A SWEET BIG SISTER... MOST OF THE TIME.

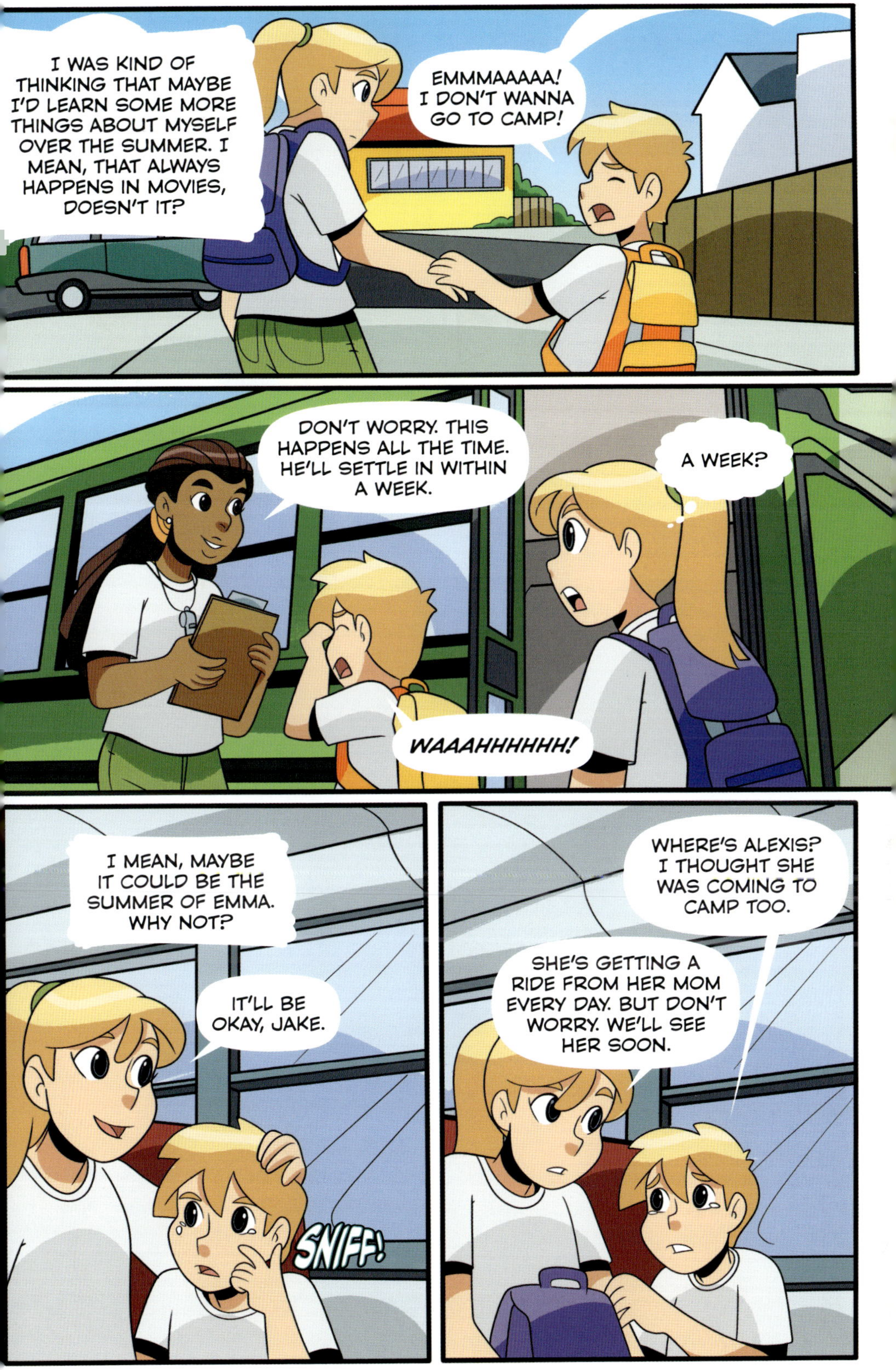
I WAS KIND OF THINKING THAT MAYBE I'D LEARN SOME MORE THINGS ABOUT MYSELF OVER THE SUMMER. I MEAN, THAT ALWAYS HAPPENS IN MOVIES, DOESN'T IT?
EMMMAAAAA! I DON'T WANNA GO TO CAMP!
DON'T WORRY. THIS HAPPENS ALL THE TIME. HE'LL SETTLE IN WITHIN A WEEK.
A WEEK?
WAAAHHHHHH!
I MEAN, MAYBE IT COULD BE THE SUMMER OF EMMA. WHY NOT?
IT'LL BE OKAY, JAKE.
SNIFF!
WHERE'S ALEXIS? I THOUGHT SHE WAS COMING TO CAMP TOO.
SHE'S GETTING A RIDE FROM HER MOM EVERY DAY. BUT DON'T WORRY. WE'LL SEE HER SOON.

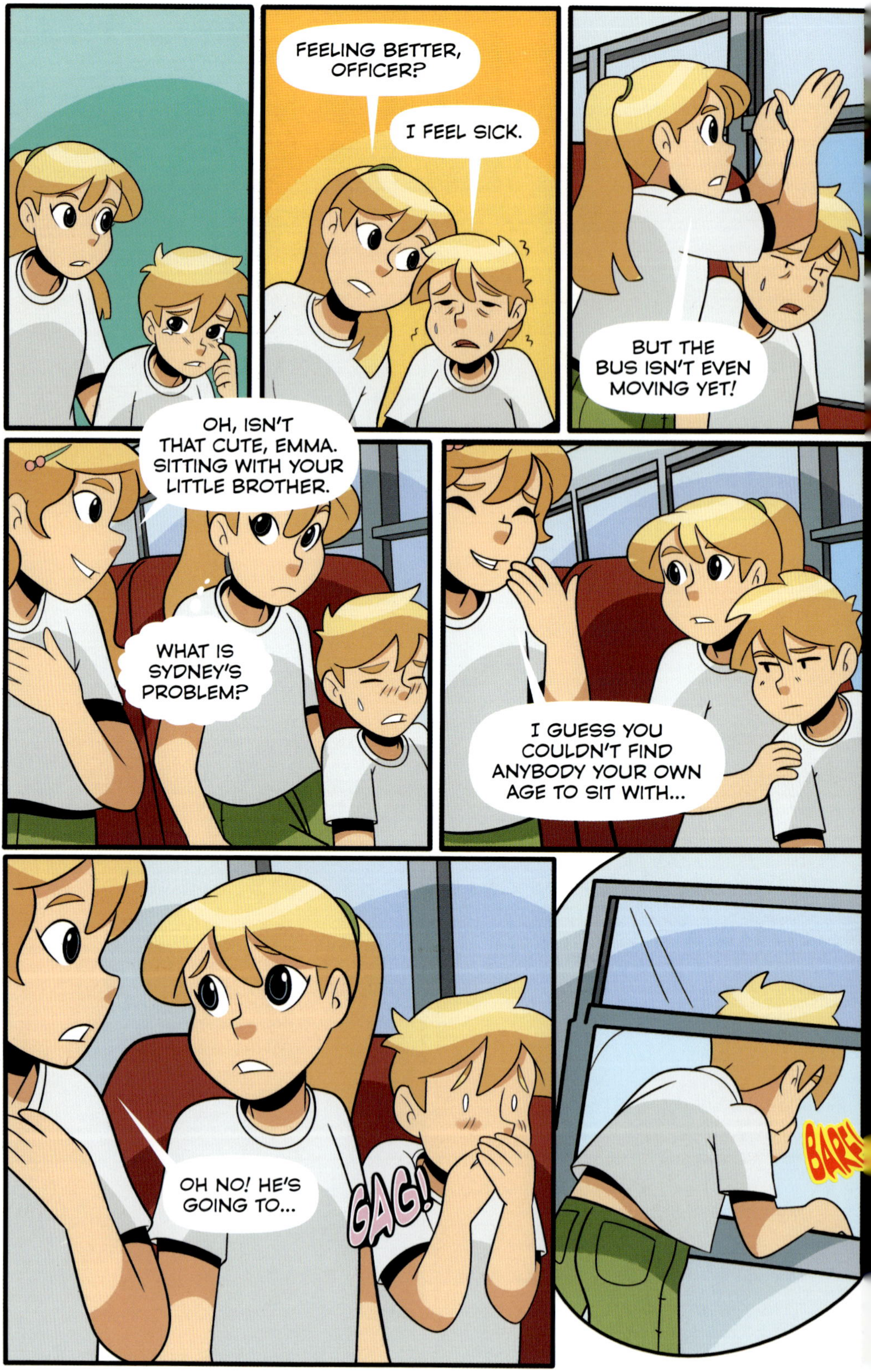
FEELING BETTER, OFFICER?
I FEEL SICK.
BUT THE BUS ISN'T EVEN MOVING YET!
OH, ISN'T THAT CUTE, EMMA. SITTING WITH YOUR LITTLE BROTHER.
WHAT IS SYDNEY'S PROBLEM?
I GUESS YOU COULDN'T FIND ANYBODY YOUR OWN AGE TO SIT WITH...
OH NO! HE'S GOING TO...
GAG!

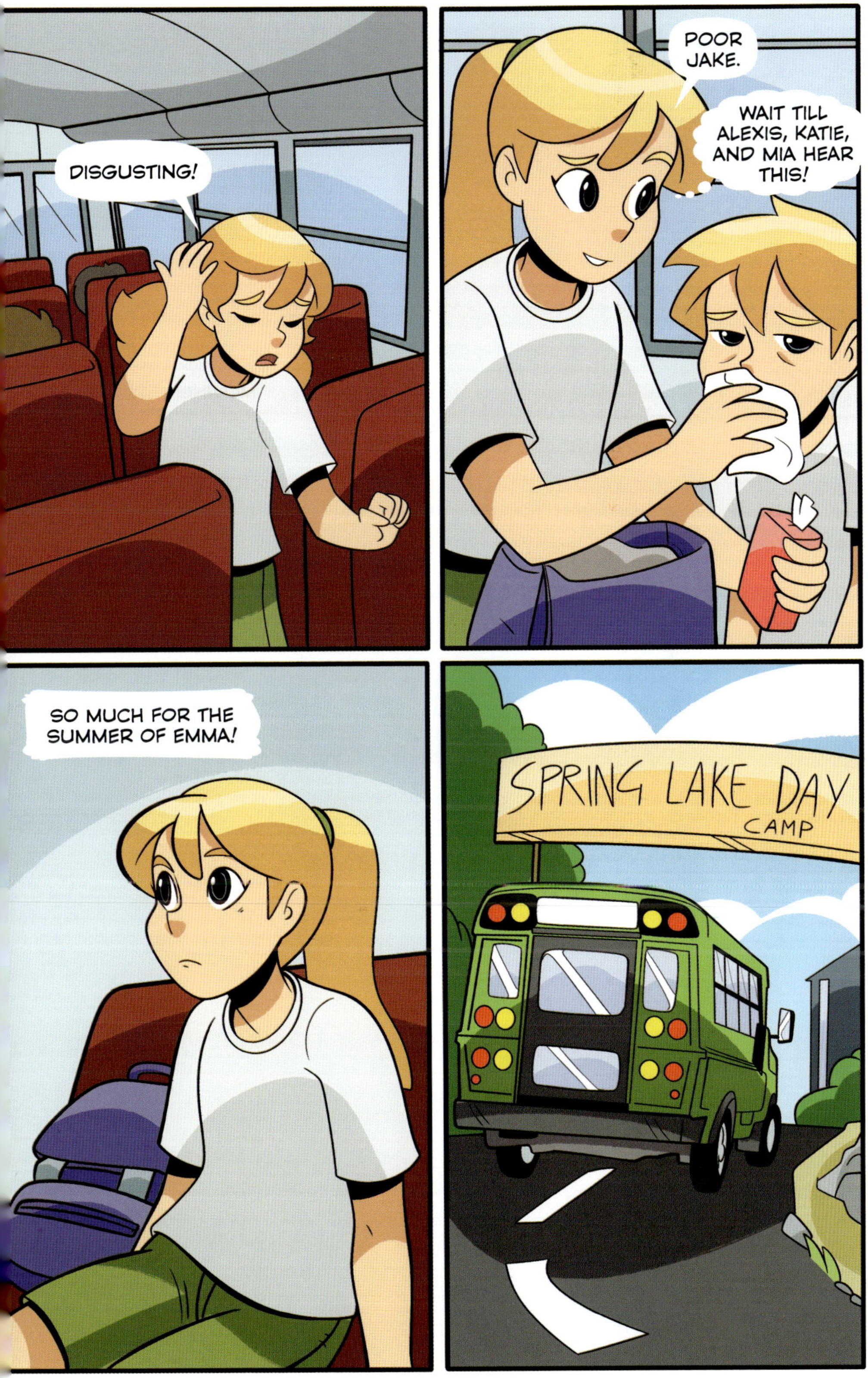
DISGUSTING!
POOR JAKE.
WAIT TILL ALEXIS, KATIE, AND MIA HEAR THIS!
SO MUCH FOR THE SUMMER OF EMMA!
SPRING LAKE DAY CAMP

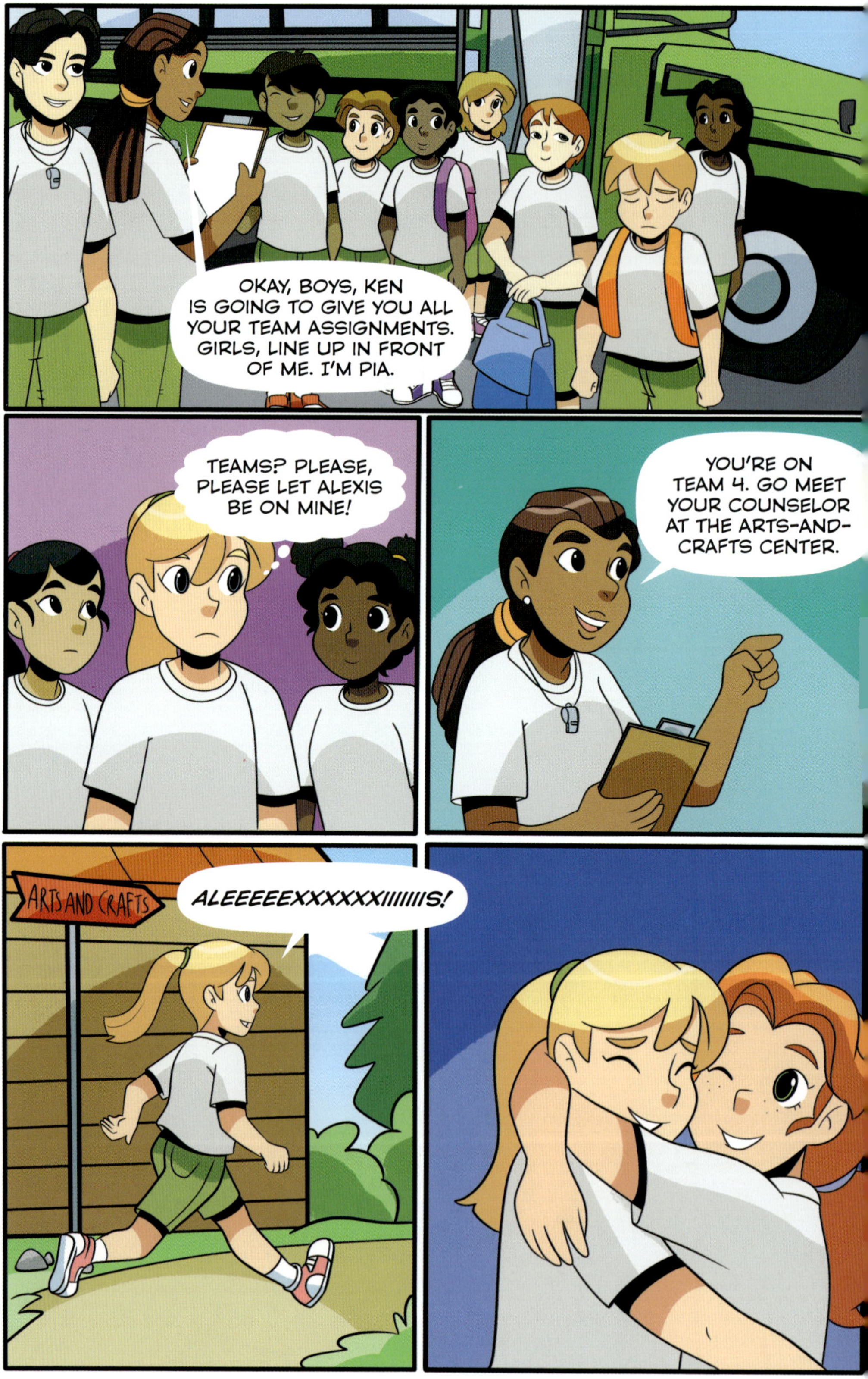
OKAY, BOYS, KEN IS GOING TO GIVE YOU ALL YOUR TEAM ASSIGNMENTS. GIRLS, LINE UP IN FRONT OF ME. I'M PIA.
TEAMS? PLEASE, PLEASE LET ALEXIS BE ON MINE!
YOU'RE ON TEAM 4. GO MEET YOUR COUNSELOR AT THE ARTS-AND-CRAFTS CENTER.
ARTS AND CRAFTS
ALEEEEEXXXXXXIIIIIIIS!

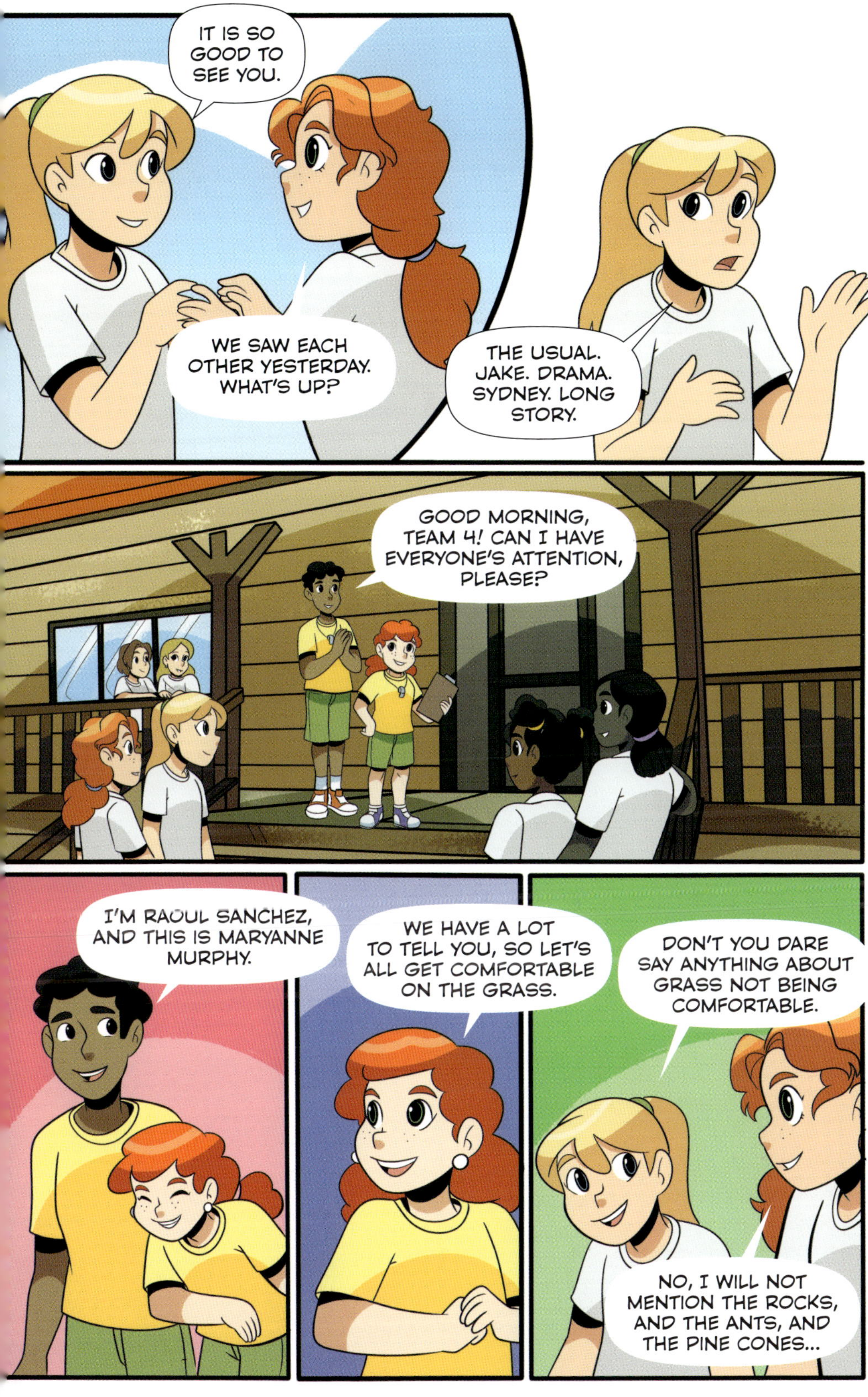
IT IS SO GOOD TO SEE YOU.
WE SAW EACH OTHER YESTERDAY. WHAT'S UP?
THE USUAL. JAKE. DRAMA. SYDNEY. LONG STORY.
GOOD MORNING, TEAM 4! CAN I HAVE EVERYONE'S ATTENTION, PLEASE?
I'M RAOUL SANCHEZ, AND THIS IS MARYANNE MURPHY.
WE HAVE A LOT TO TELL YOU, SO LET'S ALL GET COMFORTABLE ON THE GRASS.
DON'T YOU DARE SAY ANYTHING ABOUT GRASS NOT BEING COMFORTABLE.
NO, I WILL NOT MENTION THE ROCKS, AND THE ANTS, AND THE PINE CONES...

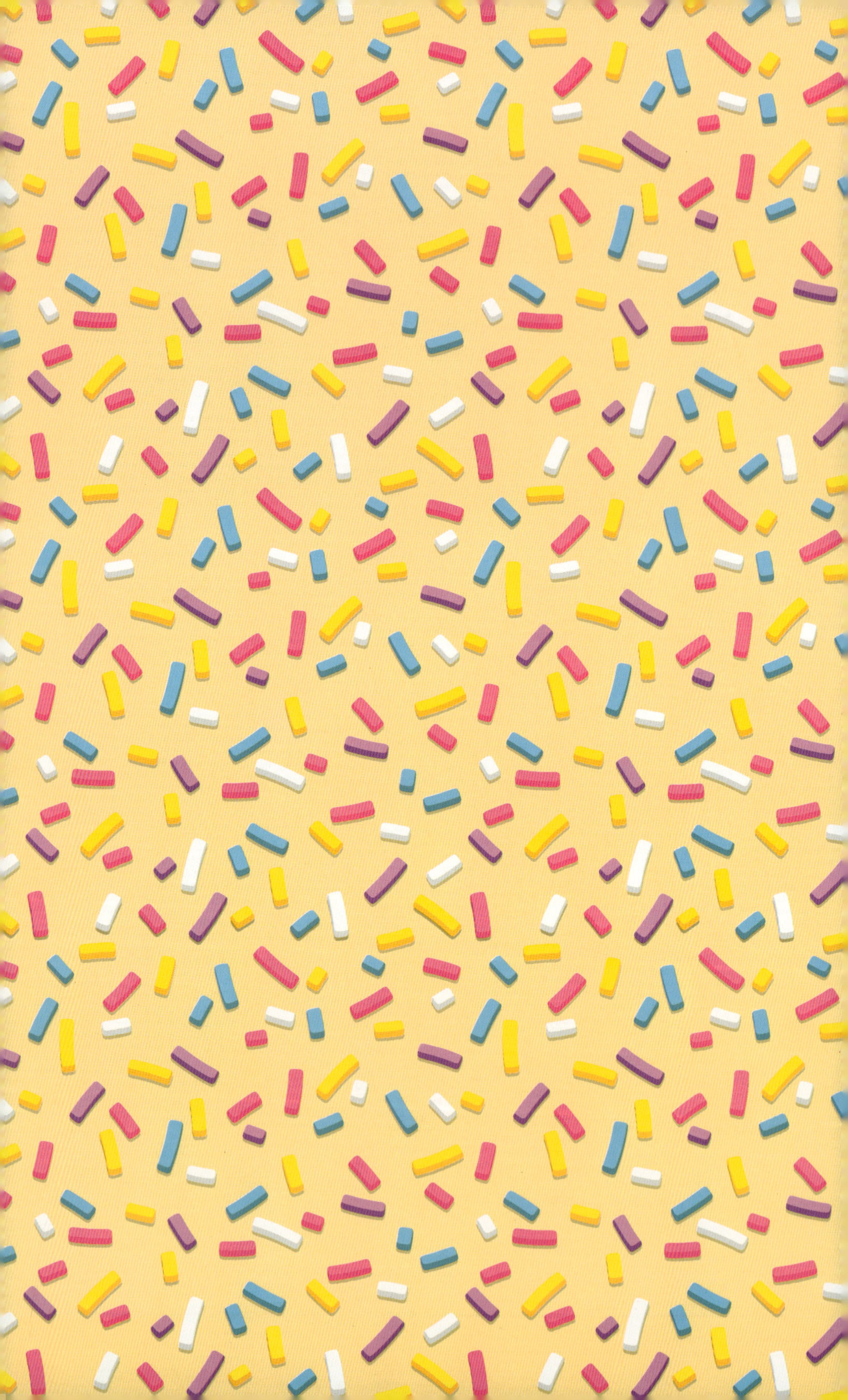

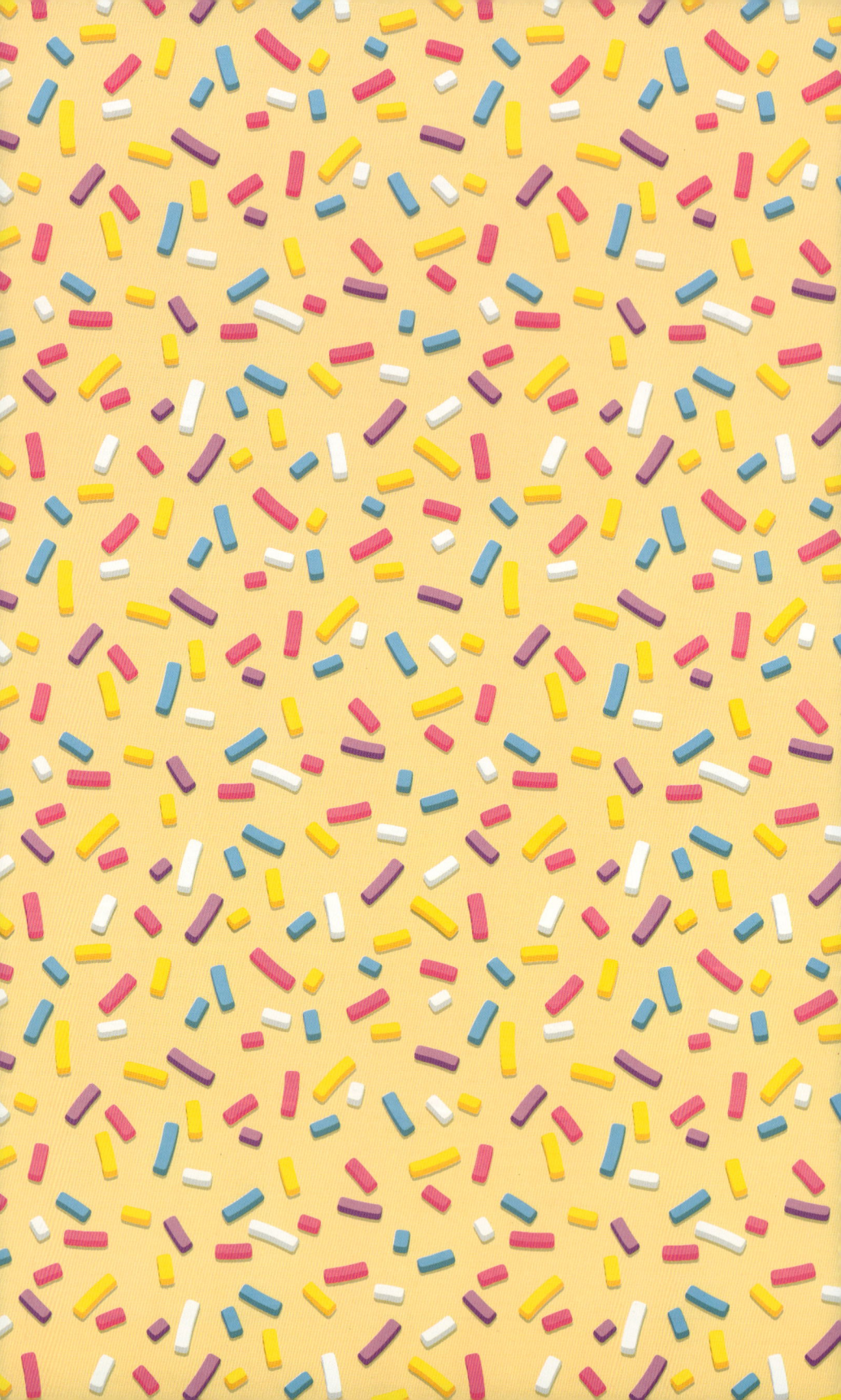